Spy's Honour

ALSO BY GAVIN LYALL

SPY'S HONOUR

Gavin Lyall

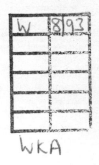
Hodder & Stoughton
LONDON SYDNEY AUCKLAND

British Library Cataloguing in Publication Data

Lyall, Gavin
  Spy's Honour
  I. Title
  823.914 [F]

  ISBN 0-340-58980-9

First published in Great Britain 1993

Published by Hodder and Stoughton,
a division of Hodder and Stoughton Ltd,
Mill Road, Dunton Green, Sevenoaks, Kent TN13 2YA
Editorial Office: 47 Bedford Square, London WC1B 3DP

Photoset by E.P.L. BookSet, Norwood, London

Printed in Great Britain by Mackays of Chatham PLC,
Chatham, Kent

Contents

THE SALONIKA ROAD

1

The journalist put down a pad of coarse writing paper on the café table, tilted and shook the chair to make sure there were no bits of broken glass on it, then sat down. A waiter put a cup of thick sweet coffee and a glass of water in front of him and the journalist nodded, but neither of them spoke.

He sipped the coffee, took out a pencil and wrote: *Salonika, November 9*. Then, feeling pessimistic about when the despatch would reach London, completed the date: *1912*. After that, he stared blankly out at the cold morning, past the big Greek flag that hung in limp folds over the door. He knew just how it felt. He sighed and began to write quickly.

Today, after 470 years of Turkish domination, the Greek Army once more trod the streets of Salonika. It has been a great day for the Hellenes, their goal is reached, their dreams realised. And no ancient army returning victorious to its native Athens ever received a more tumultuous welcome than . . .

He realised someone was standing beside him and looked up, not moving his head too fast. He wasn't surprised to see a uniformed officer – the city had more of them than beggars at the moment – but hadn't expected the uniform to be of a Major in the Coldstream Guards.

"You are English, aren't you?" the Major said. "Do you know where I can get hold of a horse?"

By the mane, the journalist thought, if there aren't any reins. But he said: "Not so easy, in a country at war. But if you've got money, anything's possible."

"Just for a couple of hours or so."

"There's a stables in the street behind this place, but don't blame me if it turns out the Turks have pinched them all to escape on. But if you want to get out to the Greek HQ down the road," he nodded to the east, "you could get a lift on a supply cart."

The Major was wearing highly polished riding boots and an expression that said he hadn't put them on to go jaunting in ox-carts. He looked around the café as if hoping there was a saddled horse half-hidden in some corner, but only saw an old man sweeping fiercely at the chips of glass and crockery welded to the floor by sticky patches of wine.

"It looks as if you had a bit of a party last night."

"It happens every four hundred and seventy years, I believe."

Unsmiling, the Major went on: "I suppose you didn't happen to run across a chap, a British officer in the Greek gunners?"

The journalist perked up. "No, but I'd like to. What's his name?"

But the Major just nodded and said: "Well, thanks awfully. I think I'll try that stables."

Left to himself again, the journalist finished his coffee, beckoned for more, and wrote:

I spent the evening observing exultant human nature from a point of vantage in the principal café, where a huge Greek flag had replaced the Turkish red and white. The appearance of officers in uniform was the signal for the crowd to rise and give vent to more cries of 'Long live'.

Then he crossed out from 'cries' and wrote simply: 'more Zetos'. If any reader of *The Times* didn't understand Greek, he wouldn't dare to show it by complaining.

The road across the coastal plain must have followed the same line between the sea and the distant snow-dusted hills for thousands of years. Alexander the Great would have ridden it often, and Mark Antony on his way to Philippi to avenge Caesar's murder. But like so many historical sites the Major had seen, it was frankly just another scruffy place. The road itself was no better than a farm track, soggy and stony at the same time, jolting the wagon at every step the oxen took.

A couple of miles out of Salonika they passed a small crossroads that had been shelled in the last hours of the battle. The road was pitted with small shallow craters that were already filling with rain, and the wreckage of a wagon had been piled at one side. A Greek working party was clearing the scatter of cooking pots, bundles of clothing and prayer mats, and lifting stiff corpses into another cart; one of the dead was clearly a woman. In the field beyond, another group was half-heartedly burying the remains of a horse; obviously the army cooks had had first pick at it.

The Major had never been on a fresh battlefield before and found it difficult to believe that Alexander's or Antony's battles had left so mundane a litter.

He got down near the tents of the Greek headquarters and after a flurry of saluting and schoolboy Greek, found an officer willing to look at the documents he had brought. General Kleomanes, the officer apologised, would much regret not greeting him but, alas, their supposed allies the Bulgarians were sending an army to dispute just who owned Salonika . . .

So the squabbling over the loot had begun already, the Major noted for his report. And perhaps Serbia, the third ally, also had its eyes on such a well-established port; what would the Emperor of Austria-Hungary, Serbia's northern neighbour, say to that? And the Czar of Russia say to any interference with Serbia? And the Kaiser say to Russian interference? The dominoes of Europe were all ready to topple, and the Major unconsciously stiffened his shoulders as he stood with Antony and Alexander.

Of course, a European war would be a terrible thing, quite dreadful, however short it must be. But it was for the politicians and diplomatists to avoid it. A soldier's job was to take what came, and if that included action and promotion, so be it. The Major had missed both the Sudan campaign and the South African war.

Good God – suppose the politicians kept Britain out of it!

The Greek officer led him through the neat lines of artillery and machine guns – drawn up not for battle, but to impress the citizens and journalists of Salonika – to a clutch of small buildings beside a railway line. These too had been bombarded, and he thought they were still smouldering until he realised the smoke came from cooking fires and looted stoves.

He paused to look at the shell damage with professional interest.

It seemed curiously arbitrary: a patch of wall had been blown apart, some of its stones reduced to a muddy paste, yet a few feet away there was unscratched woodwork and unbroken panes of glass.

A group of officers huddled round a stove glanced at the Major's papers, glared at him, and gestured out through a doorless back door towards a smaller whitewashed stone building. His escorting officer stayed by the stove.

"Colonel Ranklin?"

The man asleep on a folded tent in one corner had a round, childlike face that aged into strained lines the moment he woke. Then he worked his dry mouth and scratched in his limp fair hair, making grunting noises.

"I'm sorry to be the one to demote you, as it were," the Major said, "but it's 'Captain' Ranklin again now. I'm here to reclaim you."

The man levered himself up into a sitting position and scratched vigorously at his thighs. He was short and, despite the last few weeks, slightly tubby. He wore a long goatskin waistcoat over his Greek uniform and hadn't shaved for some days, but the stubble was so fair that it only showed where it was stained with grime.

"Who the devil are you?" he croaked.

That wasn't the way you spoke to a Major in the Coldstream. "I represent, at some moves, His Britannic Majesty."

"Good for you," Ranklin said, peering at the Major's uniform in the dim light. "How did you get here?"

The Major decided not to mention the ox-cart. "On the good ship HMS *Good Hope*, now anchored in Salonika harbour and waiting, among other things, for you."

Ranklin got stiffly to his feet. "But I'm number two in this brigade."

"Not any longer, I fear. It's all been cleared in Athens."

He handed over the documents and Ranklin glanced at the preambles and signatures.

"But I resigned my commission in the Gunners."

"And now, effectively, you've resigned from the Greek gunners, too."

Then Ranklin said what was, to the Major, a very odd thing: "Did you collect my pay?"

The Major's face stiffened with surprise. "I . . . I'm afraid it didn't occur to me."

Ranklin was wiping his face with a damp rag. "Well, I'm not leaving Greece without it."

"I was told, unofficially, to pass on a message that I don't understand: that if you don't return to London there will be civil as well as military consequences. So shall we get a move on, *Captain?*"

It wasn't quite that easy. Having conceded the Major's basic demand, Ranklin made no effort to hurry. A small boy tending a fire by a large hole in the far wall made him a tin mug of coffee, and Ranklin sipped as he sorted through his kit. Most of it, along with battered tins of tobacco and sugar, he gave away to other officers and gunners who drifted in to say goodbye and scowl at the Major. Nobody even gave him the chance to show his haste by refusing a mug of coffee.

"Who's the boy?" he asked.

"Alex? He just adopted us on the road. His parents are probably . . . " he shrugged. "He doesn't say, doesn't seem to want to remember them . . . I suppose it could have been our guns."

"Some guns had certainly caused civilian casualties at a crossroads I came through. Don't your chaps look where they're shooting?"

"Of course not."

The Major stared. "I beg your pardon?"

Ranklin stopped in the middle of packing a small haversack and looked at him. "Haven't the Coldstream heard of indirect fire yet? We've stopped the sporting habit of putting the guns and gunners out where the enemy can get a decent shot at them. Now we skulk behind hills and forests and shoot over them." He went back to ramming socks and underclothes into the haversack and said more thoughtfully: "And it works. It really did. Observation and signalling, the clock code, ranging, concentration – everything we've been practising since South Africa. It all came together and it worked. Our guns won."

"Really?" The Major held the low opinion of artillery common among soldiers who have never been shot at. "Well, that's something you can tell them back in London. And that it makes for a pretty messy war in this part of Europe."

Ranklin slung the haversack from his shoulder. "We've been using French guns, the Turks have German ones. How's it going to be different in any other part of Europe?"

The Major didn't know; he just felt that it ought to be. Then he had to wait while Ranklin went in to say goodbye to the Brigadier – and, it seemed, the Paymaster. He came out of the station ticket office counting a roll of worn drachma notes and they walked back to the Salonika road.

Ranklin stowed the money away. "I suppose you've got no idea what they want me back for?"

"Not the foggiest, old boy. But after twenty years in the Army," and he guessed Ranklin had also served nearly that long, "I'm only sure it'll be something you never thought of." He was too well-bred to have put into words his feeling about an officer who fought for money, but now he saw a chance to hint at it. "Perhaps they want you for some sort of job in *Intelligence*."

CLIMBING SPY HILL

2

The first thing he noticed when he came on deck was the smell, steam and coal smoke, that was both exciting and threatening because it was the smell of travel itself. Just as, to Ranklin, the smell of wood smoke had once meant the security and comfort of his family home.

In the four months since the gun lines at Salonika, he had got back his normal slight tubbiness and his face its clean roundness, with a wisp of fair moustache as ordered by paragraph 1696 of King's Regulations but invisible at more than a few paces. But what most people remembered about him was the permanent small smile that kept his blue eyes crinkled half-shut and gave him a look of innocent optimism, as if he were looking to buy a solid gold watch off the next stranger.

He had developed that expression over most of his thirty-eight years because he knew a more serious one looked absurd on his boyish face. But it was an expensive smile, attracting beggars and unnecessary but tippable help, and a misleading one. Ranklin leant firmly towards pessimism rather than optimism, no matter what King's Regulations implied about it being All Right On The Day.

A long shudder rippled through the ferry as its engines slowed and they came into Cork harbour, past the Army forts that guarded the entrance and then the vast steel side of a four-funnelled liner pausing briefly on its run to, or from, America. In New York it might belong; here it looked ludicrously wrong, towering above the islands and headlands that cluttered the bay and standing rock steady while the tenders and bumboats serving it pitched and rolled in the swell.

Closer in lay a row of armoured cruisers, looking less warlike than industrial: all drab, stiff complication like bits chopped off a factory and floated out to sea. And beyond them the port of Queenstown sat on terraces cut into the face of a long ridge that, low as it was, almost scratched the gloomy March sky. The western end, he knew from a map, was called Spy Hill – but so was the highest point in many ports, meaning just the place from which incoming ships were first espied.

He peered through the thin drizzle, searching for Admiralty House, and knew it the moment he saw it because he had seen exactly the same building in every port of the Empire he had visited. With its canopied balconies, tree-shaded garden and tall flagpole, it gazed out over the heads of whatever natives it happened to be guarding with that serene superiority that only the Royal Navy could achieve.

Ranklin smiled at it with renewed pessimism and felt resentfully in his pocket to make sure he had enough change for the porters and cabbies waiting for him ashore.

"Bad luck, your kit not catching up with you," the Admiral's Secretary said, politely assuming Ranklin wasn't dressed as a civilian on purpose. "Happens to us all. Sherry or pink gin? I don't suppose you know anybody; I'll introduce you."

The Secretary was a Staff-Paymaster, with a Commander's stripes and well senior to Ranklin; fiftyish, bald on top, with a ginger-grey imperial beard. The Admiral himself was at a conference at Dublin Castle: "He sends you his apologies," the Secretary invented kindly.

The rest of the dinner party was all male, all Naval, and more jovial than the first mouthful of the first drink could justify. Either there was good news around, or the Admiral's absence was good news itself.

"How's London?" the most senior – a real Commander – asked.

"Cold and wet and all the taxis on strike," Ranklin reported.

"Yes, I read something about that," a senior Lieutenant chipped in. "The cost of petrol, isn't it? Eightpence a gallon. Damn it, we must pay more than that here, don't we?"

"Since you're the only one with cash to waste keeping a car on these roads, you should know," the Commander said.

The Lieutenant shook his head. He had a face that was both lean and limp with a puzzled expression, as if the world were always moving too fast for him. "I notice you didn't turn down the offer of a lift, but damned if I know what I pay for petrol."

There was a general chuckle and a junior Lieutenant forgot himself and tried to be funny.

"Why don't you get one of your clerks to embezzle David's pay?" he suggested to the Secretary. "He'd never notice and you could divvy it up among the rest of us."

This time there was a general silence and the Commander growled: "Not in the best of taste."

The Secretary stepped in to save the bewildered Lieutenant. "You've been on leave, haven't you, Ian? Well, I'm afraid one of the Paymaster's clerks *is* up for misuse of funds – and Lord knows what else, when the investigation's complete. Sorry to wash our dirty linen in public, Ranklin."

"Oh, I think the Army's washing line's quite as busy." And they smiled gratefully.

"The funny thing," David said, "is that he got caught trying to pay it *back*."

"Ah," the Secretary said. "That's the great mistake. There's no column in an accounts ledger for repentance. If you've been clever sneaking money out, you have to undo all that cleverness to get it back – and at best you end up with two irregularities instead of one and double the chance of starting an investigation."

"I wonder what's the theological view on that?" the Commander mused. "Repent not lest ye be found out. How's that entered in the Great Ledger Up Yonder?"

"If you meet any ledgers in the next life," the Secretary said with feeling, "it's proof you've been posted to the Other Place. Shall we go in?"

Leading the way as their guest, Ranklin heard behind him David saying plaintively: "But where did he get the money to pay back?"

"Lucky with the gee-gees – at last," the Commander suggested.

"But what races – in the weather we've been having?"

3

As with the drawing room, the dining room furnishings must have been provided by the Admiralty, giving the impersonal harmony of a stage set: "Act II, a room where visiting Royalty and lesser species may sit around a large dignified table on hard dignified chairs and, when the conversation lags, stare at pictures of sailing ships where at least the rigging is accurate. A few conventional souvenirs such as a Zulu shield and Chinese vases are permitted, to show that the Admiral has actually been abroad."

But for all that, it was still a warriors' dining room, full of familiar rituals, Ranklin's own world more than any he had known. Only it wasn't, not any longer. His ease with the routines, the conversation, even the jokes, was real – but still a sham, because he didn't really belong. He himself, not his behaviour, was the pretence.

"You're Worcestershire, aren't you?" David asked quietly from his place at Ranklin's elbow.

Instantly wary, Ranklin said: "Yes, originally."

"I knew your brother John, not very well, but – I was dreadfully sorry to hear of his death. A shooting accident, wasn't it?"

"Yes."

Realising Ranklin didn't want to talk about it, David hadn't got the knack of changing the conversation completely. "Well – at least you didn't have to resign the Army to take his place."

"No." What place? he thought sourly, then accepted that he had to find a new topic for himself. "D'you know what time the *Maggie Gray* will be getting in?"

He probably should have said "moor" or "berth" but that wasn't what caused the flurry of Naval glances. The Secretary coughed and said: "I don't think we're expecting her until, ah, sometime tomorrow morning, are we?" He looked to the Commander for help, and got it.

"With a southerly wind the channel's tricky enough even by day, and it only needs to back a couple of points and she'd have to anchor in the roads. And I've known times when the big liners have just passed us by – eastbound, that is – too rough for the tenders to go out, and with a boat train to meet at Southampton . . . "

"You haven't had a signal from her, then?" Ranklin asked timidly.

The chuckle around the table was unforced, if cynical. "From a Merchant wireless operator?" the Commander said. "Most of them aren't qualified to put in a new light bulb. It's absurd that we have to transport our stores, ammunition and . . . er, everything, in chartered merchantmen. The South African war cost us . . . well, I don't know, but quite ridiculous. What we need, and it's for the Army's sake as much as anything, is a cargo fleet manned by our own people . . .

So, with the SS *Maggie Gray* apparently still out of sight and mind, the conversation sailed on through the savoury, the passing of the port and the loyal toast. Then the butler, clearly an ex-sailor from the days of wooden ships, passed the silver box of cigars. Ranklin chose the smallest, perhaps subconsciously hoping that when it was finished they could finally get down to business – although how, with this crowd around, he didn't know.

But the Secretary calmly chose a cigar like a truncheon and, when he had finally got steam up on it, started a mock-pompous tirade against the junior Lieutenant for smoking a cigarette.

"You admit it's a filthy habit and that's just the point: it's a *habit* when it should be a *pleasure* . . . "

Shut up, go away, and leave us to get on with it! Ranklin screamed silently. And, as if he had read Ranklin's mind, the Commander pulled out a large watch and went through a ritual of consulting it, saying: "Well, the Navy may be going to the dogs, but I'm going to my night's repose."

There is always something artificial about such leave-taking, with juniors following their seniors' lead, but this seemed more planned than most. Nor were there any farewells between those leaving, no "I'll see you at . . . " or "Will you be going to . . . ?" They just left, in a bunch, having made clear to Ranklin that he should stay.

Well, perhaps the Secretary had, after all, given them orders – though the whole dinner had been unnecessary, in Ranklin's view.

"Bring your glass through," the Secretary commanded. "Give them a chance to clear the table."

In the drawing room he half opened the long curtains across the French windows that led onto the house-length balcony and ornate stone steps into the garden. From there, in anything but fog, the Admiral could stare out over the whole bay, now a long low constellation of riding lights and lit portholes, threaded by slow comets that were the sparking funnels of tugs and tenders still at work.

"I wonder," he mused, "if we'll dare be showing all these lights this time twelvemonth? Or even six months?" He sighed and let the curtain drop. "Now, Captain, will you please tell me what your orders are?"

From being too polite, the conversation had suddenly become a great deal too blunt. But, Ranklin reflected, he was the junior and very much on Naval territory. And it wasn't as if he were going to tell the whole truth anyway.

"I believe you've had a signal about the rumour that the Fenians are going to make an attempt on the *Maggie Gray* and her cargo?"

The Secretary nodded. "We have full precautions in hand."

"I have been detailed, with your co-operation, to take charge of one man who is thought to be involved in the attempt. If your people catch him. Even if they kill him."

The Secretary was registering surprise and some distaste. "What an extraordinary business."

"The man is not Irish," Ranklin said quickly, "nor English, and couldn't pass for either. He's expected to be sailing for America in the next day or so, after . . . whatever happens. I spent the afternoon doing a round of the shipping offices . . . " It had been a dispiriting experience, jostling through crowds of Irishmen and –

far fewer – women, all intent on leaving their homeland and the Empire he was sworn to defend for the hope-paved streets of America; " . . . but he's used half a dozen aliases we know of and probably more we don't so . . . Anyway, we – my superiors – just want to stop him sailing but keep him out of the hands of the police."

"And lawyers and courts and newspapers, hey?" the Secretary said shrewdly. "Well I won't say the Navy hasn't done that before. But who are your superiors? Who are you, come to that?"

"Oh, I'm just a Gunner, pure and simple," Ranklin said, wishing it were true. "This is just one of those odd tasks; I was spare, between appointments . . . "

"Hmmm. I expect you'll be glad to get back to your pure and simple gunnery. If I may take advantage of my age and give some advice, don't let them – whoever *they* are – get you too mixed up in these sorts of carry-ons. There's altogether too much of it about these days, spying and so on. We may need it in India and Ireland, too, sometimes, but it's got nothing to do with honest-to-God soldiering and sailoring. We're in clean, honourable professions and it's our duty to keep 'em that way. And if they want spies, let 'em comb the jails for such people."

Like most landlocked sailors (and deskbound soldiers, to be fair) the Secretary talked a strong line in blood and thunder. But Ranklin mostly agreed with him. He nodded and said: "Oh, quite, absolutely," with sincerity, then asked: "Can you tell me what the arrangements are for the *Maggie Gray* when she arrives?"

"She'll unload at Haulbowline – that's the berths on the dockyard island in the bay."

"Is that normal routine?"

"Oh yes. Most Naval stores go ashore there, most of them are distributed to our ships by tender anyway. That's how the ammunition will get to your forts: they're the devil's own job to reach by land; the roads here aren't made for lorries, especially in winter."

Ranklin could well believe that, but still found it odd that the Navy's first thought when moving something was to do it by sea, even over a few hundred yards. But it left a delicate problem.

"This may sound absurd, sir, but unloading at the island and so on – it doesn't give anybody much opportunity to interfere."

The Secretary raised his eyebrows and smiled. "Do you want them to have a chance? Yes, I suppose you do, if you want to catch one of them. But the matter of safety has to come first, and since we're talking of five hundred tons of ammunition – "

"Almost impossible to turn into bombs. Though, of course, the Fenians might not be expert enough to realise that."

"Quite possibly, but suppose their plan is just to set the ship on fire? D'you want a blazing ammunition ship along the quayside by the town down there? You can't expect us to take any risk of that."

Ranklin nodded glumly. He had realised from the start that he could fail, but knowing nothing of the routines here could not see in detail why he would fail, so he hadn't felt too depressed. But now he saw precisely how.

Only that meant that the ambushers should fail for just the same reason, and they must have known the unloading routine here when they made their plan. And a mere explosion – however un-mere it might be considered as an explosion – didn't sound like the ambition of the man he was after.

He was in a tricky situation. "If," he said cautiously, "an attempt is to be made, is it possible that the Fenians know something that, er – *I* don't?"

"Quite impossible." Then the Secretary realised he had said that too quickly, and added: "Of course, I can't tell just how much you do know."

"When you say 'impossible' do you mean there is something, but you think it's impossible that they should have found it out?"

The Secretary gave him a cold and senior look. But Ranklin was thinking of the rest of the dinner party leaving in a bunch, perhaps with a purpose that wasn't the Commander's "night's repose". "Could it be," Ranklin ploughed on, "that you expect the *Maggie Gray* a good deal earlier than I've been led to believe?"

"If so," the Secretary said blandly, "it would be earlier than certain others have been led to believe as well."

You bloody old fool, Ranklin thought; didn't you realise that the very existence of a plan to ambush the ship means they've got a source of information inside your dockyard? And if you haven't caught that source, you've no idea what information it's passing on.

With careful calm, he said: "We – and I include my London

superiors – are all on the same side."

"But our aims are different, it seems. I want to save Queenstown from being blown off the face of the earth, you want to catch a particular man. You wouldn't care to tell me just why capturing him is so important to you – and to whoever your real superiors are?" He smiled a superior smile and puffed on his cigar. "No, I rather thought not. I'm afraid, Captain, that matters will just have to rest there."

4

Only matters didn't, because at that moment three men stepped quietly from behind the curtains covering the French windows. They carried, respectively, a shotgun, a pistol and a rifle.

"If ye'll be keepin' quiet, gentlemen," the one with the shotgun said, "we'll be doing jest the same." And he patted the shotgun barrels. He had a long face, mostly hidden by a tangle of black moustache and beard, and wore a short seaman's jacket over whipcord breeches. As his glance searched Ranklin he seemed to hesitate, frowning, and Ranklin had the absurd idea that they had met somewhere before.

The man with the rifle moved quickly to check the doors to the dining room and corridor; the third man made sure the curtains were properly closed, then turned, and Ranklin certainly knew him, although only from photographs: the man he had come to Queenstown to collect.

Then the Secretary decided he owed it to his age and rank to say something useless: "What the devil d'you think you're . . . "

"Be quiet, Admiral," the man with the pistol – Peter, as Ranklin was thinking of him – said with a faint accent.

The shotgun man chuckled. "Ah, he's no admiral. But he should be knowing how many's in the house."

"If you think . . . " the Secretary began.

"Tell them," Ranklin said. "It'll be safer for the servants."

"Yer a wise man." But the dark eyes under the matted black hair were still puzzled about Ranklin.

The count came out as the butler, a footman and a kitchen maid;

26

the cook lived out and the Admiral's servant and his wife's maid had gone to Dublin with them. That sounded right to Ranklin, and he let his nod of agreement show.

At a word from Peter, the man with the rifle laid it aside – cautiously; he wasn't used to firearms – and began searching them. He was young, not yet twenty, Ranklin guessed, and probably very scared under his aggressive pose; that made him dangerous. Then he found Ranklin's card case, opened it, and read out his rank and name.

The shotgun man gave a little satisfied grunt, then: "And now put it back. It's got a badge on it, d'ye want that and the story of it showin' in the pawnshop window?"

Reluctantly the younger man handed the case back. "And if he's a captain, where's his uniform? A spy, more like."

"Sure, sure," the other soothed. "And carryin' his cards and eatin' at the Big House for disguise." He smiled through his beard at Ranklin.

So he knows me, and knows I can't remember him, Ranklin thought. But he doesn't want to announce that; could there be an advantage to me there?

Then Peter took charge. "You will go and imprison the servants. Here, I am on guard." He was both taller and younger than Ranklin and held his sharp-faced head with a high, nervous pride. His dark hair and moustache were neatly trimmed, and when he stripped off his shabby overcoat he was wearing evening dress and, more surprisingly, a crusting of elaborate foreign decorations and honours.

This display enraged the Secretary. "How *dare* you, sir!" he erupted. "You're nothing more than a damned *bandit!*"

The pistol jabbed towards his stomach. "Do not make me angry," Peter said. "I need you for my plan but I can make a new plan." It was the very lack of anger that made them all, even the Irishmen with their own guns, hold their breath. They might kill if it meant something, Ranklin thought; Peter will kill because it means nothing.

The Secretary swallowed and shut his mouth. "Sit yourself," Peter ordered, waving the pistol to include Ranklin. They sat in deep chairs from which sudden movement was impossible.

The other two went out; Peter stationed himself by the fireplace holding the pistol – a pocket-size semi-automatic type – loosely by his side. "You," he said to Ranklin, "you are a captain of artillery. What do you do here?"

Ranklin remembered to be properly reluctant and sparse in his answer. "I'm here to inspect the guns in the forts."

"And then?"

"I report back to my superiors."

"Report what?"

"I don't know yet. I only got here this afternoon."

Peter nodded, not really interested, and then looked at the Secretary, who clenched his mouth firmly. Peter smiled. "I do not ask your secrets – I know them already. I just tell you what you must do. I tell you, and you will have time to think how to cheat me. Think carefully. Think how, when you try to cheat me, you can stop me killing you. All of you: him, the servants, the sentries at the gate – yes, I know of them – the men who bring the gold. All of them. We have enough bullets."

The *gold?* Ranklin felt his ears peaking like a rabbit's. *What* gold? Whose? – presumably the Navy's, certainly the government's – But where, how . . . ?

He hadn't controlled his expression and Peter was smiling at him. "Yes, Captain: you did not know about that. Twenty thousand gold sovereigns for the fleet out there. You think your big guns rule the world, but no: it is small guns – " he gestured with the pistol, " – and gold."

The butler came in, high-coloured and highly indignant, ushered by the black-bearded man who was now carrying the rifle. He held it with familiar ease at the high port position, finger clear of the trigger – and that way, Ranklin remembered who he was. Or had been. This time, he kept his face expressionless, but nobody was looking at him anyway.

"They're all locked up," the man reported, "and the maid so sniffling scared she'd have the footman wrapped round her like a blanket and welcome – if Mick wasn't watching. I'll be taking the Captain now, then."

Peter nodded. "Yes, take him . . . Ach, Captain: as an officer, it becomes your duty to be sure the other prisoners stay quiet – and alive."

As Ranklin was marched out, Peter began giving instructions to the Secretary and butler: "Remember now, I am Count Viktor de Bazaroff of the Imperial Russian Embassy, asked by your Foreign Minister to give information – most secret – to the Admiral who sails with the fleet . . . "

The only basement room with a proper lock was the wine cellar, lit by a single unshaded light bulb and, of course, unheated. The kitchen maid, pale, wide-eyed and tear-stained, sat huddled in a nightgown and a blanket at the end of a rack of dusty bottles. The footman, in his shirt sleeves and collarless, leapt up from his seat on a wine box as Ranklin came in. He was little more than a boy and it was only the audience of the kitchen maid, Ranklin guessed, that was keeping him calm.

And perhaps only these two who are keeping me calm, Ranklin's thoughts confessed. But of course he had to take charge of them: it was expected of him, no matter that they weren't his servants and the situation wasn't of his making nor understanding. No matter how badly he did it.

"There's nothing to worry about," he announced, then corrected himself. "Nothing that worrying will improve, anyway. We just have to wait – and keep quiet. I've been nearly twenty years in the Army and I know there's times not to try and be clever. This is one." He realised he was speaking mostly for the two Irishmen behind him, and hoped they were listening. "Now, lad, if that's a case of brandy you're sitting on, get out a bottle. There must be a corkscrew around somewhere, so we'll all have a tot to keep us warm."

"A thoughtful deed, Captain," the black-bearded voice said over his shoulder. "Though when was drinking permitted in cells?"

"Just a mouthful. And for yourself?"

"Thank ye, Captain, but I'll get by a while without. Step into the corridor when ye've finished dispensing rations."

The corridor was just as dimly lit and a waggle of the shotgun – they had swapped weapons again, and "Mick" with the rifle had gone back upstairs – suggested he shut the cellar door behind him. They stared at each other.

"Well, now, Captain . . . "

"Well, Private O'Gilroy."

A long sigh. "So ye remembered – only it was Corporal and an honourable discharge *wid* two good conduct stripes – afterwards." Was it odd that a man could be so flagrantly outside the law and yet remember, with precision and pride, his loyal Army service? Perhaps not: they had been things he had set out to do, and done; real achievements.

O'Gilroy took a paper packet of Woodbines from a pocket and tossed them to Ranklin. "Light me one – and yeself, if yez a mind. I fancy I owe ye more'n one, not counting the ones we rolled of tea leaves."

Ranklin lit two cigarettes and placed one delicately in the muzzle of the shotgun offered towards him. O'Gilroy transferred the cigarette to his mouth, then leant against the flaking whitewashed wall and breathed smoke for a while. "Garrison Artillery, is it now? Isn't that a bit of a comedown?"

"As pure gunnery it's a step up, all barrel wear and air pressure and magazine temperatures – "

" – and beer and more beer; *I've* seen them, bare able to stand for the weight of their bellies even whiles they're sober. That's garrison gunners." He breathed smoke for a while, then said slowly: "I don't know what to be doing wid yez, Captain, and that's a fact. I'm not fool enough to take yer parole, nor yet believe ye'll forget me' face oncest we're gone – so I jest don't know."

"Is it your decision? The foreign gentleman upstairs seemed to be doing the deciding."

O'Gilroy's face was shadowed in the dusty light, but Ranklin saw him stiffen. "Jest helping, Captain, as a friend of Ireland."

"Really? He's certainly a friend of gold."

O'Gilroy lifted his face to show his frown, but said nothing. Ranklin went on carefully: "I've seen his photograph on posters in London. He's wanted in Russia, as well, and maybe France and Portugal. I don't think he was helping Ireland in those places."

"I'm no child to think we're the only ones in the world wid troubles – nor yet that I'd be better off a Russian peasant. He's talked of them, and I believe him. But there can be friendship in adversity; I fancied ye knew that yeself oncest."

"There can be pilfering and hoarding and swindling, too, that doesn't get into the heroic stories in the newspapers and official histories, and you know *that*. What's he taking as his cut?"

"Are ye trying to spread disaffection in the ranks, Captain? He's taking no cut."

"And that doesn't make you suspicious? The labourer's worthy of his hire."

O'Gilroy had smoked his cigarette down to a glowing fragment; now he flicked it against the wall and said firmly: "And I think that finishes everything in orders for the day, Captain, so if ye'll be getting back to cells . . . "

Ranklin didn't argue with the gesturing gun. The cellar was windowless but had a rusty punched-metal grille in the door, impossible to see through, to let some air in to circulate around the racked bottles. Ranklin stayed close to it, listening to the key creak in the lock and then O'Gilroy's footsteps fade back along the corridor.

The footman was sitting so far from the kitchen maid that he'd obviously been much closer before Ranklin came in; now both looked at him with the hope on their faces as thin as the light. Ranklin tried a reassuring smile. "So now we go back to waiting. Did the brandy help at all?"

They over-enthused their thanks, the kitchen maid adding: "But I don't like to think what the butler will say." She was a local girl, the footman was English.

"He's got other things to worry about. And that being the case, I might take a drop myself. And for you?" From the level in the bottle, they'd had no more than a spoonful each.

The footman didn't mind if he did, but the girl shook her head. "Thank ye kindly, sir, but it's terrible strong stuff."

It was also terribly nice stuff, and Ranklin looked for the first time at the label: a forty-year-old Hines worth about twenty-five shillings a bottle, so they'd each drunk a day's wages already. Well, it was a rare luxury for himself these days, and if the Admiral really wanted to bring the matter up . . . though his years in uniform had convinced him that a few shillings' worth of misappropriated brandy was exactly the sort of thing senior officers did like to concentrate on in a crisis.

"What are your names?" He should have asked that before, if he was in charge. The footman was Wilks, the kitchen maid Bridget.

"And I'm Captain Ranklin, Royal Garrison Artillery. But I'm afraid I forgot to bring any of our big guns with me tonight." No, he wasn't good at this sort of thing. But they ha-ha'd dutifully.

"Wilks – upstairs there was talk of gold, twenty thousand pounds worth. Do you know anything about it?"

Wilks shrank back from the thought. "It's not for me to listen to what the officers are saying, sir."

Bridget looked at him with contempt. "No, but ye do, me little man, and blether it to the likes of me to show yer importance. Now be telling himself that really needs to know."

It was possible, Ranklin reflected, that Bridget's virtue didn't need as much protection as everyone seemed to assume.

"Well, sir, it's for the squadron. The cruiser squadron in the harbour. There's talk of them being sent to the Mediterranean." Ranklin was snobbishly surprised that Wilks pronounced the word perfectly – but of course this was a Naval household where such names were as common as . . . as gold, apparently. And with a new outbreak of fighting in the Balkans the Admiralty might well be sending flag-showing reinforcements. But . . .

"But twenty thousand pounds: how on earth are they going, in taxis?"

"Ha, ha, sir. No, it's for the captains, sir. They always take golden guineas to foreign parts."

Of course. A warship commander was far more on his own than his Army equivalent. He might need repairs in some out-of-the-way port, or supplies, or just the latest rumours – all easiest bought with gold sovereigns that were recognised worldwide. "But . . . is it being brought *here*? Hasn't the Paymaster got a safe somewhere?"

"He must do, sir, but it seems it isn't as safe a safe as the Admiral's here."

So it was all a cunning plan to defeat the very robbery that was now going on. And he could guess at how cunningly it had itself been defeated: the embezzling clerk in the Paymaster's office had found the money to repay his theft from the sale of that information. Finding such men and exploiting their weaknesses sounded like Peter's doing. It was just such work that spies and their ilk were expected to be good at.

But that still left the robbers with a problem: "I wonder how much it all weighs?"

Wilks shrank back again. "I'm sure I don't know, sir."

"No, no, sorry. I was just thinking aloud." He took three sovereigns from his pocket and clinked them in his palm: small but heavy, weighing – as much as an ounce? Then he remembered how recently he had been concerned with the price of gold on the market. Depending on its "fineness" it ranged from just under to just over four pounds an ounce. Perhaps that was troy weight, but he only wanted a rough figure. So four pounds times sixteen divided into twenty thousand is just over three hundred pounds in weight. Even split into three loads, no one man was going to stroll out of here with over a hundred pounds of gold in his pockets. They must have a cart or carriage nearby. Or a car.

Then they heard a car – just a distant growl filtered through an airbrick high on the outside wall. The door creaked open behind them and O'Gilroy was standing there. Holding the shotgun one-handed, he pointed it silently at each of them in turn and held a finger to his lips. It was a macabre little performance.

Then, above them, the front door slammed and footsteps – many of them – creaked the ceiling. The gold had arrived.

5

Ranklin walked to the door and listened. But O'Gilroy would be well away, probably at the top of the cellar steps and ready to intervene up there. Any noise they made down here could be dealt with later, after the slaughter in the hallway that was all they could cause.

He turned away and made a brief exploration of the cellar, finding nothing but a drain hole in one corner and a small table with a candle-holder used for decanting wines. But behind one of the tall racks, he was out of sight of anybody else for the first time in hours. He pulled up his left trouser leg and ripped loose the surgical tape that held a tiny pistol just below the hollow behind his knee. It was a two-barrelled derringer, an American gambler's sleeve gun barely three inches long and accurate no further than the width of a card table, issued to him "just in case". Just in case, he had reckoned, he needed a false sense of security. But now, maybe . . . Well, maybe.

He slid it into a pocket, hoping O'Gilroy and co. would be content with just one search, and went back wearing as cheerful a smile as he could manage.

"Begging yer pardon, sir," Bridget whispered, "but would ye be, sort of, knowing the . . . " She pointed to the door.

"Yes, but for God's sake don't mention it. He doesn't seem to want his . . . colleagues to know, so let's leave it that way." He was pretty sure by now that Bridget wasn't one of Peter's or O'Gilroy's informants, and sharing confidences was a good way to raise morale (though raise it for what, he had no idea).

"He was a soldier in an Irish regiment at the South African War. Before your time," he added. He might think of himself as still young, but these two had barely been of school age when that war began. "His battalion got chopped up before Nicholson's Nek, where I had a troop of field artillery, I was a subaltern, then. He was probably lucky that he got wounded and dropped out early: we picked him up in the retreat and . . . " They might be listening, but he could be describing the battle of Agincourt for all they understood or could imagine. "Anyway, we ended up besieged in Ladysmith with him attached unofficially to my troop, sharing roasted rat and horsemeat soup until General Buller condescended to relieve us four months later."

They might imagine that – the diet, anyway. Not the heat and flies and bombardment from guns better than their own, nor the daily death list from sickness . . . No: born in an Irish city, Bridget could probably understand that list.

"It must have been frightful, sir," Wilks said, as convention demanded.

Less conventionally, Bridget said: "And now he's the man ordering yez around wid a gun? And yeself an officer? It shouldn't be allowed."

"Er – yes. Quite." Class distinctions weren't uppermost in Ranklin's mind just then. He was grateful for the distraction of more footsteps overhead, another slam of the front door and, soon after, the rattle and chug of a car engine. The delivery of gold must be complete and the curtain ready to rise on the last act. How did they plan to get the gold out of the house? Carry it down the back garden and over the wall into someone else's garden and . . . ? He didn't know what, but it seemed chancy. And there were two sentries – Army, not Marine – at the front gate, mostly symbolic, but likely to ask questions of any cart or car at that time of night. And even then –

"Wilks," he said, speaking low and quickly, "they must have some vehicle to carry the sovereigns. Now, if they want to get it out of Queenstown, how would they go?"

He had asked the wrong person; without a local upbringing or any military training, Wilks had no concept of seeing himself at a geographical point. He could think of two roads out of town, no, three or maybe . . .

Bridget rescued him. "There's jest the one road off'n the island, sir."

"*Island?*"

She couldn't suppress her grin. "Did ye not know yez on an island, sir?"

So with all his military experience, Ranklin had managed to miss that simple fact. His one glance at a map had suggested Queenstown was on a peninsula, with a lot of shallow creeks around.

"Just one road?"

"Aye, sir, the road to Cork over Belvelly bridge, next the railway."

So whoever held that bridge could keep the gold on the island – if Peter wanted to get it off, of course.

"Mind, sir," Bridget added, quietly enjoying herself, "Wid a rowing boat ye'd be jest ten minutes acrost to Monkstown or Glenbrook. Or An Pasaiste or East Ferry on t'other side, and if'n the tide's over the mud, then anywheres . . . "

In other words, you were on an island. And, by boat, could get off it in any direction. He was still thinking like a landlocked soldier.

A yell, abruptly cut off, came from upstairs, followed by scuffled footsteps and a thump. The front door slammed again.

"What was that, sir?" Wilks asked, wide-eyed.

"Don't know, but keep quiet. And calm." Whatever it was, it had been something nasty. Ranklin fingered the hard cool metal of the derringer in his pocket. It might not profit himself, but he could leave one body as evidence for the police . . .

Footsteps clattered on the stairs and corridor and the door opened wide. The Secretary, the butler and a private soldier in a blue-grey greatcoat were pushed inside. The soldier had lost his cap, the butler was white-faced and clutching his stomach.

Ranklin got a glimpse of O'Gilroy and Mick in the corridor before the door slammed on them all.

The soldier burst out wildly: "They killed me mate! Just stuck a knife in him, the bastards!" He was young and pale and shaking.

"Steady, lad. I'm Captain Ranklin, Royal Artillery. Now, who did it?"

The soldier calmed down, but seemed struck dumb. The Secretary said: "That damned German or Russian or whatever he is. Just cut his throat from behind, when . . . and they made me call them in to be murdered! God, I'd like too . . . "

Bridget let out a sobbing squeal and clutched at Wilks. He put his arm awkwardly round her shoulders.

Ranklin said: "Right, at least now we don't have to guess at how serious they are. Here – " he poured the soldier a tot of brandy and looked around for the butler, who was suddenly sick against the wall.

"That's the *Admiral's* brandy," the Secretary said, confirming Ranklin's view of senior officers in a crisis. He just said: "Yes."

The Secretary coughed. "The one with a beard butt-stroked him with the shotgun. The man's been a soldier to know how to handle a weapon like that."

With a warning glance at Bridget and Wilks, Ranklin said: "Perhaps, but I don't advise speculating out loud. You're witnesses to a murder, now. Not the safest job on the market."

The Secretary had calmed down. "I want a word, Captain." He led Ranklin behind a rack of wine to the furthest corner just a few feet from the servants and other ranks, but now Officers' Territory.

"What do you think they'll do with us?" he whispered. Just asking a question was a slight transfer of authority.

"First," Ranklin whispered back, "how will they get the gold away?"

"They've got the keys to the stable where the Admiral keeps his car."

"Ah." Ranklin hadn't thought of that possibility. But that car, easily recognised, could be a passport to – where? O'Gilroy had said Peter wasn't even taking a share of the gold, which had to mean he planned to take the lot. Some to America now, and bury the rest, probably. He could recover it in just a two-week return voyage – or leave it as a nest egg in case he got chased out of America, too. "Where are all your people and Marines and so on?"

"Guarding the *Maggie Gray* and the ammunition. We all assumed the gold would be safe once it was in this house."

Feeling that any comment would be unhelpful, Ranklin asked: "What's the state of the tide?"

"The tide? Just past full, I think. Ah, you think they plan to use a small boat, away from the harbour. Yes, they could do that in the next hour or two."

Distantly, they heard the sound of a different car engine and the squeal of brakes; Ranklin wondered which of them could drive. "Are you prepared for me to take the lead?"

"I don't see what you might do that I can't," the Secretary said stiffly.

"Nevertheless."

The Secretary was two ranks senior to Ranklin, but only in the Navy's Civil Branch. He frowned at Ranklin in the blotches of dusty light coming through the rack of bottles and Ranklin smiled his optimistic smile back.

"You've seen action, I trust?" It was an abdication.

"Yes."

"Very well, then. I suppose you and that young soldier . . . "

"They'll be watching for that combination. Just let me make the first move." It wasn't that he had any move in mind, just making quite sure the Secretary had none either.

They heard the key in the lock once more and moved back to meet O'Gilroy in the doorway. He pointed the shotgun at Ranklin. "Ye come wid me. There's heavin' and carryin' to be done."

In the corridor, Ranklin asked quietly: "Why me?"

Just as quietly, O'Gilroy said: "I know ye for a quiet man, Captain. Not excitable. And one that can start plotting if he's got time to think."

So O'Gilroy had assumed he would take charge in the cellar and wanted to leave the group leaderless. It was an odd compliment.

He stepped through the traditional green baize door at the head of the stairs – and into a puddle of blood. He shivered and stopped, but there was no avoiding it: cutting a man's throat leaves a floor like that. The soldier's shrunken body lay scooped aside against the wall.

"Why did you bring *him?*" Peter demanded loudly; he stood just beyond the blood pool.

O'Gilroy didn't dare to explain the real reason. "Ye gave me the choice." There was a tightstrung tension in the hallway; Mick stood with his back to the front door, unable to keep his hands still

38

on the rifle. And the very fact that none of them was willing to lay aside his weapon to carry the gold suggested an apprehension, perhaps mistrust, that could have started with the murder of the soldier. Ranklin didn't think the Irishmen had expected that: perhaps a mistrust he could exploit.

But first he had to carry twenty sealed bags of sovereigns from the safe in the Admiral's office out to a blue Vauxhall tourer that sat rumbling under the lamppost in the carriageway. He stowed them on the floor by the back seat, and when the last had gone in there was a noticeable sag of the rear springs.

Peter said: "So now a few broadsides will not be fired at the poor of the world." It fell flat; nobody was thinking in such terms now. "Now take him back."

O'Gilroy said calmly: "Let Mick take him."

"What does it matter?"

"So let Mick take him." Did O'Gilroy not want to leave Peter unwatched, with the car now loaded and running?

"My friends, we do not quarrel now."

"Sure. So let Mick take him."

Muscles in Peter's face twitched. O'Gilroy was impassive behind the beard, but his thumb was on the shotgun hammers, his finger on the first trigger.

The telephone rang.

Everybody moved in one spasm, then froze in place. The ringing went on, from the Admiral's desk deep in the dim office. Peter looked around, his face taut.

"You," to O'Gilroy, "you will say . . . "

"Not me: they know there isn't an Irish manservant in the house."

"Then you," to Ranklin now. "You say – you say one wrong word and you die."

Proof of that lay crumpled against the wall, and Ranklin had no intention of giving up his life to save, perhaps, twenty thousand pounds of Admiralty funds. He picked his way through the shadows and lifted the earpiece. "Admiralty House."

"Lieutenant Colonel Kirkwood here," the telephone said. "May I ask who that is?"

An arm reached over Ranklin's shoulder and a knife glittered faintly. He said calmly: "This is Captain Ranklin. Did you want the Secretary? He's, erm, in the lavatory at the moment . . . "

"No, thank you, sir. Just checking. And would you tell Lionel that I'm doubling the guard at the next change? Just as a precaution. Good night, sir."

The knife pulled away as Ranklin hung up, frowning. "Just checking," but what could he or any man have said with a knife at his throat or a gun at his back? Then he chuckled.

Peter was instantly suspicious. "Why do you laugh? What did you say to him?"

"He called me 'Sir'. Must have thought I was a Navy captain."

O'Gilroy grinned, too, but the military niceties were lost on Peter. He pushed Ranklin towards the hallway – and into the sudden eye-stinging waft of petrol.

"Jayzus!" O'Gilroy lunged forward.

Mick stood grinning in the reeking hall, with the car's now-empty spare petrol tin lying beside the dark blood pool.

"Now isn't it a quieter way than shootin' the lot of them?" he said. "And a diversion besides to keep the English busy whiles we git acrost the channel."

"Yez never goin' to burn every soul in the house!" O'Gilroy turned on Peter. "Tell him, ye idjit! Tell him it'll be settin' the whole country alight and never a place to hide!"

The shotgun was staring in Peter's face and he made placating gestures, rather spoiled by the knife in his hand. "But, Conall, you agreed we must . . . "

"Ah," Mick said. "Me big cousin's jist gone soft." And he struck a match.

The rasp spun O'Gilroy round. Perhaps he fired at the match flame but it was in front of Mick's chest. Or perhaps he just reacted with the instinct of a man who has been controlling a situation with a gun. The blast took the match and Mick's chest in one gulp and slung the remains halfway through the baize door.

In the hall, it was like a coastal six-incher firing. It blew Ranklin's eyes and ears shut, and when he got his eyes open again, fully expecting the hall to be ablaze from the blast, he saw Peter drop the knife and grab for his pocket. Forgetting his own pistol,

Ranklin dived for Mick's abandoned rifle.

There was no sound, not through the ringing in Ranklin's ears, just a dumb show of one man trying to free a pistol from a tight-fitting pocket, another grabbing up a blood-slippery rifle, thumbing for the safety-catch – then Peter gave up and jumped through the open front doorway.

6

Now unhurried, Ranklin half-opened the rifle bolt to check there was a round in the breech, then looked for O'Gilroy. He was in no hurry to rush into the darkness that now hid Peter and his pistol.

O'Gilroy was cradling his dead cousin in his arms, sobbing wildly and, to Ranklin, silently. He hesitated, then the roar of the car's engine, cutting through his deafness, startled them both. O'Gilroy laid Mick down and reached for the shotgun.

"Did he git away?" he seemed to be asking, and Ranklin nodded. O'Gilroy snapped off the light and looked cautiously out into the driveway. The car's rear light was just vanishing past the lodge.

O'Gilroy surprised Ranklin by turning and running back into the drawing room, but he followed. And out through the French windows, down the steps into the garden and on down the sloping lawn.

"Where are we going?" he asked.

"Yer not invited."

"Shoot me, too, then," Ranklin puffed, scrambling over a stone wall on what seemed to be a familiar route for O'Gilroy. For a while he thought O'Gilroy was taking up the suggestion, since he fumbled to reload the shotgun as they crossed another garden, another wall, and ran down an alley into a lower street. But now he had the derringer hidden in his clenched hand – hidden well enough for that darkness, lit only by flares of half-moon light among the ragged clouds.

They came out under the dark stunted bulk of the spireless cathedral, and O'Gilroy turned into a darker alley and grabbed one of two push-bikes hidden against the wall.

"D'you know where he's going?" Ranklin demanded.

"I do that." He climbed on the bike. "I hope I do," he added, and rode off, not bothering with the lamps. Ranklin stared at the other bike, presumably the late Mick's, then pocketed the derringer and climbed aboard.

The bike was arthritic and loud with rust and took almost no notice of its screeching brakes as he plunged downhill on slippery cobbles. But at least Ranklin was fit: that legacy of the Balkans hadn't worn off, and as he came to the bottom of Spy Hill and on to the flat road that ran round the corner of the island, he began to catch up with the weaving shadow ahead.

O'Gilroy was riding with the shotgun held crossways on the handlebars as Ranklin came up alongside. Not too close alongside, since the road was flat only in principle, not counting details like potholes and ruts now they had left the town behind. They seemed to be paralleling the railway and the channel up to Cork, heading for Belvelly bridge.

"Have you got a boat . . . cross the channel in?" Ranklin asked in puffs.

"Niver ye mind."

"I know this man . . . he's wanted in London . . . Peter Piatkow was his name there . . . Peter the Painter, did you hear of him? . . . the Sidney Street siege . . . the Houndsditch murders before that . . . you think he's joined your cause? . . . others thought that . . . they did the robberies and got shot . . . a factory, then a jeweller . . . "

"That's not my business wid him."

"It's his business with you . . . taking his cut . . . only this time it's the lot . . . to America . . . he's booked his passage," though that was only rumour. But the rumour that had brought Ranklin there.

They trundled past the lights of a shipyard and the road closed up on the channel again. There were lights on the far shore, no more than a quarter of a mile away, and closer still the lights and skeleton masts of a windjammer being towed down from Cork on the tide.

"Piat-kow, ye said his name was?" O'Gilroy asked.

Ranklin gave a grunt of relief. He thought O'Gilroy had only been half listening, acting on another instinct that made him chase Peter without thinking whom he was really chasing, or what to do when – if – he caught up. Now, perhaps, he had begun to think again.

"The name he used . . . in London . . . Probably a different one here . . . he's used half a dozen . . . in France, too."

"And what d'ye want of him yeself?"

"I'm just along . . . to guard your back."

"Yer a connivin' liar, Captain. Is it the gold or the man ye want most?"

"We haven't got either, yet."

Ahead, the road swung sharply right and dived under the railway track. O'Gilroy slowed, then dismounted and pushed his bike straight ahead at the turn, onto an overgrown and muddy track. Ranklin got off and followed, his bike squeaking and grinding.

O'Gilroy stopped. "Leave the bikes, ye sound like a tinker's cart. Mick niver would take care of machinery, God rest him."

They lowered the bikes onto the grass, beyond sight of the road, and moved ahead beside a row of spindly trees. Beyond, Ranklin could see the dull sheen of the channel and, closer, the duller glint of wet mud. O'Gilroy moved right, inland, to avoid being silhouetted against the water and sky.

Then, dark against the mud, Ranklin saw the hard curve of a rowing boat. They stopped. The car might be in the darkness of the trees, but there was no shape, no light, no sound but the gentle wind. They waited, Ranklin curling his thumb over the derringer's hammer. It was awkward, too small a gun even for his hand, and he hadn't practised enough since he hadn't much believed in it. He wished he believed in it now. Then Peter moved.

Just a dark shape coming from the trees towards the boat, slowly, with faint mudsquelching noises. O'Gilroy took several silent paces, Ranklin following in a crouch. A hot machine smell stung his nostrils and, peering, he could see the car just a few yards away.

There was the thump of something heavy on the wood of the boat, then Peter squelched his way back towards them. O'Gilroy let him get within ten feet.

"Would ye be wantin' any help wid the gold, Mr Piat-kow?"

44

Ranklin wished he could have seen Peter's first expression. But his mind and voice recovered quickly. "Conall? You escaped also? Wonderful! Yes, help, please, into the boat." He came forward, towards the car, O'Gilroy covering him with the shotgun.

"Would that be the boat to America, then?"

"What do you mean? Who have you talked . . . who is with you?"

Ranklin said: "Take his pistol. Then talk all you want."

"The Captain?" Peter said, peering through the gloom under the trees. "Why did you bring . . . "

"I'll be takin' the pistol, all the same."

Ranklin glared at the shape that was Peter, wanting to hate him, reminding himself of the trail of blood that led across Europe to this muddy patch, of the dead soldier in the hall, wanting to want to kill him. He just felt cold.

But a soldier should feel cold. Not hate. The enemy was a thing, an obstacle, an obstruction to be removed. Think of this man as the enemy.

"The pistol?" Peter said. "Oh, it is in the car. I show you." He turned to the car, turned his back on O'Gilroy and the shotgun.

And Ranklin, abandoning wanting and trying and thinking itself, raised the derringer at arm's length and fired both shots into Peter's back. Immediately, there was a third shot.

Ranklin jerked his glance at O'Gilroy, but the shotgun hadn't fired. Peter fell, with very little sound in the wet grass and mud, gave one gasping moan and died.

O'Gilroy stepped forward, bent, and picked up the pistol that had been in Peter's waistband, that he had grabbed when he turned his back. "Ye was quicker'n me, Captain. He'd mebbe've shot me."

No, Ranklin thought dully, I wasn't quick. I shot an unarmed man in the back. I didn't know he had his finger on a trigger. I was just doing my duty.

"Only I didn't know ye had a gun," O'Gilroy went on. "Is it my turn now?"

"It's empty." Ranklin gave it to him and stooped over the body.

Surprised, O'Gilroy peered at the little pistol. "I niver saw the like before. And where was ye keepin' it?"

"Taped to the back of my leg."

"I'd've missed findin' it meself."

Ranklin straightened up holding a bunch of papers, then took out his matches and lit one of the car's acetylene lamps.

"Jayzus," O'Gilroy protested. "Ye'll have every constable and all the Army itself on us – "

"Just for a moment." He read quickly through the papers in the lamplight. "Here we are: a second-class berth in the name of Vogel, on the *Carmania* to New York, later today. D'you want to see?"

Numb of mind, O'Gilroy glanced at the ticket and nodded. Ranklin turned off the lamp.

"Well now," O'Gilroy said. He lowered the hammers on the shotgun, propped it against the car, and sat down on the running board. "And now d'ye . . . No. First, d'ye have a cigarette?"

They both lit up; Ranklin opened the rear door of the car and sat on the seat beside several bags of gold, just to get his feet off the ground. His thin evening shoes were leaking and his toes freezing.

"And what about the gold?" O'Gilroy asked quietly.

What indeed? Ranklin had already been thinking about that. If he piled it back aboard the car, drove to some corner of the island and buried it, O'Gilroy would be committing suicide if he denounced him. It would be plain theft and horribly disloyal but genteel poverty was horrible, too, and twenty thousand would just about put his family back on its feet.

And, of course, give him away, because it would be immediately clear that his family *was* back on its feet, most creditors paid off. The only reason he wanted the gold would betray that he had taken it. He sighed and put the idea behind him (but later, being as pessimistic about himself as about anything, he wondered which had been the stronger motive for leaving the sovereigns alone. Or, as it turned out, almost alone).

"When you think about it." he said, "that steamship ticket was your death warrant – and Mick's. He couldn't have left you two alive. He would have killed Mick anyway."

"I'll remember who killed Mick," O'Gilroy said tonelessly.

And I who killed Peter Piatkow, Ranklin thought. And exactly how.

"And the gold?" O'Gilroy prompted.

"As far as I'm concerned, you can take it – as far as you can get with it."

"So ye was jist after himself." He nodded at Peter's body. "Wid yer little gun. And what would it all be for?"

"He was some sort of revolutionary – Anarchist, Communist, Menshevik, Bolshevik, perhaps all of them at one time – going to America to organise things there." It was absurd to be discussing the Bureau's affairs with this man, but Ranklin badly needed to sort out his own thoughts. "I was to prevent him, arrest him separately from – anybody else."

"It sounds like somebody's been talking about us," O'Gilroy said thoughtfully, and almost stopping Ranklin's heart. What had he betrayed now? Then he realised that just by planning to ambush the ambushers, the Bureau had given away its hand, and must have withdrawn its informant already – or be sure he was above suspicion. He started breathing again.

"Arrest him – or kill him?" O'Gilroy added.

"I was prepared for that," Ranklin said stiffly.

"I see ye was. And nobody to know, is that it? And then what?"

"I do not have to explain myself to you." Ranklin hoped his stiffness hid the fact that he had no idea.

"Ye do not, and that's a fact." O'Gilroy smoked and thought for a while. "But ye wanted his ticket and papers."

Ranklin had assumed that was simply as proof, like taking Peter's scalp. But now he, too, began to wonder.

"So if ye had a man waitin'," O'Gilroy said slowly, "and wid his bags packed, he could be sailin' in Piat-kow's place. And them in America'd never know, not knowin' him already. Would that be the way of it?"

Suddenly faced with the naked idea, Ranklin knew that *had* to be the way of it. But why hadn't the Bureau trusted him with full knowledge? Because he might have been captured and talked, of course. And why hadn't he worked it out for himself? Because he had set out doggedly to obey orders he hadn't liked. And while O'Gilroy might be used to thinking in such crooked ways, he himself wasn't.

And then came the appalling shock of shame that he had accidentally revealed the whole scheme to O'Gilroy.

47

"Do you believe," he said as earnestly as he could, "that if you breathe one word of this to anybody, then if I don't hunt you down and kill you, somebody else most certainly will?"

O'Gilroy thought carefully about that, then said: "No."

7

Ranklin, who from his brief experience of the Bureau hadn't believed it either, nevertheless felt rather taken aback. But O'Gilroy took a last suck at his cigarette, pitched it into the trees and went on: "No, there's none of yez could do it, and most'd have the sense not to try. But what's to worry? Yer talkin' to a dead man, when word gets round I killed me sister's boy and banjaxed the whole matter. How far d'ye think I'll get, come the day?"

Ranklin instinctively glanced at the east, but the day was still on the far side of the world.

O'Gilroy said heavily: "And would ye believe I come along tonight jest to be sure the boy didn't come to harm – Jayzus." He shook his head. "Would ye have another cigarette? I've thinkin' to do."

They smoked in silence, except for the noise Ranklin made trying to shuffle life back into his almost-beyond-pain toes. Breaks in the cloud showed patches of vivid blackness, pinholed with sharp stars, and on the earth below, the mud flats looked like smooth slimy lumps of offal.

Halfway through his cigarette, O'Gilroy asked: "Was ye thinkin' of gettin' me strung up for the killin' of that soldier?"

Ranklin was a bit surprised that the idea hadn't even occurred to him. "No, as far as I'm concerned, that score's settled with . . . " he gestured towards Piatkow's body. "And the people I work for, they aren't really concerned with Ireland."

"Is that a fact, now?" O'Gilroy went back to thinking. Then: "Yer new to this work, then, Captain?"

"Yes." Ranklin wished he hadn't said that so vehemently.

"Ye'll be needin' some help, then."

"I need to dispose of Piatkow. The channel here should be quite deep, in the middle."

O'Gilroy nodded. "And the fact is, I'm needin' some help meself, not fancyin' bein' shot by me own friends or hanged by yourn."

A man under sentence of death from two sides has little left to lose. And, Ranklin reflected, no good reason to keep any secrets he may have stumbled on.

"I'm prepared to get you out of this," he said carefully. "But you'll have to tell me how to do it. This is your home ground."

"I mean out of Ireland, Captain."

"That, too."

"Good enough. It'll mean yer tellin' some fancy lies, now."

"I'm supposed to be getting used to that," Ranklin said coldly. "Now, can we . . . ?" He walked over to Piatkow.

O'Gilroy threw away his cigarette and followed. "Remember a dead man floats, Captain."

"Not one as rich as he's going to be." Three thousand pounds in Admiralty gold, he had calculated, should keep Piatkow at the bottom until any buoyancy had rotted.

"Jayzus!" O'Gilroy whispered as the awesome cost of the idea sank in.

"It's only Navy money. Ends up on the bottom anyway."

With Piatkow sunk, O'Gilroy rowed back to the shore. Ranklin wasn't surprised to find he was a competent oarsman: he found he was assuming the man was competent at all such things, as well as being good at dreaming up an escape plan combined with a tale for Ranklin to spin to the Navy. And even that was a form of competence, he supposed.

"What are you going to do when you reach England?" he asked. "You daren't go near the Irish communities in the big cities. The story could get there even before you do."

O'Gilroy pushed the empty dinghy back into the ebbing tide; that was part of the plan. "Been thinking about that meself, Captain. Seems mebbe ye could lend me the passage money to America . . . "

"You might be no better off there."

" . . . or give me a job."

Ranklin stared through the darkness, then exploded. "Good God Almighty! Are you *serious*?"

"Ye said ye needed help. Judgin' by tonight, I'd say yer right." He wiped some of the thick mud off his boots on the coarse grass and tramped back towards the car. Ranklin followed in a daze.

But after a time he realised his shock was more at O'Gilroy's effrontery than at the idea that the man could do the job. If tonight was in any way typical, he was perfectly suited to such work. And the Bureau's recruitment policy, he thought bitterly, was none too delicate.

He made a half-hearted attempt to clean up his own shoes on the richer grass away from the water's edge. "You didn't exactly start this evening on our side."

Perhaps O'Gilroy's shadowy figure gave a shrug. "I wasn't fightin' for yer Queen and Empire in South Africa, Captain, and I'm not offerin' to start now. I was fightin' for me pay. And for some fellas, mebbe – like yeself." He paused. "And a bit for meself, besides."

How would the Bureau feel about taking on a pure mercenary? But hadn't it found him on the Salonika road, selling the only talent he had? Hard times make for soft principles, it seemed.

"Have you got a criminal record?" He found he had said it formally, as if to a new recruit.

"No." O'Gilroy was positive enough. But that might only mean that he was cleverer than the police. But again, isn't that what the Bureau wants?

"Oh hell, this is the most ridiculous . . . " He shook his head. "We'll get to England and let *them* decide. But it could turn out to be just another helping of roasted rat."

"And ye was always a most gen'rous man wid that, Captain. Now, could ye be lendin' me a coupla sovereigns 'til payday? I'm not wantin' to go near any house or shop I'm known."

With a sour glance at the remaining bags of gold, Ranklin took them from his own pocket. "And we meet somewhere near the railway station?"

"At the bottom of Spy Hill. That sounds about right."

A LONDON CLUB

8

Lunching at this club was always a hazard for the Commander. He had just decided on the curry when an angular Brigadier-General of the Royal Artillery, wearing the red tabs of a staff job, folded himself into the chair opposite and gave him a conspiratorial smile.

Oh God, thought the Commander.

"And how are things not going in that non-existent Bureau which you don't command?" the Brigadier asked, twinkling at his own well-rehearsed wit.

This was the hazard, although even worse were the handful who honestly didn't know the secret and simply asked what he was doing these days. On the other hand, kidnapping being illegal, he depended on fellow club members for a flow of recruits.

That thought got garbled in the thinking, he reflected grimly. For "flow" read "drip", as with a faulty tap, and the results were usually as annoying.

"Well enough," the Commander said, grinning falsely. Even out of uniform, he would have looked like a Naval officer: in his fifties, solidly built, with bright eyes in a large head whose nose and chin seemed prevented from meeting only by the briar pipe he usually wore in between. His usual expression was aggressive but amused and he was trying hard to keep the balance: he did owe the Brigadier something.

"How's the recruiting drive coming along?" the Brigadier asked.

"Splendidly," the Commander began, then had to break off to order his lunch. The Brigadier chose lamb chops, was told it was too early in the season, and opted for pork instead.

"And half a bottle of the Beaune," he added. "You'll join me in a glass? Did I hear you say 'splendidly'?"

"If I were recruiting for a concert party to tour the better lunatic asylums, yes."

The Brigadier laughed. "The dear old Army game of pass the parcel; sooner or later it's everybody's turn to be the Dead Letter Office. But in all seriousness, you can't expect us to send you our best officers, chaps we've been training for fifteen or twenty years. We're only human."

"Which is more than can be said for the people you do send me."

"Oh, come now – what about the last chap I put you on to?"

"At no great sacrifice to yourself, since you'd dropped him and he was serving in the Greek Army at the time."

"Well, you can't keep a chap who's about to be hauled into court for bankruptcy, even if it was allowed. His brother officers . . . well, they wouldn't . . . it would be an embarrassment to . . . " He was grateful that the arrival of the soup stopped him.

"Anyway," he resumed when the servant had gone, "I noticed you'd got him back in the Army List as attached to the War Office. Does that mean you solved his money problems for him?"

"To an extent." The Commander was ready to leave it there, but the Brigadier obviously wanted more, so he went on: "We – our bank – offered his creditors a cast-iron Deed of Composition so that they get paid off in instalments and only care about the bank, not him."

"By that, d'you mean nothing has to come out in public?" The Brigadier fixed on the only aspect of bankruptcy he knew or cared about.

"That is correct."

"Good. We look after our own, in the Gunners." The Brigadier, who had done nothing but gossip Ranklin's name to the Commander, gulped soup smugly. "I hope he isn't resenting our efforts as being an act of charity or something damn fool."

"I think he resents it rather more as being an act of blackmail. He's not a bloody fool, not entirely. He certainly resents working for me. But he'd like the alternatives even worse."

The Brigadier frowned uneasily and dabbed soup off his moustache. "Look, I hope you're not being too hard on the chap.

He seems to have been a perfectly good officer until . . . "

"Well-travelled, languages, able to mix in respectable society – I can use all that. And he can pretend he's still got money, even to himself if he wants. I want good pretenders."

The Brigadier didn't like this turn in the conversation. "It isn't as if he was an absolute blackguard, spending it all on women and horses. I expect you went into the details, but I understood it was really his elder brother getting into the wrong crowd at the Stock Exchange and then shooting himself when it all went wrong. I thought our chap just signed some papers that got him involved, and if you can't trust your own brother . . . "

"Splendid lesson. I don't want him to trust anyone."

The Brigadier looked at him warily. "Aren't you being rather ghoulish? I know you expect your chaps to dress up in disguise and so forth, but surely you want men of good character underneath."

"Do I?" the Commander asked blandly. "You may be right, but I really don't know. Not yet."

"Good God. Why don't you go the whole hog and hire some of these Irish fanatics?"

"How can you be sure I haven't?" The Commander smiled wickedly. "They've certainly got the experience, and Irishmen make good mercenaries: the 'Wild Geese' tradition. Continental armies are full of Irish names. And all I ask is a full day's skulduggery for a full day's pay."

"Good God," the Brigadier said again. Just then their main courses and wine arrived and there was a lull of serving, pouring and tasting. The Brigadier chewed thoughtfully for a while, then said: "Of course, it is rather difficult to imagine what sort of person would actually want to be a spy."

"Agent. We prefer 'agent'."

The Brigadier raised his eyebrows, acting more surprise than he felt. "Really? I don't imagine your chaps introduce themselves as 'agents' any more than they do as 'spies'. However, if you feel their self-esteem needs such unction . . . "

The Commander said nothing.

"When I was younger," the Brigadier mused, "it seemed to me that we had the best Secret Service in the world. It never got mentioned in the newspapers, its – ah, agents never got caught, it seemed to function perfectly, in perfect secrecy. Only later did I realise that this was because we had no Secret Service at all. Oh, a few *ad hoc* arrangements in India and Ireland, but no organised Service until you were asked to set up your Bureau. And I suppose a myth has fewer practical problems than the real thing."

"Quite," the Commander said.

"Such as finding the right personnel."

"Exactly."

"Particularly if you have a clearer idea of what you don't want than of what you do." The Brigadier looked down at the haggled bits of pork on his plate. "As with this chop."

"As with that chop, you just have to make do with what you've got."

The Brigadier laid down his knife and fork. "When I reached General rank, I decided there were some things I no longer had to swallow."

"Lucky you," said the Commander.

KEEPING THE CODE

9

They got a first-class smoking compartment to themselves on the train to Newhaven, carrying three copies of the Anglo-French military code "X" parcelled up in Ranklin's hand baggage. It wasn't the genuine code: that was the "W" one, three copies of which were being carried by Lieutenant Spiers of Military Operations in the next compartment. And somewhere else on the train was a gentleman with three copies of the equally false code "Y".

It was all overcomplicated and uncertain and Ranklin didn't like it. Why, for instance, wasn't the code simply going by Diplomatic Bag?

"Because," the Commander had explained, "the Foreign Office doesn't know about it. Half the Cabinet doesn't know we've got as cosy with the Frogs' Army as to need a joint code. Their Liberal morality would be outraged and their mistresses would have told all of London by lunchtime. And we don't want two years' work thrown away.

"Mind you," he had added, "damn few secrets last that long, especially when they involve the Frogs' Ministère de la Guerre. That's why we've undertaken to deliver the code ourselves, right to their front door."

"Does the Ministère know when the code's supposed to arrive, sir?"

"Oh, yes. So if there's been any leak, it'll come from their end, and it'll be your job to prove it. Spring any ambush, fall into any trap. I envy you: should be jolly good sport."

Sport?

"I want two volunteers to go ahead until they get shot, then report back," O'Gilroy interpreted.

"Apart from that word 'volunteers', that seems to be the case."

"And just what will we be doing when somebody tries to relieve us of our precious burden?"

"We're supposed to use our discretion."

"By that d'ye mean yer little gun?"

"No, I haven't brought that."

"That's the first good news I've heard about this job. If somebody found that on ye, specially taped behind yer knee, it'd be a badge saying Secret Service. Ye don't happen to have such a badge, do ye?"

"Of course not." Ranklin was too ashamed to admit that he had once asked the Commander if such a thing existed – a distinctive signet ring or cigarette case, even something pasted inside a watch – to identify brother agents to each other. The Commander had said with threadbare patience: "I thought I told you when you joined the British Secret Service that Britain *has* no Secret Service. Therefore, how can it have a badge?"

O'Gilroy was saying: "Fine, but then what will we be doing with him? – just kick the right to vote off'n him?"

"Well, try to find out who he is and who he's working for. No, I don't imagine anybody'll just jump at us from a dark alley, that sort of thing . . . " But he had no idea of what the unknown anybody might do – nor of what he would do in their place . . .

"And don't smoke your cigarettes down that far," he snapped at O'Gilroy's lean and exasperating smile.

The idea of treating O'Gilroy as an equal – another country gentlemen, albeit an eccentric Irish one – had at first struck Ranklin as impossible, but in fact came easily. His great weakness as an officer, one which made him an indifferent leader, was that unless he treated a man as his equal, he had little idea of how to treat him at all. He had often blessed the juvenile whim that had made him pick the Artillery when the inflexible pattern of life had forced him, as second son, to join the Army.

Trying to be a conscientious infantry officer, he now realised, would have been a life of constant doubt and embarrassment. He had learnt that he could cope in battle, steadily and thoughtfully if not with much dash. He could order men to risk their lives or kill others: that, after all, was what they were there for. But listening to a man's marital troubles, or his lame excuses for horrible misdeeds, just terrified him. It wasn't the gross details, it was the expectation that he should give advice that would do some good. Why should it? Who on earth was he to judge? And the Army had far more marital problems than battles.

But in the Guns, the rapidly evolving world of breech mechanisms, recoil buffers and sighting systems, the interlocking problems of range, muzzle velocity, trajectory, convergence and probability theory – all this created a firm ground on which he could meet other minds. And, largely, let their incontinent bodies look after themselves.

Perhaps that was why he had taken to O'Gilroy at Ladysmith. Pressed into service as a replacement gun number, the lad had been unforthcoming about himself even when there can have been little to forthcome about, but hungrily anxious to learn about the guns' mechanisms and routines. In teaching him, Ranklin may have been trying to create another equal, but the infantry had swallowed him up again once the siege was lifted.

And now, after thirteen years and some weeks of careful coaching, he had O'Gilroy back – as an equal.

The equal smiled wickedly and took another cigarette from his gold case – second-hand, as were his watch and wallet and thus well worn – and having stared carefully at its length, lit it. Ranklin clamped his mouth on his pipe and said nothing.

It had been easy to get O'Gilroy shaved, barbered and into the right tweedy clothes, and not too difficult to fit him with the general air of an Irish gentleman of leisure. He had known the genuine article well, having been chauffeur for a big house in Waterford (though how he had learnt to drive, Ranklin had no idea). And he obviously enjoyed life in first class.

But there lay the problem: he enjoyed it because it had only just come to him, and constantly forgot to waste it: to leave drinks, meals and cigarettes half-finished, the change from a sovereign uncounted. Oh well, Ranklin shrugged mentally, perhaps the French would simply think O'Gilroy was untravelled. He hunched down in his seat and stared unseeing at the damp April landscape rattling past the misted windows; he had been thinking too much of O'Gilroy and not enough of the job ahead.

And after a time, he said: "I've been a bit slow: they aren't going to steal this code from us. If we knew it had been stolen, we'd change it. A damned nuisance, but nothing worse than that, not in peacetime."

"Ah-hah? I've had no dealing with codes, but what ye say makes sense. So what would they do? Try to get a look at it and copy it without us knowing?"

"It'd have to be something like that. But again, how . . . "

"I'd think we watched who tried to make friends with us, then." He held up his cigarette to make sure it was precisely half-smoked, and ground it out. Ranklin pretended not to see.

10

Newhaven was a bad photograph of itself, colourless, grimy and blurred by steam and smoke. Despite the spatter of rain and a wind that creaked the lines holding the Channel steamer to the dock, Ranklin waited to see Spiers safely on board and then acted the worried traveller by watching their luggage – registered through to Paris – unloaded from the guard's van. If they were bait, he reasoned, they should be visible.

The steamer, built narrow for speed rather than stability, was trying to roll even alongside the dock. "I've no plans for sea-sickness," O'Gilroy announced, "but I'm thinking it has plans for me." Ranklin knew better than to argue: once a man believes that, he can be sick walking through a puddle. So he found their tiny day cabin and left O'Gilroy with their travelling bags and a flask of brandy to take care of each other.

Once the steamer had lurched off in a cloud of smoke and seagulls, Ranklin joined the crowd in the first-class saloon which, less defeatist than O'Gilroy, was already ordering the first round of cognac-and-sodas. Ranklin found a corner table, lit his pipe and opened the *Army Quarterly*. As he turned each page or paused to stoke his pipe, he glanced up through the fast-developing fug – a true smoker knows that smoking is a cure, not a cause – for prospective code-copiers.

But what would such people look like? Dark-eyed enchantresses? (there were no women at all in the saloon). Humourless, bristle-headed Prussians? Oily Levantines? There seemed to be none of them, either; most people in the saloon looked like just people.

Why on earth hadn't they been given more training? O'Gilroy had been particularly scathing about how much the Bureau knew, or was ready to impart, about its own job. And Ranklin found himself loyally defending his superiors, as a good officer should, whilst privately agreeing. The Commander's attitude seemed to be that spying was just another game that any officer-and-gentleman would take to naturally – which was exactly the opposite of Ranklin's view. In the Guns they didn't expect a troop officer to invent his own orders for loading, laying and firing, so why the devil . . . ?

His mood made the gale outside seem a timid amateur.

"May I sit here, please?" The voice was a low, slow Teutonic growl; the speaker a fat, slightly younger man with a big dark moustache and spectacles.

"Of course." Ranklin's manner snapped back into perfect politeness. The man hovered in a stooped position, trying to time his descent with the roll of the ship. He didn't quite make it; his well-upholstered backside hit the chair with a thump. He grunted and took a swallow of his beer.

"Not the best of days for the Channel," Ranklin said. "Do you mind my pipe?"

"No. Please." The man stuffed a cigarette in under his moustache and waved a match after it. Ranklin held his breath: the moustache looked very vulnerable. But the cigarette caught first, and the man held out a fat firm hand.

"Gunther Arnold," he announced. "I am going to France."

Unless I'm on the wrong boat, so are we all, Ranklin thought. "Captain Ranklin," he said. "I'm off to Paris."

"Just you alone?"

"No, I'm with a friend. He's got a touch of *mal-de-mer*."

"You are going for just fun?"

"To see some friends. And . . . ?"

"There is a new hotel," Gunther said, cutting off Ranklin's polite question. "The Crillon. You know it?"

"No, I . . . "

"It is very – " he waved a hand in a slow encompassing circle, " – very much. But not as much as the Ritz, I think. You know the Ritz?"

Ranklin had eaten lunch at the Ritz once. "I've just . . . "

"It is very much." Bavarian, Ranklin guessed, and full to the gunwales with beer, a familiar Bavarian custom. Gunther spotted the *Army Quarterly*. "You are a soldier? An officer?"

"Yes." He had been told to play himself on this trip. So close to home, there was too much chance of meeting people who knew him. And the *Army Quarterly* had itself been bait, though he'd hoped for a better fish.

"I was a soldier. Not an officer. If there is a war they will make me a soldier again. I think perhaps two soldiers." He chuckled and patted his stomach.

Ranklin smiled politely and wished the man would turn into an empty chair. "Are you going . . . ?"

"I know: you are on a secret mission," Gunther chuckled. Ranklin froze inside. How the devil did he answer that? Shrug it off, laughing? Get indignant? Go along with the joke? How would Captain Matthew Ranklin RGA take it? He had learnt in a flash that the hardest part in the world to play is yourself. Only those who have deliberately invented a self can do it easily.

But Gunther ploughed ponderously on. "You are to study the French fortifications – of the Moulin Rouge, Maxim's, the Rat Mort." He rumbled and shook with laughter. "Then you will have all the secrets of France." He coughed smoke and a fine spray of beer over Ranklin. "I wish you much luck." He heaved to his feet, mistiming the roll again so that he nearly sprawled over the table, and stumped away into the crowd at the bar.

Ranklin's relief was soured by his own clumsy reaction to that "secret mission" nonsense. Lucky that he had failed only in front of a Bavarian beer-barrel.

Towards lunchtime, he went to see if O'Gilroy wanted any. He found the man and the brandy flask empty and the cabin reeking.

"If ye say 'food' to me," O'Gilroy moaned, "ye'd best say the Last Rites besides."

"At least take a turn on deck," Ranklin urged. "The smell in here . . . "

"Do me a favour, Captain. Jest one."

"What?"

"Fall overboard."

So Ranklin had a table to himself in the uncrowded dining saloon. After coffee, he walked – or staggered – for a few minutes on the lee deck. Then, with perhaps half an hour to go before they reached Dieppe, he went back to the saloon.

Gunther was no longer there, but to his surprise, O'Gilroy was. He looked pale and haggard but, Ranklin had to admit, lean and handsome in a romantic-poetic way with his long dark hair falling over his eyes and talking expansively to an American at the bar. Ranklin's stomach clenched with apprehension. O'Gilroy must already be slightly drunk – that flask of brandy on a stomach that was unquestionably empty – and now with another glass in his hand . . . But damn it, this was the part of the trade O'Gilroy was supposed to be teaching *him*: how to lead a secret life unsuspected. If the man usually babbled when he had a drop taken, Ranklin reassured himself, we'd have had him in jail ourselves long since.

"I'm not a travelled man meself," O'Gilroy was saying, "not hardly at all. My little place in the Old Country keeps me tied down. But Captain Ranklin, now – here, Matthew – he's been the world over and backwards besides." He *was* a little touched by brandy, Ranklin thought, but it seemed to do no more than roughen his accent and colour his imagination. "This gentleman's wanting to know about getting off at – at France."

Ranklin shook hands with Mr Clayburn of Detroit. "If you're going to Paris and your baggage is registered through . . . It is? then you just get on the train at the dock. The delay comes at the Gare St Lazare, the station in Paris. You have to wait about twenty minutes while they organise your baggage and then you clear it through customs and the *octroi* – all they're really worried about is tobacco and matches and food. The *octroi*'s for taxing any food brought into Paris or any French city."

Mr Clayburn bought them both a drink and withdrew to find his Dear Wife. They moved to a corner table.

"How are you feeling?" Ranklin asked.

"Just don't mention it, and it won't mention itself. I'm not thinking Mr Clayburn's one of *them* – did ye have any luck yerself?"

"All I got was a fat German – you might have seen him, big moustache, glasses? That was before lunch. He was loaded and primed with beer. But that's all. I wonder if this whole . . . " But it wouldn't do to express his doubts in front of O'Gilroy. "There's still the train to Paris."

They went on deck to enjoy the suddenness, like waking from a nightmare, as the steamer finished a roll and, seemingly surprised herself, stayed upright as she slid between the jetties, and into the channel and harbour of Dieppe. Ranklin always enjoyed the sight of a non-British port. For a country that relied so much on its sea trade and Navy, British ports were remarkably surly-looking places. Here, even in the gusting rain, the defiant bright awnings of the café-lined quay, the tall houses above them, the arcade at the beginning of the Quai Duquesne, all suggested an *interest* in the comings and goings of the cosy little harbour. Perhaps "trade" was the key: English ports were tradesmen's entrances, mere necessities.

The Paris train was puffing impatiently on the dockside, late because they were late themselves in that weather. They got their travelling bags – Ranklin suddenly remembered they had been left unguarded in the cabin, albeit locked – handed the cabin key to the purser, and joined the crowd stumbling across the gangplank.

"Capitaine Ranklin! M'sieur le Capitaine Ranklin!" A uniform waving an envelope.

Ranklin was startled, then embarrassed, perhaps more as an Englishman having to unmask himself in front of a crowd than for his mission. He showed his passport, grabbed the envelope and tore it open.

Would Captain Ranklin urgently and personally telephone Colonel Yarde-Buller at the Embassy in Paris?

Despite his unlikely name, the Colonel was the perfectly real Military Attaché to the British Embassy, and the message could only originate with the Bureau, since only it knew . . . But one thing they *had* been told about their work was not to rely on military attachés who were appointed by the Foreign Office and totally subservient to their ambassadors. And ambassadors regarded spies as being even worse than warm champagne.

The French official was looking at him with frank curiosity. Damn it, they might as well have laid on a band and flags. He showed the message to O'Gilroy who shrugged and said: "The train's looking urgent."

It wasn't so much the train as the officials and blue-bloused porters, all enjoying a loud French panic as they bustled passengers aboard. They had already seen Lieutenant Spiers get in.

"Ah, M'sieu, est qu'il y a un téléphone?" But, naturellement, all telephones were for official use. However, at the hotel which one could not see because the train was in the way . . .

"Wait here," he told O'Gilroy, and galloped off down the slippery cobblestones.

The walk back, when he came out of the hotel, was much shorter because the train was no longer in the way.

"And the Colonel isn't even in his office this afternoon. What the devil the Bureau's playing at . . . "

O'Gilroy took it calmly. "Would it have to be the Bureau at all? It wouldn't need a genius to find out the Colonel's name."

"So you think we've been spotted?" The thought was both exciting and sinister. "But we have to pretend we don't know that. And as real couriers we'd want to get to Paris quickly, but safely. But if we were real couriers we'd be pretending to be tourists, so . . . " And standing between the scurry of replenishing the steamer and the busy cafés of the quayside, he began to feel the loneliness of his new trade.

"It's a mite fancy for me too, Captain," O'Gilroy said dryly. "We'd best remember if it's them, they'll play the next card."

"But we're cut off from Spiers: have they diverted us from him, or are we diverting them from him?"

"You did not go to Paris, then?" The low, slow Gunther Arnold growl, now wrapped in a flapping grey-green cloak that made him look like a fat Christmas tree. Ranklin couldn't imagine how he had got so close unnoticed.

"Some silly mix-up made us miss the train," he said.

"Then we must have another drink! And your friend also. I have a hotel – it is not the Ritz, but – yes?"

Ranklin tried not to stare at him. Gunther was, presumably, the first spy he had met. Apart from himself, of course, and other members of the Bureau whom he couldn't think of as *real* spies. But Gunther would hardly have been born into a Fine Old Spy Family, would he?

"That's very kind," he said pleasantly. "But we'll have to find out about the next train, then telegraph to Paris to make sure our luggage . . . "

"M'sieu?" This time it was a tall man in grey chauffeur's uniform, a small gold coronet embroidered on his breast and an unfamiliar badge on his cap. He bowed very slightly. "The General le Comte de St Col presents his compliments and wishes to know if he may be of assistance. He wishes your visit to France to be without problems."

"How thoughtful of him." Ranklin looked around for the General, feeling but resisting the attraction of a fellow soldier – even a General – in problem times.

"The General is in the automobile." It was parked a few yards away, a large white landaulette being gazed at by small and apparently rainproof schoolboys.

"And a very nice automobile to be waiting in," O'Gilroy murmured, and Ranklin looked at him sharply. He had resisted the temptation, so O'Gilroy could, too. Their task was to stay in Gunther's clutches but when he looked, the man had faded away again. Trust any general to pop up at the wrong time and mess things up, he thought angrily, then found himself following O'Gilroy towards the car.

The General, obviously well past retirement age, leant forward from the shadowed back seat, gloved hands resting on a walking stick. He had a thin face but puffy red cheeks, a long thinned-out white moustache and damp blue eyes. He shook hands as Ranklin was forced to explain a version of their problem.

"Sergeant Clement will telegraph to St-Lazare for the accommodation of your baggage. It would be an error to take the next trains, they stop everywhere to Rouen. But my house is on the route to there and is at your disposal after such a crossing. Perhaps you would wish to bathe, to take a small repas – and then Sergeant Clement will convey you to a comfortable express from Rouen. There is no problem."

It wasn't an order, not quite, and Ranklin was about to refuse politely when O'Gilroy simply climbed into the car. Ranklin now had the choice of getting loudly angry or getting in also. He got in, but he also got quietly very angry as well.

11

As he'd expected, the house wasn't exactly on the direct road to Rouen, and nor was it a house but a château. Not a grand one – it got its size from the height of its witch's-hat turrets rather than its width – but perfectly sited atop a small hill with a steep lawn down to the road in front and now-leafless forests marching up on either flank. Only as they chugged up the drive which curled round to the back could he see that the lawn needed scything, the creeper on the walls should be cut back and the drainpipes in the courtyard where they arrived were dribbling rustily down the stonework. It was nice to know that it wasn't only the English landed class that had been ravaged by death duties and the agricultural slump.

A manservant in worn but well-kept livery whisked away their bags – Ranklin should have foreseen that – and the General led the way inside. After a few paces, he halted and Took Off His Hat in a gesture that made Ranklin do the same and glare at O'Gilroy to copy.

"Gentlemen," the General said, "His Most Christian Majesty King Philippe of the French."

The portrait, hung to dominate the hallway, was of a middle-aged man with a long, full-lipped face and square fringe beard, wearing ducal robes. It was a recent picture but done in the style of the old court painters, with a stylised background showing, in defiance of geography, the Palace of Versailles on one side and Orléans cathedral on the other. Ranklin's memory fixed on that clue: the current pretender to the throne had taken the title of Duc d'Orléans, not his father's one of Comte de Paris.

Please God, don't let O'Gilroy say one word, but let me say the right ones.

"We are most honoured to be received in the house of a truly loyal soldier of France," he intoned hopefully. A sideways glance showed it had been well received.

An older and stouter servant took their hats and coats, and they followed the General into a drawing room overlooking the terrace and the unmown lawn sloping down to the road. Itching with anger at O'Gilroy, Ranklin took in only a vague impression of the room: strongly masculine and military – a small brass cannon as a paperweight – the walls hung with African trophies, group photographs and decorative but useless maps. If there was, or had been, a comtesse, she had had no influence on this room.

"Would you care for some refreshment?" the General offered, as the stout servant came in with a tray. "Of coffee, tea, or some wine?"

Ranklin was about to choose tea, then recalled his mistrust of the French version and took coffee. O'Gilroy, he was relieved to see, did the same. The General sat down with a glass of lemon tea and the servant – the butler, Ranklin assumed – arranged a Moroccan shawl around his shoulders.

For want of anything better to say, Ranklin harked back to the portrait in the hallway. "Are you acquainted with the Duc d'Orléans, sir?"

"His Majesty is gracious enough to correspond with me. I have not been fortunate enough to wait upon him."

O'Gilroy was looking baffled. Let him stew, Ranklin's anger said.

"Do you know if he plans any further travels, sir?" And as the General's thin eyebrows closed at this impertinence, Ranklin added quickly: "I thought his book on Spitzbergen was quite excellent. Most informative." And for all he knew, it might have been, along with being a daft place to write a book about.

The General was mollified. "I understand he plans no further travels. He knows his destiny lies in Europe at this time."

There was something, but not quite everything, unreal about talking of France accepting a king once more. Ranklin went along with it, partly to explore the General, but just as much to bewilder O'Gilroy. "I am reassured that His Majesty's leadership will be available in these dark times."

There was a tap at the door and the butler trundled over to bring the message up the chain of command: from housemaid to butler to General, who announced: "Mon Capitaine, M'sieu, your baths have been prepared. A small repas will be waiting on your return."

"That is most kind, but we do need to get to Paris . . . " They might already have failed in their task, except in distracting Gunther away from Spiers and the true codes, but there was an interview in London to think about ("And what did you do then, Captain?" "Well, sir, we wallowed in hot baths, had a bite to eat and toddled on our way . . . ")

"I quite understand, mon Capitaine. By then Sergeant Clement will have prepared the car to join the express at Rouen."

Resigned, Ranklin let the butler lead the way upstairs.

In a first-floor bedroom, with the same view over the lawn, their small travelling bags had already been half-unpacked. Ranklin waited until the door was closed behind them, then let fly: "What the devil were you up to getting us stuck out here? Didn't you realise that fat German was just the man we were supposed to watch out for, get caught by? So now we've lost . . . "

"Ah, calm down, Captain, dear." O'Gilroy was quite unruffled. "Could ye not see they're all in it together?"

Ranklin gaped.

"Sure, the fat German was to spot ye on the boat – and did – pretending to be drunk on beer before noon. And him the size of a garrison sergeant that could drink beer the day round without it touching him. And getting word of yer name ahead . . . Now, that I can't tell how he did at all . . . "

"Wireless," Ranklin said reluctantly.

"Ah, sure, I was too bothered with me stomach to see the boat had an aerial on it. And using yer name in a message so we miss the train, then him coming round being pushy on the dockside so when a nice general turns up with a nice motorcar, if ye'd been the officer with the real code, wouldn't ye think him, another army man, was an angel sent from Heaven?"

Ranklin wasn't about to agree that O'Gilroy was right. Lucky, perhaps, but . . . but at least he seemed to have guessed how a real courier might think. Or, perhaps more importantly, how their opponents assumed a real courier would think. He shivered to recall how instinctively he had been drawn to the General.

And if they were still in the trap they had sprung, he could relax and look around as he undressed. It was a high-windowed room with white-painted panelling edged with gold, a pink and green oriental carpet and a couple of elegant pre-Empire chairs beside the beds. But the whole had the dullness of old varnish on a painting, at the brink of becoming shabby and grimy.

Putting on his dressing gown and picking up a bath towel, he peeked at the parcel in his bag. "They surely can't be planning to copy the code while we're in the bath?"

"Not even while *I'm* in me bath." Constant hot baths were the high point of O'Gilroy's new life, and no nonsense about leaving them half-finished.

Ranklin's natural pessimism caught up with him and he was back in the bedroom sooner than he'd intended, leaving O'Gilroy sluicing in suds and folk song. The bathrooms had all been built in a clump around the recently installed main drainage, which made sense but gave a rather barracks-block effect.

He dressed slowly, putting on a fresh collar, puzzling over the odd combination of French general and German spy and very conscious of his own failure to think imaginatively earlier that afternoon. At last O'Gilroy drifted in, shining pink around a small, private smile.

"Captain, did ye notice a funny smell about the bathrooms?"

Ranklin might have done, but expected foreign bathrooms to smell funny.

"Chemicals," O'Gilroy said, watching him.

"Well, that's a step in the right direction. What bothers me – "

"So I took a shufti around the other bedrooms . . . "

"You didn't!"

"Is that not in our code of conduct, then? And I found one being used, with them big brown bottles of chemicals a fella I worked for in Ireland had for his photography, and a wooden case with a big camera in it . . . "

"They're going to photograph the code!"

"I thought ye might be interested," O'Gilroy said dryly.

That made the whole thing more feasible. They could photograph two pages of the book at a time just as fast as they could change plates. It also meant that O'Gilroy was right yet again. By way of congratulation and apology, Ranklin said: "Um."

O'Gilroy smiled faintly and began to dress. "And what was that about downstairs with His Majesty stuff, then? – and me thinking France didn't have kings at all."

"She doesn't, but in the last century she's had an emperor, a king, president-turned-emperor and president again. With passing help from the Paris mob and the Army. The General's obviously a monarchist, believes in having a king again. Quite a lot of the officer corps feels the same way."

There were some things O'Gilroy didn't know.

"So he wants the code for plotting agin the government?"

"That's what bothers me. He might want to overthrow *this* government, but why should a general turn traitor?"

O'Gilroy's look said plainly what he thought of the idea that Military Gentlemen just did not do Certain Things. And Ranklin read it clearly. "No, just consider: he must have spent at least forty years working to become a general. I just don't believe any man can spend that time pretending. Life's far easier if you believe in what you're doing."

Ranklin probably knew what he was talking about there, O'Gilroy reflected. "Money, mebbe?"

"D'you really think so?"

O'Gilroy considered: the Château might be run down, but it was still a château, still with land around it, with servants and the big motorcar. Perhaps it was the car that convinced him. "Mebbe not," he conceded. "But ye said he was agin the government."

"For patriotic reasons. Not to betray his own Army to the Germans."

"Do we know that fat German's working for Germany, 'cept him being German?"

Come to think of it, Ranklin didn't.

"Or mebbe," O'Gilroy finished tying his necktie and paused to gloat at himself in the mirror, "the whole shebang's German spies and acting at General and servants, with the big house and motor-car all hired." He wasn't being very serious; to O'Gilroy an enemy was an enemy and he didn't trouble overmuch with asking why.

"Now," he went on, "would that 'repas' he was talking about have anything to do with food? Me stomach's asking if me mouth's emigrated."

Ranklin, who had never learnt to dress as fast as a private soldier must, was still working at his own tie. "Now we know they're going to photograph the code we can afford to seem in more of a hurry. But see if you can't make it easier for them. Can you undo the package a bit, without it seeming obvious?"

Nobody had done anything to make the parcel obviously tamper-proof: that hadn't been the objective. O'Gilroy picked apart the knots on the string and the brown paper fell loose. Inside was a plain manilla envelope with a criss-cross of government red tape (actually pink) held in place with a blob of sealing wax. Perhaps somebody in the War Office thought that was secure; O'Gilroy took just two seconds to bend a corner of the envelope and slip a loop of the tape free of the lightly gummed flap.

Then, since Ranklin still wasn't ready, he peeled the flap open with his penknife. It wasn't a clean job, but the enemy wouldn't be looking for signs that the envelope had already been opened.

"Captain," he said, "there's a mite of a problem here."

Ranklin turned from the mirror to see O'Gilroy handling three thin red pocketbooks, just like Army field manuals, each wrapped in a strand of pink tape. "Yes?"

"We was bringing over code 'X', wasn't it?"

"That's right."

O'Gilroy looked at the front of one book. "Code X." He dropped it on the bed and looked at the next. "Code Y." He picked up the third. "Code W."

There comes a time when it is your knees and not your will that decide you should sit down.

After a time Ranklin heard himself saying tonelessly: "I can see how it happened, of course. Some clerk at the War House was told to make up three parcels from nine books. But he wasn't told what it was about, that would be too secret for him." He read from the cover of the nearest book: "'Most Secret', in fact. So he used his common sense: obviously three addresses in France were to get one copy of each code. Oh, I *understand* it."

"And if ye understand how England ever got itself an Empire without somebody having dropped it in the street, mebbe ye'll tell me that, too. Along with what we do next."

Ranklin sat very still, shoulders hunched and thinking hard. Then he said: "We try leaving one code, one of the false ones, and hope they don't know there should be three copies." But they seemed to know so much else about this job that he wasn't too hopeful. "Wrap up the Y code, would you? See if you can make it seem it was never more than one." He stood up, pocketing the X and W codes. They were slim enough that they barely bulged in the big pockets of his travelling tweeds.

O'Gilroy started work. "But ye said yeself, if we know they've got hold of even the right one, all it needs doing is to change it."

After the French had had a hearty laugh at the bungling of the Bureau and the War Office and their wrath had been passed on to those junior enough to be thought worthy of blame.

"That isn't the point any longer. If they even suspect we can denounce them as spies . . . well, it means Devil's Island for the General. That's where they sent Dreyfus for the same thing, and he wasn't even guilty. Have you heard of Devil's Island?"

"I have that," O'Gilroy said grimly. "And I get yer meaning, Captain. I'd kill us rather than wind up there."

A freshly lit wood fire was crackling and popping in the drawing room, with the General dozing in front of it. A cosy, old-fashioned scene of the old soldier home from the wars, and Ranklin looked appraisingly at the trophies of those wars around the walls. He could handle a sword, and anybody could use a stabbing spear, but he was sure he'd be up against modern revolvers. For the moment he settled for a whisky and soda, offered in a whisper by the watchful butler.

O'Gilroy took the same and they stared silently out of the windows. It wasn't raining at the moment, but the overlong grass was rippling in the wind and the whole afternoon had been one long twilight.

The General woke with a whuffling grunt, saw them and said: "Ah, pardon, messieurs . . . " and the butler hurried over with a glass of something pink.

"I wonder," Ranklin said, "if I might place a telephone call to Paris? I was given a message at Dieppe but was unable to contact the person."

He reckoned he was running no risk: he wasn't supposed to know the message had been false. And he wanted to see how the General would handle it.

"But naturally. Gaston will obtain the number."

"Colonel Yarde-Buller at the British Embassy, please."

He was not surprised when Gaston returned to report his desolation that the apparatus did not function. So Gaston was in on the act, too (only later did he wonder why he'd assumed the telephone must really be working; his own experience of telephones was that half the time they didn't).

"I never trust these barbarous machines meself," O'Gilroy chipped in. "Begging yer pardon, General, it being yer own machine."

"But no, M'sieu, it is the company's. I agree: they are barbarisms. And now the Army is to employ them for – how do you say?"

"Field telephones?" Ranklin suggested.

"Exactly. And for how long will they function? It demands just one horse to put just one foot on the wire, that is how long . . . And you, M'sieu Gilroy, you have not served with the Army?"

"Alas no, General. I fancied the drum and the glory when I was a lad, but me poor father died early and the family and the land . . . "

Ranklin listened only faintly to O'Gilroy's fantasies. Perhaps at this moment somebody – Gunther, possibly: he was sure Gunther would be somewhere backstage – was sorting through their bags, coming up with the single code book. And being satisfied? Or realising their plot had been detected and there was only one thing to do . . .

Would they get any warning? Or would the door open and . . . ?

At that moment the door did open, and while Ranklin stood gaping, the General began to lever himself to his feet. "Ah, Madame Finn: permit me to introduce these gentlemen."

12

American, Ranklin thought, then wondered why he thought it. It
was the freshness about her – and the boldness. Not that European
women couldn't manage both, but it seemed more natural with
Americans. She was taller than Ranklin, with black hair pinned up
under a small straw hat, large dark eyes and a wide smile as she
thrust out an ungloved hand. Whoever she is, Ranklin realised, she
doesn't intend to be underestimated.

She was Mrs Winslow Finn, daughter of Reynard Sherring – the
General dragged that name in, though Ranklin already knew it. To
him, and most people, it simply meant Money, subdivided into
cartels, rings, railways – sorry, railroads – or coal or steel or oil or
perhaps all of them. It was a world Ranklin had been brought up
tacitly to despise and ignore – until about a year before. Now he
had learnt that at least he couldn't ignore it.

"Hi," she said, "I'm Corinna. Happy to meet you. General –
may I use your telephone?"

Ranklin suppressed his smile, but the General coped. "I am
desolated, my dear Mrs Finn, but it is not functioning. Captain
Ranklin also . . . "

"Oh *bugger* the silly thing." The General didn't flinch, but
O'Gilroy's eyeballs nearly exploded. He had met enough of the
gentry to know that their ladies, particularly in the hunting field,
could use language that would scald the fur off a fox, but he hadn't
expected it from this American enchantress. "I think I've found
just the château for Pop," Corinna went on. "I wanted to tell him."

"I doubt," the General said gravely, "there will be much

competition with your father if he wishes to buy."

"When Pop wants to buy there's always competition," she said crisply. Then to Gaston: "Café noir s'il vous plaît, pas de sucre." Her French accent, Ranklin noted, was far better than his own.

The General said: "Then perhaps your father will not mind the deprivation of one residence from – how many?"

"Don't be an old meanie, General. Everybody likes a few roofs over their heads, don't they, Captain?"

"They come in handy in the winter."

She grinned at him. With a thin face, high cheekbones and wide mouth she was immediately attractive rather than stand-back-and-stare beautiful. That afternoon she was wearing a plain high-necked white silk blouse and simple purple-red wool skirt, but the single ruby at her throat would, Ranklin thought sourly, make a down payment on any château in the land.

"You're staying here while you house-hunt, are you, Mrs Finn?" he asked politely.

"The General's been kind enough to put up with me for a couple of nights, but I'm through now. I'm heading back to Rouen and Paris."

"You drove down?"

"No-o. In fact, if you're talking to Pop, I didn't drive at all. But I got off the train at Rouen and hired an automobile there. It gives you more freedom, don't you think?"

Ranklin tried to keep his agreement polite, but his mind was galloping. No, driving . . .

But she spoiled that thought immediately: "All they could let me have was a little Renault roadster with its radiator in the wrong place. Why do Renaults have their radiators *behind* the engine, General?"

"My dear, you must ask Sergeant Clement. Of automobiles I understand nothing."

Corinna grinned again. "I should've known better than to ask a technical question of a man. Say, is Cort back yet? I'd like to say goodbye to him."

The General was momentarily confused. "Ah . . . no. Pas encore, I went to Dieppe to meet him, but he was not on the boat. The boat you were on, Capitaine. Perhaps he tried to call with the telephone, but . . . " He shrugged.

"Cort?" Ranklin asked.

"Cort van der Brock, a jolly fat Dutch guy," Corinna explained. "He deals in cigars."

"He had to go to England," the General said quickly. "For business."

A fat Dutchman, not a fat Bavarian. Ranklin looked at O'Gilroy, who had come out of shock, and got the response he hoped for.

"There was a fat man with a big moustache and spectacles," O'Gilroy said reflectively.

"That sounds like Cort," Corinna said. The General screwed up his mouth nervously.

"We was talking to him at the dockside," O'Gilroy went on. "Ye remember him, Matt? But ye must have seen him yeself, General."

"He was much like Cort," the General said huskily. "But he was not Cort."

"Oh . . . " but Corinna had noted the effect her language could have on O'Gilroy and checked herself. "I did so want to see his photographs. He's real keen, uses a big camera, not one of those little Kodaks, and he was doing some pictures of this Château."

"I will make sure he sends you some pictures at Paris," the General gabbled.

Corinna looked at her small gold wristwatch. "I'd best be getting on the road if we're going to be at Rouen before dark."

"Then we won't have your company at – at the repas the General has promised us?" It was an impertinence to invite her to another man's table, but his sadness wasn't pretended. While the daughter of Reynard Sherring was around, nobody would do anything violent.

"'Fraid not. But I envy you, the General keeps a great table. Are you boys staying long?"

"Unfortunately no. We have to be in Paris tonight."

"Maybe I'll see you around there." She turned to the General: "I took the liberty of asking your boys to load up my automobile."

"But naturally. I will see you to your automobile which has no radiator – whatever that may be."

"No, just in the wrong place."

"But I am sure it would be better if it had none at all."

Corinna gave an amused but despairing glance that happened to fall on O'Gilroy, who smiled nervously back. He could act the gentleman among other gentlemen, but hadn't yet found the right pose and voice for ladies. In fact, he was giving a perfect imitation of a sex-shy Irish squire, and Ranklin was quite happy: who would dream of employing anyone so gauche as a spy?

The hallway became a brief flummox of departure as the man-servant carried out Corinna's cases and bags, Sergeant Clement strapped them onto the back of the Renault, and Corinna's maid, a small, fair and bossy girl, told him he was getting it wrong. Ranklin joined in, carrying out the smaller bits of Corinna's baggage train and putting them in the wrong places, too.

Little puffs of drizzle came scurrying round the corners of the house as Corinna wriggled into her long car coat and fitted herself into the driving seat. "I'll see you around," and she gestured to Clement. He cranked the engine, the General saluted from the doorway, and Ranklin muttered: "How many servants?"

Surprised, O'Gilroy muttered back: "Not enough for a place this size."

"How many *men*?"

Realising that Ranklin was counting a potential enemy, O'Gilroy reconsidered. "What we've seen – three – and what's in the kitchen. I've seen no outside staff at all."

"And Gunther at least." He waved as the little car clattered stiffly out onto the drive and round the corner. They followed the General back into the house, Ranklin pausing to give the Duke's portrait a sour glance. This problem was a poor return for Britain having given the Duke a birthplace, a Sandhurst education and a commission in the 60th. Bloody Greenjacket.

They found that, for the moment, they had the drawing room to themselves.

"'Tis a shame she's not staying on," O'Gilroy said quietly. "Unless yer thinking she's one of *them*."

"It doesn't seem too likely."

"And did ye not think of suggesting the Sergeant could take them in the big car, warm and dry, and us take her little one?"

"I thought of it." And he had, too. "But we don't know they suspect we know who they are, yet. If they fall for that single code book they'll be anxious to have us on our way happy and unharmed. And we'll have succeeded better than anyone hoped. Planting a false code on an enemy – prospective enemy – that's quite a coup. And if they do suspect . . . Can we involve her?"

"They'd never . . . " Then O'Gilroy paused to think, perhaps about Devil's Island. "Mebbe, mebbe . . . It's a mite more difficult than saying 'Range one thousand, fire,' I fancy."

"It is," Ranklin said shortly.

"And I suppose ye wasn't lying when ye said ye didn't have yer little gun with ye?"

"Unfortunately not. If it comes to it, and they don't suddenly up and cut our throats – and I don't think they will: they'd be better off making it seem an accident, and that might take time – try and play for more time. Spin it out."

"I've no argument agin living another minute, Captain. Or for ever, anyone gives me the chance."

Soon afterwards, the General came back, punting his way with the walking stick across to his unfinished drink. They watched him cautiously as he sipped and put the glass down with a shivery hand.

"Mon Capitaine, you spoke of these dark times. And you are correct. The government of France is a rabble. The Army – my Army – is led by opportunists. Anarchists are on the streets of Paris, bandits on the highways – where is the discipline?" He grunted angrily. "You are too young to recall General Boulanger."

"The 'Man on Horseback'?" Ranklin said. "He was elected a deputy for Paris, I believe."

"That same man. And that night – it is more than twenty years – he could have rallied other deputies. The generals were with him. And they could have restored the King – the father of the Duke. It needed only for Boulanger to take the lead – and where was he that night, Captain?"

Ranklin suddenly remembered the story, but let the General tell it.

"On top of his mistress!" the General hissed.

They waited in polite silence. "His mistress," the General repeated, staring fiercely into the might-have-been. "One night, one woman – and the destiny of France. That is how weak our government has become. Enfin, there will come another night, and no woman."

There didn't seem anything to say. The wind rattled tentatively at a window. Then Gaston coughed discreetly from the doorway and announced: "Le Comte est servi."

Hanging back as the General led the way out, O'Gilroy whispered: "Was that the truth, then?"

"About Boulanger and his mistress? Oh yes. I think he was in love with her – you might say he'd better have been. Anyhow, he shot himself on her grave a few years later."

"Yer fooling me."

"No, all of that's true. Mind, I'm not saying the coup would have worked, the King would have come back. But it gives you an idea of how fragile French politics can be. And still are."

13

They sat around the end of a long walnut table, waited on by Gaston and the manservant: vegetable soup, trout, and lamb cutlets – the first Ranklin had seen that year – in aspic. The aspic was probably new to O'Gilroy, but he would have eaten the cutlets with the wool still on. The General merely picked at his food; like most men of his age, he lived in short bursts of energy and talkativeness, and being gallant to Corinna and angry about Boulanger had exhausted him. Ranklin made one attempt to ask about Corinna's husband and was told one did not talk about ladies at table. He went back to twiddling his wine glass.

Although it was still light outside, and they were eating absurdly early, the heavy curtains had been drawn and the room lit by silver candelabra. The colours enriched by the half-dark, the glints of light on china and glass, the shadows wavering in the slight draught – all gave a stagy effect. Perhaps doubly so, because Ranklin guessed that in daylight the room would seem as tawdry as stage scenery. And weren't they in a play – acting parts and speaking meaningless lines until – until what?

It came when Gaston leant down to whisper a discreet something in the General's ear and the old man gazed sombrely first at Ranklin, then O'Gilroy. Somebody, Ranklin thought grimly, has searched our room and not found what he was looking for. The General sighed. "Gentlemen, you are both royalists also."

Since O'Gilroy probably hadn't believed in any king since Brian Boru, Ranklin said quickly: "I am an officer in His Britannic Majesty's Army."

The General grunted. "In the past our countries have fought many times, honourably. Now, soon, we will fight together. But victory is only possible if France is led by a true king, His Majesty Philippe. I comprehend, Captain, that you carry to Paris a code for our Army. On behalf of His Majesty I will accept the code and you may report that it has been correctly delivered."

That simple statement would have silenced a Welsh politician; it struck Ranklin dumb as a statue. The implications of it swam blurred and dreamily round his mind; the only hard-and-fast thought he could cling to was that the General was monumentally loony.

And the only thing he could think of to do was to play – indeed, overplay – his own part in this farce. "General, you must understand that I have my orders, and as I hold the King's Commission, these orders come, in effect, from my King. I am ordered to deliver the code to Paris."

"Paris is full of traitors."

Perhaps so, Ranklin reflected, since the General shouldn't have heard of the code at all.

"The code will be safe," the General went on, "only in the hands of a loyal servant of His Majesty." And he held out one such quavering hand.

Trying not to break down into wild and disastrous laughter, Ranklin stiffened in his chair. He knew his chubby figure didn't play dignity well, but he did his best. "General, I am an officer entrusted with a mission. You have warned me that my mission is endangered, and I am deeply grateful. Now, if you would kindly permit me to contact my superiors in London and inform them of the situation, I shall obey their new orders."

The General sipped his wine, wiped his mouth on his napkin, and nodded to Gaston, who nodded towards the door. Ranklin saw O'Gilroy tense.

Gunther Arnold came into the room with Sergeant Clement close behind.

"You have met M'sieu van der Brock," the General said.

"Yes," Ranklin agreed. "But perhaps I misheard the name."

Gunther, wearing a dark suit straining at its buttons and a floppy bow tie, just smiled and slid into a chair opposite Ranklin. Gaston brought a glass and poured him wine. Clement stayed back in the shadows.

Realising they were waiting for him to speak, Ranklin ignored Gunther and said to the General: "Do you believe my superiors in London are also traitors? If so, they could have given the code to an enemy directly. They still can. Instead, they entrusted it to me to deliver to Paris."

"To the *traitors* in Paris," Gunther said smoothly, and Ranklin saw his argument crumble like Jericho's walls.

"This," O'Gilroy observed, "is getting a mite more tangled than who owns M'Ginty's cow."

Ranklin glared angrily at him and, now desperate, tried again with the General: "But if we have traitors in London who know the code, then it becomes valueless – worse, a liability – to your King."

But Gunther was wearing a small, satisfied smile and, looking at the General, Ranklin suddenly guessed why: the old relic simply didn't know the first thing about codes. In his campaigns, which in the last forty years could only have been against tribesmen in the French colonies, he wouldn't have needed codes. He might just know what they were, but saw them as things that kept an intrinsic value no matter who owned them, like a sword or a barrel of gunpowder.

And he also saw that, loony or not, the General was completely sincere. He simply wanted the code for his "King", and presumably believed it was going to get there. How? By hand of Gunther, probably, on his travels as a cigar merchant. Which in turn meant that Gunther was manipulating the General, using his royalist connections in Paris – in the Ministère de la Guerre especially – and . . .

Perhaps he let something show in his face, because Gunther said quickly: "Perhaps I might talk to Captain Ranklin alone for a moment? As a young man, an officer of little experience, he does not have the instinct of duty and honourable behaviour that you expect. As someone closer to his age, perhaps I can persuade him where his duty lies."

Ranklin was about to say in frozen terms that no rotten spy could teach him anything about duty and honour when he remembered that he was a rotten spy himself and that such words would mean nothing to Gunther anyway. And there was always a chance that Gunther didn't know Ranklin was a spy and not an ordinary officer picked by chance for a courier's job. Not that the amount of training he'd been given made that much difference, he thought sourly. But there still had to be a reason why they hadn't just been scragged, and Gunther was the man in charge.

So he said: "If the General allows it, I will listen to Heer van der Brock."

When they were outside the dining room, standing in front of the portrait of the Duc d'Orléans, who, Ranklin now realised, knew nothing of this affair, of Gunther and perhaps even the General, but had still been a bloody Greenjacket, Gunther lit a small cigar.

Then he said abruptly: "We know there should be three copies of the code and unless you show me two others, we must believe the one you left upstairs is false." His English had improved, Ranklin noted, since he became a Dutchman.

"You are new to these matters," Gunther continued. "So I will explain how they are conducted: the code is already compromised by your unfortunate delay. Would you trust the lives of men, of armies, to a code that has unaccountably vanished for a few hours? I think not. I think also it will not be of helping your career. So I will help you: you must sell me the code."

Ranklin had been determined to keep a face of stone, but this offer chipped it badly. He may even have gaped.

Gunther smiled, leaking cigar smoke. "Consider the result: you will have the assurance that I will not betray you because it would be to betray myself. And I will have the assurance that you will not betray me because I can say you sold the code for money. It will be in both our interests to pretend that nothing has happened. No?

"You look worried. I know! You think I am a German spy. Ach, that I should be so insulted. They are as clumsy and incompetent as . . . as your own new Secret Service. Romantics, adventurers, the misfits of the officer corps – cads and bounders, you would call them."

It seemed reasonable to suppose that Gunther did *not* think Ranklin was a spy.

"But I am a professional. You may choose to despise that, but be assured that your superiors do not. I have had many dealings with them, and they recognise work of quality."

That, Ranklin knew, was at least partly true. The Bureau did shop for information in the mercenary markets, notably in Vienna and Brussels.

"Also, you are thinking I will sell the code to Germany, to Austria-Hungary. Most certainly that is my plan. But consider: your War Office knows the code is no longer to be trusted; they must make a new one anyway. What I sell will be genuine; my reputation, my business, depend on that. But it will not harm your country."

"But they'll still suspect me."

"Because of the delay, what else can they do? The moving finger has written, the delay exists. But they will still prefer to blame the French Ministère than a British officer – and this way, you can tell of the General and his gang of royalist dreamers who are a danger to all secrets you share with France, not just one code. When you tell your War Office of them they will not suspect you of anything but a little foolishness. They should thank you – but perhaps that is to expect too much, no?"

"You're ready to ditch the General?"

"Fools are dangerous people. Who knows what his next dream of chivalry will make him to do? You see already he plans to take the code from you. I offer to buy it for, shall we say, four hundred pounds?"

Ranklin saw that four hundred pounds – nearly two years' pay – and he wanted it. But he also saw Gunther taking it back from his corpse, because he now knew for sure that he planned to kill them. No businessman would give up a prize like the General and the royalist network.

"There are two of us," Ranklin said, and then realised that was a mistake. He had been trying to sound properly mercenary, but had forced Gunther to reconsider O'Gilroy's position. Probably he had assumed Ranklin had brought him along as an innocent disguise: two pals out on a jaunt to Gay Paree. Now he was thinking of two couriers, and it must seem odd.

"There is only one code," Gunther said, temporising.

Ranklin had to go through with it. "I must talk to him."

Back in the dining room, the General looked up under his

eyebrows with a stern, inquiring look. Gunther said: "Mon Général, the Captain wishes to explain certain matters to his friend," and Ranklin beckoned O'Gilroy over.

However, nobody was letting them out of sight. Sergeant Clement, still in his tight chauffeur's jacket but with a large and heavy bulge in the right-hand pocket, stood blocking the door. They backed off into a corner shared with a plinth and a bust of (Ranklin guessed) Louis Philippe.

"Gunther claims he's a mercenary spy," Ranklin whispered. "He tried to buy the code off me."

O'Gilroy nodded, unsurprised. "How much?"

"Doesn't matter. If he's telling the truth, it just makes it more sure he's going to kill us. A mercenary spy won't have any feeling he's in jail for his country's sake, no back pay waiting at home. He'll just see his business going to pot and coming out to starve on the street."

"Like enough. So what did ye say?"

"I'd talk to you. What I don't see is why we haven't been scragged already."

"Ye think the General would allow it?"

It was as if a photographic flash had been set off, freezing the tableau so that Ranklin could see the relationships clearly for the first time.

He nodded gently. "You're right, of course. The old fool may not know anything about codes, but he'd know a stab in the back if he saw it. And you don't do that in a house of chivalry and honour – so Gunther's got to get us out of the house first."

"Mind, I don't say the General wouldn't have his fellas just take the code off'n ye."

"Yes, I don't think that would offend his honour. All right, I don't know how we'll manage this, but we know what we want." They walked back to their places.

"So, mon Capitaine," the General said, "have you understood where your duty lies?"

Ranklin took a sip of wine and touched his lips with his napkin, determined to do everything as slowly as possible. "Was it at your suggestion that Heer van der Brock should insult me by offering *money* for the code?"

The General frowned thoughtfully, and looked at Gunther.

"A simple test," Gunther said easily. "To see if the Captain's loyalty lay in his wallet. Unfortunately I failed to offer *enough* money."

"That," Ranklin said, "is the sort of lie one expects from a bourgeois cigar-peddler."

Despite himself, Gunther stiffened and gave Ranklin a grim look. Unfortunately, the insult misfired with the General. "The lowness of birth is of no consequence in matters of loyalty. His Majesty has chosen M'sieu van der Brock as his loyal servant. I should not presume to argue with His Majesty's choice."

Gunther bowed his head to the General, and came up with a new idea. "Mon Général, perhaps the Captain doubts that I truly am the servant of His Majesty. If so, it is a motor journey of only some hours for me to bring him before His Majesty. He cannot have any doubts about handing over the code to His Majesty in person."

It was stupendously bold, and it left Ranklin speechless – partly with admiration. And it was a winner with the General. "Parfait." He slapped a hand on the table. "You are most honoured, mon Capitaine. And surely you can have no doubts any longer. Sergeant Clement! L'automobile est préparée, n'est ce pas?"

"And what about meself?" O'Gilroy asked.

The General looked at him. "Naturally, you will accompany the Capitaine."

"Ah, the King wouldn't want to be bothering with the likes of an Irish squire. I'll wait here, 'til the Captain gets back."

Nothing showed in Gunther's face, but a hesitancy in his movement suggested he saw a problem. Perhaps, if he didn't want to leave O'Gilroy while he and Clement were away, Clement was the only one of the household truly on Gunther's team.

"It is many hours to Belgium," the General said uncertainly. "And perhaps the Capitaine will wish to take the railway from there . . . "

"I haven't finished me wine yet," O'Gilroy said.

"Who is this man?" Gunther took the offensive.

"I'm jest what ye see," O'Gilroy said contentedly.

"An escort to a courier. L'intelligence? Secret Service – which I think you despise, mon Général?"

"Absolument." The General gave O'Gilroy a despising look.

"Then," Gunther announced, "you will not want him to remain an instant longer in an honourable house. We will leave him at the station in Rouen."

"It would be best," the General said gravely.

"Nobody," Ranklin said, "has yet asked me if I want to go to Belgium."

"Mais naturellement . . . " the General seemed puzzled.

"It will be far too late to wait upon His Majesty by the time we get there tonight – and I have heard he prefers to sleep early." He hadn't heard any such thing, but was sure nobody else had heard anything either. "Tomorrow we will go to Rouen, take the train for Paris, and . . . "

Gunther jumped in. "So you can deliver the code to the traitors in Paris?"

"Mijnheer," Ranklin said coldly, "you have accused me, an officer in the service of His Britannic Majesty, of treachery and being ready to sell a code for *money*. There can be no worse insults to my honour, and only one course is open to me. I only regret that I must wait till dawn to receive the satisfaction that is my due." And reaching across the table he lightly flicked his napkin in Gunther's pop-eyed face. "Mr O'Gilroy will act as my second."

Was he right? Was the casual but implacable code of the duel part of the General's dream that they were all living?

He was right – and wrong. While everybody else was sitting dazed with surprise, the General shook his head. "Capitaine, you dishonour yourself. For a gentleman-at-arms to challenge a bourgeois seller of cigars! – no, this is not permissible. Not in a house of honour."

A small relieved smile twitched Gunther's moustache.

O'Gilroy leant back in his chair and drawled: "Meself, I'm no gentleman-at-arms. But I'd be no sort of gentleman at all to hear meself called Secret Service – which, General, ye'll agree is lower than the lowest thing that crawls in yer sewers – without seeing the foul stain washed out in blood." And he tossed his whole napkin at Gunther, now totally flabbergasted. "I'm sure the Captain will act as me second."

14

O'Gilroy flopped onto one of the beds and said mournfully: "I think I saw this play at the Gaiety. It had an unhappy end to it." He looked up at Ranklin. "Ye'd best tell me jest what I've talked meself into."

"'Wiping out a foul stain in blood', that's what. Did that come from the play?"

"It did."

Ranklin shook his head, still trying to catch up with the rush of events. "You didn't have to challenge Gunther like that."

"Ye did yeself."

"I was playing for time. Anyway, with my background – "

"Ah, I see it now." O'Gilroy's voice got a jagged edge to it. "Not being an officer and a gentleman, I'm not good enough to . . . "

"Did you have fencing lessons at *your* school?" Ranklin asked coldly. "Have you ever fired a black-powder pistol – or any pistol at the sort of distance duels are fought?"

The quivering silence dwindled into the tap of rain on the window, the breath of wind in the chimney. O'Gilroy nodded. "Permission to speak more sensibly, Captain? Does it have to be swords or pistols?"

"It's traditional. But that's all duels are, anyway."

"Are they always having duels in France?"

"Not nowadays. But it's about the only place on the Continent where they aren't still common among . . . among the duelling classes. Germany, Italy, Austria-Hungary – I think they've all got laws against it. Like the law against distilling poteen in Ireland."

"I get yer meaning, Captain."

"Anyway, Gunther doesn't want a duel any more than we do, so he might just cut his losses and run."

"I'm not betting on it."

"Nor I – Entrez!" to a knock on the door.

The manservant brought in a large tray loaded with decanters, glasses, coffee cups and pots – even a silver cigarette box. "Le Comte mon Général vous attendra en cinq minutes, mon Capitaine."

Ranklin studied the man: about forty and thickening up, but burly and stronger than himself. Sergeant Clement might be the only one on Gunther's side, but this man would be one to worry about if they fell foul of the General. The butler Gaston was strictly supply train.

He nodded, dismissing the man. "Cognac? Brandy to us."

O'Gilroy took a glass and coffee. "And what d'ye decide when ye parley-vous with the General?" He helped himself to a cigarette from the box.

"Weapons, time, place, any conditions. The useful thing about a duel is that it stops everything in place. The General won't make any move about the code, you and Gunther mustn't meet, Gunther can't meet me – nothing happens until the duel's over, and if that isn't until dawn . . . "

"I see what ye . . . Jayzus!" He jerked the cigarette from his lips and peered at it. "What am I smoking here? Frogs' legs? Ye'll observe me perfect manners in not smoking this thing to the last drag. And when ye see the General, ask if he's anything else to smoke, some oily rags from the car, mebbe."

Ranklin smiled and pulled out his watch. "Yes, I'd better go and parley. One thing: Gunther may try to dodge the duel by offering an abject apology."

"And what then?"

"If you accept – and you're supposed to if it's abject enough – then I suppose we're back where we left off."

O'Gilroy stretched out on the bed; the window was darkening, the room growing colder. He started to get his overcoat, then remembered it was downstairs: the butler had taken it. And he had finished his own few cigarettes – few because of Ranklin's warning of French customs laws – so there were only those foul French things.

He could ring the bell and demand his overcoat, perhaps other cigarettes, certainly a hot drink, but didn't want to make any move without Ranklin knowing. So he stayed as helpless as a man in a cell – or a gentleman without his servants. He smiled, as he had so often before, at that helplessness, at men who couldn't put a stud into the shirts they owned, nor their own cars into gear. Men who were so proud of despising any skill except horse riding and shooting.

"That's what keeps us in our place," an old shipyard worker had grumbled to him once, "pride in our work. That's what they teach us and all they teach us, so's we'll sleep easy and not be dreaming of painting the walls with their blood."

There had been a lot of truth, as well as porter, in that remark.

He got up and poured lukewarm coffee into his cup, then added a dash of brandy, something he had only heard of doing before. It certainly tasted warmer, though in truth it must be colder. And was that being an English gentleman – just a feeling of being better than most, and probably brought on by brandy besides?

Holy Mary, and he had offered to fight a duel for such people and their damned Empire! *No!* He threw that thought away immediately. Anybody who thought that didn't know Conall O'Gilroy. He was fighting – if it got that far – for himself, and fighting Gunther because he was Gunther.

He lived with questions – why had he joined up with Ranklin and the Bureau? why had he joined the Army before that? – which were too big to have anything but small answers, like a smile and a shrug. He had been there, he was here now, tomorrow he would be – in Hell, it seemed possible. He smiled and shrugged.

Ranklin came in with a long rifle in one hand, a scabbarded bayonet in the other and a dazed look on his face. He kicked the door shut, threw the rifle and bayonet onto a bed and said: "That wasn't dinner we had, it was the Mad Hatter's tea party."

O'Gilroy got up and reached for the rifle. "What is it? Is it loaded?"

Ranklin shook his head and refilled his brandy glass. "No. No bullets. Just the bayonet."

"*Bayonet* fighting?"

Ranklin tried to nod and swallow brandy at the same time. When he had mopped up, he said: "Yes. And we're not waiting till dawn. That, according to the General, is just a popular myth. Christ, I . . . " he shook his head. "I'll tell you what happened."

O'Gilroy was finding out how the bayonet fitted under the muzzle of the rifle. "I'm listening."

"First, Gunther hasn't offered any apology; I don't understand that. Second, I made a fuss about having a doctor there – I know *that's* standard practice – so the General sent to the village for the local quack. He must be in the old boy's pocket, not expected to report this to the gendar – the police."

"Who might also be in the General's pocket, mind."

"Ye-es. After a few hundred years in one place, the family in the Big House can grow big pockets."

"Yer not telling me anything new." And come to that, hadn't Ranklin's family – until very recently – held just such a near-medieval position in their patch of Worcestershire?

"So – then we got on to weapons. I said a country gentleman and a cigar merchant wouldn't be swordsmen or know much about duelling pistols, so why not sporting rifles, four hundred metres apart? In daylight, of course. That's when I got the bit about not waiting for dawn. And the General came up with this: the commoner's weapon. The bayonet.

"That," he added, "is the French Lebel, their standard rifle until fairly recently. He had a couple hanging on his walls as mementos of his campaigns."

The Lebel, O'Gilroy reckoned, was over six inches longer and a pound heavier than the shortened British Lee-Enfield, as well as being generally more old-fashioned. With the bayonet fixed, it came to his own height, something like a cavalry pig-sticker. He held it in his left hand, testing for the point of balance.

Ranklin continued: "Then I said you hadn't served in the Army but Gunther had told me he *had*, and the General said that was only in the Dutch Schutterij – a sort of conscript garrison force – and anybody could learn bayonet fighting in twenty minutes."

"Twenty minutes, is it? He's remembering how long he learnt to be a General."

"Silence in the ranks. Get on with learning."

Bayonet fighting is unrealistic. If you're reduced to using the bayonet on the battlefield, you might get in one thrust before some third party stabs you from behind. But armies practise it because it makes soldiers confident in handling their rifles and is a cheap way of keeping them busy. So it gets formalised into a sort of fencing, only with two-handed swords that, if Lebels, weigh ten pounds and are six feet long.

O'Gilroy moved out from between the beds to a clear space in front of the fireplace, holding the rifle firmly in both hands. He brought it slowly down to the "on guard" position, then leant gently forward in a "point" keeping himself and the unfamiliar weapon carefully balanced. At the "withdrawal" Ranklin noticed the trained-now-instinctive twist of the hands to free the bayonet from the grip of dying flesh. O'Gilroy did it again, a little faster.

Still watching, Ranklin said: "Now we don't have a truce until dawn, we have to think a little faster. I was hoping that when it was dark, everybody asleep . . . "

"There's a back door to each wing," O'Gilroy said, swinging the rifle through low and high parries, left and right. "Past the bathrooms and down the back stairs. The servants' rooms in this wing are empty."

"You reconnoitred this?" Ranklin goggled at him.

"Coming back from me bathe. Captain – " he stopped and looked at Ranklin; " – in our trade, don't get yeself inside a building without ye know another way out."

"Yes." Ranklin nodded slowly. "Yes. Well . . . If you take the codes, I can pretend to everybody you're still here. I mean, nobody expects to see you until . . . "

"Only it's not yet dark and the house wide awake, and how far d'ye reckon to the railway?"

"Five miles. About that."

"And more to a station. With them in cars after me and me not knowing a word of the language. Haven't I heard officers talking about not dividing yer forces?"

"But if you stay here, you'll have to go through with the duel, damn it!" But the glint of the bayonet went on weaving fierce, graceful patterns in the gloom.

"Oh bugger it," Ranklin said. "Well – don't believe that about Gunther and the Dutch Schutterij. I'd say German Army, maybe even Prussian. And I'm sure he thinks you were in the Army, probably still are. Only," he added thoughtfully, "as an officer. Not with a rifle and bayonet."

O'Gilroy turned, the last cold daylight from the window lodging on his thin, hungry smile. He lunged smoothly and checked, the bayonet barely quivering, a couple of inches from Ranklin's waistcoat.

"So mebbe I'll just kill him."

"In an hour. In the courtyard. By lamplight."

But I still don't believe all this is happening, Ranklin thought, even if the duel was my idea. I'd just wandered into the General's dream, feverish from the germs of a glory that infects this house where "blood" is just a fine word like "duty" and "honour", and the dying don't scream for their mothers. When there is real blood on the cobbles down there, God let me be the first and fastest to wake up.

Somewhere behind the Château a generator chugged into life, but only the ground floor seemed to have been wired up for lighting. Soon after, the manservant brought in a duplex oil lamp, vase-shaped and ornate but cheaply electroplated. He took the coffee cups and pots and left without saying a word.

O'Gilroy made another brief attempt to smoke a French cigarette and went back to the rifle – shadow-fencing with it, now.

Time ticked by. The General's car came up the drive and Ranklin went out to the window at the head of the stairs to watch the village doctor – not an old quack, as he'd assumed, but a young man with a wispy professional beard – get out with his black bag. The courtyard was already being prepared by the manservant and another – the cook? – carrying a small ladder round to light lanterns fixed to the walls on the wing sides. There was some other light source at the main door, but that was out of sight below him.

It should be flaring torches to give the proper Olde-Tyme atmosphere, he thought sourly, and went back to the bedroom.

There, he tipped a little more brandy into their glasses. "Five minutes."

"Any time. We'll get nowhere by running now."

"No, but the first chance we get to nobble any pursuit . . . Good luck."

"Mud in yer eye, Captain. Is it the right thing now to break the glasses in the fireplace?"

Ranklin brightened. "That's an idea. The more of the old loony's property gets smashed, the better I feel." He emptied his glass and threw it with feeling.

15

The whole household seemed to have turned out to watch – well, who wouldn't? Apart from the staff they knew, and the probable cook, there were just two middle-aged women, presumably wives of two of the servants. But still barely half the number a house that size needed, and no outside staff like gardeners and stablemen.

The General himself, wrapped in a thick cape and wearing a tall silk hat, stood in the centre of the courtyard with the young doctor and Sergeant Clement, who held a second rifle. Gunther, stripped to his shirt like O'Gilroy but, unlike him, wearing a silk scarf to hide the indelicacy of being collarless, stood back by the far wall.

Ranklin parked O'Gilroy by the opposite wing of the building and took the rifle over to Sergeant Clement. Everybody raised their hats to everybody and the General perfunctorily introduced the doctor.

"Does your principal wish to apologise?" Ranklin asked.

"He is ready to regret that he made the observation."

As an apology it was rice-paper thin, barely acceptable, and that surprised Ranklin. Why hadn't he made it so abject as to call off the duel and get back to the business of the code and straightforward murder?

Then he realised why and smiled thinly over at Gunther. Playing the part of His Majesty's loyal servant, he now found himself cast as King's Champion and defender of the Royal Et Cetera, and as such couldn't crawl abjectly out of duels. Not if he wanted to keep the confidence of the General and an open peephole into the Ministère de la Guerre.

Turning back to the General, he became cold and careful. "If my principal were to accept this apology, what would happen next?"

The General was puzzled. "We would, if you wish, return to complete our dinner. With coffee and cognac, and if you desire, a cigar."

"And the matter of the code?"

This time the General really was baffled. He peered at Ranklin. "The matter of the code is quite different."

And in his mind it really was, it had no connection with the duel. Ranklin said stiffly: "Very well. You may inform your principal that my principal considers his honour so deeply impugned by the accusation that he is a member of the *Secret Service*, that he believes the stain can only be washed out by blood."

And I'll bet the author of that line never thought it would play in France, he reflected. The General shuffled away.

The doctor, who must have had a little English but no idea of what the duel was about, goggled across at O'Gilroy. Standing under a wall lamp, shirt sleeves rolled up and his dark hair tangled into his eyes, he looked like a schoolgirl's dream of a romantic pirate.

Ranklin said conversationally: "Naturellement, vous avez préparé beaucoup de l'eau chaude?"

The doctor turned ice-white in the yellow lamplight, waggled his beard, and rushed off to speak to one of the women. No hot water at a duel! Mon Dieu! Shame and dishonour!

In fact, it was a serious matter: if the doctor hadn't realised that somebody was about to get hurt, probably badly, it was time he did. The General poked his way back with his stick and asked what had happened.

"He had forgotten to prepare hot water."

The General apologised. Ranklin stared at the starless sky as if asking God, that well-known Englishman, to forgive this foreign bumbling, and said curtly: "C'est de rien."

"My principal," the General puffed, leaning on his stick, "regrets that he cannot change his apology. The matter of the code is not connected."

Ranklin shrugged. "So, the moment this affaire is settled, you will order your servants to assault us. I am not familiar with this custom, but I am your guest." He gave that a moment to seep in, then: "Now, to the procedure for the encounter."

They agreed that the combatants would stand with bayonet tips touching – just like a sword fight – and begin on Sergeant Clement's word. As to finishing . . .

"First blood?" suggested the General.

"Only if the one who bleeds wishes to stop."

"It is honourable . . . "

"Our principals are not young ladies of a seminary."

They left it at that. The two principals were called to the centre and each took a rifle. Ranklin promptly grabbed O'Gilroy's and began examining it as they walked back. He felt it wasn't seemly for O'Gilroy to do so, and anyway, he didn't want O'Gilroy showing off his familiarity with weapons.

"Suspicious?" O'Gilroy asked as Ranklin tested the firmness of the bayonet fitting.

"I'm learning. It may not be the same rifle."

"I fancy ye was giving the General some of yer English-officer talk. I saw the moths flying out of his ears."

Ranklin smiled sourly. "Just a few points of etiquette."

"How come ye know so much about duelling, Captain?"

It comes with the dream, Ranklin wanted to say. And there was plenty of Army folklore about old duels, famous and infamous, but: "Most of it's bluff. Just try to sound more honourable and fair than he is, take off your hat a lot, and you can get away with – with anything. One thing," he added quickly, "is that generally duels end at the first blood, even just a scratch. Now, I'm not giving any advice . . . "

But O'Gilroy's face showed he had already taken it.

The wind still huffed from the open side of the yard where the cars were parked on the edge of the night, and the closed lamps didn't flicker but glowed and dimmed slightly, throwing multiple shadows on the glitter of the damp cobbles. Except for Sergeant Clement, standing alone and very soldierly in the middle of the yard, the staff clustered round the main door with the doctor in front trying to be invisible but visibly not a servant. Above, the house got darker with height until its turret roofs were just black peaks against the thick grey sky.

Their boots echoed unevenly as they gathered round Sergeant Clement. Ranklin looked at Gunther but Gunther was watching O'Gilroy, his face expressionless, holding the long rifle lightly in his big hands.

Ranklin raised his hat. "Your principal offers no apology?"

The General raised his. "None."

Ranklin nodded, they replaced their hats and stepped well back. The General looked at Sergeant Clement, who said softly: "En garde, Messieurs."

O'Gilroy slid smoothly into position, not quite crouched, left foot forward. More precisely, Gunther mirrored his stance, the length of the rifles keeping them a good six feet apart, the bayonets pointing slightly up towards each other's eyes. The points touched with a little click.

"Commencez."

There was a quick clattering flurry of bayonets and an indrawn squeal from one of the women, but they had barely moved their feet and neither had committed himself to a real thrust. Only the professional watchers saw that Gunther had been trying to knock aside O'Gilroy's bayonet to create an opening, and each time O'Gilroy had disengaged and parried instantly.

Then Gunther took a quick step back out of range and they began a shuffling circle to the right. Their many shadows stretched and shortened, darkened and vanished, as they rotated through the pools of light.

And now, Ranklin thought contentedly, Gunther knows. For probably the first time in what must have been a very complicated career, he is up against a man who very simply wants to kill him and can do so within a few seconds. No careful plot, no disguise or false identity can help one gramme against a common soldier's skill.

Gunther took another step back, then charged. He met O'Gilroy's parry with a savage sideways swipe, but O'Gilroy was already jerking his rifle down, so the impetus of the swipe took Gunther's point way off as he rushed in. Unable to pull back for a thrust, O'Gilroy pivoted the rifle and whacked the flat of the butt into Gunther's stomach – the butt-stroke he had used on the butler at Queenstown.

Gunther sprawled past and came down with a thump and clatter at the General's feet. Trying to step back, the General went down as well, while Clement and Ranklin shouted and O'Gilroy checked his instinctive downward stab into Gunther's back. On the battlefield, Gunther was dead.

Between them Ranklin and Sergeant Clement got the quivering General up and propped on his stick. The doctor waved an eye-watering little bottle under the General's nose, Gaston the butler put a glass into the old boy's hand and guided it to his mouth. Then Clement levered Gunther up and brushed him down, and O'Gilroy stood alone, dangling the Lebel easily but unmilitarily across his thighs.

When he had recovered enough to speak, the General spluttered: "That was not a noble coup."

"It was bayonet-fighting," Ranklin said.

Sergeant Clement looked at O'Gilroy, then Ranklin, and said coldly: "Never a soldier, hein?" and went back to reassembling Humpty Dumpty.

"I thought your cigar-peddler did pretty well, too," Ranklin said to the General, but loud enough for Gunther and Clement. "Must be his training as a salesman. Much the same thing as bayonet-fighting, don't you think — sticking people with something they don't want?"

The General turned away, unamused, and Ranklin took out his watch. It was now over two hours since Mrs Finn had driven off for Rouen, which wasn't much more than twenty miles away, by his guess.

He walked back to O'Gilroy, who had slipped his jacket back over his shoulders and was doing a shuffling dance step to keep warm.

"Are we going on, Captain?"

"I think so. How's Gunther doing?"

"He knows the game. Some officers have to." As a Gunner, supposed to despise rifles and rifle drills (it was odd how much time the military spent despising other parts of itself) it hadn't occurred to Ranklin that bayonet training couldn't just be left to sergeant instructors. If a soldier got punctured, there would have to be some officer who knew enough about it all to confuse a court of inquiry at least.

Clement was calling them back to the centre of the courtyard again. "When he goes down this time," O'Gilroy said, "ye grab hold of his rifle and we'll both go for the Sergeant. That pistol in his pocket's enough key for any door at all."

Gunther was already in position, his shirt smudged with mud and now a dogged hatred shining through his spectacles.

"Commencez."

This time, Gunther let O'Gilroy make the moves, and after a moment of fencing, O'Gilroy backed off and began circling left, as if looking for an opening on Gunther's right. It is easy to swing a rifle to your left, across your body, but far harder to swing right because the butt jams on your right hip. Gunther had to keep turning.

Then O'Gilroy thrust to draw a parry, disengaged and thrust for real, his bayonet skidding down the stock of Gunther's rifle – and then he stopped, tried to recover, and Gunther's bayonet slashed across his forearm.

"Dégagéz!" ordered Sergeant Clement.

"First blood," the General grunted happily.

Ranklin rushed up to O'Gilroy, who was swearing down at his left arm as if it were some cheap, faulty piece of machinery. The cut was neither long nor deep but was bleeding showily.

"Tie the damn thing up."

The doctor arrived with his bag and started fussing. "Monsieur est blessé."

"If he means I'm lucky, tell him . . . "

"He means you're blessé, wounded."

"Jayzus, I know that. Tell him to tie it up."

"Why did you check?"

"Because I'd have cut his hand and given him first blood and calling it all off." He stared angrily at the little group around Gunther. "We're going on, Captain. Tell them that."

"I'll talk to the General." He saw that the doctor knew more or less what he was up to, and walked across the courtyard.

"It is completed honourably," the General said.

"Really?" Ranklin exaggerated his surprise. "We agreed, you

recall, that the one who was wounded would decide that." Gunther looked sharply at the General. Ranklin pressed on: "Of course, I can understand that your principal would prefer to escape without either harm *or honour*, but may I express my sympathy, mon Général, that your King should be represented by so timid a champion?"

If you, Herr Gunther, can play on the old warrior's muddle-headedness, then so can I.

The General's face cleared and his shoulders tried to square themselves. "Your principal desires to continue?"

"He feels that his honour demands it." And if I live through tonight, he thought, I shall never be able to use the word "honour" again without thinking what I really mean by it.

But then there was the clatter of a motor-car engine and a moving glow behind the east wing. The police, Ranklin thought, and thank God for that. It's all going to need some explaining, but now nobody's going to get killed.

The lights flared in his eyes and, squinting, it seemed to him to be a small yellow Renault just like the one Mrs Finn had . . .

She was out before the engine had died, her glare searching the throng and fixing on Ranklin. "You! Yes, *you*. What the *hell* do you mean by giving me your stupid code book? D'you think I'm a God-damned messenger for your God-damned British Empire? *That* got settled more'n a hundred years ago . . . " Then her gaze expanded to take in the whole scene. "What in jumping Jesus is going on here?"

"Why didn't you just tell the gendarmes as my note said?" Ranklin groaned.

The General shuffled towards them, raising his silk hat. "Madame, I must apologise, but this is no spectacle for a lady." His mind hadn't taken in her outburst about the code, but Gunther and Clement had: they were glancing tensely from her to Ranklin to the Renault and back.

She walked forward into the centre of the courtyard, surrounded on three sides by wavering lamplight, seeing the little group of spectators by the main door, the rifles, the white shirts of Gunther and O'Gilroy – and the stain on O'Gilroy's bandage.

"Have you two been *fighting*? Have you been shot? What's going on?"

O'Gilroy said: "It's nothing, ma'am, jest a bit of a cut. I've been learning about affairs of honour."

"Duelling?" She whipped round on the General, who had shuffled after her. "Have you all lost your little tinpot minds?"

The General stiffened to rather stooped uprightness. "Madame, I must beg of you not to concern yourself with this matter. Which is, I am happy to say, completed."

"The devil it is," O'Gilroy said. "Ye said it ended with first blood only if the fella's bleeding wants it to. Ye try to stop me carving that fat bastard into dog meat and I'll serve ye up for afters."

I rather doubt, Ranklin thought, that he spoke to many generals like that in his Army days.

Corinna, far from being startled, took O'Gilroy's hardly honourable ambition as more natural than the whole duel. "Not until I've had a look at that arm, you won't." She brushed the doctor aside, asking: "What've you got in that black bag?" and, when she had looked: "Lordie, was your last patient a dodo? I've got some stuff in the automobile. Unwrap that . . . déroulez ce bandage."

Ranklin watched her go back to the Renault; now it had no luggage strapped on behind and, obviously, no maid. So she had driven to Rouen, then turned around when she found the code and note. Only why didn't women ever do as they were told?

The General was back with Gunther. O'Gilroy glanced at the doctor, remembered he didn't understand English and whispered fiercely: "Ye gave *her* one of the codes? – and wasn't telling *me*?"

"I slipped it into her muff – with a note telling her to go to the police. That was the important thing."

"'Cept she didn't and came back to banjax things more'n ever. D'ye think Gunther reckons he's got to kill her, too?"

That was something Ranklin preferred not to think about. "Well, it gives him a problem."

Which was true enough. It was one thing for the two of them to vanish or be found in a fatal "accident", but something else for a daughter of Reynard Sherring. And meanwhile O'Gilroy was giving him a look of pure contempt.

Corinna came back with a small travelling bag and began

smearing something medical on O'Gilroy's arm. He squeaked.

"Try to be brave," she said reassuringly. "But if you will go playing rough games with the other boys . . . Now tell me what the hell this is all about?"

"We were taking that code-book to Paris," Ranklin said.

"Then how did you wind up here?"

"I'd rather explain *why*. The General's a royalist."

"I know that."

"And there's quite a ring of royalists in the Army, government posts and so on."

"I know about that, too. Probably more than you do."

Really? Ranklin filed that for future thought. "I'm guessing now, but suppose somebody came one day with a message, proper writing paper and signature, introducing himself as a messenger from the Duc d'Orléans, d'you think the General could be fooled?"

She paused to consider. "I guess . . . He lives in a dream world. Yes, it would be Christmas all over again. And?"

"And suppose that somebody was really an international spy wanting to tap into the secret information the royalists were sharing among themselves. Such as a code being brought to Paris."

"And you think Cort's an international spy?"

It took a moment for Ranklin to remember Cort was Gunther. "I do."

She nodded slowly. "Cort's smart. He doesn't try to hide that. And smart businessmen don't hang around broken-down châteaux unless there's a good business reason – or they're a smart something else. But it makes me wonder how you boys earn your daily bread, too."

"I am an Army officer," Ranklin said coldly. "Naturally, a mission like this couldn't be entrusted to a civilian . . . "

"Okay, okay." She gestured to the doctor to re-bandage O'Gilroy's arm. "So how did you get him involved in a duel, for God's sake?"

"Well – it started off as a delaying tactic – while you got the police here. Gunther – Cort – knows we know about him. It gets a bit complicated, but Gu – Cort – insulted O'Gilroy."

"Called me Secret Service," O'Gilroy said with some relish.

Ranklin said: "Which, as O'Gilroy pointed out, is like

something out of the sewers."

"It sounds like you should know. And what now? You really want to go on with it?"

Before O'Gilroy could have an opinion, Ranklin said: "If you could say O'Gilroy needs to be got to a hospital and offer to drive him there, I'll be all right."

"What's to stop you just walking out anyway? The General doesn't want the duel to go on."

"The General's not in charge, however much he thinks he is. And it's gone beyond the business of the code. If we get away, we'll denounce Cort, he'll be jailed and lose everything. So once we're out of the General's sight, he'll kill us."

She thought about that. Then she said carefully and unemotionally: "And now you've told me, which Cort has to assume you've been doing, he has to kill me, too. Spying isn't exactly a gentlemanly business, is it?"

Staring at the cobbles, Ranklin said in a quiet voice: "No, not exactly."

"Then there isn't much point in me asking Please can I go home now, is there?"

"Don't you *want* to get out of this?"

"You're damned right I do. But – I don't know why, I feel safer with you two."

"Meself," O'Gilroy said, "I still like the first idea best: I kill the fat bastard."

Ranklin said: "That would narrow it down to the Sergeant."

"Clement?" Corinna was surprised. "Is he . . . ?"

"He's the one we're sure is on Gunther's side." Be damned to remembering that Gunther was Cort, or vice versa. "And he's wearing a pocketful of pistol."

She stared across the lamplit courtyard. The General was stumping towards them; behind him, Clement was fiddling with the bayonet fixings of both rifles. When he moved, his right-hand pocket quivered with the weight inside it.

"Not exactly a pocket pistol, either," she murmured as the General arrived and raised his hat to her.

"My dear lady, I understand you have a small book which rightly belongs in the hands of His Majesty. If you will permit, I will see it is properly delivered."

"Captain Ranklin passed me that book, General. I figure he decides where it goes."

"My dear, I beg of you not to concern your pretty head with matters which we men . . . "

Ranklin barely knew Corinna, but even he could have told the General he'd made a tactical mistake. However, the General found out soon enough.

"And maybe mop the kitchens and clean your boots? – while you great brains play childish games with loaded . . . bayonets that'll probably get someone killed. And all because of some jerk who belongs in an asylum for thinking he's King of France!"

Let's say a strategic mistake, Ranklin thought. The General stood there, his mouth opening and closing, then he turned dazedly away.

Ranklin hurried after him. "Mon Général we wish to go on . . . "

"I like that 'we' stuff," Corinna muttered to O'Gilroy, who'd been staring at her in wonder. "I don't see him doing very much."

"Ah, he started it, ma'am. I mean, he challenged Gunther first, only the General said 'twasn't fair, Gunther not being a gent-at-arms, which is likely all ba – not true, I mean."

"Quite so." Corinna suppressed a smile.

Ranklin beckoned O'Gilroy to the centre, Clement handed out the rifles and Ranklin came back to Corinna.

"Couldn't he just *wound* Cort?" she asked.

"No," Ranklin said firmly. "Oh, it may work out like that, but if you go into something like this without meaning to kill, you're going to get killed yourself."

She watched as the two took their positions. "I just do not *believe* this."

"Gunther admitted he was a spy; he tried to buy the code off me, and . . . "

"I don't mean that. Code-books, international spies – that's plain ordinary common sense. But all *this* . . . tell me you're really making a cinematograph film. Or I'm having a lobster dream."

Ranklin smiled thinly. "The General's having the dream; we're just passing through."

"Commencez!"

Again Gunther let O'Gilroy move, and again he moved left. Perhaps he was favouring his left arm, perhaps he was pretending to, but after the first few clashes blood was staining the bandage above his wrist.

And is Gunther's mind muddied by thoughts of how he can get scratched, and end the duel, without getting killed? Oh, I *hope* so, Ranklin thought.

Then he noticed the change in Gunther's style: he didn't seem to be really trying. He was content to stand off, making neither real thrusts nor even feints, and just fencing so that the bayonets constantly clacked on each other. O'Gilroy seemed puzzled, too, trying feints to draw Gunther into a real thrust, then changing to a right-hand circle to see if that made a difference.

If so, it was only that Gunther fenced harder, really hacking O'Gilroy's bayonet aside and – almost – leaving himself open to a thrust. Was he trying to tire O'Gilroy? – constantly jolt his wounded arm so that . . .

O'Gilroy's bayonet snapped. It sparkled in the air and clattered on the cobbles, and while everyone waited for Clement to shout "Dégagéz!" Gunther lunged.

O'Gilroy had half-lowered his rifle. Now he didn't try to parry: he stepped left, across Gunther's bayonet, let go of the rifle with his left hand and held it out one-handed just in time for Gunther to ram his ribs onto the remaining three inches of bayonet.

Gunther's point, his rifle and then himself brushed O'Gilroy's right shoulder and crashed onto the cobbles. Clement still hadn't called "Dégagéz!"

O'Gilroy yanked his rifle clear and into both hands again. "Ye stinking bastard, ye!" But Clement was busy tugging at his pocket.

The courtyard exploded with noise; the women – except Corinna – screamed, the men shouted orders and jostled to let each other reach the blood first, the General squawked: "Sergeant! Sergeant!" and Ranklin yelled: "The car! Get in the car!" as he ran to scoop up Gunther's rifle.

Corinna grabbed O'Gilroy's jacket and her bag in one hand, pulled up her skirt with the other and ran for the Renault.

Clement pulled a huge revolver free as the wave of people broke around Gunther. O'Gilroy threw his rifle, the General slashed with his stick, and Clement dropped the gun – which surprisingly didn't go off. Ranklin pulled O'Gilroy clear and shouted in his furious face: "In the *car!*"

O'Gilroy stared at him for a blank instant, then ran. Ranklin paused to take the starting-handle from the General's car, but it wasn't in place, so he threw the rifle through the windscreen instead. Corinna was already in the driving seat and O'Gilroy pushing the car back one-handed. They got it turned, then rolling forward onto the gravel of the drive and its weight took over as they tipped downhill. O'Gilroy scrambled into the second seat and Ranklin found himself on the running-board on Corinna's side.

She let in the clutch, the back wheels skidded, then the engine caught with a bang and the car surged forward.

"We left our bags. And me overcoat," O'Gilroy said suddenly.

"You've got your lives," Corinna pointed out. "Though for how much longer, driving without lamps . . . "

"Just *guess*," Ranklin said impatiently.

She slowed right down where the drive met the road by the unlit gatehouse, but even then Ranklin's weight nearly toppled them into the ditch.

She stopped. "There's a rumble seat back there, you know."

Ranklin was baffled, then realised she must mean a dickey seat under lids where the luggage had been strapped. He had only ridden in one a couple of times before: usually it was for children and servants. He lifted the lids with more haste than enthusiasm, but it would be better than clinging on the running board.

"And light the lamps while you're out there," Corinna said.

"No. Find a side road, then if we're being chased they'll go right past."

He sat down and they rattled off again; Renaults were known for their reliability but not, obviously, for their silence, and Ranklin's view forwards was just the back of the canvas hood.

Inside the hood, Corinna asked O'Gilroy: "You didn't kill Cort, did you?"

"Never at all. But that doctor's got his chance yet. Just cut him along his ribs. With what I'd left of me bayonet ye couldn't slice bread."

"Yes, what happened there?"

"That bastard the Sergeant – begging your pardon, ma'am . . . "

"That's okay. It sounds quite accurate."

"He must've filed me bayonet across, or more like put on one he'd got filed already. When ye was helping to fix me arm – and that was a real kindness of ye, ma'am."

"Any time. And Cort knew this?"

"And him hammering away at me bayonet like ye saw? And me wondering what he was doing? Ah, he knew. An affair of honour. Jayzus and Mary."

"Do you think the General knew?"

O'Gilroy thought about it. "No, not him. Not with him getting angry with the Sergeant taking out his pistol. No, he was being honourable enough. And bloody barmy besides, begging your pardon."

"Stop apologising. It was more than bloody barmy: Prospero's isle with the duel scene from Hamlet thrown in."

But she couldn't show off any more because O'Gilroy didn't ask what she meant.

They were almost in sight of the local village, showing as a faint glow on the low clouds and flickers of light through the windswept trees, before she found a track to turn into.

Ranklin clambered down stiffly to put a match to the acetylene lamps.

"What's it like back there?" Corinna asked cheerfully.

"Cold, thank you."

"I guess it's lucky you're – not too tall. You've lost your hat."

It had come off in the scuffle of their escape, and Ranklin felt horribly naked without it. One simply did not go out without some sort of headgear, and his natural instinct combined with his new trade to make him shrink from being conspicuous.

Of course, O'Gilroy was in a worse state, being without a collar, tie and overcoat as well. Any gendarme with a proper sense of values would probably arrest them on sight. But they wouldn't have to worry about that until they reached Rouen.

Corinna promptly cancelled that: "I should tell you we'll run out of gas at any time. I figured on getting filled up at the Château."

"Out of what?"

"Petroleum, benzine, the stuff automobiles drink. Any idea where we can get some at this time of night?"

The French countryside didn't go in for garages, except on a few main roads. A go-ahead blacksmith or ironmonger might stock a few tins at an inflated price, but Ranklin didn't fancy the delay of routing out one of them, not in the village of which the General was the squire. By themselves, he and O'Gilroy might have chanced it, but not with Corinna . . . She had provided the wheels, but also a brake.

"Keep going," he decided. "But head for the railway line. We've got to reach Paris tonight."

"To hand over the code? I must give it you back. But don't you want the local gendarme first?"

"Not in the General's own village. Nor anywhere in the country-side, not now. I'll explain it to people who'll understand in Paris. But why didn't you get the car filled up in Rouen?"

"Because," she said crisply, "I was so damned mad at a certain party for using me as a messenger girl that I turned right around and headed back. Does that answer your question?"

"I said you should go to the gendarmerie there."

"Hey, that's great. A total stranger tells me I should go to the cops and tell them to raid a château – a place I know, I've been staying in – for no reason at all."

"Well, I couldn't say much on the back of a card. And it would have solved all our problems."

"And if you'd been strangled at birth we wouldn't *have* any problems. Now, d'you want to stand here debating it until the motor runs dry?"

Ranklin climbed back into the dickey seat. "Stay warm," Corinna called. "I can go *fast* now."

"If Englishwomen do what they're told just like that," she said to O'Gilroy amidst an angry clashing of gear-wheels, "then . . . then they *deserve* Englishmen."

16

The car didn't die until they were through the village and coming down into the valley of the Scie, with the lights of little villages strung along the railway to Rouen. Corinna let it roll as far as it would – about half a mile from the nearest village.

"End of the line," she announced. "Change here for Rouen, Paris and the British Empire. All ashore that's going ashore. A good brisk walk will soon warm you up." Watching Ranklin climb, cramped and cold, out of the servants' seat had put her in a good humour.

O'Gilroy turned off the lamps, Corinna lent him a silk scarf to replace his collar, and they began walking.

After a while she said suddenly: "But if Cort and Clement were really going to kill you – us – it would have looked awful suspicious, wouldn't it?"

"Not necessarily," Ranklin said grumpily.

O'Gilroy said: "Ye could make an accident, with our necks broke in a car crash. Or drowned driving into a river. Or burned up."

"Or hit by a train on a crossing," Ranklin said in the tone of somebody who'd just had it happen.

"Ah, now that'd be a grand sight to see. Better'n being poisoned from smoking French cigarettes. Begging your pardon, ma'am, but ye don't happen to smoke yeself?"

"Sorry, no."

"And even if we'd been shot," Ranklin wound up, "and they had to explain away bullet-holes, they could have blamed it on French motor bandits."

"I suppose in your job you carry lists of such thoughts. And I get the general idea – but you think that's all over?"

Ranklin instinctively looked behind, but there was only darkness. "I hope so. They probably want to get Gunther to hospital. But we did mark the road for them by leaving the car back there." There hadn't been anywhere to push it off the road. "I'd rather keep worrying a little longer."

"Suit yourself." They came into the village and a patch of light from a busy café. "You know something? You two do look kind of funny, outdoors without hats. If anybody asks, you better say you've been playing tennis."

They walked on through the village to the station and found there was a stopping train to Rouen in a quarter of an hour. And yes, monsieur would find a train on to Paris tonight, pas de problème.

"It would take us longer to find petrol – if there is any – and walk back to the car. And if we are being chased, I'd rather they didn't catch us out there on the road, alone."

Corinna seemed about to suggest something, paused, and changed her mind: "Forget the automobile; I'll tell them where they can find it." And since she was the daughter of Reynard Sherring, they wouldn't raise a peep, although they'd certainly raise the bill. Ranklin bought one first-class ticket for Rouen, where Corinna's maid and luggage were, and two for Paris.

Then she went off to find the ladies' lavatory: "I was planning for that at the Château, too. Now, on a French railroad station. Lord, the things I seem to be doing for your Empire."

O'Gilroy gave Ranklin a puzzled look. "Are we in so much of a rush now? Ye really think they're chasing after?"

"We can still wreck the mission if we don't get the code to Paris tonight – now we've got the *real* code. It was something Gunther said to me in our private chat: that the War House wouldn't trust the code if it had vanished, from their point of view, for a few hours. Perhaps the War House doesn't know about the mix-up, but the French'll have the other two parcels by now and they'll damn well know. D'you think *they'll* trust it if the third copy doesn't arrive until sometime tomorrow? So they'll politely ask the War House to make up a new code please, and with two years' work down the drain the War House will have words with the Bureau, and what the Commander says to *us* . . . "

O'Gilroy shrugged. "'Twasn't our mix-up. How'd they blame us?"

"Did you leave your brains in your overcoat? And your Army experience?"

"Sorry, Captain. I was forgetting."

Corinna came back saying: "Don't ask," which deeply shocked Ranklin, who wouldn't have dreamed of asking.

"Are you returning to Paris tomorrow?" Ranklin asked, trying to restore some tone to the conversation.

"That's right. Are you going home or staying on in Paris for more spying?"

"*Really*," Ranklin protested. "Would an agent announce he's a British Army officer? And I hope we've got real agents who wouldn't get into the mess we did at the Château."

"Oh, I don't know: I thought it was pretty resourceful, forcing a duel. Just the thing I'd expect spies to do."

"Once and for all."

But then O'Gilroy, who'd been thinking and not listening, said: "If ye don't fancy the train, I could mebbe steal a car and go all the way."

"O'Gilroy," Ranklin said with a glare, "has a rather individual sense of humour. And property."

Nettled, O'Gilroy sighed: "Ah, to hear the English sorrowing about others' property is like the tiger saying sorry to the goat. Afterwards."

"I'm glad you boys are maintaining a united front," Corinna said, now thoroughly unconvinced by Ranklin. "But if it doesn't offend your professional propriety, we'll be legalistic and take the train. And speaking of tigers and goats, would either of you have a goat to spare?"

Ranklin puzzled, then realised: "D'you mean you've had no dinner?"

"Thanks to getting mad at you and your code."

Ranklin tried to recall if they'd passed an open food shop (they certainly hadn't passed a hat shop), but O'Gilroy just turned out his pockets. He came up with a bar of chocolate, some boiled sweets and what looked like two of the General's tea biscuits.

"Trust an old campaigner," Corinna said, pouncing. "May I?"

The train dramatised its arrival with a complete symphony of hoots, squeals, rattles and clanks, then sat steaming like a blown horse. It had only three carriages and barely more passengers; nobody was taking day trips to Dieppe's beaches yet, and boat passengers had their own expresses. They climbed into one of the corridorless first-class compartments, and Corinna plonked her travelling bag on the seat beside her. "Since it seems to be the fashion, does anybody mind if I take off my hat?"

The train gave a preliminary shudder, then the door swung open and Sergeant Clement swarmed in, holding the big military revolver.

He slammed the door and sat in the corner beside it, holding the pistol two-handed on his knees. At the other end of the long seat, O'Gilroy was so rigid that he swayed all in one piece as the train ambled away; his face shone with hatred.

Trying to defuse him, Ranklin said quickly: "I suppose you didn't think to bring my hat, did you? No? One just doesn't realise – "

"I think you have the code-book, Madame," Clement said to Corinna. "Please to give it to me."

Corinna glanced at Ranklin for guidance. He seemed faintly exasperated. "For heaven's sake, man, that's all over. Why didn't you run when you had the chance – and the car? You still can: I'm not going to report anything until we reach Paris. Nobody around here would believe us."

"Please, the code-book."

Ranklin sighed and nodded to Corinna. She took the still tape-bound book from her bag and tossed it on the seat beside Clement. He took another, the Y code, Ranklin remembered, from his pocket and compared them, then looked suspicious.

"These are not the same. I think you have another."

Ranklin reached – carefully, because the revolver was watching him – into his own pocket and threw across the third book.

"This also is not the same!" Clement was baffled and by now trebly suspicious. So was Corinna, but she was keeping quiet about it. "You will tell," Clement demanded, "which is the right code."

"And you'll believe me?" Ranklin asked. "What happens next, anyway?"

It was a question Corinna wasn't sure she wanted answered, and certainly wouldn't have asked.

"We get out at the next village."

Ranklin nodded, glancing at O'Gilroy. The staging of the "accident" would start from there. "But why," he said, "are you still fooling about with these codes? You'd far better spend the time running."

O'Gilroy's face twisted into a sour smile. "Running takes money, Captain. And ye'd be surprised how much, oncest others know how bad ye need their help."

"Free Trade in action," Corinna murmured.

Of course: with Gunther in no state to help, getting hold of the code was Clement's one hope of escape. A quick sale of that (or, more sensibly, a copy of it) before it was known to be discredited . . .

"It won't be any use," Ranklin said. "Unless I deliver that code, it'll be changed. Worthless."

Clement smiled faintly. "And do you think your government, and also the government in Paris, they will say in the newspapers they have lost a code and must change it?"

No, Ranklin hadn't believed that, just hoped Clement might.

"But," Corinna said, "when we're found dead, they'll sure as hell print *my* name. And theirs besides. Captain Ranklin of the British Army, travelling to Paris on official business. Somebody could read that and have time to connect it with the code coming on the market. Because if you think you're going to go into an embassy and roll out with a hatful of gold five minutes later, you know nothing about getting money out of government officials."

And at last a twitch of doubt showed on Clement's bony face. Because in all his years of soldiering, he must have learnt a lot about getting money out of officials: delayed back pay, quibbles over deductions and allotments and dates of promotion. That was one war every soldier had fought.

"But you're in luck, my friend," Corinna went on. "You want money, we want our lives. Let's deal." She plunged her hand, both hands, into her bag and French banknotes fluttered out like big moths. Ranklin could see they were big denominations, and Clement could recognise them even quicker.

"Here," she said, "take it, take the lot." And, with both hands still inside, she thrust the bag out towards Clement. He reached with his free hand and the bag boomed smoke in his face.

He was whirled back into his seat by shock, blinded by smoke, and a moment later had O'Gilroy's elbow rammed in his face, the pistol wrenched from his hand, lifted above his head.

"Stop!" Ranklin roared, and O'Gilroy paused. The heavy revolver would have burst Clement's head open. Panting more in anger than breathlessness, O'Gilroy settled the gun in his hand and clicked back the hammer. "Say something interesting, Sergeant. Like how ye file bayonets in half."

Corinna sat with her eyes shut and holding the bag, which was still pouring smoke, in her lap. "Did I kill him?"

"No, ma'am, jest his hand." Clement's left hand was dripping blood and his eyes streaming tears. A hit on the hand always does that, as Ranklin had learnt in school long before he saw it again on the battlefield.

O'Gilroy said: "Ah, Jayzus," passed the revolver to Ranklin and began wrapping a handkerchief around the hand. Ranklin picked up the bag and emptied out its smouldering papers, gloves, handkerchief, more money – and an elderly brass-inlaid pocket revolver with the unmistakable Colt butt.

"Less than Government calibre," he said, peering into the muzzle. "And black powder besides."

"Ye hear that, Sergeant? – ye wasn't more'n tickled. Proper gun like ye had yerself'd tore yer hand right off. Hold yer arm *up*, me darling; ye can hurt or bleed, it's yer own choice."

Ranklin passed over his own handkerchief to add to the bandaging, then went on standing, swaying slightly, with a pistol in each hand.

"You look like Buffalo Bill in a dime novel," Corinna said with a shaky smile, then: "I think I'm going to throw up."

"Don't," Ranklin ordered. "There's enough mess in here already."

She gave him a look of pure hate, but wasn't sick. The train slowed and rocked around a curve; peering across the inside of it,

Ranklin could see the lights of a station ahead, and took a quick decision.

"You get out here," he told Clement. He dropped Corinna's pistol back into her bag and picked up a smoke-stained 500-franc note. "Here – I don't know how far this'll get you, but just stay out of our sight for evermore. Unless you want to discuss filed bayonets with O'Gilroy."

A village station would hardly have enough staff, especially at night, to man both platforms, so they let Clement down onto the track on the empty side.

As the train pulled out again, Corinna began repacking her bag, which had a charred hole the size of a penny at one end.

Ranklin said: "I see now why you don't mind driving on French roads at night."

She stared at her pistol as if seeing it for the first time. "I've carried this around for years, but never . . . "

"Why didn't you give it to one of us earlier?" Ranklin asked gently.

She frowned. "I guess . . . I thought . . . God damn it, I don't *know* you! Except you go starting and fighting duels and stuff. Maybe I thought if I gave you the gun, you'd shoot somebody and there'd been quite enough . . . " She lifted her head with her eyes closed and shuddered. "When I got the thing cocked, I thought: maybe I'm going to kill this guy. And I thought: so! he's going to kill me. *Me*. And I shot as straight as I could."

She put the gun in the bag and snapped it shut. "Is that what happens? What you feel?"

Ranklin and O'Gilroy looked at each other, then nodded.

"Mind, why a couple of spies, of all people, don't carry their own guns and need so much help from me, I'll never understand."

"I keep telling you . . . " Ranklin began.

"I know you do. Aren't you going to put away your secret codes before someone else walks off with them?"

Ranklin began stuffing the three books into the pockets that didn't already hold Clement's revolver.

Corinna watched. "And why three of them – all different?"

Ranklin hesitated, then said: "Two of them are false." There was no need to explain it hadn't been planned just that way.

"And the one you gave me, X, is the real one?" O'Gilroy's eyebrows lifted for a moment, but he said nothing. "Because," she went on, "it had damn well better be. I didn't fancy being a messenger, but if I thought I'd just been a decoy duck . . ."

Ranklin nodded. "X is the real one."

At Rouen, they saw Corinna into a taxi and had time to buy a different brand of cigarette, since O'Gilroy believed an entire nation couldn't tolerate the things he had tried at the Château. Ranklin, who still had some English tobacco for his pipe, said nothing.

When they were settled, alone, in a rather more first-class compartment than the small train's, O'Gilroy lit a cigarette, scowled, and said: "So ye did send her off as a decoy duck for them to be chasing after."

"It might have come to that, if I thought it could gain us more time. But they'd never have caught her."

"'Cept they would, with her turning round like that to come back and blast ye."

"Damn fool woman."

"Yer a hard man, Captain."

"All right, what code am I supposed to be keeping to? Did I get a foul stain on my honour as a *spy*?" Ranklin knew his face looked childish in anger, but no longer cared.

"It's 'spies' we are now, is it?"

"Of course it is. All that bloody nonsense about 'agents' – we're spies and that's all there is to it. And not much bloody good at it, not me, anyway. Nearly getting you killed in a duel."

"Nearly killed, was I now?" O'Gilroy changed gear into high indignation. "I could've bested six of him with one hand tied behind me back – and I *did* have one hand tied, nearabouts, and turned out there was two of them. If'n ye want *me* killed, try a regiment of cavalry next time, and a few machine-guns besides."

"Sorry."

"Save yer sorrow for the times we lose. We beat them bastards,

Captain, and yer own War Office besides. Only – I'm wondering why ye volunteered for such work at all."

"Don't worry," Ranklin muttered. "I'll stick with the job."

"I'm not worried, Captain. Knowing yer a man of honour."

17

The next afternoon they took tea with Mrs Winslow Finn at the Ritz. Ranklin had expected O'Gilroy to be overawed, but he just strolled in, smiling appreciatively. Perhaps, Ranklin reflected, it was like telling a man you're going to give him a bucketful of gin: he's never seen such a thing before, but when he gets it, it's exactly what he expected. O'Gilroy would simply have been disappointed if there had not been a high decorated ceiling, twinkling chandeliers, potted palms and soft music.

Obviously of her own choice, Corinna was tucked away at a quiet corner table talking to a young man in a dark suit who was taking notes. She wore a peg-top dress in ultramarine silk – most of the women around the room were in pastel shades – with a short white jacket and flowerpot hat. The young man got up and melted away as the Maître brought them across.

"One of Pop's assistants," she introduced the retreating back view. "You boys have been shopping."

Ranklin smiled painfully; she could only be referring to a rather erroneous tie O'Gilroy had insisted on buying in the Avenue de l'Opéra.

"Yes, we had to replace quite a lot of kit that we'd left at the Château."

"And did you deliver your precious code?"

Ranklin nodded. Last night he had handed over the W code to a professionally gloomy Colonel Huguet who was on the brink of giving it up as compromised – and still needed a lot of persuading that it had never left Ranklin's person. But he had listened, puzzled, intrigued and finally outraged, then launched Ranklin into a long night of interviews with officers of the Service de Renseignments, who knew something of "van der Brock" already, and an artist who drew Clement's face from Ranklin's description.

Ultimately they had agreed that the War Office's "little error" (about which Lieutenant Spiers and the other agent knew nothing, having delivered their parcels intact) just about balanced out the French carelessness about the General and the royalists in the Ministère, and that perhaps written reports would cause needless worry . . . Huguet had sealed the pact by giving him the X code-book as a souvenir. And Ranklin had drunk too much coffee and cognac and slept badly.

"And you had to tell them about the General?"

O'Gilroy looked up from his lemon tea. "Was ye thinking we owed him any better, then?"

"Fools on that scale are dangerous," Ranklin said. "He was trying – unwittingly, perhaps – to commit a blatantly treacherous act. Next time . . . "

Corinna nodded and smiled sadly. "I suppose so. But he was kind of sweet, with his old-fashioned honour and duelling . . . "

"If you look carefully at any history of duelling," Ranklin said, "you'll find that, except where both parties were just drunk, most were legitimised murder forced by an expert swordsman or pistol shot."

O'Gilroy stared, then chuckled to himself. Corinna said: "Bye-bye King Arthur. But what'll happen to the old boy?"

"They daren't have a trial, it would get the royalists up in arms. So, a few nods and winks behind closed doors, perhaps somebody of more certain loyalty taking over Clement's job – and no, nothing heard of *him*." Then, trying to change the subject: "Was your father taken with any of the châteaux you saw?"

"Was he – ?" For a moment she looked blank, then remembered the reason she'd given for being at the Château. "Oh, yes, well . . . I don't know that he's very serious about it. What he might be serious about is knowing just how cosy the British and French armies are, and how close they think a war is."

"Armies always think a war is close," Ranklin said quickly. "It's

127

their job. And we'd rather yesterday's doings weren't shouted from the rooftops."

"Just nods and winks behind closed doors? Well, that's how Pop usually does business. And you press-ganged me, Captain, when you slipped me that code: I'd say you owe me pay for the voyage. I'd also say I'd got you boys over a barrel, knowing how you earn your daily bread."

O'Gilroy stopped eating tea biscuits – just for a moment – to stare hard at her. Ranklin said amiably: "If I understand the expression aright, you may well have. But if you really wanted to help your father, why not suggest he tries to get involved in placing French Government bonds in America? – as Pierpoint Morgan would be doing if he hadn't just died? They'll need a new issue to pay for the third year of conscription they're proposing. Mr Sherring would be delighted to know what an intelligent – sorry, smart – business-woman he'd got for a daughter."

That lunchtime Ranklin had had a friendly chat with a man from the Paris branch of an English bank. They had touched on the career of Reynard Sherring, private banker: not in the class of a Rothschild or the late J. P. Morgan, perhaps, but well respected and with no worries about where his next steam yacht was coming from. And now his daughter sat and listened, a polite smile held on her usually mobile face.

"Because it struck me," Ranklin went on, "that a smart businesswoman might have a smart business reason for wasting time in that crumbling old Château. Such as finding out whether the royalists really have any political future. Not directly from the old warhorse himself, but from the names he'd let drop when trying to impress a pretty young face. Stuff that your father would like to know but daren't be seen trying to find out, not if he wanted any slice of the French bond pie or anything else from the government. Because if there was even a whisper of royalist sympathies, they'd rather dig up poor Mr Morgan than give any business to your father . . . you're letting your tea go cold, Mrs Finn."

She sat back and stared, apparently at nothing. Around them, the waiters glided as if on skates, the music soothed, the laughter twittered like the bird house at the zoo. Just another Ritz teatime.

"You know something?" she said finally. "I just clean forgot something Pop once told me: never try to skin a live wolf. Stupid of me." She leant forward, smiling. "It's Matthew – Matt – isn't it? And Conall. I'm Corinna. We must take tea again, some time."

WHITEHALL COURT

18

"It is very good of you to see me," Lord Erith said, smiling gently as he looked around for a place to put his silk hat. In fact, it was very good of him to say that, because the Commander had had no choice but to see him. He could fend off politicians and diplomats by threatening to tell them secrets, but Lord Erith came – at least on this occasion – from the Palace, and saying No to him would be saying No to the King.

"I suppose," Erith went on, "that since your Bureau does not exist, neither does this room. A most remarkable illusion of reality."

The Commander found a space for Erith's hat and gloves between a model of a futuristic warship and an experimental chronometer on the work-table. The whole attic room was cluttered with such things, together with a shelf of technical books, a row of telephones, and a flock of maps, charts and seascape pictures roosting on the walls.

It looked, as the Commander had intended, like the office of the Chief of the Secret Service Bureau.

Erith seemed about to flick invisible dust off the padded dining chair kept for visitors, but then just sat, draping the skirts of his frock coat away from his thighs. He had a face that was very fashionable at the time, virtually just a profile with a thin beaked nose, high forehead and sharp chin. Senior diplomats, generals and some admirals all wore it, although not so many politicians; perhaps the voters needed some way of telling them apart. Erith's version was balder than most, but with a fuller moustache.

"Are you to be involved in Monsieur Poincaré's visit?" he asked politely, but rather hoping not, if the Commander would be wearing what appeared to be a mechanic's uniform. Whoever had designed the Naval officer's working dress had held a bitter grudge against sailors.

"No, My Lord, no reason for me to be embroiled in pomp and circumstance." The Commander pulled his own chair out to sit beside rather than behind his desk. He didn't mind looking like a mechanic, but never like a blasted banker.

"And I trust that none of your, ah, agents will be doing anything *interesting* in France at the time of the visit?"

The Commander lowered his brows and reached for his briar pipe, rather like a man instinctively resting his hand on his sword hilt. "None of that got into the newspapers, not even the French ones."

"So we were pleased not to see. But your profession seems to be rather in the public eye at the moment, with the Colonel Redl affair in Vienna, and now the release of . . . dear me, I forget the names – "

"Brandon and Trench." Three years ago these two, one a Marine, the other a Naval officer, had been imprisoned for snooping round the forts of North Germany. Last month they had been released as a gesture when the King went to Berlin for the wedding of the Kaiser's daughter. The British press had made quite a fuss of the two men; the Admiralty had not.

"I know they were none of your responsibility, but still . . . "

The Commander growled: "Damned Naval Intelligence sending out total amateurs who think it'll be a jolly jape to spend their leave doing a bit of *spying*. Mind, the Army can be just as bad."

"My dear Commander, I do so agree with you (please light that pipe if you want to). For years I've been arguing for a secretariat that wasn't dominated by generals and admirals to handle co-operative planning and intelligence."

The Commander knew that was true. Somehow Erith, holding just some obscure post in the Royal Household, and with no background as soldier, sailor, diplomat or governor of this or that, managed to be in the centre of everything, including, from its inception, the Imperial Defence Committee. Too fastidious to be a leader, too intelligent to be a docile follower, what he clearly enjoyed was being an Influence.

I wouldn't be surprised, thought the Commander as he squinted through his pipe smoke, if I wasn't looking at a happy man. Remarkable.

"And what we got," Erith went on, "was your Bureau. A big step but not, I'm sure you'll forgive me, a seven-league stride. What do you feel the next step should be?"

"The right men and more money," the Commander said promptly.

"Hmm. I was afraid you'd say that. Aren't you forgetting our national custom of giving the means to do the job as a reward for having done it without them?" He smiled gently. "Now, if you could achieve some earth-shaking – but of course quite confidential – coup, such as discovering the secret fleet with which Germany plans to invade us . . . ? Indeed, I recall that collecting and giving an independent assessment of such invasion rumours was an argument we used for setting up your Bureau. May I ask how the invasion is coming?"

The Commander gave a pained smile. "Apart from a dozen shilling shockers, about the same amount of wordage masquerading as journalism and a successful stage play – no, I have no evidence of any coming invasion at all."

"Then let me ask this: could you produce evidence that such an invasion is *not* coming?"

The Commander waved his pipe in a helpless gesture, leaving an S of smoke drifting in the air. "Evidence of a negative? Can I produce evidence that a witch is not about to fly down the chimney and turn us both into toads? I can offer reasoned argument, but to those of your Committee determined to believe in witches . . . "

Erith's nod encouraged him to go on anyway. He clasped both hands on the bowl of his pipe and said firmly: "Can we start by forgetting this secret fleet of shallow-draught barges being built in the Ostfriesland creeks? It simply isn't necessary. All that's necessary to invade Britain is to sink the Royal Navy. If you can do that, you can invade; if you can't, you can't. It's that simple.

"And may we also forget the notion of distracting the Navy just long enough to sneak an invasion ashore somewhere? An invasion isn't an assassination, one-shot-and-away; it's just the start of a campaign – one that needs reinforcement and resupply just as any other. What happens when the Navy wakes up and cuts the supply line – which would have to be a regular steamship service across two hundred miles of open sea? You'd have tens of thousands of Prussians stranded in Norfolk or Lincolnshire, running out of ammunition and not a decent Bierkeller or brothel within miles."

Erith frowned. "I beg you, this is a serious – "

"I am being quite as serious as those Committee members who persist in believing in an invasion without, apparently, believing that the Navy would have to be defeated first."

Erith sighed and gazed out of the window at the already smoke-stained cupolas of the new War Office building across the street. "You're quite right, I'm sure." His voice and thoughts seemed distant. "But there is some excuse for those military and naval gentlemen who have cried 'wolf!' without really believing in invasion at all. The public at large does not see why we might have to become involved in a Continental war. But it does believe – thanks to those shilling shockers – in the wolf of invasion (uneducated literacy has much to answer for). And we must be thankful that they accept increased expenditure on the Army and Navy for any reason, right or wrong. But now . . . "

"Now, the wolf having scared the taxpayer into emptying his pockets, you want my agents to hunt it down?"

"Not kill it, by no means kill it. But cage it, tame it, at the very least get it out of the hands of the Lords of Admiralty. Have you heard their latest ploy?"

News of the misbehaviour of his nominal masters at the Admiralty always cheered the Commander up. He grinned impishly. "Usually I have, by this time of day, but please continue."

Men of Erith's age – past sixty – and dignity did not spring to their feet, but he rose impatiently. "They want two whole divisions – forty thousand men – out of the seven we plan to send to the Continent in the event of war, left behind to guard against invasion. Forty thousand of our best men, nearly a third of our whole regular force!" He stalked himself restlessly round his chair. "And when no invasion comes? – then, I wager, the Admiralty will affect to notice those troops for the first time and say: 'But we can't have these fellows standing idle, let's carry them off on an invasion of our own. On the islands of Heligoland or Borkum, or even the German coast itself.'"

The Commander leant back puffing contentedly. "Well, I hope they remember to sink the German fleet on the way. Jackie Fisher's been hawking schemes like that for years – or is it young Winston wanting a cavalry charge by sea if he can't get one by land?"

Erith sat down again and said sombrely: "I grant you this isn't a new idea of the Navy's. The new idea is how to lay hold of the troops. Forty thousand of them!"

"Unless I can cage the wolf. I can submit another report . . . "

"It would have to be convincing enough for the Army members to over-ride the Navy's dire warnings. I'm afraid that simply re-phrasing the old lack of evidence of invasion won't do it."

"What you need is a new lack of evidence? That my agents have scoured the German coastline within the last few weeks and found nothing?" The Commander frowned. "There is one problem to that." He thought carefully, then said: "Whenever I go on a picnic, I try to remember to take a near-empty jar of jam or honey along. This I half fill with water and set aside for the wasps. They swarm in to reach the jam, fall into the water, and drown. And I am left to eat my hard-boiled egg unstung.

"The Germans know all about our obsession with invasion from the sea. They also know that any invasion, theirs or ours, involves just eighty miles of their coast, from the Dutch frontier to the mouth of the Elbe. It's a coastline that's well worth our attention, since it holds three major naval harbours, most of their ship-building yards, one end of the Kiel Canal and all those fortifications that Brandon and Trench got caught looking at. But . . . " He paused to relight his pipe. " . . . but I sometimes wonder how many German invasion rumours that so excite your Committee are pure jam, spread deliberately to get my agents – and the Navy's – swarming in to drown themselves. And not in trying to learn something useful about their battle fleet or the Kiel Canal, but just pottering about looking for a non-existent invasion armada in some muddy creek. That is the problem."

Erith sat very still and silent. He hadn't thought of that at all. And to do him credit, he was thinking very hard about it now.

Finally he said: "Thank you for pointing that out. I shall most certainly pass it on to my colleagues." And if the hints I drop to certain admirals and cabinet ministers that they may be dupes of the German counter-espionage system are not phrased delicately enough . . . well, doubtless they will let me know.

"So," he added, "you do not propose to send our agents pottering up those muddy creeks?"

"Not of my own choice, My Lord."

Erith's circle of influence was probably wider than any in the country; men who would defy the King might defer to him. But in the end, it was only influence, not power. He could give orders to nobody but his own servants, and the Commander had just shown he knew it; had in effect said: "Find someone who can give me orders, and influence *him*."

He sighed to himself. Was powerlessness the price of influence? Well, he had been offered power often enough, as minister, editor, governor, but had shied away from the hurly-burly of command. He had chosen; he could live with his choice.

He stood up and let the Commander pass him his hat and gloves. "With the situation in the Balkans, the storm could break on us almost any day now." It was one last dignified plea.

"Indeed," the Commander said, just as gravely. "I shall need all my men – and more – on that day."

When he had escorted Erith to the more public part of the building, the Commander pushed his chair back behind his desk and took out a sheaf of papers hidden under a Naval logbook. He read each one carefully, then signed it in green ink, a single bold letter: C.

He enjoyed that signature.

A POSTCARD FROM KIEL

19

Ranklin was gazing courteously rather than studiously at a large canvas of Admiral Tromp trouncing the British fleet in 1653 when an English voice beside him said: "I must say I prefer flower paintings myself."

So would any true-blooded Briton, of course, but all Ranklin said was: "It's odd that they never show any seagulls in such pictures. Probably assume the cannon-fire would scare them off."

A mention of flowers had been answered with a mention of birds, so they wandered on together, and soon out of the Rijks-museum.

The new man was some years younger than Ranklin and seemed some years brisker, with curly fair hair and a fresh open smile. He wore a hairy brown tweed travelling suit that looked far too warm for the day.

"You know," he said thoughtfully, "those pictures give quite the wrong impression. The Navy didn't do at all badly in that year. The Dutch outnumbered us in most of those battles."

"Unsporting," Ranklin agreed, steering them back into the city in the general direction of, but not getting too close to, the Rembrandts Plein. Then he led the way into a small smoky café where the tables were covered in strips of patterned carpet – the patterns by now being mostly foodstains and tobacco burns.

"I thought there were two of you?"

"He'll be along," Ranklin said, and ordered three beers.

"I'm Dickie Cross – sort of ex-RN." Ranklin had already guessed the Naval connection.

"Ranklin," he said, then added: "And O'Gilroy," as he appeared and sat beside him with a little shake of his head that Cross intercepted with a smile.

"So nobody was following us? Jolly good." He pushed across a folded copy of *The Times*. "I don't know if you'd like to see what you missed at Ascot . . . " Ranklin moved the paper to one side, feeling the bulk of the packages inside. So despite looking like an overgrown schoolboy, Cross actually knew something about their trade. Probably a lot more than he did himself.

Cross insisted on ordering Ertwensoep, which they had eaten themselves the night before as part of Ranklin's plan to force-feed O'Gilroy with typical dishes wherever they went. But a thick pea soup crammed with leeks, sausage and pigs' feet wasn't his idea of lunch on a warm June day, so they chose bread, ham and cheese.

When the waiter had vanished into the chattering gloom – a journey of about three feet – Cross said: "You're going on to Brussels, I believe?"

"Yes."

"I don't want to interfere, but have you had much of a brief?"

"Hardly anything," Ranklin confessed.

"Pushing you in the deep end. Well, it *is* the deep end in our trade – along with Vienna. A lot of information for sale and not all of it twenty-four carat. So unless you want trouble with your expenses . . . Among others, you might run across somebody calling himself van der Brock."

Ranklin let a small puzzled frown show on his face, then turned deliberately to O'Gilroy to see if he could help.

"I might know the man," O'Gilroy seemed to recall. "Would he be fat and dark and wearing glasses?"

"Well, one of them is," Cross smiled. "It's a name they pass around a little group. If you challenged one of them, he'd say: 'Oh, you must have met my brother; he's in the firm, too.' Cigars is their shop front. That's quite real: they've got a place here, in Amsterdam."

They knew that already, having looked up the address and strolled past it, but not risked doing anything more.

"The one you met," Cross said, "actually he hasn't been around for some time. Been ill, I heard."

"Has he, now?" O'Gilroy was politely uninterested.

"So they say. What I was going to say was, they're the upper end of the market. Purveyors of secrets to the crowned heads of Europe, you might say. So if they offer to sell you anything, it'll *probably* be genuine, just as somebody else's probably won't be. But I can't help much more than that. The best way to judge information is to have most of it already as I'm sure you know."

Their lunch loomed out of the atmosphere and kept them busy for a time. Then Cross, who had been frowning and hesitating for a time, suddenly said: "I'm going on to Kiel."

Knowing at least that unnecessary questions and volunteering unnecessary information was Not Done, Ranklin was a little surprised.

"For Kiel Week?" He must remember to explain to O'Gilroy that this yachting regatta was Germany's answer to Cowes Week, but held in a harbour that was also German Naval HQ, had several warship-building yards and one end of the now-being-enlarged Kiel Canal.

"I've been going for years," Cross said. "My club's got an arrangement with the Kaiser Yacht Club, so they're quite used to me by now."

"I hope it won't be too warm for you there," Ranklin said politely. Kiel had to be a sensitive place at the moment, and particularly for anybody with a British Naval background.

Cross acknowledged the comment with a brief smile. "Yes – but, you know, it isn't a crime to be an agent. Only to be caught doing some – well, agenting. They may suspect, but if they can't prove anything . . . "

O'Gilroy smiled sourly at the idea that the police would never touch you on mere suspicion, but said nothing.

"Anyway," Cross went on, "I've got some unfinished business there – and it's the Russians that worry me as much as anything."

"I thought the Russians was on yer side?" O'Gilroy said, puzzled, but maintaining Irish independence.

"The Czar may be, but I wouldn't vouch for his Okhrana – their secret service. Too many of them are playing a double game, making sure whatever happens in the next revolution, they'll be on the winning side. There's some pretty entomological specimens involved."

"Insect-like," Ranklin interpreted to O'Gilroy.

"Maybe we met one," O'Gilroy said, looking at Ranklin. "Back in Ireland. But he died before we could be sure."

"What's happened to that waiter?" Ranklin asked, not quite loud enough to be heard in St Petersburg.

As they shook hands on the pavement outside, Cross said cheerfully: "Those smoky little dens seem so secret – but I suppose that's their trouble. People can get too close. I prefer an open-air café, wide-spaced tables . . . "

The galling thing was that O'Gilroy had said exactly that earlier, and Ranklin had overruled him. And O'Gilroy hadn't forgotten: "Knows the trade, that boy. Good to know he's one of ours."

"Well, he isn't," Ranklin said ten minutes later, in the security of the hotel room. He was reading a note included in his envelope, which O'Gilroy had checked to make sure it hadn't been opened. "He's Naval Intelligence, not the Bureau. Our people had asked if there was anyone coming this way who could act as courier."

"I see if the Navy's got a good man they wouldn't let him go," O'Gilroy rubbed it in.

"Quite. What did you make of that business about van der Brock? I suppose it means Gunther wasn't actually a German spy."

"He didn't learn his bayonet drill in the Dutch Boy Scouts."

"No, he could still be German by birth . . . could have been working for them on that occasion . . . " He was trying to prepare his thinking to cope with professional spies-for-hire; it sounded as if they might meet more than one in Brussels – indeed, they were being sent there to sample that world. And what, after all, was O'Gilroy? But that was a question Ranklin had long since decided not to ask, nor force O'Gilroy to ask himself.

He hastily emptied the rest of the envelope onto the table by the window and unfolded his new passport. It showed him to be James Spencer, merchant, of Lahore, India, travelling with his servant Terence Gorman.

"Just like I was yer dog," O'Gilroy commented, realising he had to give up having a passport of his own.

"It would be the same if you were my wife or child."

"English gentlemen surely love owning people."

"Look, we talked this *over* . . . "

And had agreed to experiment with a master-and-servant act to widen their social coverage. O'Gilroy might now pick up gossip from other servants and go unnoticed where a gentleman would arouse suspicion. And, within limits, they had been free to invent their own new selves.

Ranklin's had been the trickiest, since a gentleman leaves a well-marked trail of family, schools, university or one of the services, job – if he has one – his clubs and London friends. Now each such footprint he had left in Time had to be considered, then altered or erased.

Spencer had once been real enough, a schoolboy friend who had vanished from Oxford after a scandal that had been called "unspeakable" because, no matter how hard people had spoken of it, nobody could understand its complications. However, if only half those complications were true, it was reasonable to assume that Spencer was long dead, and the only relatives the Bureau could trace were in Canada. Ranklin had simply given him a new life in India where he had served for three years himself – and the Bureau had rounded it off with the proper passport, driving licence, calling cards, letter of credit and tailors' labels to replace those on his clothes which, of course, bore his real name.

Ranklin now looked at these gloomily. Like his clothes, he was used to an identity that fitted and was his alone, and James Spencer did not really fit. He was second-hand and awkward, and like most short people, Ranklin hated seeming awkward.

But perhaps worst of all, he was quite incompetent with a needle and thread. "Can you sew?" he asked.

"Yez asking a soldier with ten years' service?"

"Of course! Then would you be so kind?"

O'Gilroy's new identity had excited him: he liked being secret and unknown. The Bureau had found his problem to be the very opposite of Ranklin's: to leave his background as vague as he preferred it, would, they thought, itself be suspicious. So they had added longer periods of service with Anglo-Irish ("West British" as they called themselves) families, and a misspelt letter from a sister in America urging him to emigrate after her.

O'Gilroy read this through twice and announced: "She's convinced me. Anything's better than sitting here sewing for a black-hearted scoundrel like yeself, Mr Spencer."

"I observe the sitting but not yet the sewing. I think we agreed you didn't have to be a good valet, but you had to be seen to be trying."

Replacing the tailors' labels apart, all they now had to do was leave a trunk of unsuitable clothes with the hotel, lodge their old passports and papers at the bank and catch a train to give their new identities a trial run in Brussels.

Oh yes – and Ranklin could shave his upper lip for the first time in twenty years. His moustache was the one aspect of his Army background he didn't mind leaving behind. And the risk of being mistaken for a Naval officer was, he reckoned, very slight.

20

DID YOU HEAR POOR RICHARD DIED ACCIDENT KIEL
QUERY CROSS SENIOR TRAVELLING VIA HOOK STOP HE
WOULD MUCH APPRECIATE YOUR MORAL SUPPORT
KIEL STOP CONTACT THROUGH VICE CONSUL STOP
REGARDS TO MATTHEW AND CONALL ENDS SIGNED
UNCLE CHARLIE

"Bloody hell," Ranklin croaked sleepily. Then, to the sombre
night porter: "Allez reveiller mon domestique, chambre cinque
zéro quatre, s'il vous plaît," and pushed some coins at him.

They must have been enough because he came back for more,
along with a rumpled and dressing-gowned O'Gilroy, and Ranklin
sent him for a large cognac. Then he gave O'Gilroy the cable.

"Richard? Would that be the feller we was talking with in
Amsterdam?"

"Must be. Died in an accident. Christ. How?"

"D'ye think this is real?" He flapped the cable.

"I do. That 'Matthew and Conall' . . . If anybody else knows as
much about us, how much more can we give away by going to Kiel?
You get dressed and pack up, then come back and pack for me. I'll
be downstairs feeding francs into the night manager to get us on the
next train."

The cognac arrived as Ranklin was tying his necktie. He
swallowed half, pretending it was late yesterday instead of early
today, and left the rest to stoke up O'Gilroy. The next half-hour
was as fraught as he'd expected, but then they were in a cab and
almost galloping through the empty dawn streets to the Gare du

147

Nord. Perhaps no city in Europe becomes so much a fortress against the night as Brussels, but now the heavily shuttered windows seemed deliberately blind to the bright new day. And on the whole, Ranklin's feelings were with the windows and not the day.

The station platform was barely more wakeful, with hunched sleepy figures standing oblivious to the shrieks, clanks and drifting smoke from the busy shunting engines.

O'Gilroy lit a cigarette. "And what are we doing when we get there?"

"I don't know yet. Can he expect us to investigate how Cross died?"

"That'd be telling the Germans who we are – if they knew who he was."

Ranklin reread the crumpled telegram (should he be sure to destroy it or be sure to keep it? – but have a ready explanation for who Uncle Charlie was? Oh Lord, the complications). "'He would much appreciate your moral support'. How's your moral support?"

"I forgot to pack it."

"I wonder if this doesn't decode as 'Find out if Mr Cross knew what his son was up to, stop him making a fuss, and pack him off home with the body at the double.'"

"I'd prefer it that way. Speaking of codes, is that the best the Bureau can do?"

"In a rush like this, I imagine it is. We don't want the hotel getting a cable in five-figure cipher groups. Anyway, the cable companies won't send them except between embassies and governments. And we were told our worst problem would be communications."

"I could've told them that meself. But when I was . . . " then O'Gilroy shut up firmly.

"Europe's a little bigger than the back streets of Dublin and Cork, but if you've any suggestions . . . ?"

It was doomed to be a long, hot, crowded day. The train, second- and third-class only, much to O'Gilroy's disgust, took four sticky hours to crawl the hundred miles to Cologne. At first, Ranklin just sat and watched Belgium's industrial towns waking up, step by step, town by town, like heavy smokers rolling out of bed and lighting the first cigarette, then the first pipe . . . by Liège, the windless sky had a false ceiling of smoke from thousands of kitchen and factory chimneys. After that, he read a newspaper.

There was nothing about an Englishman's death at Kiel, but after two weeks of frontier incidents and skirmishes, real fighting seemed to have restarted in the Balkans. Who had started it was uncertain, but Ranklin's money was on Bulgaria. They were fighting the Serbs near Kotchana and the Greeks on the river Mesta. He got angry at the lack of certainty and detail, then remembered how much, much less those actually fighting would know of what was going on. So he tried instead to get angry at the stolid pipe-puffing faces around him who thought of this as a distant peasant squabble and didn't realise that war could run along a telegraph wire faster than fire along a fuse. But if they did realise, what could they do about it? So he glowered at O'Gilroy for having the good sense to fall asleep again.

They were roused for a long Customs check at Herbesthal, where Ranklin tried to look, casually, for the rumoured signs of preparation for an invasion of Belgium, but saw none.

At Cologne they had to wait an hour between trains, so they had a late breakfast and then Ranklin changed some money, bought tickets to Kiel and a newspaper while O'Gilroy had an early lunch.

"I imagine I'll know when you're dead when you've stopped chewing, not just breathing," Ranklin said tartly, not having found any mention of Cross's death in the German paper.

"How long before we get to this place Kiel?"

"Um . . . another ten hours."

O'Gilroy said nothing and Ranklin went to buy himself a tin of Nürnberg teacakes.

They travelled first-class to Hamburg, but even so the last day of June was no time to be going on an unplanned journey. Too much competition with holiday-makers who had booked their campaigns of pleasure months before, and were now spraying chatter and cake-crumbs all around them.

Ranklin passed some of the time by trying to teach O'Gilroy some everyday words and phrases in German. He was a quick learner, though at his age he would never master another language, and his Irishness would always show through. But being Irish was itself a form of disguise for his present job, and Ranklin was ready to exploit it. He assumed O'Gilroy knew that, but it was too delicate a matter to be mentioned aloud.

The rest of the time, Ranklin just grew irritated at the journey and the vagueness of their task. At one stop, when they had the compartment briefly to themselves, he grumbled: "They should have *some* way of getting more information and instructions to us. Once we're there, we're bound to be under suspicion – if they suspected Cross – and difficult to get in touch with safely."

"Like ye said, the problem of communications." O'Gilroy was taking it all too equably for Ranklin's mood.

"If it is just a clearing-up job – well, they should have somebody stationed permanently in a place as important as the German Navy's headquarters town. Or they could have sent somebody along with Cross senior."

"Mebbe they just don't have the men. If they could find better than yeself who doesn't like the job and me who doesn't belong in it, d'ye think they'd be using us?"

That, unhappily, was unanswerable.

At Hamburg, where they changed trains and stations for Kiel, Ranklin bought another newspaper and at last found a reference to Cross's death. At dawn on Sunday – yesterday – he had been found in one of the new and still empty locks at Holtenau, the Baltic end of the Kaiser Wilhelm Kanal (just Kiel Canal to the rest of the world) a mile or so north of Kiel city. He was a retired Royal Navy lieutenant, aged thirty-five, a keen yachtsman and a regular visitor to previous Kiel Weeks who had been staying at the Imperial Jachtklub. Sad, tragic, unfortunate – but no explanation or specu-lation. Ranklin guessed it was a simple rephrasing of a police statement.

He translated to O'Gilroy, who thought it over and said: "A sea lock, it'd be. Deep. How deep?"

"For the last few years they've been dredging the Canal and building these new locks to take the biggest battleships."

"Forty foot, nearer fifty foot from the dockside, then." Ranklin had forgotten how close to the sea the Irish lived – closer than the English, since literally every Irish city was a port. And hadn't there been a hint that O'Gilroy had worked in the shipyards of

Queenstown or Kingstown?

"A long way to fall, anyhow," O'Gilroy observed. "D'ye mind me suggesting something? That ye don't read nor speak German too well while we're here. That way ye might be hearing things people don't expect ye to understand."

It was a lesson Ranklin seemed to be relearning constantly. His new job could use every skill he had, and many he hadn't, but use them best in secrecy.

21

Kiel was boisterously overcrowded during the biggest event of its year, which meant there wouldn't be as much as a mousehole left to rent. Nor were there any motor taxis: they simply hadn't reached Kiel yet. So by the time they had packed themselves and their bags into a cab, Ranklin was reduced to clinging limply to his James Spencer identity and taking everything else one step at a time. The first step was the vice-consul.

Only, at that time of the evening, he wasn't there and Herr Kessler was. "You are of Herr Cross a long-term friend?"

"Ah, yes," Ranklin agreed, hoping one lunch covered the idea. "I was."

"He is dead."

"That's why I'm here. Has his father arrived?"

"Yes. He is not here. He with Herr Sartori eats."

The Sartori family clearly had a whole fistful of fingers in the pie of Kiel, being both British and American vice-consuls as well as Lloyd's agents, before you started counting the shipping interests and incomes housed in their solid, dark waterfront offices. Kessler was just some senior clerk, but he had the stout unflustered dignity that comes with working for a long-established firm. And death was just another, probably not unfamiliar, commodity.

"Do you wish to see the police report?" he offered. "Herr Cross did not wish to see."

Ranklin could imagine that the details of a beloved son's violent end might lack appeal, but took the two-page document for himself.

"It must not this office leave," Kessler warned.

So Ranklin stood at one of the high ledger desks in an empty office and picked his way carefully through the report. At least the police side of it was clear and concise: the Nachtwächter at the (new) Holtenau locks had telephoned the local police at 1.43 a.m. They arrived at 2.02, helped get the body out of the lock, and called the Kiel police at 2.17. Hauptmann Lenz arrived from Kiel at 2.39 and confirmed identity of the body (so a police captain, a big fish in a small city like Kiel, already knew Cross; that was bad news). Body sent to the Lazarett by 3.15, a cable sent to Cross's parents' home by the vice-consul as soon as the telegraph office opened at 8, medical report received at 1.30 p.m.

It all looked too neat and precise, but so did any report, including hundreds Ranklin himself had written. He copied all the times down without believing they were more than approximate, and moved onto the medical details. After ten minutes chewing his empty pipe and guessing at German versions of medical Latin, he deduced that Cross had broken almost every bone in his body, but predominantly his arms, skull and kneecaps, ruptured most internal organs but died – and was there a hint of expertise triumphant here? – of asphyxiation due to inhaling water and blood. Water in an empty lock?

He gnawed his pipe some more, wrote a few more notes, and took the report back to Herr Kessler.

"You understand?" Kessler asked.

"I think so. When will Herr Cross come back?"

"He does not come back. He stays at the Jachtklub or Hotel Hansa."

"*Thank* you."

"Please."

Kiel harbour was a long inlet with the shipyards on the far, east, side, and most of the town and the docks on the west. Quite apart from the regatta, it was a busy place, the docksides lined with small steamers and Baltic trading schooners, the water crammed with homing fishing boats, ferries and important-acting motor launches. The Yacht Club, which Ranklin decided to try first once he had routed O'Gilroy and their baggage out of the nearest tavern, lay further out, almost on the edge of town and halfway to the Canal mouth and Holtenau.

"How's it looking?" O'Gilroy asked, once they were clattering north in a cab.

"Good and bad." He gave a rough outline of the report, adding: "The fact that they gave it to our vice-consul – in effect, to our Foreign Office – suggests it'll stand up to scrutiny."

"Sure, but is it the report they put in their own files?"

And come to think of it, Ranklin realised that the police and medical reports must originally have been separate. "Umm, yes. Well, the Canal and its locks aren't secret, but they're government property so it's a suspicious place to be and a suspicious time to be there."

"Did ye find out how easy it is to get to it?"

"No, but we'll have a look tomorrow. The Navy probably wants a report from the Bureau so we'll need all sorts of useless facts to pad it out. But what worries me more just now is Mr Cross Senior. He's never heard any talk about dear old chum, Jim Spencer."

"With being in the Navy, the boy'd be away a whole lot and making all sorts of friends," O'Gilroy said sagely. "Anyhow, best mumble and be short on words. Ye know? – just like an Englishman."

The big bright windows of the Yacht Club gazed out across its railed garden of well-clipped shrubs, across the harbour road, and onto a gently swaying plantation of bare-masted yachts. And a larger-than-life statue of Krupp the Cannon King gazed with them, justifiably, since he had paid for it all.

The front rooms were all laughter and loud talk. In a small, quiet back room, Mr Cross, seventyish and with a sad spaniel face and big white moustache, half got up to shake Ranklin's hand and say: "Very good of you to come," without much meaning it.

The other two men introduced themselves: Kapitanleutnant Reimers, slim with a sharp imperial beard in uniform mess dress, and police Hauptmann Lenz, a burly man of about forty who, oddly, had a more weatherbeaten face than Reimers the sailor.

Ranklin sat down. Cross went on staring at a full glass of

schnapps, then said wearily: "You knew my boy?"

"We hadn't met for some time, until the other day in Amsterdam. And when I heard . . . I still can't believe it. How could it happen?"

Cross obviously wasn't going to say anything, so Lenz had to. "On Saturday," he announced formally, "there was much drinking . . . " Cross shook his head; Lenz went on: "Perhaps Leutnant Cross also – here at the Club he was with friends, then they to the Weinkeller went. I do not know why he is at Holtenau. The nightwatch telephoned."

"And you went out there?" Ranklin asked, adding quickly: "I saw the report at the vice-consul's. You knew Lieutenant Cross already?"

"Do you speak German well?" Reimers asked. His English was far more fluent than Lenz's and, oddly to Ranklin's ear, had a slight American accent.

"Just schoolboy level," Ranklin said, trying for a charming smile.

A servant quietly put an unasked-for glass of schnapps in front of Ranklin and three of them drank with polite formal gestures. Cross did nothing.

"I had met Leutnant Cross when he visited here before," Lenz said firmly, looking squarely at Ranklin.

Ranklin just nodded, closing the subject, and asked Cross: "Is there anything I can do, sir? Anything at all?"

"Very good of you," Cross mumbled automatically, but then roused himself. "Yes, there's one thing: if you could go through his kit in his room, get it packed up and sent home – and if there's anything – like letters, you know – you think his mother shouldn't . . . I can't face it."

"Of course." It was what you did for the battlefield dead: sifted out letters, photographs, perhaps a diary, that didn't fit the image of a young hero so heroically dead.

But he instinctively glanced at Reimers for permission, and got an official nod, confirming his feeling that the Naval officer was in charge. But in charge of what?

Cross levered himself to his feet. "I'll get back to the hotel. Will you be here in the morning?"

"I don't yet know where I'm staying . . . "

Reimers said: "You can take Lieutenant Cross's room, if that suits you."

That was a stroke of luck. No, it wasn't: it kept Ranklin where Reimers could find him.

And it confirmed Reimers' influence: Club rooms would be rare pearls in Kiel Week, even to Club members. But it still suited Ranklin – particularly the idea of getting at Cross's papers.

"That's very kind of you. Perhaps the Club could suggest a small hotel for my man-servant?"

That flummoxed them. Perhaps they hadn't thought of a spy (and he must remember they would suspect him if they had suspected Cross) bringing along a valet. That might reduce the suspicion. Anyway, another nod from Reimers dumped the problem on Lenz.

They escorted Cross to the entrance hall and into a waiting cab, then got O'Gilroy summoned from down among the kitchens. Since Reimers was quite blatantly listening, Ranklin had to stay in Character.

"Gorman, I'm staying here tonight to sort Dickie Cross's things. They're putting you into some hotel. Have you got enough money?"

"I wouldn't be knowing, sir." O'Gilroy did mournful truculence infuriatingly well.

"Here's a double crown, then. It's worth about a pound and I expect plenty of change. And don't go off boozing in the waterfront bars. They may speak English, but they're no place for you while you're in my service. How you behave reflects on me just as much as the state of my shoes does. I shan't need you until 8.30 tomorrow, but I expect you on the dot and sober. Good night.

"These Irish," Ranklin complained, once O'Gilroy had gone off with Lenz, "they're completely lost once they're abroad. Or they behave as if they're in the jungle."

"You have not had him long?"

"I haven't been home long."

A Club servant picked up Ranklin's bags and Reimers led the way out: the room, it appeared, was next door in a large annexe covered with gable roofs, turrets, bay windows, wooden-railed balconies and all the other trimmings of a grand German guesthouse.

The room itself was high-ceilinged if not very big, with heavy curtains hiding the view east across the Harbour. And there were enough of Cross's belongings scattered about to give it an occupied look.

"Put them down anywhere," Ranklin told the servant. "Don't bother to unpack." He wanted nothing disturbed until he could do it himself.

Reimers dismissed the servant but showed no sign of following. In fact, he promptly sat down in a comfortable flowered-chintz chair and took out a small cigar. "Do you mind? Thank you. You don't live in London, then?"

"Oh, no. India. Lahore."

"And you work for the Government?"

"I was in the Civil Service until a few years ago. D'you know India?"

"I'm sorry to say, no. Only America." Since Germany's few colonies were all in Africa or the Pacific, Reimers's sea-going career sounded rather misdirected. "And what do you work at now?"

"I supply stuff to the Government," Ranklin said casually, knowing how that would strike Reimers, although James Spencer probably wouldn't have. He had confessed to being a Kaufmann, a merchant, definitely not of the officer class. No matter that Krupp himself had been a Kaufmann, nor that this Club, the whole sport of yachting, existed only because of rich merchants obeying the Kaiser's drang nach the sea. The Prussian officer class wanted no part of such nonsense.

And absurdly, Ranklin wanted to wink and confide: "I'm only pretending; really, I'm an officer." Perhaps Prussian and English attitudes weren't all that different.

To his surprise, Reimers just nodded. "Government contracts? A good foundation for any business. If you don't rely on them too much."

Turning to the corner washbasin to scrub off the day's travel, Ranklin felt unsettled by Reimers' refusal to be a typical officer. And increasingly wary of him. As he dried himself, he looked around the room: there was a large sealed envelope on the table by the window.

"That is what Hauptmann Lenz took off the body," Reimers said. "Mr Cross senior had it sent up here." He stayed where he was as Ranklin opened the envelope, so presumably he'd seen it all before.

Anyway, there was very little to see: some coins, a packet of cigarettes, a box of matches, a broken watch, some bank-notes and a restaurant bill. Clearly, all the papers had got wet: they were crumpled and stained and the cigarettes had dried to a solid cake.

"Damp? In a dry lock?"

"No lock's ever really dry. The bottom is thirteen metres below the sea, and with rain and seepage . . . They keep pumping it out, but . . . "

Ranklin nodded. Just a few inches of water would do nothing to cushion a fifty-feet fall, just add the final touch of asphyxiation to a fast-dying body.

The watch appeared to have stopped at 1.45 (wasn't that about the time the night watchman had spotted Cross's body?) but when he picked it up, the minute hand swung loosely all round the dial. So much for the watch as a clue: that would never have happened to a *proper* detective, he thought sourly.

There were two 100-mark notes, the bill was from the local Ratsweinkeller for three dinners on the Saturday night – and that was all. No passport, card case, wallet, keys – none of the innocent freight that cluttered his own pockets. He was about to ask if this were really all, but then didn't. Reimers wouldn't like the implication.

While he was there he opened the table drawer – and found the answer: passport, wallet and all the rest. But it was an answer that posed a new question: had Cross stripped for action, as it were, on his last night?

"What was Lieutenant Cross wearing when he was found?" he asked casually.

"I can't say."

"Then probably he's still wearing it. I hope you cleaned it up a bit before his father saw him."

"The Club gave the police a suit and other things for the body," Reimers said stiffly.

"What a good idea." One of the papers, when unfolded, turned out to be a 200-mark bond for a local land development company. What would Cross want with such a thing? He hurried his thoughts, trying to think if there was an incriminating aspect to it, in which case he shouldn't mention it, or . . . He recognised that the moment for showing surprise had passed, so just dropped it back into the drawer and went around the room collecting other bits and pieces.

There were only a couple of shilling-edition English novels (neither of them on the popular German-invasion-of-Britain theme, thank God), British and German yachting magazines, a new Baedeker Guide to Northern Germany (which he planned to keep for himself), and a hectographed list of visiting big yachts on Club paper.

He also wondered how to get rid of Reimers. He considered asking if Mrs Reimers had run off with the window-cleaner, or whether the bailiffs had taken the bed, but before he could think of something more diplomatic, Reimers asked: "Have you visited much of Europe?"

"Not on this trip, not yet. Just Paris, Amsterdam and Brussels so far. I thought of going on east, Vienna and so forth, unless there looks like being a war down there."

"Do you think there will be?"

"Me? – haven't a notion, old boy. But Emperor Franz Josef doesn't seem to have much grasp on his Empire, these days."

"I think all Empires of many races have problems today."

That was probably a jibe at India and the rest of the British Empire, but Ranklin just said: "Very profound. Wise of you to have an Emperor and no Empire."

Reimers's politeness became controlled. "I do not advise you to say that to Hauptmann Lenz, who served His Imperial Majesty in the Schutztruppen of the Cameroons."

It was no surprise that Lenz had been an army officer – just about all German police officers had to have been – but few came from the tough school of African soldiering. He asked: "What's his job here?"

"Lenz? He is head of the detective bureau – and, at this time, most concerned with the safety of His Imperial Majesty. And," he added, "other royal visitors, of course."

Ranklin had quite forgotten that the Kaiser would have to be around, Kiel Week being his own invention. Probably his steam yacht was parked out in the harbour right now. And had there been a whisper of warning? – that anything happening in Kiel this week was *serious*?

Ranklin started piling Cross's clothes on the bed and sorting through the pockets. "And what's your job?"

"Lieutenant Cross was found on Imperial property that is not open to the public."

"And what do you make of that?"

"I do not know. Do you?"

"D'you think he was spying?" James Spencer was turning out to be rather tart and blunt. Which might be useful, as long as he didn't get Spencer thrown into jail.

"Why should we think an officer and a gentleman was spying?" Reimers asked smoothly, if a little belatedly.

"Wasn't that what you were hinting at? You can't have thought Dickie was trying to steal your locks. Not even pick them." He chuckled at Spencer's wit.

Reimers stood up, walked to the window and pulled aside a curtain to show the fairground lights of the steam yachts moored in the harbour. "It is Kiel Week. There are ships from all Europe and America also. They are all welcome, and welcome to this Club and this city. Why should we think they are spying?"

Ranklin stared out. "Impressive. No, I dare say they aren't all spying. Sorry I brought it up. Captain Lenz thought he'd been drinking."

Reimers let the curtain fall back. "Perhaps. But you know him better than Hauptmann Lenz: what do you think?"

Ouch. Then, airily: "Oh, Dickie could take a jar or two, but in company . . . I say!" he grabbed for the restaurant receipt. "Look, it says Abendessen for three. So he ate his last meal with two other chaps. Now, why didn't Lenz find who they were and ask them what happened?"

"Their names were Younger and Kay, both young Englishmen and small yacht racers. They say they all stayed drinking at the Ratsweinkeller until eleven o'clock. Then Lieutenant Cross went to the lavatory – and did not come back. They waited, they looked for him, then they went back to their hotel – the Deutscher Kaiser, very close. That is all they know."

"Oh." Spencer's triumph was only matched by his despondency. And now truculence: "Then why the devil didn't Lenz tell Mr Cross?"

"He told him before you arrived."

"Oh. Well – didn't he have any other friends around as well?"

"Sure. He had one other friend." Reimers took out his pocket-book and passed over a folded piece of writing paper, crumpled and stained like the banknotes and restaurant receipt. It said in large script:

Kiel, June 28
Ich bin gekommen im Namen der Freiheit von der Tyrannie
Dragan el Vipero.

The writing was slow and careful, perhaps uneducated. "And who is this Dragan who comes in the name of freedom from tyranny?"

"You haven't heard of Dragan el Vipero? But it is clear that Lieutenant Cross had – no?"

Ranklin shrugged. June 28 had been Saturday, Cross's last day. "And this was on his body, too?"

Reimers nodded. "But we did not show it to his father. We did not want him to know his son knew such a monster."

Dragan the Viper certainly sounded monstrous, but: "What sort of monster? Have you caught him?"

Reimers frowned quickly. "No, he has not been caught yet. I suggest you don't try to catch – or meet – with him." He tucked away the note. "This may be evidence, but – we hope not. Good night, Mr Spencer."

When the door had closed, Ranklin grabbed a pencil and wrote down the names Kay and Younger of the Deutscher Kaiser hotel. Then he sat back and thought. Reimers was almost certainly Naval Counter-Intelligence. And he suspected Cross of something, and by now suspected Ranklin/Spencer, too, though that transfer of suspicion had been inevitable. But most of all, Reimers suspected Dragan el Vipero – and who the devil was he!

22

There can hardly be such a thing as a "feeling" that you are being followed – except for nervous people, who are usually wrong. For O'Gilroy it was an awareness, tuned by experience, that close behind him in the babbling patchily lit streets there were footsteps and a shadow that copied his own. He shrugged mentally, knowing he would pinpoint the follower eventually, and strolled on whistling 'The Wearin' of the Green'.

The old town was a tangle of short narrow streets overhung by decrepit old houses, and to prowl it O'Gilroy had changed his "pepper-and-salt" valet suit for his oldest clothes, with an untied handkerchief in place of collar and tie. In such streets, he wanted no slip-knots round his neck.

He had turned perhaps half a dozen corners at random when the whistled tune worked as bait. A soft, slightly blurred voice asked: "Are yez lookin' for comp'ny or jest a fight wid an Englishman?"

"Me stomach's empty and me pocket's full and not a word of the lingo to change one for t'other."

"Ah, ye've come to the right man." He had the short squat build of a seaman, a rolling gait due more to an evening in town than a life at sea, with dark smelly clothes and a knitted cap – unlike everybody else on the streets, who seemed to be wearing peaked sailor's caps no matter what their trades. "Is it yer first voyage to Kiel?"

"Me first time anywheres in Germany," O'Gilroy said, letting him lead the way. "And I'm no sailor."

"I t'ought the clothes was wrong, but ye might be a nancy-boy of'n Lord Arsehole's yacht."

"I might throw ye in the harbour," O'Gilroy said pleasantly, "but it looked too clean to be fouled wid Galway men."

The tavern or café or whatever – just a single room with a bar and furniture too heavy to break easily – was kept by a Wicklow man named, at least professionally, Paddy, and his German wife. O'Gilroy introduced himself as Terence Gorman.

Paddy nodded and started drawing two Pils. The Galway man said: "I knew a Gorman oncest," to begin the ritual of swapping names until they found one they both knew or had heard of.

"So did me mother," O'Gilroy said, stopping the ritual dead. Then to Paddy: "Me passin' acquaintance here sez ye can feed me."

"Me wife can."

"And a fine job she makes of it," O'Gilroy said with true respect. Indeed, he had never seen a fatter Irishman. That apart, Paddy was about sixty, with thin white hair and a barman's way of asking inoffensive questions that you could answer or ignore according to mood.

Such as: "Are yez in town for Kiel Week?"

"He's a nancy boy off'n a yacht," Galway said.

"Shut yer mouth or buy yer own. I'm valet to an English gent – "

"Jayzus! Ye *are* a nancy boy!"

O'Gilroy ignored him. "And we was touring about and heard of a man – we'd seen him just a week gone in Holland – was killed in an accident here. Did ye hear of it?"

Paddy nodded, his eyes looking over O'Gilroy's shoulder at someone who had just come in. "Up in one of the new locks. Bin in the Royal Navy, they said."

"He'd be a spy, then," Galway said firmly. "And who's yer gent? – a detective?"

"Does he ever," O'Gilroy asked Paddy, "spread the story that somebody's normal, or would that be too wild at all?"

Paddy said and expressed nothing, just picked up a tin tray and bar-rag and went over to the new customer. Casually, O'Gilroy turned to watch. The man was youngish, heavyish, in rough longshoreman's clothes and well-kept boots. He had brought a newspaper along so that he could look self-contained and unaware; they usually did.

Paddy came back and started drawing a mug of beer. "'T'would seem yer good for me trade."

Galway looked puzzled, O'Gilroy just shook his head sadly. "Ah, sounds like me gent's bin asking questions. And him taking the dead boy's room at the Club to pack his things, and shoving me in a stinking guest-house."

"Ye prefer the Adlon or the Ritz, do ye?" Paddy wore a wisp of a smile as he poured spilt beer from the tray into the mug.

"I've slept hard in me time, but I prefer soft and someone else doing the paying. And ye can spread that wild story about me," he told Galway.

"Ye should try sleepin' in a wet bunk in a North Sea gale wid a cargo o' timber creakin' in yer ear," Galway said sullenly.

"Yer a secret recruiting sergeant for the Merchant Navy. I knowed it all the time."

Before packing Cross's clothes, Ranklin pretended he was Cross himself, getting up in the morning and going through the day, to see if there was anything missing. He was sure that, on one excuse or another, Lenz or Reimers had searched the room: had they taken anything? But apart from clothes and shoes that Cross had died in, or that he now wore in the coffin, nothing was obviously lacking.

He sat down and stared at the meagre paperwork – particularly the bond certificate. The Wik Landentwicklungsgesellschaft had issued it in 1905 promising to pay four per cent on a scheme to develop the land on the south side of the new locks in the district of Wik (Holtenau was a village on the other side of the Canal, beside the existing locks). The plan was shown in an elaborate and imaginative engraving – doubly imaginative, since it was from a bird's or balloon's viewpoint some distance up in the air, and showed the new locks and attendant buildings finished and ships busily shunting to and fro – which wouldn't happen until some time next year. In the lower foreground was a small lighthouse and a building fronting onto the long inlet of the harbour.

All very picturesque, but why should Cross want four per cent per annum of 200 marks-worth of it – an income of just eight shillings?

Baffled, he rustled the papers and magazines and came up with the list of visiting yachts and their owners. That at least made one thing clear: that a hurricane in Kiel that night would leave Lloyd's of London sleeping on a park bench wrapped in newspaper. Looking up, he realised that what he saw through the window was a city of floating palaces, belonging to kings, emperors, princes as well as mere Kaufleute such as Krupp von Bohlen, Pulitzer, Armour, Sherring . . . What name? But there it was: SY (for steam yacht, presumably) *Kachina*, registered at Newport, owner Reynard Sherring.

Instinctively, he leant to peer harder at the harbour, but had no idea what the *Kachina* looked like even by day. Well, well. There was a good chance that Mrs Finn would be on board, unless Pop left her to mind the bank whilst he went boating. He wondered if, and how, he could approach her as James Spencer. It would do no harm for Lenz and Reimers to know he had a powerful friend at hand – and he could use her financial knowledge in the matter of that baffling bond.

O'Gilroy had chosen the one hot dish that Frau Paddy had to offer. "Now what d'ye call that again?" he asked, helpfully bringing his empty plate back to the bar. The Galway man had drifted off when he found he wasn't being offered a free meal.

"Labskaus," Paddy went on rinsing beer mugs in what looked like harbour water. "Pickled meat and pickled herring and beetroot and fried egg."

"Sure, I recognised the egg. Very nourishing. What would I drink to keep it down?"

Irish whiskey turned out to be far too expensive for Terence Gorman's pocket, so he tried the local Korn. And left his mouth open to cool.

Paddy asked softly: "Your gent: does he have any ideas about that accident?"

"I wouldn't be knowing. But he's got the time to waste."

"Now, if the police have the idea he's having ideas . . . " Paddy's eyes flicked to the follower; " . . . ye've already got them trailing ye. So let them and let them be. And never in this world hit a one of them."

"Ye mean they wouldn't take it for a joke, like in the Old

Country?" O'Gilroy's smile was mostly a sneer.

Paddy looked down at the slopped beer he was rearranging on the bar with a soaked rag. "Ye can find out for yeself, like some I've known. They'd pick on six, mebbe eight, poor defenceless policemen in their own cells, just for the fun of it. Sure and ye could hear them laughing right up to the Canal where yer friend had his accident. Now, he wouldn't have been a man that liked a joke, would he?"

"I wouldn't be knowing. He wasn't my friend."

Paddy looked at O'Gilroy carefully, then said: "Another thing: near midnight Saturday, the police was in here – and every place, I heard – askin' about a man could be yer friend: English, with a pink boating jacket and straw hat. Sudden keen to find him, they was. Mind ye," he added, "I've said nothing."

"Never a word," O'Gilroy agreed, and walked out thoughtfully and slowly enough to save his follower from hurry.

Ranklin had just finished packing Cross's luggage when a servant knocked and asked if the Club could offer him anything? Ranklin said that was very civilised of them, and asked for a Pils and a sandwich – no, of course, this was Germany – well, just something to nibble on. So why had the Kaiser, in his youthful passion for things British, imported such useless ideas as a navy and a yacht club but ignored the vital concept of the sandwich?

When the beer and a plate of cold ham, sausage and black bread arrived, he asked about communicating with the yachts. It turned out to be very simple: the Club acted as poste restante for them all, and owners sent boats ashore to pick up the day's post. As to finding out who was on any one yacht, that was in its own way just as simple: impossible. People came and went and didn't always want their comings and goings noticed.

Alone again, Ranklin took a sheet of the Club's writing paper, thought carefully and wrote:

Dear Mrs Finn,

You may recall our taking tea at the Ritz in Paris after you kindly helped me secure a rare first edition before it came on the market, and solved a travel problem in an admirably practical fashion. It would

give me the greatest pleasure if I might call on you to repeat my heartfelt thanks for your beneficence. Many things change but not the deepest gratitude of
  James Spencer
PS My man Gorman wishes me to convey his humble respects.

German drinkers didn't prop up the bar the way British ones did: they sat down at tables and got on with it. It wasn't so far to fall, perhaps, but it made making new friends a more deliberate effort. It ran against O'Gilroy's grain not to conform and try to be inconspicuous, but he was there to make his presence known. So he usually started by asking the barman for the lavatory – to check the back way out, just in case – and then asked what to drink and as much more as he could without seeming too suspicious.

The snag was that the barman usually assumed he was shyly asking for a brothel, and when O'Gilroy refused that, he was offered more expensive and startling alternatives. He had thought himself a man of the world, but realised he wasn't a man of Baltic seaports.

Then he just sat, drank and smoked. So did his policeman, only he had his newspaper – though by now he must be reading the Lost Dogs column.

At the third tavern, a youngish Nordic-looking seaman came in soon after him and went round the room trying to sell dirty pictures. He got a lot of comment but no takers until he reached O'Gilroy. The women in the photographs were voluptuous and apparently very happy, but when the seller hissed: "This one your master like," he flashed a postcard of warships firing their guns. And, with his back to the room, turned the card to show a number pencilled on the back.

Without knowing the phrase, O'Gilroy knew all about agents provocateurs, and that this could be evidence being "planted" on him. He decided he'd swear he thought he was buying only "artistic poses" and the seller had cheated him, so paid a few coins for three pictures. The seller tossed a coin on the bar as commission and scuttled out, leaving the other drinkers chuckling contemptuously at O'Gilroy's naivety.

He brazened it out for a while by studying the pictures happily, but then pocketed them and left.

The streets were emptier but the Old Town wasn't asleep yet: singing, loud voices and laughter seeped out from ill-fitting shutters and scanty curtains. At one corner he was nearly trampled by a group of, presumably, visiting yachtsmen in evening dress, slumming and drunk, but still sensible enough to stick together as a group. And always, behind him, the copycat tread of his follower.

Then suddenly there were other footsteps, a scuffle, a squawk, and O'Gilroy turned to face two men running at him. Behind, his follower was slumping onto the pavement. He got his back against the wall.

But the nearest man just grabbed at his arm as he rushed past, yelling: "Komm schnell!" As O'Gilroy's childhood training had been strict on not lingering near beaten-up policemen, he ran too.

They had rounded two corners and he was just thinking of not lingering near the beaters-up of policemen either, when they grabbed him. Looking back, he admired their planning.

One held his upper arms from behind, the other poked a knife against his side, and between them they forced him on round another corner and into a narrow alley. It was a breath of perfume rather than what he could see of the stocky dark figure that told him the person waiting there was a woman. They were crowded close in the alley, the breath from the man behind rasping in O'Gilroy's ear.

The woman spoke in a low growly voice and the man with the knife passed her something – a box of matches, since she struck one to peer at O'Gilroy.

He shut his eyes to avoid the dazzle, but caught just a glimpse of her wide face and the glitter of green stones at her ears. She said something else and O'Gilroy felt a hand go into his jacket pocket. His eyelids darkened and he opened them just as the knife man took away the photographs.

The man then tried to see what they were in the darkness – a mistake, since O'Gilroy promptly kicked him in the balls. The reaction of the kick threw O'Gilroy backwards, squashing the man holding him against the wall and loosening his grip. O'Gilroy jabbed his elbow back, twisted, and stiff-armed the heel of his hand into the man's face, slamming his head onto the wall again.

Then he grabbed the photographs and ran.

Five minutes later he walked into Paddy's and said: "Gimme an Irish whiskey and I'm not asking what it costs."

Instead, Paddy passed him a bar-rag. "I should get the blood off'n yer hand first. Ye didn't go and hit that policeman?"

"I did not. But somebody else did."

"Would he think it's you?" Paddy poured the whiskey and O'Gilroy gulped it.

"He was still watching me back when they caught him."

"And what'll ye be doing now?" Paddy was obviously worried it might involve his premises.

"Go back to me hotel, lock me door and sit with an open knife in me hand. Ye keep a rough town, here."

Relieved, Paddy nodded absently. "If it means anything, I've heard there's a feller called Dragan el Vipero around."

"Who?"

"The feller that killed the King of Greece just the other month. So they say. Mind, I've said nothing."

23

Ranklin was already shaved and half-dressed when a servant brought in a tray of coffee and bread. He took his cup out on to the little balcony, nodded Guten Morgen to a clubman in a Chinese dressing-gown on the next balcony, and leant on the railing to sniff the air.

It was a perfect sailing day, blue and sparkling. Already there was a crowd on the quayside across the road, with yachts flapping and fluttering away from the mooring poles to join others already jinking full-sailed among the graceful white steam yachts. He still couldn't identify *Kachina*, but knew the Kaiser's *Hohenzollern* by its size, twin yellow funnels and old-fashioned ram bow. And, in the middle of the channel, rigid and many funnelled, the German fleet at anchor.

Suddenly he realised somebody had been pounding on his door and hurried inside just as Mr Cross stumped in. He was dressed in what could only be "travelling" tweeds, and was followed by Hauptmann Lenz. Cross looked as if he'd had a restless night, Lenz restless in a different way, suspicious and annoyed.

"I've got Richard's kit all packed." Ranklin gestured at the bags. "There's only . . . "

"May as well take them with me, then. I'm heading for home. Nothing for me to do here, and his mother . . . " Cross put a pipe in his mouth but didn't light it, just stared around, discontented.

"If there's anything more I can do . . . " Ranklin said.

"Yes there *is*," Cross burst out. "You can ask some questions about this damnable business. I'm just not satisfied. Are you?"

"Ah . . . " Ranklin was conscious of Lenz's glower.

"Well, I'm not," Cross said firmly. "Why the devil should Richard get drunk – and that's what you were implying," he snapped at Lenz, "and go fooling around those locks in the middle of the night? It's ridiculous: he wasn't some idiot midshipman. I want you to look into it, for his sake if not mine."

Ranklin had no idea of what to say. Both professionally and personally, his first instinct was not to offend Lenz.

However, it was a bit late for that. "Herr Spencer is not befugt – he has no rights to – "

"Oh, get out!" Cross barked. "Buzz off. Go and arrest a stray dog."

You do *not* speak to Prussian policemen like that. An English one might have apologised, saluted and buzzed; Lenz just goggled at Cross as if he'd spat on the flag.

"Herr Cross is distressed," Ranklin said anxiously. "*If* you could leave us alone for a minute . . . "

Clearly unable to believe what he was doing, Lenz turned and slow-marched out.

"Bone-headed flatfoot," Cross said loudly.

"Quite, but he's not a village bobby. He could be back with the Horse Marines. Before he is, is there anything specific that makes you suspicious?"

"Just what I said: why should Richard behave like a backward schoolboy? If you want to know what I think, that pompous dog-catcher decided Richard was a spy and he and his bullyboys – and, damn it, the last thing I want said of my son is that he was a filthy spy."

"Quite," Ranklin said again, but more faintly.

"But there is something odd . . . " Cross took a sheaf of cablegrams from an inside pocket. "I was getting these all last week – all from a place called Korsör in Denmark. Only about eighty miles from here. They don't make sense to me, but obviously something Richard arranged."

"Have you shown these to Lenz or anybody?"

"No. They'd just make something nasty out of them."

Ranklin pocketed them quickly. "Thank you. I'll do what I can, but you heard Lenz, and it's his town. One thing – " he offered the bond; " – does this mean anything?"

Cross frowned at the stained, crumpled document. "I can see what it is, but . . . was it . . . ?"

"He had it with him when he died, yes. But you can't think of any connection with the firm, or that line of business?"

"Nothing. Richard was never interested in speculation – or in building."

"What was his line, in the Navy?"

"Signals, mostly."

Not a bad background for . . . He said quickly: "The bond's part of his estate, but I'd like to hang onto it just to see if . . . "

"Good God, man, do what you like with it."

"Thank you. Here's the rest of his stuff, passport and so on. I didn't have to burn anything. Richard had nothing to hide."

Except that he was a filthy spy, of course.

"Thank you," said his father.

Cross must have passed Lenz and Kapitanleutnant Reimers on the stairs, but any conversation had been brief because Ranklin had hardly got his jacket on when they were inside his room. He braced himself.

But Reimers, wearing his best everyday uniform, was as sunny as the day. "Good morning, Mr Spencer. Now I hear you are to be the Sherlock Holmes of Kiel."

"Oh, Lord," Ranklin groaned. "The old man's taking it very hard and . . . "

"I get it." Reimers held up a hand in blessing. "And you are welcome. Unlike your Scotland Yard, Hauptmann Lenz will give you all assistance. Most willingly," he said to Lenz, who was having trouble with his willing expression. "And maybe it's best for an Englishman to investigate also. Then there can be no international misunderstandings."

It was a shrewd point. He wanted Ranklin to investigate – and find nothing. Which meant he thought there was nothing to find, or nothing that reflected on the German authorities, anyway. But on top of that, he was inviting Ranklin to display snooping abilities that, as James Spencer, he shouldn't have.

"I am not Sherlock Holmes," Ranklin said wearily. "But – I'll go through the motions. For Mr Cross."

"Excellent. But I am afraid you cannot use the Club as Baker Street (I forget the number). It was a kindness for only one night, but Hauptmann Lenz will find you a hotel room."

"That's very kind." It was nothing of the sort: they just wanted him in a room of their choice, probably with their own man next door, stethoscope pressed to the wall. But at least it meant a place to sleep.

"Now all you need is your Doctor Watson. Hauptmann Lenz has some unhappy news, I'm afraid."

Looking happy for the first time, Lenz reported: "Room-servant Gorman did not obey your order not to go to Kneipen. Also, he spent more than twenty marks. So he has money of his own."

"Mine, you mean."

"Yes, perhaps from you he steals." That thought made Lenz even happier. "He went to three Kneipen, perhaps more."

The imprecision of that "perhaps" surprised Ranklin. A little embarrassed but more indignant, Lenz explained: "The detective who was protecting Room-servant Gorman was attacked in the street, from behind, and made unconscious."

Ranklin froze inside. Surely O'Gilroy hadn't been fool, or drunk, enough to . . .

"We hope," Reimers said sternly, "that Gorman did not arrange this attack."

Ranklin drew himself up stiffly. "I hardly think that a stranger with barely a word of your language could arrange such a thing, particularly with Captain Lenz's trained detective looking on. Now, has Gorman broken any law?"

Reluctantly, Lenz had to admit not.

"Very well. Thank you for your information, Captain, but provided no law has been broken, then a servant's behaviour, no matter how ill-advised, is a matter for his master."

Lenz might be disappointed, but Ranklin was playing the scene for the more cosmopolitan Reimers, who smiled in his beard and said: "But would the good Dr Watson have behaved so? Now, I think you want to see the locks at Holtenau."

"Yes, but not until I've solved the case of what yachtsmen have for breakfast."

•

Over breakfast in the original Club building, he read the Balkan news in the *Kieler Zeitung*. The Serbs were resisting strongly, and though it said nothing about the Greeks, he was reasonably sure they wouldn't have been caught dozing. In a few days, Bulgaria was going to regret starting this war, no matter what secret encouragement it had been getting from Vienna. But supposing that encouragement became more open? Austria-Hungary wanted Serbia slapped down, but if one major power joined in, could the others stand idle?

Morosely, he joined a crowd of suntanned men in identical blue blazers and white trousers all harassing the hall porter for their mail. The impact of loud-voiced wealth depressed him further: each man here, he thought, could dip into his pocket and buy all I own. If, that is, I legally own anything but my own clothes. And even they – a dark town suit – aren't the right ones for this occasion.

He was passed a single envelope and stared gloomily at the SY *KACHINA* embossed on the flap; if he hadn't got the right clothes for the Club, they were even less right for a steam yacht. Then the gloom was swept away by pure terror: his own note had been innocent enough if steamed open, but what about her reply? *Dear Spy . . .*

No: *My dear Mr Spencer – Delighted to hear from you again. If you would care to join us for lunch on board, be at the Club landing at noon. And by all means bring Gorman to carry your umbrella.*

Yrs Affectionately, Corinna.

He let his shoulders sag with relief – a mistake in that muscular crowd, since he immediately got squashed flat. Wriggling his way out of the crush, he reflected that it was odd that she didn't use her married name even to sign letters. American practice, perhaps. But now it was half past eight and time to find O'Gilroy.

There was no hint at all of Army experience in O'Gilroy's posture: he was upright, but apart from that as relaxed as a tired snake. He barely managed to flick away his cigarette end and raise his bowler as Ranklin came out into the sunlight.

"Stand to attention," Ranklin muttered, "and look as if I'm taking off your balls with a blunt knife. I'm sure you know you had the police trailing you last night – and what happened to one of them. I've been hearing all about it. Don't answer: they'll expect me to rave on at you, and we have to assume we're being watched, everywhere. I think their Naval Intelligence is in on the act, too, and I fancy they got Cross's number. Now his father wants me to play detective and the police are co-operating. It makes it easier for them to keep an eye on us."

He remembered to keep his expression angry and to punctuate with savage gestures. By now O'Gilroy was at attention and looking like a dog trying to charm its way out of a whipping.

"One bit of good news is that Mrs Finn's on her father's yacht in the harbour and we're invited to lunch. You'll probably have to eat with the crew, so d'you want to come?"

"When else would I be seeing the inside of a boat like one of them?" O'Gilroy asked mournfully.

"Fine. Now we'd better take a look at these locks."

Just then, Lenz came striding out of the Club, touched his hat to Ranklin, gave O'Gilroy a disdainful up-and-down look, and went to a small but well-polished blue tourer that he cranked and drove away himself.

"Lenz," Ranklin said. "Their captain of detectives."

"I saw him watching from just inside the Club.

"Assume he's always around. Get us a cab, please."

There were plenty of other cars parked at the quayside, but still none of them taxis. So they ended up in another open horse-drawn four-wheeler, O'Gilroy sitting upright under his bowler, Ranklin slumped under his straw boater (at least he had the right hat) and both far enough from the cabby to talk freely, they hoped.

Of course, Sherlock Holmes wouldn't have taken the first nor the second cab on offer (did the man never miss a train thereby?) but there was hardly any secret about this journey. Still, Ranklin hadn't realised the Holmes stories were so well-known in Germany – unless they were just prescribed reading for Naval Intelligence.

Watching the harbour jog past, he realised how spoilt he had become by the motor taxis of London and Paris. A few years ago, he would have relaxed, knowing he was going as fast as possible; now, he fidgeted with impatience that slowly dissolved as O'Gilroy reported his night in the Old Town. Ranklin half admired his tenacious depravity, half feared he would have done most of it from choice anyway.

"You seem to have had a most educational time," he conceded finally. "And about all I did was count Cross's socks. Would you know either of the two men again?"

"Surely." O'Gilroy smiled nastily. "One'll be walking bent over and holding himself private-like, and t'other's got his nose spread right across his face."

"Ye-es. I suppose it is more practical to have a description of people *after* they've met you than before. And the woman?"

"Mebbe. The voice I think I'd know. D'ye want to see the pictures?" He passed them over. "That's the one the feller said ye'd like best."

"And quite right too." Ranklin quickly covered some square metres of female flesh with the German High Seas Fleet. It was an ordinary postcard showing a salute being fired at some earlier Kiel Week. Perhaps five ships might, to an expert, have been identifiable through the smoke clouds. So saluting guns didn't use smokeless charges: the Admiralty wasn't likely to award him a pension for that news.

"There's a number on the back," O'Gilroy said.

The scrawled figures said 030110. Ranklin looked blankly at them, then blankly at O'Gilroy. "Well? – you bought it."

O'Gilroy shrugged. "He just said ye'd like it. Didn't say there was a couple of hard boys outside wanted it as well."

"Just another damned mysterious bit of paper." He realised he hadn't read the cablegrams Mr Cross had given him, not wanting to produce them in the Club breakfast room. He took them out, gave one to O'Gilroy, and they both read for a while. The cab turned inland and began to climb through wooded parkland past the Bellevue Hotel.

Three cablegrams had been sent at two-day intervals during the past week, each from Korsör to Mr Cross Senior at his Essex home. But one was about commodity prices, timber, grain and coal, another gave the results of the early yacht races and the third was about the times of boats and trains for young Cross's journey home.

They stared at each other.

"Code?" O'Gilroy suggested.

"Yes, except his father couldn't understand them. Perhaps it was a trial run to see if the cable office accepted such messages."

"Lots of numbers in them."

"That's true." Ranklin began counting. "Exactly twelve figures in each message, not counting times and dates put on by the cable company."

"That sounds like something."

"Damn it, everything *sounds* like something – even Dragan el Vipero."

"Ye've heard of him, too?"

"Yes – and you? Reimers, their Naval Intelligence, I think, said he was in town."

"Paddy the barman told me. Said 'twas·him killed the King of Greece."

"Another ?" Brussels had been full of stories-for-sale about that assassination. The shot had been fired by a loony, but that left the question of who hired the loony, then who hired whoever hired the loony . . . Dragan sounded as if he belonged in such rumours; it seemed the sort of name which, mentioned in a Low Dive, would cause half the customers to slink out white-faced and the other half to knife you.

O'Gilroy took a more robust view. "Most fellers call themselves names like that're just piss and wind. Worry about the ones that tear yer arms off without introducing themselves."

"I'll try to remember. Oh, and one other thing." He hadn't planned to mention the bearer bond, high finance not being O'Gilroy's strong point, but if they were sharing paper puzzles . . . He explained what the bond was, officially.

O'Gilroy looked it over and grunted: "Pretty picture. Is this where we're going?"

"Yes. Mind, all that isn't built yet."

"Tell me something, Captain," being called that again immediately made Ranklin wary; "are we trying to solve what got him killed?"

"No, we are *not*. No matter what his father thinks. And quite apart from what it would do to us, we aren't in the business of revenge. Cross knew the risks he was running, he knew he was on his own." But, forced to think about it, he realised he was assuming

Cross *had* been murdered – probably because he assumed that spies on active service didn't die accidentally. But for that very reason, he had to convince Lenz and Reimers that he accepted it as an accident.

"I expect the police did it anyways," O'Gilroy said equably. "And how would ye prove that?"

"Hold on. The Prussian police have a reputation for thinking with their fists, but they'd rather have the kudos of catching a spy."

"They was looking for him, just before he got dead."

"So you said. They didn't say why they were looking?"

O'Gilroy gave him a pitying look. "Since when did the police say why they was doing anything?" Their different backgrounds had given them very different outlooks on the police – of any country.

"What happened that night that they should suddenly want Cross?" Ranklin mused. "Or had they been watching him and lost him?"

"And him in a pink jacket."

"That sounds like a Leander Rowing Club blazer." In Kiel's Old Town, that would have stood out like a lighthouse on the darkest night.

Ranklin shook his head and summed up: "I'd *like* to know what Cross was up to; I *want* to be sure he didn't leave any dangerous loose ends – the Bureau'll expect that much. But we may end up just burning all these papers and catching the next train. Or ship."

"I second the motion – if it comes to a vote."

24

Their first sight of the Canal came near the bottom of a long slope down through the village suburb of Wik. On the far side, the red roofs of Holtenau glowed like embers amid the fresh summer greenery, but to the right on this side there was a pall of smoke, dust and steam hanging over the ravaged land that would become the new locks.

From ground level it was difficult to see any shape to the project, particularly since the work was going down and not up. But as they turned towards it and the road broke up into a wide trail of ruts and sandy dust, a broad pattern emerged. Two gigantic open-ended brick-and-concrete graves lay side by side, each over a thousand feet long and more than fifty deep. At this end, and presumably also at the other, where the locks would open into the harbour, a great basin had been hacked out to the same depth, its sloping banks lined with rough stonework.

In a few weeks the last bank holding back the waters of the Canal would be blown or chopped through, and the basin and locks would be flooded. But now the excavation floor was still crossed by a light railway track and duckboard walks, and dotted with carts and unrecognisable lumps of machinery.

"And what more," O'Gilroy asked softly, "would a man see by getting close enough to fall in?"

Ranklin shook his head. Any idea he might have had that Cross had planned to sabotage the locks was crushed by their vast simplicity: it would be taking a hat pin to sabotage a steamroller. "We came here to ask questions. We'd better find someone to ask."

179

At that point, the cabbie decided the going had got too rough, so they left him – as yet unpaid – and began walking. The site was far too big and needed too many entrances to be fenced properly, so relied on dozens of those warning notices the Germans do so well. But finally they found a sort of gatekeeper's hut and Ranklin tried to explain themselves.

The gatekeeper's suspicious stare turned to: "Ach, die Engländer," which told them that Reimers had telephoned ahead. They were then led up to the lockside and handed over to a man with a complicated title that boiled down to overseer: a muscular body crammed into a black suit, a large moustache on a wind-rouged face topped with a black bowler. If he wasn't delighted to see them, he was at least resigned.

He spoke loudly and carefully against the cross-rhythms of half a dozen pieces of pumping, digging and hauling equipment. It seemed that the other Engländer had fallen over *there* – from the far side, up towards the harbour end. So they walked along the paved lockside studded with great iron bollards and electric-light poles, past a new and obviously temporary wooden viewing stand, and stared solemnly and pointlessly at the Fatal Spot.

There was still a shallow pool of water on the lock floor, covered with a film of oil that moved in colourful art nouveau swirls as a pump tried to guzzle it up. The far lockside from which Cross had fallen was in effect a free-standing wall dividing the two locks, and Ranklin couldn't see how he could have got there. It wasn't until the overseer explained that Ranklin understood how the lock gates worked.

Instead of swinging on hinges, as with smaller locks, these gates were massive slabs of metal that slid across the lock on rails from deep slots in the walls. And there were three of them, one at each end and one not quite in the middle – presumably so that the lock could be used as a smaller, quicker one when handling only a few small ships. At the moment all the gates on both locks were open – slid back into their slots – but over the weekend the central gate of the far lock and the harbour-end gate of this lock had been closed. Cross must have come across the walkway atop that centre gate, then turned towards the harbour-end gate to cross that to where they now stood. But coming from and going to where?

From somewhere not too far off came the boom of a single cannon, and several workmen ran past them towards the harbour end. The overseer gave a half-exasperated smile and began to explain, but Ranklin was already looking: in the middle of the harbour four big yachts, sharp-edged clouds of bulging white sail, were heeling to starboard and heading north in an irregular pack. The day's big race was on.

The overseer named each one: the Kaiser's *Meteor*, the *Hamburg II*, *Germania*, and some Englishman's *Margherita*. Ranklin recalled his coastal gunner's experience and estimated them as a mile off – no, 2,000 yards, and only then grasped how big they were. Their simplicity had made them seem no more than models on the Round Pond.

"One hundred and fifty-foot masts on them," O'Gilroy commented, and he should know: yacht racing had virtually been invented in Cork bay. But for all their size, they *were* just toy boats, Ranklin thought.

The overseer listened to the workers' loyal "Hochs!" with mixed feelings. As he explained, he could hardly stop them cheering the Kaiser's yacht, but he would rather they got on with preparing for the Kaiser's visit here the day after tomorrow, along with the King and Queen of Italy. Hence the viewing stand, the new duckboarding being laid below, bunting being strung from light poles.

(In the midst of yacht-racing we are in diplomacy, Ranklin noted: Italy, the lukewarm ally, is to be impressed with the seriousness of the German Naval programme).

The workmen finally drifted back to work and the overseer to the events of early Sunday morning. Yes, one of the night watchmen had seen the body and telephoned both the Wik police and himself at the workers' lodging house. He had –

O'Gilroy had been taking notes from Ranklin's interpretations as an excuse for a valet being in on the conversation. Now he muttered: "And why did the watchman know to look down into the lock?"

Ach, that was simple: they had been pumping throughout the night and every hour he went around topping up the pump engines with petrol and looking down to see that they weren't sucking dry.

O'Gilroy gave a faint nod, satisfied.

So, the overseer arrived to find the body had been brought up and searched but no identification found. So he himself had telephoned the Kiel police to say they had found the body of a seaman, so if any were reported missing . . .

"But, mein Herr," Ranklin interrupted, "what made you think it was the body of a seaman?"

The way he was dressed, naturally.

"But the pink blazer?"

He saw no pink blazer.

Mystified, Ranklin protested: "But surely you must have known it was the body of a gentleman?" He knew he was sounding pompous, but this final humiliation in Cross's damp and undignified death riled him.

The overseer's voice easily drowned out any construction noise. The corpse was just a muddy, bloody, oily wreck and all it had in its pockets were some money, a watch, cigarettes, a restaurant bill and a meaningless bit of radical writing. Any seaman could be carrying such things and so he told the Kiel police he'd found the body of a seaman, that was all. And he was a busy man with a lock both to build and keep clean enough to be inspected by the All-Highest on Thursday, so . . .

They parted with feathers ruffled on both sides. When they were almost back to the cab, O'Gilroy asked: "So what did we learn?"

"That Cross wasn't wearing his blazer, and that he probably came from the Holtenau side. So I suppose we go over there."

To reach Holtenau they had to go back nearly a mile along the Canal and cross by the new high-level bridge, higher than the masts of the newest warships. From up there they could see the layout of the locks plainly, the old smaller ones nestled up against Holtenau village and separated from the new locks by what would become a man-made island once the water was released through the locks themselves.

Going from Holtenau, Cross must have passed through the clutter of constructors' huts, dumps of building material and half-built structures of the "island". But why? To look at – or sabotage – the one finished building, the power station needed to shunt those great gates to and fro?

Far behind, an old car with its hood up against the sun and moving no faster than their cab, turned onto the bridge behind them. It was still behind and only reaching the crest of the bridge when they turned right into Holtenau and Ranklin told the cabbie to drive them through the village along the Canal side.

Here, the solid old houses and equally solid trees were a calm contrast to the racket and rawness of the site they had left on the other side. The old locks were busy, but nobody can rush a lock. Cargo steamers, schooners, barges and their tugs all oozed gently in and out with no more fuss than a few hoots and commands and some deft rope-handling.

"A big business," O'Gilroy commented. "Must cost a mint."

"They must charge tolls," Ranklin said, "but the Canal was really built for the Navy. Probably they could shift the whole fleet from the Baltic to the North Sea in twenty-four hours. In two days, a dreadnought could go from harbour here to bombarding London – our Navy permitting."

Abruptly, they were past the locks, through the village and with the wide inlet of Kiel harbour ahead. The land ended in a slight knoll topped by a stubby lighthouse and a statue of Wilhelm I, just as shown in the engraving on the bearer bond. Ranklin also remembered the two-storey mock-medieval building alongside, which turned out to be a café-restaurant. The cabbie had assumed that was where they were heading, and since it was never too early for O'Gilroy . . .

They ordered coffee – perhaps O'Gilroy was still recovering from last night – and sat on a sunny terrace overlooking the inlet. Around them, a small crowd of expensively dressed race-watchers stared through binoculars at the four big racing yachts, now slow-weaving white triangles on the northern horizon.

"Ye know," O'Gilroy said softly, "if'n I was a spy, which thank God I'm not, I'd mebbe set here and watch everything that happened with the German Navy."

He had a point: without moving more than his head, Ranklin could see every ship that came in and out of Kiel harbour and of the Canal as well – and as far as Britain was concerned, it was the Canal that mattered; a fleet ignoring the Canal and sailing out into the Baltic would only be bad news for the Russians. But you could watch the Canal itself more easily and less conspicuously from elsewhere along its 60-mile length: perhaps rent a room in Rendsburg, just a few miles inland, right on the Canal bank.

He nodded and asked: "But how would you get the information out? By letter? In wartime when it mattered?"

"The old problem," O'Gilroy agreed.

"Of course," Ranklin remembered, "Cross was a signals specialist in the Navy, his father said."

O'Gilroy raised his eyebrows. "Was he, now? Wireless?"

For once, Ranklin had some technical knowledge that O'Gilroy hadn't picked up. "Somebody told me that most ships can't send wireless signals for more than a hundred and fifty miles. I doubt you could have secret equipment for sending over twice that range."

"And he wouldn't have laid a secret cablewire, neither."

"No – *but*," Ranklin remembered the cablegrams, "the public cable from Denmark would still be working in a war. From Korsör, just five or six hours by ship."

O'Gilroy's eyes widened, then narrowed as a wide shadow fell across the table.

"Is frei?" Gunther Arnold asked, but sat down anyway.

25

Ranklin's heart stopped, but his mind raced frantically down a list of possible next moves. O'Gilroy's mind chose one: in a blink of thought the terrace became fighting ground, he mapped the chairs and tables as obstacles, hunted for weapons, assessed escape routes.

Then, as Gunther's moustache-topped smile widened, the same realisation seeped into both of them: if Gunther was here on business, they could betray him just as he could them.

"Since you do not ask, I am very well, thank you," Gunther said, smiling. "Or not so well, thank you to Mr O'Gilroy. It was a mistake to trust so much in information from those royalist dreamers. They are not so great a loss."

He was wearing white: flannel suit, shirt, shoes, grass homburg hat, together with lime-green spectacles. Given his size, all that whiteness brought an unreal lightness, like a huge empty egg. He turned to the hovering waiter and ordered a round of Pils.

"Are you driving an old green car?" Ranklin asked as calmly as his now over-compensating heart allowed.

"You have shaved your moustache. I prefer it. So you saw me behind you?"

"I assumed it was the police."

Gunther winced. "To be seen following is not good, but to be mistaken for the police is an insult – No! I do not pick any more duels."

"The police are probably following us – perhaps here already or at least going to check on who we talked to." If they weren't going to betray each other on purpose, Ranklin didn't want it to happen by accident. If Gunther was known in Kiel, it wouldn't help their own shaky pretence.

But he was unworried. "I am a simple merchant from Munich, as many there will testify. It is not my fault if I loyally come to see the All-Highest sail his magnificent yacht (probably built by funds borrowed from the Guelph treasure) to victory and happen to meet two disguised British agents."

Odd, Ranklin thought: even among ourselves he says "agents" and not "spies". But so had Cross. Odd. The waiter brought the beer, Ranklin lit his pipe, and O'Gilroy glowered. He was annoyed that Ranklin had spotted the car and he had not, and he liked enemies to stay enemies: the cool, confident Gunther provoked him.

Unnoticing or uncaring, Gunther swallowed half his Pils, grunted contentedly and wiped froth off his moustache. "I trust you come from the proper Bureau, and not those Naval or Military departments? Please to give my respects to your Chief. And when we have more time, you must explain to me the organisation of the Bureau, it can only be my fault it seems most muddled in my mind. And you are not offended by my unkind remarks about British agents when we met at the General's Château? Good. A business-man does not speak well of his competitors; I am sure you are both most excellent agents. Now, you wish to know who killed Lieutenant Cross, and you want only the most reliable information. So, I am at your service."

Ranklin gave him a boyish smile. The hail-spy-well-met act was, he fancied, because he was a New Boy. But it was attractive, in the way that army officers feel a kinship with their enemies who have suffered the same danger, mud and imbecile superiors.

He didn't think Gunther knew, or cared, who had killed Cross: it was barely marketable information. But he might well be interested in what Cross had been doing to get himself killed – in effect, buying whilst pretending to be selling.

"I hear Dragan el Vipero is in town," he said casually, and was ready to swear that Gunther hadn't known that. "But I'm still not convinced he killed the King of Greece."

"Do you believe it was Apis?" Gunther asked, just as casually. "Apis" – the sacred bull of ancient Egypt – was Colonel

Dimitrijevic, head of Serbian Intelligence and perhaps scalier organisations.

"I believe anything of Apis," Ranklin said, "except that he pulls the trigger himself nowadays. But Reimers . . . "

"Steinhauer," Gunther corrected him gently. "Strutting about in a Kapitanleutnant's uniform."

"Whichever you prefer," Ranklin said, thinking quickly. So Reimers also called himself Steinhauer. "He prefers Reimers. But whichever, he seemed worried about Dragan."

The game was just the posturing of cock birds, flaunting feathers of secret knowledge, but an essential preliminary (they had learnt in Brussels) to an exchange of real information.

"Maybe," O'Gilroy chipped in, "he's worried about the King of Italy going the same way as him of Greece. A left and a right, ye might say."

That suddenly struck Ranklin as a very likely worry, though perhaps for Lenz rather than Reimers.

"You forget there are one hundred and fifty Schutz des Königs also in town," Gunther reproved. "With such a bodyguard the All-Highest can surely spare some protection for that poor midget of Italy."

So the Kaiser had brought a bodyguard of a hundred and fifty men. Ranklin wondered what was left for Lenz to do – if he was supposed to be ensuring the Kaiser's safety that week.

The yacht watchers began to bustle about and pay for their drinks. The race had gone out of sight behind some headland and now they were going to jump into their cars and rush off to the next café with a view. It seemed to Ranklin a very civilised approach to yacht racing.

"You have not asked me," Gunther said softly, "who set the dogs upon Mr O'Gilroy last night?"

O'Gilroy froze, but his eyes glittered.

"All right," Ranklin said evenly. "We're asking."

"Four hundred marks."

"Trade prices, please. Two hundred."

"Three hundred? Very good: Anya die Ringfrau. Her circus is in town for the Week."

Ranklin and O'Gilroy swapped glances, but neither of them

could evaluate the information – except that there *had* been a woman in charge.

"All right," Ranklin said again. "Do I owe you? I mean . . . " he gestured at the little crowd around them.

Gunther smiled and turned to a tall yachtsy-looking gentleman. "Bitte, mein Herr . . . " What, he asked, was the original American name of the yacht *Hamburg II*, one of those in the race?

"*Westward*, natürlich." He was surprised anyone didn't know.

Gunther thanked him and turned triumphantly back to Ranklin. "You hear? I was right. You owe me three hundred marks."

The race watchers smiled sympathetically as they streamed past. Whatever you might say about the English, they paid up promptly on a bet.

They sat, alone now, over the dregs of the Pils and the coffee.

"Anya – what-was-it?" O'Gilroy asked.

"Die Ringfrau. I suppose it could translate as 'Ringmistress' as in 'Ringmaster'. Did he mean a real circus?"

O'Gilroy shrugged; from what he'd seen, anything could be in Kiel that week. "But what's she want?"

"I should have asked more," Ranklin confessed. He had been trying to appear a more experienced spy than he was, trying to uphold the reputation of the Bureau. But so much of their job was bluff that it was difficult to know just when to stop. "We're assuming she wanted the postcard of the warships. She – I mean one of her men – saw the man who sold it to you. Did they recognise him? You said a sailor: German?"

"Not English, anyhow. Younger'n me, fair-haired . . . "

The waiter was hovering again: did they want more beer, or coffee? – something to eat? No – or rather yes, another round of Pils and see that their cabman got one, too, as Ranklin decided to be expansive. And did the waiter ever see an Englishman in here, aged about . . .

He ended up talking to the manager in the cool dark restaurant behind the terrace, having carefully explained that he was there by kind permission of Hauptmann Lenz. Fiftyish and surprisingly lean for a man who spent his life around German food, the manager obviously wanted as little as possible to do with the police and sudden death. But if brisk, his answers seemed honest.

And he didn't remember Cross. Certainly he might have been in, but half their diners were visitors up from Kiel, by car or cab or the frequent ferryboat. Fifty and more a day, in the season, and others just for coffee or a drink, like himself.

As for the death itself, all the fuss had been in the new locks, half a kilometre away, and he had known nothing about it until the Sunday morning.

His mind wandering to how one would go about counting the ships through the Canal, Ranklin asked if they had any rooms to let.

That wasn't so certain: there were rooms, but usually let for long terms, unless he needed them for his staff, who might give them up to visitors in Kiel Week . . . anyway, there was nothing free now.

Hardly disappointed, since he had hoped only for luck, Ranklin went back to the terrace. And, on impulse, asked the waiter when the next ferry for Kiel was due. In about ten minutes, it seemed.

"Cross must have been thinking about Kiel from the sea aspect," he explained to the devoutly anti-ship O'Gilroy. "So we ought to, as well. We'll take the ferry, go and pay off the cabman."

The ferry, wide, blunt and very un-shipshape, waddled away from the jetty burbling smoke ahead of itself, since the wind was now going faster. Looking back from the top deck, Ranklin was reminded of how little one could see from a ship. He was lower now than on the terrace of the restaurant, whose row of top windows stared out well above his head – and stared, he noted, at the sea and passing ships, not at the Canal at all. So if those were the rooms to let, they weren't good places from which to count Canal shipping anyway.

He passed this thought to O'Gilroy, who nodded and said: "And what was ye saying about sending cablegrams from Denmark? Where's that, now?"

"I thought you'd been studying a map of Europe? It's a country – and a collection of islands – just to the north. All this area was part of Denmark less than sixty years ago."

"Would it not be in a war?"

"I doubt it. It's too small and hasn't got anything to gain from getting involved. So you'd be able to send cablegrams to Britain even in a war."

"Ye think that was what the Lieutenant was practising?"

"Well, probably not himself. From the dates, he'd have had to spend most of last week there, or coming and going."

"There's a steamship service there, then?"

"Bound to be. Daily, I'd imagine." Wasn't Korsör the end of a railway line from Copenhagen? So a steamship from here and then a train would be the fastest link between Germany and the Danish capital – and important enough to keep going in wartime, when Germany would need all the foreign links it could get that were safe from the Royal Navy's blockade.

"Mebbe somebody on the boat was sending the cablegrams for him, then?"

"Ye-es." Ranklin nodded thoughtfully. "Crew, it would have to be one of the crew, to make it a regular series of cables. And you say it was a sailor who gave you the postcard last night?" He fumbled for the postcard of warships. "And the number on the back?"

"There was numbers in the cablegrams. Ye said a dozen in each."

Excited now, Ranklin snatched the cable forms from his pocket and held them fluttering in the breeze. Ideas whirled and danced like gnats above a river bank; his mind tried to photograph them, stop them in flight so as to study their pattern, their links – numbers, figures, twelve in each cablegram, six on the postcard: 030110.

O'Gilroy took it and frowned at the smoke-wreathed ships. The Bureau had given Ranklin a lecture on warship recognition and a copy of *Jane's Fighting Ships* to study, but O'Gilroy had spent half his life watching the Royal Navy steam in and out of Irish ports.

"He was wanting to say something about ships like these, is that what we're thinking? I make them three old battleships, one armoured cruiser and one light cruiser. Three, one and one – is that it, then?"

030110. "That," Ranklin said, "*has* to be right. He chose six rough classes of warships: the first must be new battleships, the dreadnoughts. Then old battleships, pre-dreadnoughts. Then probably battle-cruisers. Then armoured cruisers, then light cruisers – what about the last? Destroyers? Torpedo boats? Submarines?"

O'Gilroy shrugged; that detail hardly mattered. "But what's he saying about them?"

"I suppose . . . that so many ships of each class – he can't say more than nine in any class, but nine's a lot of battleships anyway – went through the Canal in the last . . . well, since the last message, say."

"Which way through the Canal?"

Ranklin missed a heartbeat, then remembered the cablegrams. "But there were twelve figures in each cable. Say, the first six mean westbound, the second six eastbound. Or vice versa." He pondered. "It may not matter if we don't understand the system exactly, as long as the people working it understand. Cross was never going to be part of it himself, just setting it up and recruiting the people to run it."

"If he'd finished doing that. So we know what the messages will mean and how they'll reach England, but are we thinking one of those Denmark fellas'll be sitting by the Canal counting every ship for all of every day and night?"

"It doesn't seem too likely," Ranklin agreed. "So we don't really know if he'd finished his recruiting – or whether we'll be expected to."

The first thing Ranklin did when they reached the Club was to go to the lavatory, burn the warship postcard and the cablegrams, and flush away the ashes. From being puzzling bits of paper they had become ticking bombs. And the two of them had passed that subtle divide between being men with suspect intent to ones holding secret knowledge intended to harm the German Empire – or some such legal phrase. They had begun to tick themselves, and he hoped Lenz and Reimers couldn't hear.

They went up to Cross's room next door where Ranklin intended to pack – or rather, have O'Gilroy do it – and leave his bags for the Club to worry about until he knew where he would be spending the night. Thieving was rare in Germany, near impossible in this Club, and, he thought wryly, inconceivable in his peculiar position. That was one small compensation for being under police suspicion.

There was a large, shapeless brown paper parcel on the bed and a servant hurrying in behind them to explain. They were the clothes Cross had been found dead in, sent by the police to the laundry or cleaners, now returned to Cross's Kiel address. Just one of those little wheels that keep turning after death. And one of those little bills to pay.

Ranklin paid the servant and wondered what to do with the parcel. It was hardly worth sending to England, and he didn't want to take it with him. In the end, he tore it open just from curiosity. Just underpants, a white shirt without a collar, dark flannel trousers torn at both knees and what looked at first like a dark blue sailing jersey, except made from thin cotton. Even without its rips and splits, it would have been no more protection against sea breezes than a spider's web.

It was easy to see how Cross, dead, bloody and dirty, could have been mistaken for a seaman. But there was another aspect to those particular clothes; O'Gilroy put it into words: "Wearing them trousers and jersey he'd be near invisible at night. Cat burglar's kit."

Probably Cross had worn the jersey under his shirt at the restaurant, then changed vice versa when he abandoned his pink blazer. The jersey had a German label, so could have been bought for just that, very suspicious, purpose. And one which the police certainly wouldn't have overlooked.

"But all that, prowling the locks at night, the connection with Dragan, suggests sabotage or something violent like that. Nothing to do with observing what warships use the Canal, which sounds much more what I'd expect him to be involved in. I don't see how the two go together."

26

By noon, they were waiting on a small wooden jetty that stuck out into the sea just across the road from the Club, among a small crowd that was mostly men in the usual white trousers and blue blazers. Although not vain, Ranklin was horribly conscious of looking wrongly dressed. He was sure his plain dark suit and waistcoat, perfectly cut, left him looking like a debt collector.

A dark mauve – or light purple – motor launch wallowed up to the steps and a sailor with KACHINA across his chest called up: "Any of youse gennlmen for the *Kachina?*" and then helped them aboard.

The boat was powerful, so they ripped across the crowded anchorage in a swerving charge, but not very big, so they rolled and slammed as they crossed the wakes of other boats. From the fittings fore and aft, Ranklin deduced it was carried on the *Kachina*'s davits: hence the small size.

Nothing in Ranklin's background had given him any connection with the sea, but he had an eye for beauty, and those private steam yachts were simply the most lovely powered craft ever built. Indeed, they had no other purpose except to look and feel elegant. Their hulls had the sweeping length and sharp bow of clipper ships, carrying only long low deckhouses, tall raked masts and slim single funnels. Against the column of warships anchored in mid-channel, they looked like debutantes visiting a seedy boxing gym.

Even O'Gilroy, who could usually find a bad word for how the rich spent their money, was moved to comment: "If they was horses, I'd be wanting to back them all." And the Irish do not joke about race horses.

The purple/mauve colour was repeated on *Kachina*'s funnel, the lettering on her white hull and the Sherring house flag at the mainmast. They managed the tricky stride to the accommodation ladder slung down the ship's side and were met at the top by a salute from the ship's Captain. At least, a white naval-cut uniform with four gold stripes and a goatee beard presumably wasn't Sherring himself, although you could never be sure with rich men playing sailors. Just behind him was Corinna, grinning broadly.

"Well, hello, Mr Spencer. And good day, Gorman." She was clearly enjoying the charade – and the day. She wore a plain white dress under a Sherring house-colour blazer, the same colour headband, and tennis shoes. Ranklin felt even more like a debt-collector and glowered internally.

"First, I'll show you around, then we'll have a drink," she announced. "Follow me."

Inside, the *Kachina* was even more elegant. Ranklin had expected something of a cross between the Spanish Main and the Bank of England: dark, heavy, ornate. But this was all lightness and light.

"Tell me," he said, "how much did you have to do with decorating the interior?"

She grinned. "Quite a bit. Pop wanted something like the partners' room at the bank, but I said this was where he got some value from what he spent on my education, so kindly step aside. And he did."

"Wise man."

"Except for his own suite. Maybe you'll see that later."

"Excuse me, ma'am," O'Gilroy asked, "but what would 'Kachina' be meaning?"

"It means 'spirit' in the Hopi Indian language. There's hundreds of them in their religion: the spirit of the wind, of the sun, the moon, the eagle. Strictly, Pop should have picked just one, whatever he wanted protecting the boat. But he said that was thinking small: he'd take the lot. And we haven't had a complaint from a Hopi Indian yet."

Alone in one of the corridors, she lowered her voice and said: "Say, I don't know how you're playing this, with Conall being your valet . . . "

O'Gilroy said: "Best keep it going. We're doing it for a good reason and there's trouble in forgetting it only a moment. I'm his servant and that's all of it."

"Okay, if you say so. I'll get Jake – our chief steward – to look after you. I think they do themselves pretty well." She hesitated, then asked mischievously: "Is he a *good* master?"

O'Gilroy rolled his eyes to heaven via the deckhead. "Oh, ma'am, the things I could tell ye and ye wouldn't believe . . . "

"I feared so. I know the English."

She and Ranklin wound up alone on the Main Deck – the top, open-air one – in cane armchairs padded with removable cushions, sipping a mint julep, a drink Ranklin had heard of but never met before. It suited the day perfectly: the gentle sway and creak of the big boat, the small yachts scudding about on some race of their own, the north-west breeze that pushed the stuffiness and smell of the city back on itself.

Corinna pointed out the other private yachts: the Italian *Trinacria*, waiting for the King and Queen to arrive tomorrow, the Prince of Monaco's *Hirondelle*, the Archduke Karl Stefan's *Ui* . . . "And all with their wireless sets buzzing away, trying to keep up with what's happening in the Balkans. That's what Pop's doing right now; you'll meet him at lunch." She gazed at the sky. "The air's fuller of wireless messages than smoke and seagulls. Do wireless messages go *through* seagulls?"

Ranklin blinked and said he hadn't thought about it.

She smiled. "When I was a girl, I thought these yachts were just toys, like the fanciest carriages and then automobiles. When I got more involved, I saw what they were really about. On this boat, Pop can be more private than anywhere else, his offices, our homes, anywhere. No journalists on the front steps, no Congressional committees listening at the windows. Just privacy."

"What did you tell your father about us?"

Her face was very expressive: now it flicked like a lantern slide into serious stillness. "Just what I know, not anything I may have guessed. That you're a British Army officer but not wearing uniform. Today, when I told him you were coming aboard, I had to say you were using different names. He's more used to that than you might think. He didn't say anything. What he thought, I don't know. You're just friends of mine. And I suppose I have to guess what you're doing here?"

Ranklin had thought hard about that already, and found he had a narrow and tricky path to walk. He lit a cigarette – and had to wait while a distant but observant servant hurried up with a heavy pedestal ashtray – then told about Cross's death and tried to give the impression that they were more interested in that than in what Cross had been up to.

He said nothing about warships passing through the Canal nor O'Gilroy's night on the town. However, because Reimers had mentioned it and it was a colourful detail, he did bring up Dragan el Vipero.

She pounced on it. "He sounds just marvellously wicked. Who is he?"

"I have no idea. But according to a barman in the Old Town, he was involved in the assassination of the King of Greece last March."

"And was he?"

"Again, no idea. But one thing I'd like your views on." He handed her the bond. She immediately unfolded it to see if there were anything inside, made a face, and started reading.

Finally she said: "Well, I guess you know this is a bearer bond, although they're more common in Europe than England or America. I guess we have more stable societies: with a bond like this, you don't have your name on any shares register, it's as portable and anonymous as cash, only this isn't worth a wooden nickel since it doesn't have the coupons you exchange for your half-yearly interest. Does that help any?"

Ranklin nodded, but uncertainly. Being valueless only made it more mysterious. Just then, Jake the Chief Steward came up to refill their glasses and tell Corinna that lunch would be in a quarter of an hour.

When he had gone, Ranklin asked: "Have you heard of the land company?"

She glanced at the name again. "No, it's too local. But owning land like that, it must be pretty valuable by now. I tell you what, why don't we ask at the bank this afternoon?"

"Are we going to the bank this afternoon?"

"Sure. Then we'll buy you a blazer and tennis shoes so's you'll blend with the background more."

Ranklin had always hated ready-made clothes; now, he also hated the idea of expense he might not get reimbursed. Lucidly she misinterpreted his expression. "I know all men hate buying clothes and Eve started it all with that fig-leaf, but you just be a brave soldier and it won't hurt too bad."

27

Sherring was a large, broad-shouldered and rather ugly man with a big man's precision of movement and a confident man's disdain for "correct" dress when it didn't matter. He had good reasons for owning a steam yacht, and that was enough: unlike some emperors and kings, he didn't think that meant he had to dress like an operetta sailor. Today he wore a plain linen jacket such as his clerks might be allowed in hot weather, a collar-attached "polo" shirt and a bright silk choker.

He shook Ranklin's hand and waved him to sit down on Corinna's left. On her right was a short, stout middle-aged man who made his dark blue blazer seem formal enough to meet the Kaiser in – which he had probably done, since he was Albert Ballin, head of the Hamburg-Amerika shipping line, the biggest in the world. This didn't stop his rather flabby face looking distinctly sombre.

"Bulgaria doesn't seem to be doing too well," Sherring announced. "The Serbs are definitely counter-attacking."

"Good news for the Czar," Ballin said gloomily. "But not so good for the Emperor in Vienna. He must have hoped – ah, but this is boring and troublesome for you, Mrs Finn," he added with heavy gallantry.

"Not at all," Corinna chirped. "What d'you think, James?"

Ranklin agreed with Ballin (on Vienna's reaction) but James Spencer probably wouldn't know enough to care. "After ten years in India, the Balkans seem a bit distant to me. Every time I get home on leave, there's another new country popped up there. It all gets confusing."

Sherring, who wore his eyes half-closed anyway, narrowed them further and started pulling a bread roll apart. Ballin looked reproving of such colonial flippancy.

"In India you are more concerned about Russia, no?"

"Oh, that old myth. No, we've stopped worrying about that."

"That's official, is it?" Sherring asked.

"I don't know about official, sir, but I do know that somebody finally went and looked at just how Russia could invade India. It turned out they'd have to travel Lord-knows-how far on a single-track railway, and then hike it over the Hindu Kush for another two hundred miles. That's good country for mountain goats but not so good for artillery."

Sherring smiled privately into his soup spoon, but Ballin was unwilling to let go the idea that Britain could never ally herself with Russia just because of the Indian question: "But can you really trust the natives to fight for England?"

Ranklin shrugged. "We're devils they know."

After that, they finished the soup as quietly as it allowed. The dining saloon, two decks down from the one they had been sitting out on, could hardly be furnished too lightly – good food needed some richness of setting – but Corinna had chosen a plain dull gold for the carpet, ivory painted wood panelling and faded rose silk for the curtains and upholstery, leaving the richness to small exquisite bits of wood carving. It gave the comfortable feeling that the room had been crafted, not just decorated.

Whoever had chosen the menu – again probably Corinna – had remembered that Germans like to eat well at lunch. There was a choice of cold lobster and salad or a hot chicken dish – or both, as Ballin decided. With equal tact, the wines were German, and Ballin forgot his troubles for a moment when he was poured an '86 hock from the Prussian Royal Domain. Ranklin thought he saw a tiny nod of approval from Sherring to Corinna.

Trying to keep the mood going, Ranklin said: "Tell me, we have the most frightful trouble with wines in India; how do you keep them aboard ship?"

"Ah," Ballin put down his knife and fork carefully before he answered. "We have an advantage in our liners: German wines travel better than French. If passengers on Cunard, White Star, CGT, American, if they ask for a good claret in the middle of a storm – ha, they will travel by Hamburg-Amerika next time."

"You can't rock claret and Burgundy in the cradle of the deep," Corinna said firmly. "I don't let Pop even try. We have it waiting at any port we're likely to call."

"So drink only German wines in India, Mr Spencer," Ballin summed up.

"And maybe you should stock up," Sherring said, provocatively, "in case export gets to be, let's say, difficult."

Corinna gave him a furious look, but it bounced off. Ballin sagged and made a helpless gesture with one pudgy hand. "Yes, we cannot escape today. Perhaps Vienna will do nothing, the Czar will do nothing . . . it will be peace this year. Despite your diplomats and spies," and he looked sorrowfully at Ranklin.

"I say, old boy," he protested, "they're hardly my diplomats and certainly not my spies."

"What have the Britishers been doing now?" Sherring seemed amused.

"Ach, always talking that we will invade them and sending spies to see if this is true. And that permits our generals and admirals to talk war to his Imperial Majesty. But you cannot understand what war in Europe will be in these times. You think the siege of Paris – and Metz – were bad things, but Dr. Krupp tells me now he has a land gun to fire a shell of 350 kilos more than ten kilometres. To destroy a house with one shell is now easy."

"Would they shoot at a house?" Corinna demanded, truly shocked.

Ballin smiled sadly. "In a siege it will happen. Enemy soldiers will be in that house or at ten kilometres they cannot see what they shoot at, they just shoot. It will happen. It is happening now, today, in the Balkans. Do you understand that?" And he looked squarely at Ranklin.

Ranklin had had the Krupp guns firing at him, both in South Africa and Macedonia, which was more than Krupp himself had experienced. And he had seen the results of the little 7-kilo shells fired by his own guns: men turned into bloodstains on walls and scattered boots you picked up carefully because there might still be a foot inside. But James Spencer would know nothing of that. "Doesn't everyone say a war will be over very quickly? Nobody can afford a long war, that's what I thought."

"Perhaps." Ballin stared morosely at his plate. "But to believe that is dangerous, it becomes the belief that Europe can afford a war because it will just be great charges of cavalry and clever ma- noeuvres like those at Tempelhof, flags and trumpets – and the losers will pay for it. But when a war starts can we be sure when it will end? Or that it will not end with the trade of Europe in ruins?"

Corinna leant back in her chair. "I think there's better reason for avoiding war than *trade*."

Ballin looked at her over his pince-nez with dark sad eyes. "Yes, dear lady. There are other and better reasons – such as God, perhaps. But we must find a reason people believe in. They do believe in trade."

Corinna nodded slowly.

"And what about these British spies?" Sherring was determined to keep the pot simmering.

"When King George of England came to Berlin for the wedding of the Princess Victoria Luise two months ago, His Imperial Maj- esty set free the English spies who had been caught on the Ostfriesland coast. It was a great and noble gesture by a good man. Great-Admiral Tirpitz was not pleased."

Sherring looked at Ranklin. "And what did you British do in return?"

"I've no idea."

"They arrested a German dentist," Ballin said lugubriously, "and convicted him of trying to buy secrets of the English Navy."

It was true, Ranklin knew, but the ludicrous image it conjured of admirals trying to babble secrets through mouths stuffed with drills and swabs brought stifled laughter all round the table. Ballin retreated into a huff of extravagant praise for the hospitality but soon went off in his launch, having invited them all to visit his ship that evening.

"And which is that?" Ranklin asked, since he couldn't remem- ber having Ballin's yacht pointed out.

"The *Victoria Luise*." Corinna pointed to a four-funnelled, white-painted liner that Ranklin had assumed was just part of Kiel's scenery. "He takes it out of service and parks it here as a floating hotel for his pals and whoever the Kaiser wants entertained in the Week. We like to think the *Kachina* is more exclusive."

"And serves better brandy," Sherring said. "Come and have one." It was an order.

Sherring's day cabin was clearly outside Corinna's jurisdiction. Here was dark wood panelling, rows of old books, heavy buttoned-leather chairs and a tiger skin on the floor; here, the time was always just after dinner. Ranklin instinctively put his pipe in his mouth and accepted a brandy from a cut-glass decanter. Corinna, by contrast, faded into a dutiful daughter sitting demurely in one corner.

Sherring stretched his long legs from his chair and puffed alight a long cigar. "Tell me, Mr – Spencer, do you have an opinion on the situation in the Balkans? How likely is it to spark off a European war?"

This is where I sing for my lunch, Ranklin thought. But it was a good lunch. "At this season – yes, it could."

"This *season?*"

"Yes. Armies work on a yearly training cycle, aiming for a peak of readiness for their big manoeuvres in August or September, when the weather should be dry for easy movement and the harvest's in and they can mobilise the farm boys who are reservists. In Southern Europe the harvest comes earlier. This year it was in June, and now they've gone to war. In about a month, Northern Europe should be ready, too."

Sherring glanced across at Corinna with a look of bemused horror, but when he looked again at Ranklin, it was with respect. "I appreciate hard-headed thinking, but I guess I'd expected something more political."

Ranklin smiled modestly. "You must know far more experienced political advisers than me. But as I see it, they have something of a power vacuum down there, caused by the decay of the Ottoman – now Turkish – empire. Countries like, first, Greece, then Bosnia, Rumania, Bulgaria, Serbia, and last, Albania, bobbing up as the Turkish tide flows back. And now squabbling over their frontiers."

"And Austria-Hungary?"

Ranklin frowned. "I can only make a military guess. They picked up Bosnia and Herzegovina, but that might be part of an overall defensive strategy. They're scared of a group of Slav states stretching west as far as the Adriatic, and waking up one morning to find a Russian fleet (they're more or less Slavs, too) based in a port there and bottling their own up in Trieste further north. So they're all for Serbia, the Slav ringleader, getting cut down to size."

"You make it all seem neat and clear," Sherring observed.

"Then I apologise, because I must have got it horribly wrong. I believe it's as I said, all right, but all soaked in a broth of local nationalism, religious persecution, trade interests and personal ambitions. And, of course, Italy, Germany, France – and Britain, I suppose – all trying to tune the Balkan piano to their own key."

"And what happens when they give up trying and throw the piano down the back stairs?"

Ranklin nodded. "That's the day I'm worried about."

They sat silent for a little while, then Sherring asked: "And how d'you reckon this new war in the Balkans will go? Will Serbia do well?"

"I think so. The Bulgarian Army's a poorly disciplined lot."

Sherring's eyes narrowed again. "Do you know that part of the world?"

"I was there at the end of last year, when the fighting first started. With the Greeks before Salonika. Just observing," he added.

Corinna said gravely: "Would that be on your way home from India, Mr Spencer?"

"Of course." He had completely wrecked the Spencer pretence. But perhaps even a distant acquaintance with Reynard Sherring was worth more.

Anyway, Sherring just smiled lazily. "Maybe it's that Indian trick of studying your navel rather than the newspapers that brings wisdom. I'll see you again, Mr – Spencer. Now you kids get off shopping."

28

With O'Gilroy back on the strength, the launch took them further down into the harbour, landing them at the Schloss pier just before the fish market. The Schloss itself, home of the Kaiser's brother Prince Heinrich, was a stolid square building that Ranklin would have assumed to be a learned institute. But perhaps the Prince liked it.

"Now," Ranklin told O'Gilroy, "can you head on down the waterfront and find out about the service to Korsör?"

O'Gilroy nodded. "And where else?"

Ranklin frowned, then saw the point: the question needed to be buried in among others. "Then ask about all the regular routes to both Denmark and Sweden. There should be half a dozen. And what ships – whose – run them."

"I can get somebody to do that for you," Corinna offered.

"No." It came out more abruptly than Ranklin had meant. "Sorry, but I don't want you to be involved in this."

"Oh? The last time we met – the time before that, anyway – you didn't seem too worried if I got shot. This could be worse, could it?"

"Yes."

"Ah, a fate worse than death? I've always wanted to be saved from one of those. Whatever they are. Let's find this bank."

It turned out to be the local branch of the Dresdner, and Corinna turned out to have a small wad of paperwork in her purse that sent bank employees hopping like fleas. Oblivious or accustomed to this, she sat with Ranklin in the manager's office, sipping coffee and assuring him that indeed her esteemed father was well, enjoying Kiel Week but, as ever, busy.

Her German was as good as her French, Ranklin noted, with an accent he knew but couldn't quite place.

"Perhaps you could also tell me something," she continued. "Do you know the Wik Landentwicklungsgesellschaft?"

The manager blinked, frowned, concentrated, then remembered with a grunt of laughter that he apologised for. "It is a long time ago, but now I recall. A sad and instructive story. The man thought he had a legal option to buy the land that would be on the south side of the new locks. He formed a company to get money to buy the land and then to build on it or perhaps to sell to the Government for offices of the locks. He was right that the Government wanted that land, but wrong that his option to buy was good in law. So, he lost everything, the company was finished, all who had bought shares also lost."

"Do you recall the man's name?" Corinna asked, in case Ranklin wanted to know.

"No. It is too long ago. But he committed suicide anyway."

Corinna glanced at Ranklin, her eyes wide.

"Drowned himself," the manager added, to show he was trying. "In the old lock. The north one. Your father was not interested, I hope?"

"We just came across the company name. I thought if it still existed, it must be doing well."

"Ah, indeed it would have been, but for a fine legal point."

"It can be a mistake to argue the law with the lawmakers," Corinna agreed. "Thank you for your time, and the coffee. Come along, James."

On the pavement, she let out a long breath. "Woof. Sorry I can't remember the poor bastard's name, only the exact spot he dived into the hereafter. Jesus wept."

"I suppose I can remember the details of some deaths – some nasty ones, in the war, but I can't remember the names."

"I guess inhumanity's only human. Anyhow, you've most likely got the guy's name on the bond, as chairman of the company. Is it important?"

"I have no idea at all." Ranklin wondered just how many times he had said that or something like it already that day.

"Well, if it can wait, it's the Holstenstrasse we're looking for now."

"If you don't mind, while we're in this district, I'd like to drop in at the Deutscher Kaiser hotel: there's a couple of Britons there who dined with Cross on his last night . . . "

And who, with a bit of luck, might spin the afternoon out until Corinna remembered something more urgent than helping him buy clothes. But neither Kay nor Younger was in, so he left them notes explaining simply and untruthfully who he was. He took his time about writing those, but it couldn't be nearly enough.

It was a blazered, white-shoed, new-necktied and distinctly grouchy Ranklin that she delivered back to the Club towards the end of the afternoon.

"Well," she said, "now I know what your fate worse than death is. I knew men didn't like clothes shopping, but . . . "

"I'm sorry. Rather a lot on my mind." He was looking around for O'Gilroy.

"D'you want to visit the *Victoria Luise* this evening?"

"Ah – I'd like to very much, but it rather depends on what O'Gilroy's found out about those steamship services. Can I get a message to you on board?"

"You can hire a boat to send one. Or get the Club to run up a signal hoist."

"Er . . . ?"

She indicated the complicated flagpole in the corner of the Club front garden. There were several signal flags fluttering from one of its many ropes. "Get them to hoist KAC – that's us – then the 'affirmative' flag, then just sign it J."

"I doubt I belong there sufficiently for them to do that."

"Then just hang a bath towel out your bedroom window," she said impatiently. "Which is it?"

He pointed it out.

"One towel if you're coming and I'll send the launch here at nine. Oh, hell." She relaxed and grinned. "I know you've got problems you can't talk about. Don't worry about being the perfect gentleman as well. I've met enough of them already."

She strode away across the road – a cab horse wisely conceding her the right – to the jetty. Ranklin turned into the Clubhouse.

There was no sign of O'Gilroy but there was a message. It was on official police paper and simply said: *Herr Gorman has been arrested. J. Lenz, Hauptmann.*

29

Lenz's office had that institutional look of grime scoured in by
constant cleaning. The desk was big and worn, the papers on it
neatly stacked, the large photograph of the Kaiser as an Admiral
stared down sternly from the wall behind. But the framed photograph of his wife and sons on the desk was turned so that the visitor
would realise the Hauptmann was a loving family man really, one
to be trusted.

"A man has given evidence," he said unemotionally, "that he
heard Gorman asking in a Kneipe for a man to attack the detective
who was following him. He has signed a statement."

"I see." Ranklin was being at least equally calm. "The detective
himself didn't see or hear this happening?"

"He may have gone to the toilet, he cannot say. He was hit on
the head and does not remember for half an hour before he was
attacked."

"Yes, I was wondering how you'd get round that problem,"
Ranklin agreed. "Very neat. The man who so dutifully came
forward to bear witness – he's of good character and so forth?"

A little warily, Lenz said: "Why must he come to us if he is not
telling the truth?"

There had to be a reason, of course, but Ranklin didn't think the
police had provided it. And that wasn't his gentlemanly view of the
police prevailing, either. Why should they trump up an assault
charge for O'Gilroy when to let him run loose might prove him a
spy?

"Did you know this man already?"

Lenz allowed himself a small smile. "No, he is not from Kiel. From Hamburg."

"Ah, yes. Now, may I see Gorman?"

"When the doctor has finished."

Ranklin's voice hardened. "He resisted arrest, did he? So the magistrate may infer from the marks on his face that he's of a violent disposition?" I'm beginning to think like O'Gilroy – at least about the police. Lenz may not have started this affair, but he's making sure it finishes his way.

There was a clatter in the hallway outside and the door sprang open, letting in the protests of some junior policemen and, ignoring them, Kapitanleutnant Reimers. His face was set and his eyes angry. He saw Ranklin, calmed himself with a quivering effort and asked very politely: "Mr Spencer, would you do us the great kindness of waiting outside for just one minute?"

Ranklin almost hurried out. So, he guessed, Reimers had not been consulted about arresting O'Gilroy. That seemed to make it an odds-on bet that O'Gilroy would soon be floating free. Bruised, but free.

He leant against a wall and lit a cigarette. But just how, he thought, is a Captain of detectives expected to feel when one of those detectives gets hammered flat? And how would the other detectives feel if the Captain does nothing – even when somebody rolls up with a sworn statement about who caused it? How would I feel if it was a man from my battery who'd got pulped by local townees?

Lenz is no Sherlock Holmes, and no cow'rin', tim'rous beastie either, but he's been in command of men all his working life. So he instinctively did the right thing for his men, his service – and forgot the bigger task.

The door opened again and Reimers said: "Please come in, Mr Spencer. I fear we have not quite got this problem sorted out yet . . . "

Lenz was behind his desk looking doggedly righteous. Ranklin sat down without being asked and went on with his cigarette.

"The situation," Reimers said, "appears to be that the witness will say he overheard Gorman attempting to hire a man to attack the detective. Gorman will obviously deny this – "

"Excuse me," Ranklin said, "but in between, the witness will be asked to describe the man Gorman spoke to and the police will be asked why they have not found that man. The witness will also be asked why he did not warn the detective – obviously he has no fear of approaching the police – or take some other action to prevent this attack. Some questions about his character, his trade, his Hamburg address may also be gone into. *Then* Gorman will deny it happened and ask how he could have benefited from it."

Reimers nodded and looked at Lenz.

Lenz said: "The evidence of the detective . . . "

"Excuse me again," Ranklin interrupted, "but the evidence of the detective will be that he remembers nothing. Nothing to clear Gorman, nothing to convict him. As far as he knows, he may have been knocked down by a cab or struck by a thunderbolt."

Reimers stroked his whiskers, hiding a small smile. "A more complicated case than we imagined, Herr Hauptmann. Perhaps one for the highest court in the land."

"We have a sworn statement," Lenz growled.

"Perhaps it would be well to question the witness further. At best the case is not complete: you have not found the attacker – or the cab or thunderbolt. And as Mr Spencer was kind enough not to say, the detective can tell the court nothing except that he did his work so badly that he was identified by a foreign servant, and that he could not defend himself on his own streets. Should we force him to say that – for so unsure a result?"

It was a crafty argument, and Ranklin warmed to Reimers. Then realised that was just what Reimers wanted.

What Lenz might have said then was lost in a growing hubbub in the corridor outside, a perfunctory knock and the immediate entrance of a stout white-haired man in a black suit and very high collar.

Lenz knew him. "Rechtsanwalt Loder – Kapitanleutnant Reimers – Herr Spencer . . . "

Behind the lawyer came two younger men, one obviously Loder's clerk, the other wearing a blazer and an eager expression. He pounced on Ranklin. "Mr Spencer. I'm Don Byrd with a Y, Mr Sherring's secretary. We got here as fast as we could. Mrs Finn's outside in the automobile. Loder's supposed to be good, we got him through the vice consul. Now what's the situation?"

As far as Ranklin could tell, the situation was a fast dialogue between the lawyer and Lenz, with Reimers looking as if he had just dropped in to report a lost battleship, his naval uniform having nothing to do with this case at all.

Before Ranklin caught the pace of the dialogue, it ended. Lawyer Loder shook hands with Lenz, then turned: "Herr Spencer?" He reached out his hand slowly and ceremoniously, shook Ranklin's hand, bowed slightly, and announced in a polished mahogany voice: "Your servant is free."

"Boy," Don Byrd whispered, "I never saw even a lawyer make a buck so fast before."

The only visible sign on O'Gilroy was a split lip, but he was moving stiffly. "They knew enough not to hit me where it'd show, not with me clothes on. But I'm all right, ma'am."

Corinna was all for laying charges and lawsuits against the police. But Loder preferred winnable cases and was learned enough in law to know that every policeman not proven to have been home in bed would have witnessed O'Gilroy's resistance to arrest. And Ranklin was learning: "Call it experience – for us. The one who got it didn't need it."

Then he got Don Byrd on one side and muttered: "I want the name and any address of that 'witness', if you can."

Byrd looked at him sharply, but then smiled. "Sure. We must have paid for that much already."

In the back of a big, and presumably hired, Mercedes tourer, Corinna was arranging cushions and rugs around O'Gilroy who leered at Ranklin and murmured: "Jest like the sergeant-major used to do."

"Shut up, you," Corinna said briskly. "You're both moving aboard *Kachina*. It isn't safe to walk the streets of Kiel," she announced to the street. "Especially with police protection. Antreiben," she told the chauffeur.

They went a quarter of a mile to O'Gilroy's guesthouse and then had to unpack him so that he and the chauffeur could go in to collect his luggage. Waiting in the car, Ranklin tried to thank Corinna for her help.

"Oh, skip it. From what Don said, you'd done most of the work already. But why did the police pick on Conall?"

Ranklin told her a censored version of O'Gilroy's night on the town: no artistic poses or warships and no mention of the attack on O'Gilroy himself.

"If they were following him, that means they suspected you from the moment you hit town, doesn't it?"

"I'm afraid so."

"Because you knew this Navy man who died?"

Ranklin nodded.

"You're walking on eggs. So what happened today?"

"Somebody went in and laid evidence that he'd heard O'Gilroy trying to hire someone to scrag the policeman."

"So who'd do that? – and why?"

"I'm working on a theory."

After that, they drove to the Club for Ranklin's belongings; there was also a message from Mr Kay, saying he would be there at six and happy to answer any questions Mr Spencer might have for him.

"If you don't mind," Ranklin said, "I'll stay here and meet this chap, then hire a boat and come out later."

"Okay." But she looked dubious. "You're sure there won't be any more trouble?"

"No. I mean, yes. If there is, I'll signal you. I'll set the Clubhouse on fire, all right?" He turned away, then suddenly remembered O'Gilroy's mission. "What about the services to Korsör?"

"There's two every day – one German, one – Danish, d'ye say? That one's the *Son-den-wind*, or something like that." Sensibly, he hadn't written anything down.

"*Sondenvind*, I expect."

"Could be. She goes out about now, be back noon tomorrow."

"That'll have to wait until then." But as he watched them walk out onto the jetty, the chauffeur almost invisible under the luggage (he must be well paid for that loss of dignity), he began wondering about how to board the *Sondenvind* unseen. Because if that link was as vital as it might be, it was one that Lenz and Reimers must never even suspect.

30

On the hallway of the Club there was a small rack of picture postcards for sale. Ranklin bought a handful, including two that had other views of warships on parade in the harbour. Then he sat in a wicker chair on the verandah to wait for Mr Kay.

110200, he thought, idly trying the 6-class coding system on a postcard of, he thought, one new battleship of the Kaiser class, one three-funnelled old battleship, and two four-funnelled ships he assumed were armoured cruisers (though some light cruisers had four funnels and some armoured ones only two or three, he remembered). You know, he told himself, whoever sits by that Canal, day and night, rain and shine, counting the German Navy go past, must know that Navy better than most. Better than I do, anyway.

Perhaps Cross simply hadn't found anybody to do it before he died: he had everything else worked out but not that. Does that mean we've got to scour the city for a volunteer traitor? Not double-bloody likely.

It wasn't the way they had been taught to work, anyway. You found out where the information you wanted was, then investigated those who had access to it. Did one of them have money problems? Woman problems? Little boy problems? – anything that marked the soul "For Sale" to those trained to read souls.

But he couldn't see himself going up to an angler on the Canal bank to ask: "Excuse me, mein Herr, but are you an expert on German warships who seduces choirboys?" There had to be an easier way.

Only he couldn't find it. Did it lead somehow through Dragan who cast a remarkably wide shadow for a man who was invisible? Or through the bearer bond issued by the suicided company promoter? What was his name? He was about to take out the bond and consult it when a blue blazer loomed up in front and asked if he were Mr James Spencer.

Mr Kay was a pleasant young man whom Ranklin came to believe had no ambition except to sail boats until he became a pleasant old man. He apologised, pleasantly, for the absence of Mr Younger. They had dismasted their own small yacht and he was over at Laboe seeing it repaired before . . . Ranklin didn't really listen, just waited until Cross's name came up.

"Are you sort of . . . well, actually . . . investigating how Cross got killed?"

"His father asked me to do that, and the local police are being, well, sympathetic . . . " Would Lenz recognise that description of himself? " . . . but I'm really a duffer at that sort of thing."

"Yes, I suppose you would be," the young man said seriously.

Ranklin, who was prepared to be modest but not to welcome any help at it, clenched his teeth. "I just wonder if you could run through that evening for me?"

"Of course. We started off with a few jars at the Club here, then we said we'd like to try the dinner at the Ratsweinkeller, and Cross said he'd change and meet us there only he didn't. Change, I mean. It seemed the laundry hadn't brought back his dress shirts, so he was still wearing the Leander blazer. I must say it made him stand out rather, and the head waiter got a bit stuffy about it being an insult to the Kaiser – who wasn't even in Kiel that night, as Cross told him – and wouldn't have gone to that sort of place anyway; it had some jolly weird pictures on the walls. It was all a bit of a laugh. Anyway, we had a jolly good dinner and then – it was about eleven o'clock – Cross went off to the lavatory and didn't come back. That was all, really."

"Did you look for him?"

"Oh, yes. We thought he might have gone dizzy from the grape-juice so we went looking, but not a sign. So we toddled off, too, and next day we heard he'd been found dead, poor chap, so we steamed round to the Polizei and told them – well, what I've just told you."

"Who did you speak to there?"

"A chappie called Lenz. Looks a bit of a bruiser, but almost a gentleman. I've seen him around the Club a couple of times."

Lenz was getting very favourable reviews that evening. "Did Cross say anything about what else he might do that night? Mention anybody, anywhere?"

"Well – " Kay hesitated. "I don't know if we should have said this to the Polizei, but with Cross dead and it might not be an accident, you know, we told Lenz about a chap Cross had talked about at dinner. Dragan the Viper."

Ranklin opened and then closed his mouth, and then said: "El Vipero?"

"That's the chap. Sounds frightfully wicked, doesn't he?"

"Did Cross say he'd met him?"

"Er, no, I don't think so. Only that he was around, I think."

"Did he tell you anything about this Dragan?"

"Just that he was all sorts of a bad hat. An assassin and so on."

What the devil had Cross been up to? "And how did the police react?"

"Oh, absolutely fascinated. Lenz wrote down everything we said."

Not in the report Ranklin had seen, he hadn't. But perhaps it's wiser not to mention villains you haven't managed to catch.

"Did he mention the name Anya die Ringfrau as well?"

To Ranklin's astonishment, Kay went a deep red. "No, no, I don't suppose he knew anything about her. No reason at all."

"Well, hold on, I don't know anything, either – except the name."

"Neither do I. I wouldn't . . . it's not . . . It was just something I heard."

"What?"

Kay went on looking as if he were trapped in a steam bath. "She runs a house," he muttered.

"A house? . . . Oh, of ill-fame. A brothel."

"In Hamburg. Usually. A chap said."

"She brings the circus to town for Kiel Week?" How very logical. Of course Kiel's resident girls couldn't cope with the influx of young yachtsmen and their healthy appetites. Whores from

Hamburg were as inevitable as champagne salesmen from Reims. Indeed, interdependent.

"High-class girls?" he asked.

Kay barely nodded, being deeply fascinated by his own shoe-laces. Ranklin tried to keep his round face straight. It was rare to find a young man embarrassed about visits to such houses; for subalterns in Army messes, it was just part of a night on the town. But Kay had the faintest trace of a Cornish accent; perhaps they were stricter – or less well provided for – down there. He changed the subject: "Did you mention Dragan to anybody else?"

Kay brightened. "I think so. I mean, he sounds a bit of a card, doesn't he?"

After Kay had gone, Ranklin just sat. Homing yachtsmen clumped past him in seaboots, carrying bundles of clothing and picnic baskets and chattering loudly, but he just sat, drained. It wasn't the effort of talking, he reckoned; he could make conversation all day and night. But then you didn't care if you were listening to a liar, even a murderer, as long as the conversation flowed. It was the effort of weighing every word, even the feather-light ones of young Kay, for Real Truth, that wore you down. How on earth did Great Detectives keep it up? By keeping it fictional, he supposed sourly, and leaving fact to the Lenzes who could find all the Real Truth they wanted with one swift kick in the kidneys.

He yawned, then made a last effort and hauled himself across the road to find a motorboat out to *Kachina*. Already half the people waiting there were in evening dress and diamonds; the yachts were moored but the social race had barely begun.

Ushered into his cabin one deck below the dining room and Sherring's suite, Ranklin found his bags already unpacked and his clothes hung in the closet. But he gave himself the luxury – and a luxury it was, after the hasty packing in Brussels and the very temporary night at the Club – of rearranging everything just so. He liked a clean, settled room, and could live as long as necessary in a dirty battlefield tent, but it was the in-between half-dirty half-tidy life that unsettled him.

Then he had a bath – in fresh water, he found, an exceptional luxury on a ship – wrapped himself in a dressing gown, rang for a steward and asked for "Gorman" to be sent up.

The steward said: "He's taken a beating. Can't you dress yourself for once?"

It was as if a gun had said: "No, thank you, I don't want to be loaded and fired today." Ranklin gaped, wondering if this were Bloody Mutiny or just the American way of doing things. He was, after all, on American "territory".

"I can tie my own necktie," he said coldly, "but I want to see how he is."

"That's okay then," the steward said cheerfully. "Anything else you want?"

"Yes: two whisky-and-sodas, *please*."

"Coming right up."

O'Gilroy came in walking stiffly and lowered himself carefully into an upright chair. "I had a bath and it brought out all the bruises in me. But the doctor says it's nothing more."

Of course *Kachina* would have a doctor on board. "Did he say you could drink?"

"He's Irish." Again, of course, like almost every other ship's doctor Ranklin had met. And they only prescribed abstinence as a last, baffled resort.

They drank. "Are they treating you well, below – what d'you say on a ship? Below decks?"

"Ah, they're being new mothers to me, a poor Irish slave to an English milord, not knowing the English gentry for the kind generous folk they really are."

"How difficult for you," Ranklin said coolly.

O'Gilroy grinned and started rolling a cigarette. "Mrs Finn was saying ye'd done more than the lawyer fella to get me out. Thank ye."

"Part of the job. But I think Reimers did more than either of us: he wants us running free to hang ourselves on a bigger charge. Have you any idea who denounced you?"

"I'm thinking it was the boyos from last night again. Had to be somebody knew what had happened to make up he'd seen something that didn't."

Ranklin nodded. "I learned a little more about Anya and her circus."

O'Gilroy listened, smoke trickling from his nose. Then: "Yes, when ye've fancy women like that, ye've always got hard men to keep them and the customers in line. But what's she got against us?"

Tired of saying "I just don't know". Ranklin shook his head. "It started when you bought those pictures in the pub. Somebody else must have been watching you besides the detective."

"Seems like we marched into town with a flag and drum saying who we was."

Ranklin decided it was his duty to do a little morale-building. "Well, we're safe enough aboard here. Things'll look better in the morning."

O'Gilroy's expression wasn't convinced. "Did ye think 'twould be like this? – the whole job? Like always being on the run and wondering which of yer friends'll sell ye to the police for the price of a drink?"

"I think I prefer a proper war," Ranklin admitted.

"At least ye can shoot back." A dressing gong rumbled in the corridor and O'Gilroy stubbed out the wisp of his cigarette. "Are ye going to the shebang aboard the liner?"

"I think so – if Mrs Finn does. It's the sort of thing James Spencer would probably do. D'you want me to try and wangle you . . . ?"

"No thank ye; I'll stay home tonight." He got up and flexed his shoulders cautiously, then went to peer at the one painting in the cabin. It was of a canoe on a forest stream, and so dark that Ranklin hadn't at first realised it was a watercolour. "D'ye see how she's done up the cabin from it? Clever, that."

Only then did Ranklin see that the painting's blue-green forest was repeated in the cabin's curtains and carpet, the glimpse of a sunset sky in the pale gold wallpaper, the paddle blade by the elm furniture.

He finished his dressing bemused both by Corinna's imaginative decorative touch and O'Gilroy's ability to spot it. What else am I missing, he wondered uneasily? Oh well, I'm a better artillery commander than either of them. Only I'm not even allowed to be that, now.

31

The four-funnelled *Victoria Luise* had started life, Ranklin learned, as the *Deutschland* and fastest ship across the Atlantic, albeit shaking her passengers' teeth loose with vibration. So she had been refitted with slower and smoother engines, fewer and less urgent passengers, renamed after the Kaiser's favourite daughter, and sent cruising. And acting as host ship during Kiel Week.

Corinna dragged Ranklin straight onto the dance floor – perhaps, he thought, just to check up on his range of social graces. He was quite an adequate dancer, of course, certainly not a good one – that was for gigolos and, in their own barbaric way, Scotsmen. But he felt they must make a grotesque pair, with her towering over him, and was happy when she was ready to retire to the inevitable fruit punch.

It was odd to be in a ship so big and in water so still that it was only when the band and dancers paused and he could feel the rumble of the generators that he remembered they were afloat. Most of the uniforms were Navy – as Ranklin expected, the Prussian officer class had stayed away – and the women, while expensively dressed . . . well, it wasn't Paris. I wonder if the Kaiser himself will drop in, he thought, then realised that the same half-exciting, half-sobering thought dominated the ballroom.

"Not the most lively crowd," Corinna commented. She was using her height and a very simple ballgown of dark red to look stately – perhaps flying the American flag. Then she spoiled it by whispering: "How much d'you think it would take to bribe the band-leader to play a tango?"

"I don't know just what the tango is . . . "

"It was invented in an Argentinian bordello."

"What a remarkable *depth* of knowledge you do have. But I do know the Kaiser's forbidden his officers to dance it."

"I know. The Pope doesn't like it, either."

"You surprise me. But since we're probably within earshot of the Kaiser, I'd suggest a bribe of not less than a lifetime job for the band aboard the *Kachina*. And pensions."

"Nope," she decided. "They aren't good enough. Maybe they know a hootchie-kootchie though."

"My ignorance of the world's vulgarities is positively embarrassing. Where was *that* invented?"

"In some US bordello, I guess. Just 'hootch' means home-made liquor, from some Alaskan Indian tribe who were good at it."

"You seem very knowledgeable about Red Indians. Were they your favourite subject at school?"

"Matter of fact, yes – kind of. It was in Switzerland and all the other girls were always telling me about how old their countries and families were, so I got hold of some books on pre-Columbian America to balance things up."

So now he knew where her accented German came from: a Swiss finishing school. "You didn't offer to demonstrate scalping on them?"

"I came close. Good evening," she abruptly swung round to face a German Naval officer who had been not quite eavesdropping; it was Reimers, of course. "I saw you outside the police station."

Reimers would far rather not have been seen on that occasion, but clicked his heels and bowed over her hand. "Mrs Finn – and Mr Spencer. Kapitanleutnant Reimers, at your service."

"Delighted to meet you, Captain. I see you know James."

"Indeed. But he had not told me you and he were buddies."

Reimers' Americanisms still startled Ranklin, who believed all foreigners should learn the King's, not the President's, English; Corinna seemed not to notice.

"Why, James," she said, "haven't you been boasting of our acquaintance?"

"Mea culpa. Somehow, we got stuck on less important matters."

"And Mr Finn?" Reimers continued. "Is he in Kiel?"

Mr Finn was somebody Ranklin had wanted to ask about himself, but Corinna had never given him an opening.

"No, he's back home in the States."

Ranklin hoped Reimers would press for more information, but he just bowed and said: "May I ask you for this dance?"

Corinna turned pointedly to Ranklin, who should have been asked for his permission first. "If Mrs Finn isn't too tired," he said with automatic tact, then added: "and if she doesn't mind anything so old-fashioned as a waltz."

Corinna made a graceful scalping gesture with her fan as Reimers led her away. Watching her go, Ranklin glanced past her and seemed to catch the eyes of a squat middle-aged woman in a green gown. But she looked away immediately.

He left his unfinished punch – he mistrusted mixed drinks – and intercepted a passing glass of champagne, then looked round for conversation. He agreed with an Austrian that the champagne was fine and the international situation poor, and with an Italian Naval officer that both weather and champagne were fine – but all the time had the idea that the woman in green was watching him. Probably, he thought, she's just interested in who Corinna's with tonight.

The waltz ended and Reimers escorted Corinna back.

"Guess what?" she chirped. "The Captain knows America well; he was at their Washington Embassy."

"Really?"

Reimers smiled but changed the subject. "And how is your investigation progressing, Mr Spencer?"

Ranklin shrugged hopelessly. "Oh, that. I've talked to everybody you suggested – and nothing. I'll write a long letter to Cross, then . . . "

"But what about the strange bearer bond he was bearing?"

"The Landentwhatsit?" Ranklin remembered he didn't know German that well. "We asked at the bank about it this afternoon – " was Reimers surprised that Corinna had been included in that? " – and just learned that the company failed long ago. There was a legal problem, the government got the land and the promoter killed himself."

"I've got it!" Corinna lit up. "All these years, the promoter's son broods on how his father was treated, ruined, killed. It gets to his mind. Then one night he meets your Lieutenant Cross and decides *he's* one of the officials ruined his father, lures him to the lock and pushes him in. And leaves the bond as a sort of teaser clue."

"For heaven's sake," Ranklin said. But Reimers was laughing aloud.

"I did say he was crazy," Corinna defended.

"Wonderful!" Reimers was still laughing. "You drive Sherlock Holmes out of business. But – I hate to bring bad news – he had no son. Only a widow, to whom the government most kindly gave a job later. And the bank was also being kind, or maybe they forgot the real story, but it was a plain share swindle. A fraud. The guy found the Government was buying the land quietly, didn't want it announced, so he cashed in on that by claiming he had the right to buy, and sold shares on that claim. The legal problem was if he hadn't killed himself, he'd be in the hoosegow."

"I think you've spoiled it," Corinna pouted. "That's dull. I prefer my version."

"And so do I, dear lady, so do I. But my poor brain can take no more. Will you excuse me?" He bowed and retreated, still chuckling.

Corinna's face did one of its lantern-slide changes. "Washington Embassy, my ass. He knows the States, but he didn't pick up that lingo at diplomatic parties. How long's he been a Navy officer?"

"To reach that rank, twenty years."

"Horse shit. Navy officers – any country's – have better manners."

"You mean their language in mixed company?"

"They're diplomats, much more than Army ones. Don't look stuffy: they're trained for it. They spend half their time in foreign ports at receptions and parties and dances. Whatever he was doing in the States it wasn't Navy officering." She glanced at Ranklin. "You don't seem too surprised."

"I'm pretty sure he's counter-intelligence." Gunther had said something about Reimers being "Steinhauer strutting in Naval uniform", hadn't he? Which meant that, whoever Reimers was, he was important enough for their Navy to let him play at being a fairly senior officer.

"Ah," Corinna said. "He was trying to get me to talk about you. Don't worry: I said we'd met in Paris. You haven't congratulated me on my detective stories."

"I'm supposed to be taking Cross's death seriously. Well, at least we found out that the late company promoter wasn't quite the poor innocent he seemed."

She cocked her head on one side and gave him an odd little smile. "Did we? I thought we heard a government man say the Government did nothing wrong – in fact, even gave a job to the widow of a con man to keep her from starving. It couldn't be to keep her from talking, now could it? Shall we circulate among the guests?"

Half an hour later, Ranklin was pushing scraps of meat around his plate in the supper room – it was too soon after dinner to be eating again – and half listening to the wife of a director of the Norddeutscher-Lloyd shipping line. Corinna was listening, apparently wholeheartedly, to the Herr Direktor himself. Words like "Hapag", "Immco", "Cunard" and "Morgan Trust" seeped across the table.

The Frau Direktor had the latest gossip on the maiden voyage of Hamburg-Amerika's new *Imperator*. "One doesn't like to say it whilst supping on board one of Dr Ballin's own vessels, but surely it is a scandal that the biggest ship in the world, named for the All-Highest, should roll like that in June weather. Just think of the poor passengers in winter," she gloated.

"Dreadful," Ranklin murmured, listening to Corinna saying: "Naturally, Herr Direktor, I understand none of this, but I'm sure my father . . . "

"If only I could speak to him privately . . . "

"But he's doing nothing right now. Why don't I take you over to the *Kachina* to have a nice quiet chat with him? I'm sure he'd be delighted. It would be no problem at all."

Nor was it. Don Byrd appeared and vanished after one quick order, the Frau Direktor was handed over to the care of the other directors and their wives – and that left Ranklin.

"You'll manage, won't you James? If the launch isn't at the gangway, they'll signal for it."

"Naturally, I understand none of this . . . "

"But we *all* have our little secrets, don't we?" With just a hint of a tomahawk in her smile.

And a few minutes ago, he thought ruefully, I believed I was at the centre of any intrigue going on here. Back to the kindergarten.

In fact, he found himself in the restfully dim smoking-room with a weak whisky-and-soda in one hand, tapping an empty pipe against his teeth with the other. And exhausted. Part of it was the day, part Corinna. She was . . . well, he hadn't known a girl, a woman, like her before. Their joking had a depth to it, unlike the flirtatious banter he played as mechanically as polite tennis with the Englishwomen of his circle. Sorry, his late circle. Perhaps because it was born of that dangerous night at the Château. A battle was the time for joking; nobody wanted to make it more serious.

But there was more to it than that. It was the way she thought, the things she thought and knew, that opened his mind's eye wider than he found comfortable. And he felt it wasn't just her being American; it would be easy to accept, and dismiss, that. It was her; she was . . . different.

And that was a cowardly backing-off thought. But, he pleaded to himself, it's been a long hard day.

So then Don Byrd had to appear beside him, smiling and offering a light for his cigarette – he had pocketed his pipe, not feeling settled enough to enjoy it.

"The guy who laid evidence against Gorman: he gave his name as Heinie Glass, address at a guest-house in the Old Town. But somebody went in this afternoon and paid the account, and Herr Glass hasn't been seen again. In fact, he paid the account for two others as well, who'd gotten themselves hurt last night, maybe in a fight. It could be they've all three left town."

"Thank you. And the man who paid their bills?"

"It's my guess that he paid more than just the account, because nobody can recall how he looked at all."

"I see."

"My pleasure." Byrd had a sharp face, bright dark eyes and sleeked-back hair, the face of an eagle except with a ready smile. But he didn't smile as he went on: "There's a certain lady wants to meet with you – she knows your name – the Gräfin von Szillert.

I've asked around and it seems she isn't noble herself, in fact she was a trapeze artiste in a circus when she met up with the Graf. He's dead now. However . . . "

"Is her Christian name Anya?"

"That's right. However," and Byrd gave him an intense stare, "you don't have to meet with her if you don't feel that a guest of Mr Sherring and Mrs Finn should meet with her."

Either Byrd was being polite rudely, or rude politely, probably he'd had a university education. Ranklin considered. "How does she come to be invited here?"

"She knows a lot of influential men in Hamburg, one way or another."

"What's the other way?"

"I don't know," Byrd said grimly.

"Well, I don't really think I'll do Mrs Finn or Mr Sherring too much harm just by saying Good Evening to the lady."

Byrd didn't agree, but looking like an eagle looking stoical, he led the way.

By now Ranklin wasn't surprised to find that Anya was the squat woman in green. She sat, a tasselled black shawl thrown round her heavy shoulders, at a small table in the corner of the cards room, playing patience and watched by a bulky young man with a mournful moustache in rather too elegant evening dress. Her watchdog, Ranklin assumed.

Byrd introduced Ranklin, who took her white-gloved hand, bowed over it and murmured: "Gräfin." The hand inside the glove was wide and firm.

"Sit down," she growled, nodding dismissively to Byrd. "James Spencer," she said, but to herself, tasting the name. Then: "D'you want another drink?" Her voice was deep, her accent perhaps Slav.

"No, thank you." Ranklin put his half-empty glass on the table and waited. The other tables in the room were busy with whist or bridge, and a round table in the middle was even busier with a poker school. It seemed as if many guests were behaving just as if they were on a voyage – but that was what the ship was equipped for; if they didn't go ashore, what else could they do?

"How do you know the daughter of Reynard Sherring?" Anya

asked finally.

"We met."

When he didn't say any more, she glanced up from her cards for a moment. Her face was as squat and muscular as her body, with pronounced cheekbones and dark, still eyes. Not quite a peasant face and even further from being a stupid one. She looked back at her cards and growled: "Where's Dragan?"

"Oh, Lord – I don't know."

She picked up a glass of ice tinged with the dregs of some green liqueur. Ranklin wondered if she drank it just for the colour, since she wore emerald earrings, too. She cracked a piece of ice loudly between her teeth and said: "I know you, I knew Lieutenant Cross. The good honest sporting country *gentlemen*," she spat the word, "playing at the sport of *spying*. Steinhauer knows you. Even Hauptmann Lenz by now. To save your own neck and Europe's – where is Dragan the Viper?"

"In the Captain's cabin playing backgammon with Santa the Claus and Rumpel the Stiltskin."

She slammed the glass down on the table. "They will put you in prison a thousand years and then shoot you." Her voice crackled like a loose power wire. "Only I will have you shot first, before you destroy Europe."

Ranklin nodded, as if this were interesting but irrelevant. "Have you met Dragan?"

"No. But I know him, I know his breed. Better than you do. Why?"

"I'm just collecting people who haven't met him, that's all. I feel we have something in common."

"Do nothing until you hear from your Department," she said. She moved two of her cards. "Go away."

Ranklin stayed put. "So far, madam, you have had your men attack my servant and get him imprisoned. The only result is that you've had to send three men back to Hamburg, two of them shop-soiled. And got Hauptmann Lenz angry, of course."

"Lenz does not worry me. But do you think your Reynard Sherring and his skyscraper daughter will protect you when they can prove what you are? Now go away."

"Why should I need their protection, when you seem to believe I have much better?"

The watchdog stood up, then leant stiffly forward from the hips to whisper mournfully: "The Gräfin said to go away."

Ranklin stood and smiled up at him – he was several inches taller. "And you won't even recognise Dragan when he catches you."

The watchdog's eyes widened suddenly, and Ranklin went away smiling. Whoever and wherever you are, Dragan, you've at last done me a bit of good as well as harm, he thought.

Byrd, who had been watching play at the poker table, fell into step beside him.

"I don't think I disgraced the House of Sherring," Ranklin said.

"I'm sure you did your best," Don Byrd said coolly. "Did the lady . . . ?"

"She really just wanted to tell me to go away."

In that, Byrd was obviously on the Gräfin Anya's side, but he said nothing. Ranklin walked on thoughtfully.

Come on, he thought to the brain that was slumped against the back of his skull with its eyes closed; come on, one last stab at Great Deduction, and I'll leave you alone until morning.

He was back in the slow-paced half-dark of the smoking room, among groups of elderly men recalling past yachting triumphs – as he could hear – or business adventures, which he could only guess at. He slumped into a horseshoe-back leather chair and tried to think logically.

She had talked of Reimers as 'Steinhauer', just as Gunther had, and of the 'Department' – presumably our Naval Intelligence: she thinks I belong there, like Cross. So she's clearly one of us (but Good God! – what company "us" is turning out to be). I've heard of traditional links between high-class brothels and espionage – she probably buys official tolerance with gossip her girls have picked up horizontally, and if they suspect (as I do) that she's working for the Russians, she's convinced them that she's working for the Revolution against the Czar.

But why is she so worried about what Dragan could get up to? "Destroying Europe" sounds a pretty big –

"So now you have met Anya die Ringfrau?" Gunther's slow deep voice gave everything he said an extra importance, as if it were carefully gold-lettered on wood.

"Yes. She wants me to go away."

"It is good advice. But of course you will not take it. It is your duty to stay. That is most correct. You have been trained to do what you are told to do, report what you are sent to find. I do not criticise that, I admire it. But, as you are finding, the world is not so simple when one does not wear uniform. And when there is not always someone to turn to for orders."

Obviously Gunther's soldiering had been largely confined to the parade ground. But Ranklin was learning that an attitude of agreement and ignorance was more useful than trying to seem a know-all. So he asked: "Do you know what Reimers/Steinhauer was doing in America?"

Gunther paused whilst he got his cigar well alight, then: "He was a detective for Pinkerton's."

"For . . . ?"

"Their most famous private detectives. President Lincoln hired them to be his secret service in the war of the states."

That made sense – and explained Reimers' American vocabulary. And the fact that Gunther hadn't tried to sell the information told him something, too. He waited.

Gunther took a deep satisfied puff at the cigar. "You find, I know, that not all intelligence is in neat parcels like – shall we say – a code-book. You must dig and throw away many things your Bureau does not want to know, would order you not to waste time in telling them. And you will think: but why throw this away? It does not matter to the Bureau, but it must concern some person. So, I will give it to that person. I will make him my friend. Perhaps he gives me money, perhaps he gives me intelligence that my Bureau wants – perhaps not that day, but one day, because he is now my friend. So by doing this, I am working for the Bureau as it wants."

"For example?"

"Ah, yes: an example." Gunther looked critically at the lit end of his cigar. "Let us think of Immco and the Morgan Trust . . . "

32

With the Norddeutscher-Lloyd director and her father settled over the brandy and cigars, Corinna changed into tennis shoes, threw a wrap around her shoulders and climbed to the open main deck. The harbour around her was a blaze of light and sound, half a dozen gramophones and at least one band ashore competing with the *Victoria Luise*'s dance music, and all with the hive-like buzz of ships' generators. But gradually she felt she was at the still, quiet centre of things, unobserved.

Except by Jake the chief steward. "Is there anything I can bring you, Mrs Finn?"

"No, thanks, Jake – yes: send up Gorman with a white wine and seltzer. And his own drink if he's got one." And that'll add to the gossip down below, she thought. But when you took on servants, you gave up privacy; she had known no other adult life.

O'Gilroy appeared beside her with both hands full. "Sorry, ma'am, I spilt some of it, not being used to climbing around things that roll about."

"Rolling?" she said indignantly. "You wouldn't know you were on a ship."

O'Gilroy muttered something.

She grinned. "You just don't like ships. Have you ever done any long voyages?"

"Only to the War. South Africa," he added, since most foreigners didn't seem to know where *the* war had been.

She sipped at her glass, leaning on the rail while he stood stiffly beside her. "Relax. Light a cigarette if you want to. Was Matt –

Captain Ranklin – in that war?"

"Where I met him." Out of deference to her he lit a ready-made cigarette – "tailor-made" as the crew called them – rather than his hand-rolled version. "I was wounded and left behind by my reg'ment – lucky, it turned out, with them most soon dead or captured – and his section picked me up, and when I was mended and without a reg'ment, he recruited me as temp'ry gunner. Shut up in Ladysmith we was by then."

"Was he a good officer? – honestly?"

O'Gilroy reflected, draped on the rail like an abandoned piece of rope. "He was younger then, o'course, but I'd say yes. Explained something and left ye to get on with it. The Gunners was more like that – and 'twas the first chancst I'd had to work with machinery. Tried to transfer after the war, but I didn't have the trade qualification."

"But you do have the qualification to be a secret agent."

O'Gilroy made a complicated but wordless noise.

"I hadn't known you'd been down in the Balkans last winter, observing on that war. He was giving Pop – "

"We wasn't."

"Oh?" She was surprised at her own disappointment; her image of Ranklin, pale and disjointed though it was, hadn't included heroising himself. She had felt an odd sort of bond with him, oblique to the normal planes of friendship, in knowing almost from the start a vital secret of his life, almost before she knew anything of his public self. In fact, the public self seemed mostly to be "James Spencer" facades. But why pretend to her?

"I wasn't there and he wasn't observing," O'Gilroy went on. "He was fighting for the Greek Army, second-in-command of an artillery brigade. Helped capture some city there."

"Salonika?"

"Sounds like it."

"And this was all part of your games?"

"No, no, 'twas before he got into all this. He was still in the British Army, only he wasn't then, if ye get my meaning."

"If you weren't Irish I'd say that was very Irish. No, I don't get you."

O'Gilroy considered, pitching his cigarette end over the side and then watching it burst in sparks on the hull below.

Corinna said: "And you haven't the qualifications to be a sailor, either. Throw things over the lee side. What did you mean?"

"He'd resigned the Army. They hauled him back and made him . . . ", he shrugged, " . . . a spy"

"*Made* him? I thought that was one thing you had to volunteer for."

In the man-made starlight of the harbour she could see only one half of O'Gilroy's cynical smile at the Army meaning of "volunteer".

"But it sounds," she persisted, "well, adventurous, exciting . . . "

"And work for a gentleman? He'd choose his big guns any day."

"Then why did he take it on?"

"I wouldn't be knowing, ma'am, but . . . " He felt he was being disloyal to Ranklin, yet at the same time defending him. "I can tell ye one thing: he's broke."

"Broke? Busted? Bankrupt?"

"Call it what ye like. Just no money, not like he used to have."

She stared down at the twinkling water, then asked quietly: "Did he tell you this?"

"Him? Never. But can ye look at a man on a horse and say he's not accustomed to it? I tell ye, the Captain's never ridden a horse called Stonybroke before. It's the small things, a man being careful with money that doesn't know how to be. I've been in service before – real service, that is – and I know the signs of it."

Now she could see why buying the blazer and new shoes hadn't been the cheerful spree she had planned. She had never thought of Ranklin being rich, not by her own family's terms, just as one of those English gentlemen whose long-owned land always gave them enough for their own ideas of comfort, their depressingly limited ambitions, their boringly formal pleasures – and the right clothes. She had no quarrel with the Englishman's sense of dress, nor with Ranklin's.

"It can only be recent, then," she mused. "D'you know what happened?"

"No . . . but there was talk of his older brother doing some fool things with shares and stocks – and then shooting himself cleaning a gun. In a family that would be learning guns in the cradle."

"Oh Lord, how conventional the English are. Why didn't he go farm sheep in Australia? I suppose sheep cost more than cartridges. But how did this make Matt a secret agent?"

"Spy. He says we're spies and be damned to it."

She grinned. Ranklin was determined to wear his secret crown of thorns with style. "D'you get paid more as a spy, then?"

"I wouldn't be knowing – but the Army doesn't like officers to be broke."

If that meant bankrupt, she could understand it: an officer should be beholden only to his job, not to his creditors. Her father was creditor to too many politicians for her not to know what influence that could give.

"And how did you come to team up with Matt again? By chance, or did he recruit you?"

"That's right. He recruited me – by chance."

"Clear as an Irish bog. Why did you let yourself be recruited?"

"The money," O'Gilroy said too promptly for her to believe him. "And travel. A boat like this . . . "

"And the inside of Kiel jail."

"That's right." His expression was set and she knew she would learn no more. Men's motives can be terribly complicated, she thought. Don't forget they can also be terribly simple.

Ranklin came aboard soon afterwards, greeting them warily as Mrs Finn and Gorman while the crew fussed around. "The Kaiser didn't show up, so you didn't miss anything."

"Who did you find to talk to, then?"

"Oddly enough, a lady who runs a bordello."

"No kidding? Did she offer you any free samples?"

"Not even of the new dances. She used to work in a circus."

Corinna caught O'Gilroy's reaction. "You want to talk privately?"

"It can wait. I was also talking to an old friend of yours – van der Brock."

Corinna's mind – and heart – whirled. "But he knows who you

are! How are you going to . . . I can get you on a boat to . . . "

"Whoa, whoa. It's all right: we know more about him by now. He doesn't belong on any one side, he's a mercenary. Now: is that Norddeutscher-Lloyd director still here?"

"Yes."

"Then it might be better if he didn't go back in *Kachina*'s launch. I've been learning a little something about the shipping business."

"Tell me more."

"Well, it seems – and I should have thought of this for myself, I suppose, but I've had other things on my mind – that if there's a war, whether it's long or short, the immediate loser will be the German merchant shipping. The Royal Navy will see to that. So far-sighted German ship-owners like Dr Ballin might be thinking of coming to some sort of arrangement with a powerful neutral country. And it seems there's already a thing called Immco – "

"International Mercantile Marine Company."

"Which is a cartel – "

She winced.

"I do apologise. A purely social club of owners of North Atlantic shipping lines?"

"Much better."

"Involving Hamburg-Amerika, Norddeutscher-Lloyd, White Star and Leyland in Britain, and some American lines. Formed by the late J. P. Morgan and, oddly enough, not doing very well even before he died."

"Your government made Cunard stay out."

"Oh, dear. Anyway, with Morgan dead and perhaps a war coming, whither Immco? There's talk of what your father might be doing talking to Ballin, whether he's talking to Norddeutscher-Lloyd . . . It was put to me that any knowledge I picked up here would find a ready market. That's all."

"Thank you, Matt," she said gravely. "If you'll excuse me, I'll tell Pop right now."

She made her way down the companionway – carefully, in that long ball gown – thinking: he pays what debts he can, anyhow. When he could have used what he learnt here to pay debts closer to home. An honourable man. She almost giggled; an honourable

233

man and a reluctant spy. I wonder which he is alone in a lady's boudoir?

Behave yourself, Corinna girl, she thought.

On the other hand, she thought, let's just wait and see, shall we?

33

"And how did you sleep – apart from long?" Corinna asked.

"Rocked in the cradle of the shallows, very well, thank you."

"This ship does *not* . . . oh, let it pass."

It was another vividly bright day and the breakfast table was laid under an awning on the main deck. Corinna had long finished, but was lingering with coffee and a batch of American magazines that had just been brought off shore. Jake poured coffee for Ranklin and asked what he would like to eat.

"Bacon and eggs?" Ranklin suggested, more in hope than expectation, but Jake agreed and went away to organise it.

"Hah!" Corinna snorted. "The Englishman abroad. None of these native customs."

"Just staying in character."

"That's your normal breakfast in India, is it?"

Ranklin remembered some ghastly attempts at English breakfasts in the Lahore cantonments and admitted that it wasn't. "Let's say it's what I came home for. Tell me: do you think we can get ashore without being seen?" There was no hurry – the *Sondenvind* wasn't due until around noon – but since he could think of no way to get aboard without walking up the gangplank, he wanted to be certain they weren't being followed at the time.

"The launch is running around the harbour all day," she said. "We could get you into her cabin out of sight of the shore – if you think they're watching from there – and stay there until it touches at wherever you want to get off. They can't cover all the landing places round the harbour. Is that good enough?"

It would have to be, and Ranklin accepted with more enthusiasm than he felt.

"Are you looking for the widow of the company promoter?" she asked.

Ranklin had almost forgotten about that, and admitted he wasn't.

"Why not?" she demanded. "I'd like to hear her version of the story. And you've got all the excuse you need: that Reimers was talking about her, and the mysterious worthless bond. A *real* detective wouldn't pass her up. D'you know her name?"

"On the bond it says Wedel, but I don't know where she lives."

"Then if *I* find out where she lives, will you go see her?"

Ranklin didn't want to drag Corinna any further into the situation – but, damn it, who was doing the dragging? "Very well."

"Promise? Spy's honour?"

Ranklin winced. "I promise."

The *Sondenvind* was about the same size as a Channel steamer, but single-funnelled and wider to accommodate the cargo that was now being unloaded. They stood in the shadow of a warehouse with O'Gilroy scanning the ship's deck and Ranklin looking agitated, which was no problem, and explaining it by frequent glances at his watch.

"That's him," O'Gilroy said suddenly. "That's the boy."

The lad, of about twenty-five, was now dressed in a Third Officer's uniform, so either he had been disguised when he went ashore selling artistic poses or O'Gilroy was wrong. But he seemed convinced enough, and Ranklin nodded him ahead.

O'Gilroy strode up the gangway, brushed aside a suspicious bo'sun, and handed the Third Officer a warship postcard as if it were a ticket. A few seconds later Ranklin followed, hoping his city suit made him look like one of those self-important officials who constantly bustle on and off ships in harbour but never go to sea. A minute after that they were in the tiny stuffy sea cabin of Captain J. Helsted.

Then, for a long moment, nobody said anything but probably everybody was thinking the same thing: if I say the wrong thing now, I may spend years regretting it in a German jail.

Captain Helsted was perhaps sixty, clean-shaven and with a thin face strongly lined with concern rather than age. He frowned at them, but looked as if he frowned at everybody and everything. And at last he said just: "Yes?"

"The night before last," Ranklin said, "your officer sold my servant some photographs. He got one he did not expect. Personally, I preferred it to the ones he did expect."

The Captain held the new postcard; now he turned it to glance at the number on the back, then to compare it with the ships in the picture.

He asked: "Did you write this number?"

Ranklin nodded.

"Who are you, please?"

Ranklin took out his – Spencer's – card case and handed over a card. Captain Helsted dropped it on the little table unread. "Who are you really?"

Ranklin took back the card and put it into the case. "Really we are not here, we do not exist."

After another moment, Helsted smiled, although the lines on his face made it more like a sneer. "Good. With men who do not exist, I can have talk that is not talked." He nodded past them and the Third Officer vanished, closing the door with a firm click. His going made the cabin remarkably more spacious.

Helsted sat down and waved Ranklin to the only other chair. Ranklin hesitated, looking for a place for O'Gilroy until he growled: "Sit down and let's get on."

"Do you know," Helsted asked, "who killed Lieutenant Cross?"

"No, and we're not trying to find out. We only want to finish his work – unless you tell us it is finished."

Helsted frowned again. "No, it is not finished."

Well, that had been too much to hope for. "What more do you need?"

Helsted got suspicious again. "What do you know?"

"Perhaps not much: Cross didn't leave any last will and testament. We know about the code for warship movements on the Canal and the cablegrams from Korsör, but that's all. Who collects the information and how it gets to you, we do not know."

Still frowning, the Captain got up and took a bottle of clear liquor from a wall cupboard and scattered three shot glasses on the table. "Since this aquavit does not exist – there are no spirits on this ship – it is perhaps good for men who do not exist." He poured. "Skol. Now I may tell you: I do not know either."

Ranklin looked at O'Gilroy, who took a second swallow, sighed, and said: "Well 'twas kind of ye to give us this before telling us that."

Ranklin said: "Did he give you any idea . . . ?"

"No. He did not want me to know. I think also he did not want the other person to know about me. He said only it would come to me by signal, that I would not have to go ashore."

All that was highly professional of Cross, making sure neither of his sub-agents could betray the other – and reassuring them by letting them know that – but it left a complete dead end.

"Did he give you another address – not his family's – to send cablegrams to?"

"No. He said that also would come to me."

"Do you think he had even arranged the other person and the signals?"

"I think yes. He said he would leave Kiel the day after, after that he was killed, I mean. And he would go by train and ship to meet me in Korsör and give me everything there."

So Cross had finished, or was about to finish, the job when he died. At least he had done the impossible: found his Canal-watcher – but that achievement seemed to have died with him.

Ranklin unfolded the bearer bond and passed it to Helsted. "Does this mean anything to you?"

The Captain's face grew even more and deeper lines as he studied it. He shook his head slowly. "It says nothing. How did . . . ?"

"It was among Lieutenant Cross's things. And I imagine he must have picked it up in Kiel, so . . . The company doesn't exist any longer. It may have been a fraud anyway." He put the bond away, musing. "I can get a cablegram address for you to use; that won't be a problem. And if we can revive the plan, can we reach you at Korsör?"

"By the steamship office."

"All right, that seems to be . . . "

"One thing," O'Gilroy interrupted. "The officer ye sent to sell me the pretty pictures: some rough things happened after that, and he could be recognised by them making them happen. I'd keep him aboard until – " he glanced at Ranklin, " – until the circus has left town, mebbe?"

"Until Kiel Week is over, anyway."

"This was not the police?" Helsted frowned.

"No. It was – perhaps some visiting Russians. I'm not sure. But you trust your officer?"

"I trust my own son," Helsted sneered his smile again. "Perhaps he will live to see Kiel a town of Denmark once more. Who knows?"

Ranklin very much doubted it, but was grateful for the hint at Helsted's motive in working for Britain. The unwritten rule book told him to use other people's patriotism – or misuse it – wherever he could find it.

"Indeed I hope so," he said solemnly.

On their way back to the jetty where the *Kachina*'s launch would pick them up, they passed the railway station which was being hung with bunting and flags for the arrival of the King and Queen of Italy that evening. A squad of Schutz des Königs, drably uniformed except for their helmets, rehearsed in the square and, as old soldiers, they had to stop to watch. They approved the uniforms – keeping the best unsullied for the real ceremony – and even the drill. Only the basic idea, that an escort of troops could prevent an assassination, was mocked by the history of the last ten years.

"Get them standing top of the steps there," O'Gilroy murmured. "Perfect target."

Most assassinations took place where the victim was raised up: on a horse, in an open carriage, on a balcony or . . . "Or up on that viewing stand at the locks, tomorrow?" Ranklin suggested gloomily.

"Sure, grand place." And Cross had been found within short rifle-shot of that stand, a letter from Dragan in his pocket. It simply didn't make sense – but here was no place to be overheard discussing it.

The chauffeured Mercedes was also waiting by the jetty and the launch delivered Corinna and her father, both dressed smartly but soberly and off to lunch with some business acquaintances.

"Jake's expecting you back to lunch," she assured Ranklin, "and you can use the launch *as long as* it's back here by three. Or you sleep in the bilges tonight – whatever they are. Oh yes – the Widow Wedel lives at Holtenau, Tiessenkai 16. You promised and I've done my bit."

"What was that about?" O'Gilroy asked as the boat scorched through the busy harbour.

"I promised to look up the widow of the man who formed the land company that issued the bond. You needn't bother, it's just to keep Mrs Finn happy."

"Ye be going to ask her how the Lieutenant picked up the bond? What it might be meaning?"

Ranklin made a face. "It's worthless, it's been worthless for years. He could have picked it up anywhere."

"Ye think? Last week's newspaper's not worth much, neither, but tell me where ye'd find one."

Ranklin was about to suggest library files or the newspaper office, but then saw the point: somebody had to make a deliberate effort to keep something that had lost its value. He nodded; it was a topic for the useless conversation with the Widow.

If the Widow worked in a government office, she wouldn't be home until the end of the afternoon, so Ranklin sat under an awning, read newspapers, listened to the starting guns of various yacht races, drank lemon tea – and worried. O'Gilroy, it turned out later, had been in the earthly paradise of *Kachina*'s engine room. Everything mechanical fascinated him; he belonged in the modern world far more than Ranklin, who welcomed improvements warily and viewed change with suspicion – except in military matters. As a soldier he wanted the latest and best fighting tools, but to defend and preserve his world as it was now, not to reshape it. O'Gilroy just preferred the stink of a petrol engine to that of the slums and assumed in some romantic way that the one must conquer the other.

"Put the turbines of this thing in torpedo boats," he enthused, having brought up Ranklin's latest glass of tea, "and ye'd have better than any navy in the world."

"Splendid. But getting back to the navy we see parked around us – " he gestured at the rigid columns of grey ships (a colour the Royal Navy seemed to be adopting) " – we're still looking for somebody who can tell what ships have gone through the Canal and has the means to signal it to the *Sondenvind* when she passes. How? like the Yacht Club's mast?"

A string of flags was displaying an unreadable message to some ship in the harbour.

"Not like to allow that – in a war," O'Gilroy said.

"Hardly." He remembered Corinna's suggestion of hanging towels on his balcony as a signal, but that had been a simple Yes or No, not a dozen different figures. And yet it must be something like that, a signal that didn't look like a signal. Red Indian smoke puffs from a chimney? He had been worrying at it all afternoon and hadn't found a better answer.

"And when ye say 'looking', I'd say we was jest standing, or sitting, here," O'Gilroy said calmly.

"But where? If we go ashore and just prowl about, all we'll do is get Lenz and Reimers on our heels, growling about Dragan. *Dragan.* I just don't see why Cross got mixed up with him. We now *know* what Cross was up to: good, sensible, naval espionage. Nothing to do with assassination. That just stirs things up – Good God, it would start a war tomorrow!" As Anya had been telling him last night, he now realised.

"If yer plotting to steal the knives, get them to counting the spoons," O'Gilroy said, as if quoting an unimpeachable authority.

"And what does that mean?" Ranklin asked crossly.

"A feller like Lenz, ye'll never stop him suspecting yer up to some deviltry. But ye may get him thinking it's a different deviltry and be looking the wrong way. So the Lieutenant didn't want Lenz thinking about battleships on the Canal . . . "

"You think he teamed up with Dragan to create a diversion?"

O'Gilroy shrugged. "He was talking enough about him, it seems."

Ranklin sat silent, frowning busily. Finally he said: "I wonder how much Dragan would like that."

"Not so much, with it getting Lenz and his detectives looking all over for him. And, ye notice, the Lieutenant did end up dead."

Dragan the murderer? If he were an assassin he wouldn't hesitate to blot out some walk-on player like Cross. And leave Lenz's suspicions to be transferred to themselves. Good God! – the man thought they were planning to kill the Kaiser! No wonder Lenz had locked O'Gilroy up on the flimsiest evidence, rather than let him get on with that plan. And probably, but for Reynard Sherring's unwitting protection, they'd both be in "protective custody" or expelled from Kiel. Either was allowed under German law.

He found himself glancing around furtively, earning a contemptuous scowl from O'Gilroy. It was a bit craven, but they were in German waters, and he was the next one to go ashore.

34

The government and province offices in Holtenau turned out at six, so assuming that the Widow Wedel didn't stop off at the nearest Biergarten then by twenty past, Ranklin reckoned, she should be home and ready to receive.

Only she wasn't either, because Tiessenkai 16 was no longer her home. And getting her new address from the dragon guarding what turned out to be a boarding-house for respectable widows and spinsters called for every ounce of Ranklin's own respectability, charm – and a few hinted lies about a business connection with Herr Wedel, deceased.

The Widow had, it seemed, just come into a small inheritance and moved to rooms above the restaurant by the lighthouse where they had met Gunther the day before. And while the rooms there might be bigger, the view better and the restaurant itself respectable, living above *any* restaurant, next door to *strangers*, quite likely *men*, was, Herr Spencer must agree . . .

Ranklin agreed with everything but it still took five minutes. After that, however, it was easy. He asked at the restaurant and a waiter pointed immediately to a corner table.

She looked very much like a pre-Raphaelite painting of The Widow: middle-aged but slim and sitting very upright, with a thin ascetic face and flaxen hair drawn tightly back to a bun. She also seemed, like such a painting, very detailed in the modest lacework of her blouse, the metal brooch at her throat, the fine pattern of her pleated skirt. The respectability of Tiessenkai 16 certainly hadn't worn off yet, and Ranklin approached her with caution.

He was, he said, most apologetic for approaching her so improperly, but he was pressed for time. She had doubtless heard of the unfortunate death of the English Naval officer, a friend of his, and he had been asked by the officer's father . . .

He spun it out, giving her time to react and for him to see her reactions; Corinna, he guessed, would be as insistent as the Commander on a complete report. At first the Widow seemed to tense, but then – almost with no visible sign – relaxed and listened carefully. When he had finished, she asked him to sit down, called for another cup and poured him coffee.

"It is so much more convenient to come back after work to a home that is also a coffee-house," she said. "Naturally, I read of the English officer's death, but knew nothing of him. Have you spoken to the police?"

"To Hauptmann Lenz and also a Naval officer, Kapitanleutnant Reimers. It was he who mentioned the unfortunate death of your late husband."

"Really? I thought the government had forgotten all about that. Why was it mentioned?"

"Lieutenant Cross had among his papers a bond issued by your husband's company."

"Truly? It would be without value now. I wonder how he got it?"

"I wondered also. Being so out of date, it would not be easy to find."

"Naturally I have several old unissued ones – as ridiculous souvenirs. But I cannot think why anyone else should keep one."

Really I'm getting nowhere, Ranklin thought, and even Corinna would have to admit it. Time to stop bothering the Widow.

"More coffee, Herr Spencer?" she suggested.

So he stayed just one cup longer. While he was trying to think of fresh but harmless conversation, she asked: "And what was the English lieutenant doing in Kiel?"

"Oh, I think only for the races."

"And you are not also in the Navy?"

"No. Just a friend."

"Not a comrade of his, then."

Ranklin said carefully: "No, but we had many interests in common – naturally."

"Naturally." She permitted herself a small prim smile, then glanced over her shoulder at the windows. "It is a charming view, is it not? It is one of the reasons I moved when I got my unexpected inheritance."

"Most charming," Ranklin agreed. "May I express my pleasure at your good fortune? – if it was not outweighed by the loss of a relative."

"Oh, I felt no loss. Indeed, that I deserved it." She put down her cup. "Come, let me show you the view from the terrace."

The last yachts were trailing home, heeled gently to port by a dying west wind and dodged by chugging ferries crammed with home-going workmen. "Charming," she said again. "And even better from my windows. See, those are my rooms up there."

A bit surprised, Ranklin turned and looked up. The windows were also fake medieval, divided into several smaller panes of glass by lead strips. Several panes were almost blanked out by coloured decorations on the inside.

"I like to decorate my windows," she explained. "To make them more interesting against the morning sun. But I cannot decide how to do it, so I change them often."

There were six windows, he counted, and nine panes in each. In each window there were no more than two decorations, each of a different colour.

"This building has not changed," she said, "from how it is in the engraving my late husband put on the bond certificate."

"Most interesting," Ranklin said very, very calmly. "And what work is it you do for the government?"

"Very dull. Every day at the locks office I must prepare for the invoicing department a complete list of all ships which have passed through the Canal in the past twenty-four hours . . . "

Coming away from the restaurant, Ranklin wanted to tell everyone of his triumph and simultaneously thought everyone was staring straight into the guilty knowledge in his head. He hesitated at the roadside. He had solved it! – well, Corinna had sent him up to the Widow Wedel, but he'd surely have visited her sooner or later anyway. And he deserved a cab back to town: if he waited, he must catch one setting down dinner guests at the restaurant. But if he wanted to cover his tracks, best to go back on the anonymous ferry, there must be one soon.

As he hesitated, an elderly but very well-kept town car drew up beside him and the chauffeur leant out to say he was heading back to Kiel empty, would the gentleman like a ride – for a consideration? A taxi! An unofficial one, but chauffeurs did it all the time. And the curtained rear windows suggested more luxury than the average motor taxi. He deserved this. He agreed and opened the rear door –

– and a hand yanked him all the way in. A pistol glinted dully in the curtained light, and at the other end of it was Anya's mournful watchdog of last night. Sherlock Holmes would never have got caught like this, Ranklin thought.

35

Corinna might have waited dinner for Ranklin, but her father wasn't used to waiting for anyone. They were into the fish course when Jake appeared at her shoulder and murmured: "A man – I wouldn't say a gentleman – wants to speak with you, ma'am. Urgently, about Mr Spencer."

"Police?"

"I wouldn't say police, ma'am. More the opposite."

Mr Sherring hadn't heard all of this (he hadn't been supposed to hear any of it) but asked: "Are your guests bringing us trouble with the authorities, Corinna?"

"Nothing like that, Pop. I'll handle it."

As they went out onto the deck, Jake said gravely: "I have a pistol in my pocket, ma'am."

"Oh? *That* much not a gentleman, is he?" She thought for a moment. "Give it to O' – to Gorman, and send him up."

The man had been leaning on the rail watching the sun prepare to set behind the Bellevue Hotel, but turned as they came up. One glance at the sad dark eyes and mournful moustache would have braced Corinna in other circumstances for an equally sad, long and untrue story of Slavic misfortune, price 1,000 marks or near offer. But now the face was trying to look cheerful, even triumphant.

"We have Mr Spencer as prisoner."

O'Gilroy had expected that, Corinna hadn't quite brought herself to. She said: "We haven't met before, have we?"

"My name does not matter."

"Nothing about you *matters*, but you must have a name."

247

The man shrugged. "Caspar."

"Okay, Caspar, what's the deal?"

Caspar seemed uncertain which of them to address. "You give us Dragan, we give you Mr Spencer. It is simple."

If somebody had asked Ranklin what he most disliked about being a spy and he had answered with the sort of honesty he was, as a spy, trying to discard, he would have said that it was the prospect of being tortured by Anya and her crew. His objections to his new trade as ungentlemanly and even dishonourable paled as she explained how much he would suffer if O'Gilroy didn't produce Dragan and she had to torture his whereabouts out of Ranklin. She hadn't been specific, just said she would use methods perfected by the Czars' secret police over many decades and which she believed were reliable. Ranklin had been told something of these methods and agreed completely.

And there was no hope of them believing the truth – that he knew nothing of Dragan, since he had threatened them with him last night. So he might well set a record for resisting under torture, even discredit those secret police methods . . . The thought was *appalling*.

He tried thinking about what they might believe about Dragan, where Dragan might actually be. He didn't know what Dragan looked like – nobody did. Nobody claimed to have met him, except possibly Cross, who had used him as a diversion. And that letter signed by Dragan, saying he had come in the name of liberty from tyranny. Which hadn't told Cross anything new and was a weird thing to be carrying on a night when he had chosen what to carry so carefully . . .

Then he came to a very simple explanation. It was obvious. It was also literally painful that Anya wouldn't believe a word of it.

"I never liked the matter of being mixed up with Dragan," O'Gilroy said as the hired launch puttered up to the Bellevue jetty. "But if I give him to ye, I want to be sure ye keep him. Not coming back for me after he's painted the walls with yeself."

"There will be three of us with pistols. And you will help," Caspar said. His vivid blue blazer, ornate shoes and tie added up to a music-hall imitation of a yachtsman, and suggested a misplaced self-confidence that O'Gilroy welcomed.

O'Gilroy nodded, his face still sombre. "All right, then – where d'ye want him?"

Caspar dipped into his breast pocket and passed over a large calling card. It was a very smooth gesture, and O'Gilroy guessed that passing out the address of Anya's circus was probably Caspar's usual line of work.

This jetty served the rich suburb, and Bellevue hotel itself, well north of the city centre. Now it and the road beyond were almost deserted while Kiel society was at dinner; the only car was a chauffeured limousine with curtained rear windows waiting at the end of the jetty. Mostly used, O'Gilroy guessed, for the circus's best customers.

"This place," he said, flourishing the card and then putting it into his side pocket, "'tis a house, is it? And ye jest want me and Dragan to walk up to the front door?"

"Ah, no. You go to the gate for servants, yes? Then to the . . . left, the door by the side. It is open, understand?"

"Servants' gate and side door," O'Gilroy confirmed. "And Mr Spencer's there."

"But sure."

O'Gilroy glanced round, as if looking for the tram Caspar expected him to take. There was nobody within clear sight. Without any haste, he took the pistol from his pocket and said: "Fine. So let's jest take a look at this gate and door, then."

Caspar looked not angry but immensely shocked, as if O'Gilroy had made some monstrous social blunder.

O'Gilroy sympathised. "Yer jest in the wrong job. But I don't think she'll be asking ye to do it again."

The four-storey house stood at the very north-western edge of town, isolated enough in its own walled garden not to annoy any neighbours. Such establishments are quiet places anyway: just a little piano music, refined laughter, at worst a breaking champagne bottle. And this was Kiel Week, after all.

Ranklin was in a small ground-floor room that Anya used as her office, dropping in to answer the telephone or file some paperwork.

He was roughly tied to an upright chair, but that was just a token: his real captivity was ensured by a large crop-haired man in evening dress who sat and fiddled restlessly with a large revolver. Ranklin hoped he might fiddle enough to shoot himself; he was reduced to hopes like that.

From the distant sounds, the rest of the house continued business as usual. At sunset Anya came in and lit the gas mantles and drew the curtains.

"Is your mouth dry?" she asked Ranklin. "It is a good sign – fear. It means you will not last for long. Bravery is no use, and most painful."

The door was part open and they heard the clump of heavy feet in the hall. "Caspar is back," she said. "We must hope for good news."

Caspar stumbled – in fact was pushed – through the doorway gabbling, and behind him O'Gilroy with a pistol in each hand and shouting: "Don't do nothing!" Anya shouted something herself.

None of the shouts affected the crop-haired man: he jumped up, instead of shooting from where he sat, and levelled the revolver. O'Gilroy fired four times, his face very intent since he mistrusted the killing power of pistols.

A vase on the mantelpiece shattered, but the bullet had gone through the crop-haired man first; all four had. His knees gave and he crumpled quite gently onto the fragments of vase that had reached the floor already.

O'Gilroy looked down at him, shaking his head as if he disapproved of something. "Fucking amateur night," he said.

It took time to restore the house to the profitable calm of a well-run brothel. But it is fundamental to such a place that neither the staff nor clients want anything dramatic and attention-getting to happen there and so are eager to believe that it hasn't. Whatever Anya told them – Ranklin suggested a young officer getting drunk and playing cowboy with his pistol – worked. Then they were back in the little office room – along with the chauffeur whom O'Gilroy had beaten near unconscious and left in the car to simplify his entrance – and Anya was glowering savagely at Ranklin.

"You started this . . . this circus act," he pointed out. "Don't blame us for topping the bill. And we both want the same thing: no assassination attempt on the Kaiser. Well, there won't be, that was just a rumour spread by Cross to get Lenz and Reimers looking the wrong way. And to give it weight, he invented Dragan. D'you know anybody who's met Dragan? Had you heard of him a week ago? Cross banked on the fact that we're all in the business of trading rumours, and it worked."

After one flash of surprise, O'Gilroy was laughing quietly but delightedly, though not forgetting to keep his pistols vaguely pointed.

"The note from Dragan to Cross," Ranklin went on, "if you heard of that, makes more sense if you see it as a threatening letter he planned to leave on the viewing stand at the locks that last night. But all this still leaves Lenz believing in Dragan, that he's going to try an assassination, and that we're involved."

"Lenz does not worry me," Anya said dismissively.

"Stop saying such silly things. Lenz has got a police force behind him and a chief constable above him and he thinks the Kaiser's in danger. D'you think your influential friends count for anything alongside *that*?"

"So now you plan to tell Hauptmann Lenz that sorry, there is no real man Dragan?" she sneered.

"Of course not. I'm going to show him how to catch Dragan."

36

The explosion which woke citizens of Kiel last night was the righteous end of a shocking plan to assassinate His Majesty the Emperor and those good friends of Germany, the King and Queen of Italy. The vile would-be assassin, that notorious anarchist Dragan el Vipero, was justly destroyed by his own bomb, detonated by a vigilant patrol of the Schutz des Königs returning fire when the cowardly Dragan had shot at them from the darkness near the new Canal locks.

The bomb had been composed of dynamite stolen from a store on the site, and had been intended for use in blasting through the earth banks to flood the locks next month.

Hauptmann Lenz, our distinguished Captain of Detectives, said that he had anticipated the attempt since coming into possession of an old bond certificate illustrated with a picture of the planned locks. Close scrutiny revealed to him near-invisible pinpricks marking on the picture a route to the place where the Imperial viewing stand is now erected, under which the dastardly Dragan undoubtedly planned to plant the bomb. Hauptmann Lenz assures us that he always had the matter under complete control and that the Emperor was never in any danger.

The infamous Dragan, described as a large man with close-cropped hair, may also have been responsible for the death last Sunday of the English Naval Lieutenant who could have encountered Dragan on a midnight reconnaissance of the locks . . .

Corinna put down the paper and blinked several times. "Lordy, that Gothic typeface makes your eyes water. But it makes it all look very solemn and true – is any of it?"

"I shan't be complaining to the editor," Ranklin said.

"Then I guess none of it is – except the explosion. That woke me. And it ties up – maybe I mean blows up – every loose end: lets you boys off the hook, even solves your murder for you." She sipped her coffee. "Pop's gotten the idea that you two were in there somewhere, helping to save the Kaiser, maybe preventing a war."

O'Gilroy unbent from his rigid stance by the rail to refill her cup. "Is that a good idea, then?"

"I'd say so. The idea he had before was that you were stirring things up to the point where the cops were likely to raid this ship. He would not have liked that – and neither would you. Better to be unsung heroes."

"And who sang the unsung song for us?" Ranklin asked.

She just smiled. Then: "Oh, in all the excitement, I forgot to ask how you got on with the Widow Wedel."

"Ah, yes, that . . . "

"Did she tell you anything about her husband and the land company?"

"Well, she wasn't all that forthcoming . . . In an awkward position, employed by the government. But reading between the lines, I'd say she's pretty bitter. Very loyal to the late Wedel."

In fact, once she knew she could trust Ranklin, the Widow had become vitriolic about the authorities who had "murdered" her husband. By now it was probably self-justification for the secret revenge she was taking, but Ranklin had had the sense to agree with every word.

"What work does she do?"

"Oh, some routine office stuff."

Her face set. "And that's all you found out? You just don't take women's work seriously." She swept off to the companionway.

Before going down, she turned and looked back. Ranklin, who had scrambled politely to his feet, was now leaning on the rail beside O'Gilroy, and neither of them looked in the least abashed. Indeed, they both looked rather smug.

She walked – almost stalked – back, and her face was still set.

"All right. I'm not a damned fool and neither are you two smirking schoolboys. I don't think you came here to stop the Kaiser getting assassinated, not you nor your Navy pal before you. I think you came here to do something to the German Navy. I don't know what, but it's something you wouldn't do to the French Navy or ours, I hope. I think you've done it, too. And with all this talk of war, are you quite sure you haven't gotten started already?"

Neither of them said anything. The *Kachina* shuddered, rumbled, and began to inch forward as the rope from the mooring buoy was hauled aboard. That morning, Sherring himself had decided to motor to Hamburg, leaving the yacht to follow through the Canal; Ranklin and O'Gilroy had chosen to stay for the voyage. Hauptmann Lenz was happy: there was no point in risking another meeting with him.

When Corinna really had gone below, O'Gilroy asked: "Is she right, then?"

"I don't think so. Let's say we're just rearming – with knowledge that won't help or hurt unless a war really starts."

"And what about the boy, Cross, and his father?"

"I'll write to him. I must remember to keep that article from the *Zeitung*."

"So he'll think Dragan killed the boy?"

"With Dragan dead, as you might say, it's the best solution we can hope for. Remember, Lenz knows Dragan and Cross were connected, with the letter being in his pocket. He suppressed that in return for me letting him solve the great bond mystery."

"By sticking pin holes in it and sending me to get me head near blown off with bullets and dynamite."

Ranklin shrugged. "It needed explaining away. And when I asked if Dragan could have killed Cross, he jumped at that, too."

O'Gilroy chuckled thinly. "I damn bet he did."

Ranklin looked at him. "Now why d'you say that?"

"Ye don't think it odd that a Captain of Detectives turns out and goes miles in the middle of the night to see a murdered Royal Navy Lieutenant. But he didn't: he turned out for a poor nobody of a seaman dead of an accident. That's what the locks feller reported; told us himself."

"You think Lenz knew it was Cross already?"

"Cross was important to him: he'd been spreading word on Dragan and assassination before he got dead and the letter found. So mebbe Lenz was at that eating house, too, separate from his detectives. And when they were fooled with Cross changing his fancy blazer, Lenz wasn't. Mebbe he followed Cross out to the locks and they met there – and he's a big strong feller. It's only guessing, mind. But I'm sure that after that, Cross wouldn't be assassinating anybody whatever."

Ranklin pondered, watching the lumpy town coastline glide past. "Why would Lenz go back then, to do the investigation?"

"Safest to be in charge yerself, wouldn't ye say? Could be worried he'd left a clue – he'd've left hurried the first time."

They had reached the wide inlet to the Canal and were curving in towards the old locks, past the raw earth bank that was due to be blown next month to flood the new ones. Beyond that, there was a flicker of colour from the flags and bunting where the Kaiser and King of Italy had just finished their sightseeing.

"And Reimers," O'Gilroy asked, "d'ye think he's content?"

"He wasn't around last night, thank God. I'm none too sure how much he'd have believed about Dragan and all. Or how much he does believe." Avoiding a meeting with the Naval counter-intelligence agent had been an even better reason for staying aboard the *Kachina*.

"But," he mused, "if Cross hadn't invented Dragan and his plots he'd probably still be alive. In a way, Dragan did kill him, after all."

"Sure," O'Gilroy said. "Isn't it in the papers? – it must be true."

CAVENDISH SQUARE

37

Immediately after the State Ball at Buckingham Palace, everybody began to leave London. The King went to Goodwood, the Duke of Devonshire to Buxton for the cure, others to the Continent for more exotic cures and tours, to Cowes for the yacht racing or just to their country places.

Not quite everybody, of course. Parliament had to stay at the bedside of the Irish Home Rule Bill, and the Foreign Office was busy trying to reconvene the conference of ambassadors to re-agree the Balkan frontiers they had agreed on just before they were outdated by the new war. Seven million other Londoners also stayed throughout that clammy hot July, most of them without even being invited to the dinner given by a leading political hostess who had thoughtfully decorated her house as "A Country Garden" for the evening.

"I'll leave you to persuade Sir Aylmer about Votes for Women," she said to the Commander. "But do try and settle it before Leon gets just a little too tipsy to play the piano."

It was part of her political talent not just to arrange useful "accidental" meetings but to leave on a slightly outrageous remark that broke the ice.

"*Are* you in favour of women's suffrage?" Sir Aylmer Corbin asked.

The Commander put a match to his pipe. "Anything to keep 'em out of politics."

"Ah . . . quite." Corbin smiled politely. "In point of fact, I'm glad of the chance for a word – do you mind talking shop?"

"Depends on whether it's about goods in the window or what we keep under the counter." The Commander sat down on a rustic bench planted on the black-and-white marble of the hallway.

"It's the Colonel Redl business." Corbin stared suspiciously at the bench: he thought he had seen something wriggle in among its rough timbers. Then he sat anyway. "Do you think you could explain it to my simple diplomatist's mind?"

The Commander grinned as if recalling a great meal. "Ah yes. For a start, just about everything you've heard about it is probably true. For ten years the Russians – Military Intelligence, not their Okhrana – had on their payroll the man who became second-in-command of Austro-Hungary's own Military Intelligence. In fact, we believe he nearly became its chief."

"As much as ten years?"

"So it seems. Originally it was blackmail because of Redl's boy-friends, but over ten years it had become something much deeper than that. They built him up: gave him some unimportant secrets and codes, let him catch some of their minor agents – they *made* him a success. And gave him the money to go with it (he explained it as an inheritance): a place in society, a fancy flat, new motorcars, gifts for the boy-friend. Delicious! Can you imagine a more perfect relationship?"

Corbin looked as if he had detected a bad smell. "Are you saying that the Russians actually betrayed some of their own agents just to build up Redl's reputation? I find that . . . " he searched for the correct Foreign Office word, " . . . bizarre."

"Precisely why nobody would believe it. And with that reputation for catching agents, every counter-espionage case came across his desk, so he could head off anything that pointed to himself."

"Then what ultimately unmasked him?"

"That came after he'd left Intelligence to become chief of staff in Prague – but we think it was a minor investigation he wouldn't have heard of anyway. The police stumbled across the money chain and traced it to him. And even then, the High Command did their best to bugger it up; Redl himself would never have handled it so crudely. But I suppose that shows how indispensable he'd made himself."

"They sent some brother officers to give him a pistol and tell him to shoot himself, did they not?"

"Not even his own pistol! And in a hotel room! *That* was their idea of keeping it all quiet."

Corbin nodded. "Yes. We heard the resulting . . . silence loud and clearly. But how, would you say, Redl himself would have handled it?"

A Japanese lantern hanging awkwardly in a potted tree across the hallway burst silently into flames. A servant came, barely hurrying, and sprayed it with a soda-water siphon; a small group gathered around another bench applauded.

The Commander's voice became a soft recitative. "Taken him off to some quiet place, not unpleasant, just neutral: you should always leave a man the hope of talking himself out of it – and talked to him. Sometimes threatening, what could happen to his family, his boy-friends, sometimes sympathetic, offering excuses, ways to make amends. But always talking, questioning, until he's ready to sleep on his feet. But never allowing him enough sleep until he's talked back, all ten years' worth of names, places, times, dates – everything."

"And then?"

The Commander shrugged indifferently. "Oh, then give him the pistol."

"And that is how Redl himself would have handled it?"

The Commander smiled. "We can only guess."

Corbin sighed. "I find it all a little tawdry. But thank you for clarifying the, ah, professional aspects of it all. The repercussions on Viennese society and the Army were fully reported by our Ambassador. They were considerable."

"So I understood."

"Particularly with the situation in the Balkans at this time. The great Austro-Hungarian Army made to look foolish, the resultant outcry for revenge on Russia – and since then, Austria's ally Bulgaria being trounced by Russia's ally, Serbia, so deepening the humiliation. Disturbing, most disturbing. It was about such repercussions of espionage exposés that I wanted a quiet word with you."

The Commander had sensed the curve of the conversation and, like the yachtsman he was, had his mental sails loosened to meet the shift of wind. He waited to see how strong it would blow.

Corbin said: "We are not often taken by surprise. A prime task of our diplomatists is to ensure this, to report changes of attitude in their host nations before they harden into action. Any change of policy usually grows from a broad base, is widely canvassed and debated, so we have timely warning of it.

"This is not so in the case of an espionage scandal. Its root cause – perhaps a single error by a single spy – is so minute as to be quite unforeseeable. Yet within days, perhaps even hours, it can be inflated into a major crisis, if only by the public." Like most senior civil servants, Corbin had a deep horror and distrust of the frivolous and uninformed "public", whether British or any other nation's.

"And," he concluded, "if it is we who have sent the spy, we are de facto in the wrong for having done so. Now, can you persuade me that I am mistaken?"

The Commander thought carefully. "Perhaps not – but let me ask: in time of war, would you say we needed secret agents as well as battleships?"

"I would say yes."

"Yet you don't expect the Admiralty to wait for the outbreak of war before starting to build such ships."

Corbin nodded. "A valid point. Although the building of warships in peacetime can be extremely provocative – as we wish the German Emperor would realise. But what else can you offer me?"

"In mitigation, our current policy: that we never admit to employing agents, deny we have a Bureau to do so, claim any agent caught was acting on his own misguided initiative, and say that while we regret the misbehaviour of one of our citizens . . . "

"Almost invariably an officer."

"But just as invariably – and provably – on leave from his more normal job and merely showing an excess of professional zeal in his spare time . . . As I say, offer that explanation and accuse the accusers of overplaying the incident."

"But the incident will still have occurred. And will recur."

"I can't deny that. Perhaps the root question is whether the intelligence our agents provide is worth the embarrassment of their – very occasional – unmasking."

"An embarrassment entirely borne by our Diplomatic and Consular Services."

Aha, the Commander thought, the wind has steadied: it's to blow only from the direction of the Foreign Office. Now I know, I can sail on this wind.

"Borne on behalf of the nation as a whole," he said, "just as the secret intelligence benefits the nation as a whole."

"But can you evaluate that risk and that benefit?"

"No," the Commander said bluntly. "But luckily it's been done for me, just by setting up my Bureau. That said the risk is worth it."

"Oh, come now," Corbin protested. "You surely wouldn't say that the existence of a motorcar – even a Rolls-Royce – implied only a fixed amount of risk, regardless of how it was driven?"

Since the Commander's driving of his own Rolls-Royce (which came from his second marriage, not his Naval pay) was recognised as one of the greater dangers of London life, he smiled grimly. But said blandly: "I'm sure we all believe we do our jobs as well as we can within the limits imposed by others."

"But in the case of your Bureau," Corbin said smoothly, "what limits? – imposed by what others?"

"Ultimately, we must be judged by results . . . " But the Commander was floundering, and Corbin sailed past.

"I do appreciate your problem," he said with the reassurance of a dentist about to make his fortune. "Being officially nonexistent has its handicaps as well as its benefits. For example, there could be no public outcry should your Bureau cease to exist: disbanded or, in more typical fashion, quietly starved of funds until its nominal functions were absorbed by some larger and more stable institution."

Such, the Commander assumed, as the Foreign Office. It didn't really disapprove of spying – it had its own secret budget – but merely of spies it didn't control. Meanwhile, the Army and Navy would be just as happy to regain undivided command of espionage in their own areas. And that would be the end of Lord Erith's vision of a Secret Service as a Broad Church with secret missionaries anywhere and everywhere.

But it wouldn't happen yet, not unless he made some terrible mistake. He might be new to political dinner parties but he had learnt a lot about political timing. Erith and others who had sponsored the Bureau were still at large, still with influence. Their successors might decide it had all been a mistake, but not they.

Did Corbin know that he knew that? He struck another match, breathed smoke, and said mildly: "Aren't we looking rather far ahead?"

"Then let me suggest what one might call 'spheres of influence'. That your agents concern themselves solely with the engines of war – the Zeppelin airship, Krupp's cannon and the like – and, at the *very* most, such matters as mobilisation timetables and the order of battle. And leave all political and diplomatic issues severely alone – this to apply with the utmost particularity to the Balkans. If we are to persuade the other Powers that we are disinterestedly seeking a peaceful outcome there, the very last thing we can risk is the revelation that we are conducting a spying campaign in parallel."

The Commander was feeling rather Balkan himself, so recently liberated, so beset by hungry empires. Well, well, he thought: first he threatens to annex me, now he merely wants a treaty. Now there's a true diplomatist at work. He said: "And you see military matters as less sensitive?"

"Oh, the *public* gets inflamed about somebody stealing the plans of a new warship – the concept's so easy to understand – but it passes, it passes. And they accept muddy morals along with muddy boots as natural consequences of military life. But while our ambassadors may have to live with the risks inherent in that form of espionage, it is quite unthinkable that an ambassador should know a spy may be reporting on the same matters as himself, behind his back and beyond his control. *Quite* unthinkable."

The Commander chewed this over and found the unswallowable bit. "But what about journalists?" he asked politely. "If a report in, say, *The Times* contradicts what an ambassador has been saying?"

"That happens far less often than you might think. An experienced ambassador cultivates any serious journalist who appears on his doorstep. Invites him to embassy functions, passes him titbits of information, flatters him by asking his advice. That way, the journalist winds up reporting to the ambassador before his own editor and his articles reinforce the ambassador's own views.

Diplomacy can be applied to any misguided person, not just foreign-born ones."

The Commander grinned widely, delighted at any deviousness. He also saw, in this "treaty" the very faint hope of something he had long wanted. Putting on a worried frown and hoping it showed in that light, he said: "It may be that an agent will stumble across something of political or diplomatic significance. Would it then be his duty to tell the nearest ambassador or consul-general?"

"It would be his duty," Corbin said firmly, "to have no contact whatsoever with our people. He should report as usual to you, and I assume you would pass the information on to . . . to an informed and sympathetic ear in the Foreign Office for proper assessment."

It was a grandiose way of saying "me", but Corbin clearly believed that particular me deserved it. He went on: "You are, one might almost say, *in trade*. A very poor way of putting it, I fear," but he wasn't withdrawing the slur. "You collect intelligence and you pass it on, it has no intrinsic value to you since your Bureau cannot act on it. That's for others to do – the Navy, Army, our humble selves at The Office."

"Perhaps we should be negotiating a trade treaty. You do have such things, don't you?"

"I believe so," Corbin said coolly. "Do you feel we have reached an understanding?"

Distantly, someone was tactlessly checking that the piano had been tuned by playing a series of scales. Their hostess came zigzagging down the hallway collecting her guests with a smile and a gesture.

The Commander said: "It may also happen that one of my agents needs to send a very urgent and secret message. In such very rare circumstances, in the interest of the nation as a whole, would you agree . . . "

Corbin understood perfectly and disagreed totally: the Commander wanted to use embassies as postboxes, since the only truly secret codes accepted by the cable companies, or the governments that licensed them, were the diplomatic codes. But from there it would be but a step to embassies becoming, or being assumed to have become, which was worse, nests of espionage. Not in my time, he thought, nor in the time of any successor – unless the

Foreign Office controls that espionage.

But he was too much of a diplomatist to say "No". "An ambassador is in the same position as the captain of a warship: he accepts total responsibility for each and every message sent from his embassy. It follows that any such decision would be entirely up to the individual ambassador."

"But you want me to forbid my agents from going anywhere near your ambassadors."

"We think that would be most advisable." Corbin stood up. "I repeat: do we have an understanding?"

"Oh, I understand all right." The Commander banged his pipe on the pot of a flowering shrub, sprinkling it with hot ash. "I suppose now we'd better go and listen to this Leon. Who is he?"

The diplomatist shrugged. "Just some dago."

THIS FAITHLESS TIME

38

"*Two* bowler hats for Mr O'Gilroy?" the Bureau's accountant said, politely mystified. "I quite see that when posing as your manservant he would need a bowler hat, but two, both purchased within the space of two weeks?"

"The first one got a bullet-hole in it at Kiel," Ranklin said evenly. "He happened – quite properly, in my view – to be wearing it when he was helping incite a patrol of German troops to open fire one night."

"Oh, quite, quite." The accountant seemed used to such explanations. "But if the second hat was a *replacement*, then you should have stated that, along with a brief outline of the circumstances leading to its loss or irreparable damage. Until then, I'm afraid . . ."

He laid the bill on the growing pile of rejected claims and picked up another paper. He was a small, affable man in his forties who smoked one cigarette an hour and wore a Norfolk jacket because, to most Englishmen, Paris was a permanent weekend. He would not have minded in the least being told that he looked like an Englishman in Paris; that, he would have said, was what he was.

"You seem," he said, "to use motor taxis a lot. Do you find the motor-omnibuses and underground railway inadequate?"

"We use those too. It just doesn't seem worth writing down the fares."

"Oh." The accountant put down his pencil to think about this radically new approach to life. Then he said: "I think you should," and began doing sums on his pad.

Ranklin sipped his lemon tea and stared up at the little square of
blue sky that showed above the hotel courtyard. Then, his eye
followed one of the many trickles from the hotel plumbing, down
to a despondent potted tree in a damp corner, to the rusty metal
table with its load of papers, and the accountant again.

He had finished the sums. "If you were to buy a bicycle – "

"A bicycle?"

"Yes. And if the price of a good second-hand machine were the
same as in Britain – let us say one hundred and twenty-five francs –
then with the saving on motor-taxis, you would have fully
recouped the cost of the bicycle in just twelve and a half days – by
your own figures."

"Quite often O'Gilroy's with me in those taxis," Ranklin
pointed out.

"Ah yes. Then it would have to be two bicycles and an amortis-
ation period of twenty-five days. Of course, that isn't quite . . . "

"I AM NOT GOING TO A RECEPTION AT THE AUSTRO-
HUNGARIAN EMBASSY ON A SECOND-HAND BLOODY
BICYCLE!"

The hotel cat, which had been asleep in the one dry corner of
the courtyard, sprang up and gave Ranklin an outraged look, then
began to lick itself. The accountant seemed just mildly surprised.
"Are you going to a reception at the Embassy?"

"Tomorrow night."

"Do you consider it wholly necessary?"

"If you know anything about the political situation in . . . Look,
it'll cost just two taxis. And I get a free supper."

"Aren't you forgetting the laundering of the collar of your dress
shirt? Perhaps even the whole shirt? You see? – it's these little
overlooked matters which can add up to considerable sums. I fully
appreciate the, ah, peculiarities of your work and that I have to
take many things on trust. But trust, I say, has to be earned. And
what better way to earn it than assiduous attention to details such
as these?" He smiled amiably, even trustingly.

The hotel waiter, thinking Ranklin's shout had been for him,
had decided after two minutes to come and see what he wanted.

"Let me pay for this," the accountant said, reaching for the
wallet that held his personal money. "Would you like another

lemon tea?"

"No, thank you. I would like a large cognac."

"That might turn out to be a very expensive drink," O'Gilroy said judiciously.

"Be damned to it. Saying I should *earn the trust* of a snotty little clerk! He was questioning my integrity! I've spent half my Army life having rows with the Quartermaster and Ordnance branches about pennies, but they were conducted as between gentlemen!"

O'Gilroy, who believed the solution to a storm in a teacup was to steal a new teacup, asked: "What's the damage, then?"

"About half of what we paid to replace the kit left at the General's Château, no first-class travel for you when you were being a manservant, about half our taxi fares disallowed – we'll be living out of our own pockets for months unless they send us on a new task. Damn it all, we didn't join the Bureau to *lose* money." He was stumping angrily around his small bedroom, picking up and throwing down clothes.

"We know where he's staying," O'Gilroy said. "So, jest suppose he met a young lady tonight, and suppose there was something in his drink to make him especial careless, and suppose ye happened by his room and found them in bed – a respectable man like himself, ye'd have him by the balls."

"The very last place I'd want to touch him in that circumstance. And you'd need to hide a whole rhinoceros in his drink, not just a bit of horn, to bring him to life . . . " But the very thought had calmed him; he sat down and mused, smiling. "It's a pity blackmail can be so unpredictable . . . isn't there any other crime we can commit?"

"It's come to that, has it?"

"We're learning to be a sort of criminal, aren't we? And we can't go on doing our job without proper financing, so let's use what we've learned."

It was logic that O'Gilroy accepted without a blink, but knew Ranklin would have rejected it out of hand a few weeks ago. We're learning, all right, Captain, dear – but I wonder if ye realise how much?

"Think, man, think," Ranklin urged him. But in the end, he

thought of it for himself.

"To count all acts of war as normal because all must be driven by necessity, to count none as exceptional, resorted to only *in extremis*, in short to deny the existence of Kriegsraison and say that all is Kriegsmanier, is to me to deny the role of conscience in the waging of war. And yet this is what Professor Westlake would have us do. But it is my profound and considered belief, ladies and gentlemen, that when we lose conscience we lose judgement – no inconsiderable trifle in matters of law. Professor Lueder has drawn the analogy with the criminal law: that a man may commit acts contrary to that law, yet be excused on grounds of dire necessity such as self-preservation. This does not destroy the law. So it is with nations: we must continue to recognise the Kriegsraison, to accept the exceptional for what it is, and still call it for judgement in the forum of conscience."

All this was rather far removed from the battlefields Ranklin had known, and his attention was wandering around the room – the ballroom, presumably, since the Hôtel de Matignon had been built as a private house – practically a palace – and become the Austro-Hungarian Embassy only thirty years before. Now the room was crowded with spindly gilt chairs (not enough: Ranklin was leaning against a pillar), the Diplomatic Corps, Parisian lawyers and distinguished guests to whom the Dual Monarchy was showing off its latest catch.

He himself was there because of Corinna, now sitting a few yards away wrapped in green watered silk and a modest spattering of rubies and listening with a bright but rather fixed smile to Professor . . . er . . . let me think . . . oh yes, Hornbeam, Gerald Hornbeam. The American expert on international law, you know. You *must* have heard of him.

Well, I have now, and would have spotted him for an American lawyer anyway, he decided. Pink-cheeked, comfortably stout, with a full white moustache, and mane of hair (it was odd how successful lawyers kept their hair; Hornbeam must be past sixty), the dress clothes slightly out of date and rumpled to show academic soundness.

He had moved on while Ranklin's thoughts had sneaked out for a smoke, though still in pursuit of Professor Westlake. "In the event of an uprising in a neighbouring state, he would brand as lawless any intervention to quell what he is pleased to call 'the mere contagion of principles', citing as his authority the famous despatch by Canning in 1823 which justified intervention only in the face of a physical threat. Yet what navy or army today could mount an invasion more potent than one manned solely by principles? And in denouncing one side of the coin, he fails entirely to observe what is inscribed on the other: that if we grant principles the power of evil, may we not also grant them the power of good? And if this indeed be so, may it not also be so of intervention in support of principles? Or must we shackle ourselves with laws obdurate to the finer judgements of conscience?"

He ended amid a burst of eager applause, a few cheers and a grim mutter from behind Ranklin: "Parce que c'est fini." Hornbeam took one question, phrased as if it were being read from an old parchment, and then several women in the audience simply stood up, forcing the men round them to do the same, and in a moment the talk was over and supper could begin.

Ranklin hung back, waiting for Corinna and watching a small crowd gathering to congratulate Hornbeam. Among them was a shortish, slightly dumpy girl, perhaps in her middle twenties, who was nevertheless dressed to stand out anywhere – except a Paris reception. She took Hornbeam's arm and smiled possessively out at the crowd.

"Matt, come here and meet Mr Temple," Corinna called. She was with a lanky bespectacled young man – American, from the way his figure drawled as his voice might.

"From our Embassy," Corinna confirmed, introducing them.

"And what did you think of Professor Hornbeam's address, sir?" Temple asked politely.

"Most interesting," Ranklin said promptly, and left to himself he would have said no more. But he owed it to Corinna not to be too much the country clodhopper, as her expression was now pointing out. So: "I think his lectures should be well received in Austria-Hungary."

That didn't satisfy Corinna, but Temple saw the drift and nodded seriously. "Exactly. His views on intervention in a neighbouring state . . . "

"Such as Serbia." And Ranklin was immediately aware that he had said a Very Rude Word. Temple winced and actually glanced around.

Now Corinna had got interested. "I thought that intervention stuff was just about Cuba and maybe now Mexico; he's a great Teddy Roosevelt man. But I never thought of *Serbia*."

"Mrs Finn, we are on Austro-Hungarian territory here," Temple hissed. "I'm sorry the matter came up."

"My fault," Ranklin said. "Still, he doesn't speak for your government and you didn't invite him to Europe, so if anything he says might be construed as endorsing any prospective act with unfortunate consequences – Good God! I'm beginning to speak like him. Anyway, you can disown him."

"We'd rather not have to," Temple said. "He's a very eminent academic. And our job is to protect our citizens abroad, not rap their knuckles. Still . . . "

"I was planning to go to Vienna soon anyway," Corinna said cheerfully. "Maybe I'll hitch myself to his wagon and see if I can't tone him down a bit."

"Mrs Finn," Temple said, beginning to sound anxious, "we have a perfectly good Embassy in Vienna."

"Why, of course you do – but they're all *diplomatists*, aren't they, old boy, what ho? Anyway, Lucy would welcome some help shopping, I'm sure."

"His wife?" Ranklin asked.

"Daughter, stupid. Mrs Hornbeam's an invalid, doesn't travel."

"Ah. Tell me," Ranklin turned to Temple, "who's the Major in Cuirassiers' uniform?"

Temple squinted across the room at a blond young man alternately laughing and dipping his moustache in champagne. "Oh, their temporary Military Attaché, I forget his name. The real one's back in Vienna."

"He looks," Corinna said, "as if he has a very muscular brain."

Ranklin nodded, hoping she was right.

39

The Embassy's windows had all been opened wide, bringing a confusion of warm fresh air and warm bad breath from last night's reception. Or at least the Temporary Military Attaché found it confusing as he picked his way through the cleaners and sweepers to stare at the man waiting in a small side room.

The visitor was lean, his hair sleeked back with some disgusting-smelling oil, and wearing thick-rimmed spectacles and a suit that was almost a diplomatic incident. He looks like a servant – or worse, the Attaché thought. Who let him in? *Who* said he could *sit down*?

Unsure of what language to use, he made an international noise in his throat. The visitor looked up and asked: "D'ye spaik English?"

"I do."

The visitor reached into a bulging pocket. "D'ye want to buy this, then?"

He didn't even say "Sir". The book was red, slim, pocket-sized and in the front it said MOST SECRET – CODE X – TRES SECRET. The Attaché opened it, then sat down abruptly.

I will attack, he read – 11647 – Je vais attaquer. His hands shivered and he took several deep breaths to subdue his hangover. Despite being a cavalryman and enjoying the image of himself as a "devil of a fellow", the Attaché was not stupid. Perhaps a good deal of what he mistook for intelligence in himself was really ruthless ambition, but in some military circles that is just as good.

I am attacking – 45151 – J'attaque.

If this is a foul joke perpetrated by an unspeakable Magyar in the Commercial section, I will personally see that he is posted to Manzanillo.

I attacked – 31847 – J'ai attaqué.

"Where – " his voice started as a croak and he coughed: " – where did you obtain this?"

"It belongs to me master, but him busy being dead drunk this fine morning, I'm handling his affairs for him." He leered like a gargoyle.

"Who is your master?"

"Ah, now. I was thinkin' names, specially mine, needn't come into this. Just say he's the sort of man uses this sort of book. And a bastard of an Englishman besides."

"You are not English?"

The visitor stood up, snatched back the book, and sneered down at the Curassiers' uniform. "I ask for an officer and they send the lavatory attendant."

"No, wait please. You are Irish."

"A genius. And in uniform."

"A good Catholic, like us Austrians."

Apparently mollified, the visitor sat down again.

"But how," the Attaché asked, "can I be sure this book is genuine?"

The visitor shrugged. "How would I know meself. – except me master jest got it for special cablegrams. D'ye want it or not?"

"This is a more complicated matter than you understand. I cannot just buy this book. I do not have the authority. And to buy the book itself would make the code useless, because . . . "

The visitor studied his fingernails, perhaps to make sure none of the dirt had fallen out.

"I want a thousand pounds," he said.

"And I said ye wouldn't be awake before one o'clock so he went charging away with the code – to get it photographed – and then asked me a lot more questions and then stuck me to wait out in the garden. Jayzus! ye should see the size of that garden – "

"I believe it's the biggest private park in central Paris," Ranklin said. They had met in a large students' café near the Place St

Michel and, for their own peace of mind, in a dark corner of it.

" . . . and gave me coffee and cream cakes – ah, those cakes, ye've never tasted the like in yer life."

"That's fine, but are we going to get the money?"

O'Gilroy considered. "From what he was saying, he was serious about it: telling me not to leave your employ sudden and go drinking it all up at oncest, or ye'd be suspicious."

"He knows something about the business, then."

"And he gave me a hundred francs."

"Four pounds? Well, it's a start. From what we heard in Brussels, a thousand's a bit high for a code, but we should get six to eight. Do you think they managed to photograph the whole book?"

"They had three hours, and was talking of getting them on a train to Vienna . . . "

"That's at least twenty-four hours. It'll take time." Their own "proof" of the code had already gone: a bribed operator had telegraphed a coded message to the British Embassy in Vienna. Tomorrow or the next day, the Kundschaftstelle would have the photographs of the code book, would take the intercepted telegram from the "unsolved" file, and behold! – it was solved. Actually, all they would learn was that it was a test run of a new code, in future to be used only in moments of crisis (which would explain why they wouldn't get a flood of telegrams in the new code) and no acknowledgement was needed. And they would conclude, Ranklin prayed, that they were being offered a bargain.

The only risk, he reckoned, was that the Vienna Embassy would have an unreadable telegram, would complain to the Foreign Office, who would suspect the Bureau and scream that their diplomatic virginity was being threatened. But that was just too bad: if the Commander didn't want trouble with the Foreign Office, he shouldn't send accountants to insult his agents' financial probity.

He picked up a short list of questions. "You said you wanted the money in cash, either pounds or francs?"

"Yes."

"And that we were leaving next week and you wanted it prompter?"

O'Gilroy nodded.

"That if they didn't pay, somebody else might?"

"Ah, they gave me a lecture on how it would ruin the value of the code if word of it got about, and I took a long time to understand what they meant by that." Ranklin's sympathy was entirely with the Austrian Attaché; O'Gilroy being stupid was a top-of-the-bill performance.

"But ye're still sure," O'Gilroy added, "ye don't want me to try it on the Germans as well?"

"No need to take the risk. The Austrians are the ones. After the Redl affair they want, they *need*, an Intelligence success – just for their own self-esteem. And," he ticked off the last question, "did they try to follow you?"

"Oh yes. But the Rue de Varenne's a straight long street and they daren't keep close, and I lost them in that tangle around the Rue du Bac and the Boulevard."

If O'Gilroy said the followers had been lost, they were lost. But what now impressed Ranklin more was the way O'Gilroy had picked up the geography of Paris; he mispronounced the street names wildly but walked them confidently. And he could sense the mood of a district the way a gnarled old countryman could smell a change in the weather. The man was just a natural townee, which wasn't much of a compliment in Ranklin's old circle, but now . . .

He rolled the list of questions into a spill, lit it and lit his pipe from it. "Well, in a few days," he puffed contentedly, "solvency should stare us in the face. And you need never put that foul stuff on your hair again."

"And me thinking to lend ye half a pint of it the next time ye was stepping out with Mrs Finn."

Ranklin shut his eyes and shuddered delicately.

There was nothing new or brash about the office of the House of Sherring in the Boulevard des Capucines. It had the quiet solid look of an institution that had been there a long time, as, in terms of the financial world, it had. Sherring's father had been of that generation of American financiers who had learnt the business in Europe, steering the old money into the railroads and iron mines of America, long before they reversed the flow to finance Europe's wars.

Puzzled why he had been summoned there, Ranklin was further surprised to find Temple, from the American Embassy, already drinking coffee in the dark-panelled private office. He wore a fawn summer suit and bright necktie, but his thin bespectacled face looked diplomatically sombre enough.

Sherring shook hands, offered coffee, and got straight down to business. "I got a telegram from Corinna. I won't bother showing it to you, you wouldn't either of you understand it, but translated and reading between the lines and so on, she's worried about Professor Hornbeam. Seems like he's getting the à la carte treatment, belle of the ball, and Corinna thinks they're up to something."

"Excuse me, sir," Temple said, "but who is 'they'?"

Ranklin was also thinking of the many levels of "they" in Vienna.

Sherring flipped through the telegram – several pages long – and frowned. "Doesn't rightly say, just big names in the court and government. And the Professor is always getting asked for legal opinions, and she's suspicious of the motives."

"It could be just flattery," Temple suggested. "Viennese society usually says more than it means."

"Sure, but Corinna's no damn fool. If she says there's something to worry about, I'd back her."

Nobody knew what to say next. Ranklin was watching Sherring and wondering why he looked American. In fact, of course, he didn't: he looked like the bosun of a tramp steamer dressed in banker's clothing. Perhaps it was that in Europe such a man could never have become an international banker, never been accepted by financial families, well-bred (in their own way, his county blood added) through generations of handling and mishandling big money. They would never have shed their jackets on the warmest of days, nor sat lounging back with thumbs jammed in their waistcoat pockets.

"Well?" Sherring said.

Temple coughed and said carefully: "If she feels an American citizen is being tempted to make statements that could embarrass us, then our Embassy in Vienna could . . . "

"She says our Embassy is . . . " Sherring reached for the telegram again to get the exact words, then decided they were too exact.

"She isn't so impressed," he concluded.

Temple smiled lopsidedly. "If this is about possible Austrian intervention in Serbia – as I believe Mr Ranklin feared when we met at Hornbeam's talk here – I don't really believe Austria is going to start a war just because an American lawyer says it's okay to do so."

"No," Sherring admitted, "but . . . "

Temple went on: "If they do go to war, sure they'll use every justification they can get a hold of. Nations always do. But I'm just as sure that no American Foreign Service officer is going to try and deprive Hornbeam of his First Amendment right to speak his mind. And I'd guess that Hornbeam, as a lawyer and Republican both, knows that also."

Sherring looked at him expressionlessly, which meant his face was just normally craggy and serious. "Okay, son. D'you want to be excused school?"

Temple stood up. "I think I'd better be, sir, if this conversation is going to continue."

When he had ushered Temple out, Sherring walked carefully back towards Ranklin. Like many tall, heavy men he had a delicate, almost tiptoe, walk.

"D'you still think like you did at Kiel?" he asked. "About what would happen if Austria charged into Serbia?"

"Yes."

"Would you go there to help Corinna figure out what's going on?"

Ranklin swallowed. "I – I'd like to. Tell me, though: what's your interest in this?"

"Finding out what's going to happen before anybody else," Sherring said promptly. "And keeping it to myself as long as I can. We might be in the same line of business." He allowed himself a little bleak smile. "Corinna wants you to meet them in Budapest – they'll have moved on from Vienna by the time you could get there. Seems he's giving the same lecture in both places."

Vienna tried – at least in unimportant matters – to treat the capital of Hungary as an equal.

"We'll pay all your expenses," Sherring went on, "both you and your Irish whatever-he-is. Okay? And would you like a drink?"

"It's rather early for me," Ranklin said. "But yes, I would."

He had expected a servant with a silver tray. Instead, Sherring simply opened a mahogany cabinet and started pouring; perhaps he valued his time and unbroken privacy more than any display of stature.

When they were settled again, Sherring said: "It's still the war season, by the reckoning you used in Kiel. D'you think it'll happen this time around?"

"You don't need me to tell you that Europe's littered with heaps of loose gunpowder and dry tinder, the Balkans particularly, even with a peace conference starting in Bucharest. But whether somebody's going to drop a lighted match, accidentally or on purpose . . . " He shrugged. "Perhaps I'll have a better idea after Budapest, but only perhaps."

"Uh-huh. If it happens, d'you figure it for a long war?"

Everybody who talked about war talked of a short one, but perhaps those who thought otherwise kept their pessimism quiet. And militarily, Ranklin had no idea: a war on the scale he foresaw hadn't happened in Europe since the days of the Brown Bess musket and wooden men-o'-war. He shook his head helplessly.

"If you get yourselves a war," Sherring said slowly, "it's going to be different. I don't just mean your new dreadnoughts and big guns. I mean it won't just be about shifting frontiers: it's going to be about shifting ideas, too. We had ourselves a war about ideas just fifty years back – like in most things, we're ahead of you here in Europe." He smiled thinly. "I was still just a boy when it was over, and my father took me on a trip through the South, to see what business was left. There wasn't much of anything left. Except hating, and that's still there.

"You get yourselves into a war like that and Europe's going to end up different. How different, I don't know, but . . . " He looked at Ranklin in an odd, reflective way. "But maybe you'll be lucky and not live to see it, not in your job. Whatever," he added politely, "that is."

Ranklin took great care with his cablegram to the Bureau, and it took them twenty-four hours to reply:
APPROVE INVESTIGATE BUSINESS OPPORTUNITIES

BUDAPEST STOP LETTER OF CREDIT AWAITS AT BANK
STOP DO NOT REPEAT NOT TRAVEL ORIENT EXPRESS
OR STAY EXPENSIVE HOTEL ENDS UNCLE CHARLIE.

"Did ye mention that Mr Sherring was paying for it all anyhow?"
O'Gilroy asked.

"In the end, no. I felt it would make my cablegram too expensive
if I explained."

"That accountant would be proud of ye."

"Still, Uncle Charlie is going to expect a full report, and some
new stuff, from all this. But with the Sherring connection, we
should meet some interesting people."

"We play that up, do we?"

"It's both our disguise and our opportunity; we're Sherring min-
ions now. Don't talk of money in less than millions – unless
somebody's trying to cheat you out of a halfpenny."

But it was the Austro-Hungarian Embassy that nearly caused the
real hold-up. Reluctant as any government institution anywhere to
hand out money, it didn't pay for the code – just over £700 – until
the afternoon of the day they were due to leave. That left no time
to deposit the cash in the small, obscure bank Ranklin had chosen
in Versailles. While he wasn't too concerned about carrying the
money to Budapest, and could telegraph it to the account from
there, he would have liked to leave the code-book in a deposit box.
He thought of simply destroying it, but that would have to be done
very thoroughly and there were no hotel-room fires in July. So
rather than try to hide it in their rooms, he simply took it along.

He wouldn't actually be breaking any law, he reflected in the
taxi taking them to the Gare de l'Est, even if the Austro-Hungarian
officials found it on him. He would simply be followed every
waking minute by twenty men in cheap boots and blank expressions.

40

Until he became a spy, O'Gilroy had never worn evening dress. He now accepted it as just another part of his disguise, but the idea of dressing for dinner on a train, even the Orient Express, struck him as going a bit far. It was Ranklin who insisted; the Wagons-Lits staff could hardly make such a rule when so many of their passengers were Orientals who had their own styles of finery, though they could certainly make anybody in travelling tweeds feel out of place.

But after a few minutes, he had to admit, to himself only, that Ranklin had been right. With the orange glow of the gas lamps deepening the colour of his champagne, it was nice to feel he belonged in such company, that it would have been incomplete without him. And even nicer to feel that the bad-tempered Turk with a voice like a parrot belonged less. But what could you expect? Bloody foreigner.

"Hors-d'oeuvre?" Ranklin was suggesting. "Then I'm having the Chateaubriand with Béarnaise – would you prefer the sole and stay with champagne throughout?"

"Ah, why not?" O'Gilroy said, surprising even himself with the ultimate luxury of not having to choose his luxuries. He finished his glass and waited – not long – for somebody to refill it.

Ranklin smiled, a little enviously and only out of the window at the twilit hills beyond the Marne. For him it had been just lifting the knife at his place setting, the remembered weight of solid silver that had brought back the mess nights at Woolwich and other tables of the Regiment where the lamplight had glinted on the trophies of old campaigns and he had once belonged. At least

O'Gilroy knew just what had got him here: money. It had taken Ranklin twenty years to learn that. Never rich, yet never wanting for cash, he hadn't realised that those mess nights, the cheery outings in London and Ascot, the very comradeship itself, had all been founded on money. And when it went, they went. Nobody had been unkind, but they no longer looked him in the eye, didn't know what to talk about. It was over.

He woke up to find the waiter asking for their order. He gave it, then pulled his hand away from his pocket where, he realised, he had been clutching and fingering the gold coins.

"It doesn't last," he said. But of course that was so obvious to O'Gilroy that he misunderstood.

"Are ye thinking there'll be a train smash?"

"No, no – though they've had a few in the past. And I dare say some close calls when the King of Bulgaria insisted on driving."

"He didn't that?"

"Why not? It was going through his country . . . " And he chattered on with legends about the train as they swayed east towards night and the German frontier. " . . . and did you know – I should have mentioned this earlier, of course – that if you felt lonely, the conductor could have telegraphed ahead from one station to have a young lady waiting at the next to see you through the night?"

He thought he caught a flash of interest in O'Gilroy's eyes before he decided to be shocked instead. "Ye never could."

"Look around you. D'you think some of these gentlemen wouldn't want such a thing from time to time? Trains like this exist to supply wants. It would cost you something for the, er, ride in both senses, and I'm sure the conductor would expect more than the telegraph costs. Be cheaper if you could find a duchess escaping from her mad husband on their honeymoon trip . . . "

"Captain!"

"I swear it. I heard it from . . . "

They awoke in the bright picture-postcard scenery of South Germany, breakfasted, and settled down for a smoke in the armchairs in the salon half of the dining car. Ranklin found a newspaper which had come aboard at an earlier stop and translated the news of the Balkans to O'Gilroy. The fighting had now officially stopped; Bulgaria, which had attacked Greece and Serbia, having lost not only to them but to Romania and Turkey who were happy to rob a man when he's down. Peace talks were going on in the Romanian capital of Bucharest much to the dismay of Austria-Hungary, which would rather be celebrating a Bulgarian victory and lording it over the peace conference.

He tried to explain, without pretending to understand all the nuances, the "Dual Monarchy": the frigid marriage of Austria and Hungary, with their forcibly adopted brood of Bohemia, Galicia, Croatia, Bosnia and all the others, with no common bond of race, religion or language.

"What seems to hold them together is the Army – and the Emperor. Don't refer to him as that in Budapest, by the way: he's Emperor of Austria but King of Hungary . . . But now with Serbia – they're Slavs – winning a string of victories, the Slavs inside the Monarchy are getting restless. There's a Pan-Slav movement, talk of a Greater Serbia reaching to the Adriatic coast. That's another thing that worries the Monarchy: finding its fleet bottled up in the ports up the coast. The Army's been mobilised for months, ready to march into Serbia."

"Sounds like they'd be swallowing a live snake to stop it biting 'em on the outside."

"And that's only the beginning. Russia will probably back Serbia: she's been egging them on. After that, the whole European house of cards could fall in."

"In a war, would ye go back to the Gunners?"

"It won't be my decision but I hope so." His mind drifted on ahead of the train, south to the shattered railway station outside Salonika. "If it lasts more than a couple of months, it'll be a gunners' war, not a spies' one."

"Mebbe Mrs Finn was right and it's our war now."

But a dark puzzled look had come over Ranklin's boyish face and O'Gilroy guessed he was trying to see too far into the future. For himself, he was content in the present: a comfortable armchair, the unreeling scenery outside and the promise of a Munich beer when they passed through that city.

•

They finished lunch just as the train pulled out of Salzburg and hurried back to reclaim their armchairs and order coffee. As O'Gilroy was turning to sit down, the door just behind him banged open and a stout solid man in a high-buttoned dark suit marched in and seemed about to march straight on through O'Gilroy. Then a uniformed arm reached past the marcher and pitched O'Gilroy aside among the chairs. Ranklin stepped back, recognising the blunt face, straight hairline and wide-winged moustache, bowed his head and murmured: "Your Royal Highness." The four men, two in Army uniform, tramped past into the dining area.

O'Gilroy bounced up like a boxer who has been foully tripped. "Jayzus and Mary! I'll have the guts out of – "

Ranklin reached up to lay a restraining hand on his chest. "I don't think you've met the Archduke Franz Ferdinand before, have you? Well, you've met him now. Sit down and have a cognac."

O'Gilroy let himself be pushed, more gently this time, into a chair, and sat there fizzing like an unexploded shell. Ranklin filled the time until their coffee and cognacs arrived by lighting, then relighting, his pipe; it was an unfamiliar French tobacco and he had packed it too loosely.

When O'Gilroy had gulped half his brandy and sipped most of the rest, he had calmed down enough to say: "So that fat dogrobber's the Emperor's son, ye say?"

"No, his nephew, but still the next Emperor. Franz Josef's son committed suicide nearly fifteen years ago (you can take your pick of stories about that one). Then the Empress got murdered a year later. When you think of it, the old boy's had a tough row to hoe. And people respect him: the old-fashioned virtues."

"Like having more manners than a bedbug."

"So I believe."

"Be an interesting day when *that* bastard comes Emperor."

"Ye-es, I fancy it'll take more than a drill-corporal's manner to hold the Monarchy together: the Hungarians loathe him, you'll find. And he's supposed to be one of the War Party – anxious to take on Serbia, even Russia – along with the Army chief, Conrad. But if it doesn't offend you too deeply, I can tell you one sympathetic story about him."

O'Gilroy looked at him with quiet but total disbelief. "Make it with the Little People and pots of gold and mebbe I'll listen."

"He married for love, and not the right woman to be Empress. Just a countess – though she's a duchess now – Sophie Chotek. They tried everything to dissuade him, but he went right ahead. So he had to sign away her right to be Empress and their children's rights to become anything. That's what true love does for you."

"The tears are running down me leg. And what did he give up for himself? – not becoming Emperor, I observe."

"That's true," Ranklin admitted, not having looked at the story from that angle before. "But he became a bit of an outcast. Viennese society's very catty about them, and her in particular. He spends most of his time with the Army."

"God help the Army, then."

That, Ranklin accepted, was a reasonable request. But Franz Ferdinand was presumably heading for Vienna today – and presumably on Army business. Why right now?

Most of the European passengers ended their journey at Vienna, being politely delayed until the Archduke and his colleagues had gone. There was no ceremony, only two men waiting for a quick exchange of salutes and bows, then all striding away through a crowd of dipping heads.

When the other passengers had gone, Ranklin and O'Gilroy got down to stretch their legs and buy newspapers and illustrated magazines: along with news, Ranklin wanted to put faces to the names of Austro-Hungarian society and hierarchy. They were still pacing in slow circles when the Hornbeam entourage arrived: Corinna, Hornbeam himself, daughter Lucy, various well-fed grandees and enough porters to help discover the source of the Nile.

Corinna greeted them. "Evening, boys. Is this the right train for the mysterious East? Don't walk in step, you look like you've been in the Army."

She was a meadow breeze in the warm grimy air of the West-bahnhof and they both grinned as they raised their hats. So did the Chef de Brigade as he saluted and bowed simultaneously – a gesture that only the French can do with conviction.

She recognised him, of course. "Good evening, Monsieur

Claude. Have we got time for coffee before we dress? Hop aboard, boys; what news on the Rivoli?"

They had already been treated as the élite – as they should have been, on that train – but for the next few hours to Budapest Ranklin foresaw they would be the select élite. Probably there still remained the especially select élite treatment, perhaps reserved for polite archdukes, if one ever got born, but Ranklin wasn't complaining. He hopped aboard.

Corinna dictated the seating for dinner, so that Ranklin shared a four-place table with Hornbeam and Lucy whilst she partnered O'Gilroy at a two-seater.

"Do you know Budapest well, Mr Ranklin?" Lucy asked. "Somebody told me it looks a lot like Paris." She had a sharp, intelligent, but not yet sensitive, face and manner. Her dress and hair style were perfect but not quite part of her, as if she were an understudy suddenly called on to play the leading role.

"Budapest's got a number of wide boulevards," Ranklin recalled, "and was mostly built in the last century, so . . . "

"But in Vienna they said it's just a poor imitation of Vienna."

"They would. Yes, there's a lot of rivalry – "

"Do you know Vienna well? I think it's a wonderful place. The people are so gallant and gay, and the palaces! – only they don't let you into them, like in Paris."

"I told you, sweetheart," Hornbeam said, quietly amused, "you'll have to wait until they see the light and become a republic. Then you'll be able to visit the palaces."

"Well, I think it's just mean of them. And the Emperor was out of town and the Archduke. We met a couple of archdukes – did you know there were seventy archhdukes? – but not the wicked Archduke Franzie."

Hornbeam winced; Ranklin said gravely: "The Archduke had lunch in this very dining-car today on his way to Vienna."

"Oh, he *didn't*! What was he like?"

Ranklin thought of referring her to O'Gilroy, but perhaps she was too young. "Very Archducal," he said lamely.

"We'd heard," Hornbeam said, "that he was hunting near Salzburg."

"That's where he got on. You didn't happen to hear why he might be in Vienna just now?"

Hornbeam shook his head, perhaps reluctant to get involved in gossip. But Lucy waded in, lowering her voice and almost licking her lips. "They *say* he has crazy rages sometimes, that's why he has to stay in the country, and people won't go hunting with him because he's shot one servant already and had to hush it up."

"Sweetheart," Hornbeam looked uneasy, "I don't think we should believe every story we heard in Vienna – do you, Mr Ranklin?" he appealed.

"I think one should take most Viennese stories as plots for operettas rather than as factual reports."

"Well, that's what we heard," Lucy said firmly, "and *I* believe there's no smoke without gunfire, *so*. Are you staying in the same hotel as we are, Mr Ranklin? It's on a place called Margaret Island. Do you know it? They say it's very peaceful but right in the middle of the city like living in Central Park . . . "

Just how Lucy had managed to hear anything in Vienna above the sound of her own voice baffled Ranklin. But for the moment he was happy for her to answer her own questions, since his own knowledge of Budapest came from recent reading on top of a brief tourist visit many years before.

The train moved more slowly and swayed more as they trundled out of Europe's drawing-room country and into its darker and more exotic back parlours. Onion- and half-onion-domed churches raised their silhouettes against the darkening sky, and Ranklin watched O'Gilroy watching the landscape jog by, attentive but non-committal.

With Lucy for once trying to be silent, since she was eating a peach, Ranklin had a chance to prompt Hornbeam: "I hear your talks went well in Vienna, sir?"

"Why, yes, I'm inclined to believe they did. And maybe did a little good, too. I think it's time for the countries of Europe to be considering matters of international law right now. Did I understand from Corinna that you were at the Embassy in Paris last week?"

"That's right, sir. I found it fascinating – though I confess some of it was rather deep for me."

Hornbeam smiled benignly and stroked his white moustache. It was the same voice coming across the table as had filled the Embassy ballroom, only the volume was precisely controlled – as you might expect of an experienced lawyer. Ranklin saw why actors and lawyers studied each other's delivery.

"I don't believe in talking down to any audience," Hornbeam said. "My real message is that international law touches us all, and increasingly so, since it grew primarily to govern our conduct in the making of war and the making of trade."

"Very true," Ranklin said, rather over-sincerely. "But tell me, sir, when you discussed intervention in a neighbouring state, did you have any particular situations in mind?"

"No, my boy, I was talking purely of principles. But I know what you're getting at. Back home it's assumed I was referring to Mexico, over here I find it applied to the Monarchy's relations with, in particular, Serbia."

"Do you find that embarrassing?"

"Indeed not. One of the experiences I hope for from this trip is to observe international relations in the field, so to speak, to meet those gentlemen applying such law to their everyday dealings. And perhaps be given the opportunity to comment on those dealings. Law should never become the house rules for life in an ivory tower." He gave a little grunt of satisfaction whenever he felt he had ended on a telling phrase.

Ranklin also grunted, but just as another way of saying "very true". "And it obviously gave you the opportunity to meet some interesting people?"

"We surely did. I believe I can say I met with almost all their leading jurists – but Lucy, of course, was more taken with high society." He smiled indulgently at her and she hastily replaced her napkin in her lap before he could see the stain of lip rouge as well as peach juice.

"Oh, yes, we met Prince Montenuovo: he's the . . . the Chamberlain at their court, and the boss of the Army, von . . . von . . . "

"General Conrad von Hotzendorff, usually just General Conrad."

"That's right. And Colonel Urbanski, I recall his name, and

Herr Schwarzenburg – "

When the waiter asked if they wanted coffee at the table or in the salon, Hornbeam pulled out a large gold watch and calculated. "We should be in Budapest in under two hours and there's sure to be a welcoming committee and hand-shaking – I think I'm going to rest up a while. But you stay on and keep Mr Ranklin company, sweetheart." He got up clutching a legal brief-case that seemed to go everywhere with him.

Lucy looked quickly around the dining-car. "Have you met any interesting people here, Mr Ranklin?"

Since, even if he'd been found "interesting", Ranklin would rather talk to Corinna, he said sadly: "I'm afraid all the interesting people got off at Vienna, Miss Hornbeam."

She wrinkled her nose. "It looks like you're right. They all look like spies – isn't this supposed to be the spies' express? – except you and Mr O'Gilroy, of course. I guess I'll rest up, too."

Ranklin had brought an envelope of papers from Sherring's office, and Corinna picked through them over her coffee to mask their talk as business.

"And how," she asked, "did you get on with Lucy?"

"I listened well."

Her voice got tart. "Lucy is a *very* sweet girl, she just happens to be the type who needs a husband to decide what sort of woman she's going to become."

"I'd suggest 'silent'."

"A husband who knows his own mind, no matter how little of it there is. Like an Army officer."

Ranklin retreated behind a cloud of pipe-smoke, muttering: "Well, let her get on with looking, then."

"What the hell d'you think she's trying to catch around Europe? – smallpox?"

There was silence until O'Gilroy said: "At the end of Round One, the challenger, Matt Ranklin, was carried back to his corner in a bucket."

She burst into laughter. "Oh shut up, Conall. Now, what did you make of Hornbeam himself?"

Ranklin reflected. "He doesn't know much about European

politics, but says he'll be happy to offer them a comment if they'll listen. I can't say that improves my peace of mind."

She nodded. "Yes, if he hadn't got such a good opinion of himself I think he'd be surprised at being invited over. A guy I got speaking to at our Embassy certainly was surprised: said there were several lawyers in Washington and Harvard who were better informed."

"Could it be that his naivety was part of his attraction? – to whomever asked him across. Who did, by the way?"

"Their sort of Bar Association."

"But he was speaking at their Embassy in Paris. He wouldn't be doing that unless somebody high up in their government approved."

"*Everybody* seems to approve, with the people he's been meeting. And it all seems a bit forced for a man who isn't top in his field."

"When ye got a circus come to a small town in Ireland," O'Gilroy recalled, "they always had the Strongest Man In The World with 'em. And sometimes I'd wonder why he wasn't in Dublin or London or Paris instead. But most folks jest liked to believe it."

Corinna smiled a little ruefully. "Yes, society sets out to catch swans, but whatever they catch they'll call it a swan."

Ranklin said: "If all they wanted was to quote him on intervention, the damage is already done. He's said it out loud, in public, on Austrian soil. What more can they want?" Then another thought struck him. "Is anybody making money out of the Strongest Swan In The World?"

"I thought of that. No, he's getting well enough paid, but his lectures are free, by invitation only. I'd be happier if I could see some financial racket going on – but maybe it's nothing more sinister than being nice to influential Americans: Hornbeam's quite a voice in the Republican Party. But with a Democrat just installed in the White House . . . "

"They said they'd met a Colonel Urbanski. Did you?"

"No, I don't recall . . . Who is he?"

"Head of their Secret Service." Corinna's eyes widened; Ranklin went on: "On the other hand, such people take evenings off, like to be seen at society shindigs talking to the right people; colonels want promotion, too."

Corinna sat back, brooding. The parrot-voiced Turk came past, pausing to give her an unmysteriously Eastern look. Her return glance nearly unmanned him.

"Poor Lucy," she sighed. "I fancy this train's headed the wrong way for her ambitions."

"Aren't they breeding plenty of cavalry officers in these parts?" O'Gilroy asked. "Ye could fix her up with one of them. Or his horse, if she wants more high-toned talk."

Corinna gave him a look. "I wasn't being as serious about Lucy's problem as she is herself. Trouble is, too many of her class at school have got English or French titles by now. And most of the Hungarian aristocracy, as I understand it, is broke and landless. So, back to business: how well d'you know Budapest?"

O'Gilroy shook his head, Ranklin said: "Hardly at all."

"Me, too. I guess you don't speak Magyar?"

"Who does?" Magyar was almost unique, related only to Finnish both in its grammar and its utter uselessness outside its own country. Most Hungarians they were likely to meet would speak German, too, but thought of it as the language of tradesmen and Austrians. English and French were acceptably "neutral".

"You're going to be great business advisers," she observed.

"Both the iron business and banking," Ranklin said solemnly, "are, effectively, what one does *not* call cartels. Even the Rothschilds, despite having a branch in Vienna, are losing their part in the government loan business to the German-backed banks. On the other hand, if that's partly anti-Vienna sentiment, there could be room for an American player."

"It's light industry they're short on," O'Gilroy said, just as solemnly. "D'ye know they can only make clothes for a third of the population? And God knows it doesn't take much money to start a sweat-shop, nor run one, neither."

"You boys have been doing your homework," Corinna admitted, smiling broadly. "But remember your real job is to turn your nasty suspicious minds on whether somebody is really trying to swing something by using Hornbeam."

Ranklin said nothing. Their real job was being spies for the Bureau, and she couldn't think they were for private hire. But they had accepted Sherring hospitality – did that limit their scope, the risks they could take with involving the Sherring name? He began to feel awkward.

She sensed that and said reassuringly: "I'm sure you'll behave like perfect gentlemen. Now I'm going to change out of this finery before we arrive."

O'Gilroy quickly grabbed her small travelling bag, kneading it briefly in his hands before passing it to her.

She smiled. "Yes, I still carry it on journeys like this. I believe virtue is its own reward, but a Colt's Navy Model also helps."

41

It was another bright day when Ranklin and O'Gilroy came down to breakfast on the hotel terrace, or at least a well-trampled area of dust surrounded by trees. They were led to a large table in the centre under a spreading plane tree: obviously for the Hornbeam party, although so far there were just two men there, both unfamiliar, both drinking coffee, reading the same copy of the morning paper and arguing good-naturedly about it. They got hastily to their feet and introduced themselves.

The squat dark one in a dark suit was Dr Johann Klapka, the thinner, younger fair one in a rumpled light suit was Stefan Hazay.

"You," Klapka suggested, "are the Englishmen?"

"Yes and no. No for Conall O'Gilroy, he's Irish, yes for me, I'm Matthew Ranklin." Everybody bowed and shook hands, then sat down again and Klapka issued orders for, Ranklin hoped, breakfast.

"And I believe you work for Mr Reynard Sherring? Very interesting. Are you looking for investments? – perhaps I can help you." Klapka was quite exceptionally ugly, despite having a third of his face hidden by a black moustache, but his cheerful quick expression and movements – followed, reluctantly and out of step, by his sober suit – made it unimportant.

Ranklin smiled but said firmly: "That's up to Mrs Finn. We await her orders."

"Then do not let Stefan hear your orders, or all will be published in his newspaper." He waved the morning paper. "But he will get it wrong, as ever, so it will not matter."

Ranklin felt smug that, mainly from the piece of bordello curtain

295

the young man wore as a necktie, he had identified Hazay as either a poet or a journalist – which in Budapest, he recalled, were often the same thing.

O'Gilroy said: "And what d'ye do yourself, Doctor?"

"Of course, I am a Doctor of Law. I am to help, to guide, Professor Hornbeam. Have you met Professor Hornbeam before?"

O'Gilroy shook his head. "Only on the train last night. But Matt heard him speak in Paris."

Hazay asked diffidently: "Do you know if his lectures in Vienna were the same as in Paris?" His English was better than Klapka's, and Ranklin suspected the puzzled diffidence was purely professional.

"I think Paris was a rehearsal, so I imagine it was much the same. Are you here to interview him?"

"If he'll talk to me. I only want some facts about his career."

Just then the coffee arrived and Ranklin grabbed his cup. "I don't know more than I read in the Paris papers, and can't recall much of that."

"Do you think he believes he has a message for us? – or for Europe?" Hazay had a way of putting a question that suggested it was already there, needing to be answered, none of his making.

But all Ranklin said was: "Ask him." Then added: "Or his daughter Lucy – here they all come." Corinna leading and looking very vivid with her black hair, wide smile and dark red skirt, Lucy, Hornbeam and a tall woman in her thirties who held herself with the buxom stiffness of a ship's figurehead.

She might have been at the station last night, but so had half Budapest. Now she was introduced as the Baroness Schramm, Hornbeam's interpreter and secretary, who had come on from Vienna by an earlier train. By the time the introductions had been made and they had sat down again, Ranklin and O'Gilroy had got themselves reasonably isolated.

"What're we doing, then?" O'Gilroy asked between mouthfuls.

"Having a look round the town, I suppose, but after that . . . "

"Not much to see of it from here." From either side came the hoot of ferries and tugs on the Danube, but there was no glimpse of them nor the twin cities of Buda and Pest on the banks beyond. Their view was a choice of the hotel – or trees. It was indeed isolated, and by more than just trees: they were almost the length of the island, about a mile, from the bridge that led to both the Buda and Pest sides. Ranklin wondered if somebody had planned for Hornbeam to be so much out of touch.

Corinna, smiling brightly and enjoying the bustle of organisation, sat down beside them. "Orders for the day – is that what you say? Anyhow, Hornbeam's staying here to talk to Dr Klapka about Hungarian law. Lucy and I are going shopping. Hornbeam's lunch-ing with the American Consul General at some club, Lucy-and I will be at a new café called the New York, remember Hornbeam goes to a lawyers' dinner tonight, none of us invited, maybe we'll go to the opera – okay, Conall, you don't have to – then his big lecture at the Palace tomorrow – " she raised her voice suddenly: "So you see Miklos at the bank, and if he's got any queries let him telegraph Pop in Paris. Have you met Mr Hazay?"

The journalist was standing beside them, looking diffident again. "I have a fiacre waiting to take me back to Pest, if you gentlemen care to . . . "

"Why not? " Corinna said. "A penny saved – Lucy and I aren't ready yet. See you at the New York if you've anything to report."

Being bossed about by a woman, and an American at that, was a near-perfect disguise for British spies, Ranklin decided – and then wondered if he was deciding that just to salve his dignity. But it was true anyway.

A fiacre was just a two-horse four-wheeler like a British victoria, except that both the horses and the driver thought they were in the Hungarian cavalry. By the time they were slowed by the toll-house on the Margaret bridge, even O'Gilroy, with his Irish love of fast horses, was wishing he'd staked his money and not his life on this pair.

That was where the city really began, sweeping away down-stream with the gentle curve of the wide and busy Danube. On the right were the short steep hills of Buda: Castle Hill with the palace and old town, with the true fortress of the Citadel lowering from the crest beyond. Opposite, behind the wharves and jetties of the left bank, was the neo-Gothic Parliament, far more impressive than anything its politicians were allowed to decide. And behind that, the flat city of Pest with its houses, factories, shops – and banks.

"Which bank do you wish to visit?" Hazay called above the clatter of hooves on cobbles.

Ranklin had been silently cursing Corinna for her glib "Miklos at the bank": an improvised lie is a petard lurking to explode later underfoot. But he hoped he had solved it: Sherring had given him a letter of credit on the Hungarian Commercial Bank in Ferencz-Jozsef Square, so he could draw some korona there, hand in the wad of notes to be cabled to their Versailles account – and all that should take as long as an imaginary interview with the imaginary "Miklos".

"If you leave us in the square," he said, "you can take the cab on to your office."

"There is no hurry – for me. Perhaps I can show you some of our city? But we walk, no?"

Perhaps to Hazay's surprise, and certainly to O'Gilroy's, Ranklin agreed, and they waited for him at a nearby café. But if they were there to pick up information, Ranklin reasoned, where better to start than a bright and talkative journalist? He must know things he couldn't print but might like to gossip away.

Hazay's idea of sightseeing was remarkably relaxing. He stood in the square and pointed out the beloved Chain Bridge, which led off it and across to a tunnel under the Palace to the South Station (in the west, since, as he explained, the West Station was in the north). He then named the statues in the square – von Eötvös, Deák and Széchenyi – nodded at the Academy of Sciences and police headquarters as they passed them for a quick tour of the Museum of Commerce, then back through the square and along the river on the Ferencz-Jozsef Quay.

It had taken barely half an hour and Ranklin wasn't sure his cultural appetite hadn't been deeply insulted, but he recalled the Quay as being one of the pleasantest boulevards in Europe. Tree- and café-lined, it was as if a one-sided Champs-Elysées had been laid out along the Seine – and shorn of its new motor showrooms as well.

He was just savouring this when somebody tried to drive a herd of pigs through the side of a tram, and the romantic image got a little clouded. But he had quite forgotten the music that was everywhere: violins and pianos from the cafés, even this early, a gypsy band on a pleasure steamer, street musicians with cornets and urchins with fifes. It gave the whole city the sound of a smile.

They had strolled no more than half a mile when Hazay led them to a café table in a triangle of trees around yet another bronze statue.

"Who's the gentleman?" O'Gilroy asked.

"Sándor Petöfi, the poet and soldier." Hazay's face had lost its diffidence. "He was killed in . . . 1849," translating figures is always tricky; "fighting the Russians."

"Who were helping the Habsburgs keep control of Hungary," Ranklin said unemotionally.

"That is right. He wrote then, the year before . . . " They waited as his face twisted in the effort of more translation; "he wrote:

'Liberty, in this . . . faithless time,

We have been your . . . thy . . . last and only faithful sons.'

I am sorry I do not translate it very well."

But it had been quite good enough for O'Gilroy, who was nodding gravely. "I like the sound of that."

The waiter brought their coffee, a plate of cream cakes and a newspaper. Hazay was immediately apologetic again: "Excuse, please, but I must see if in a Vienna newspaper there is a report . . . " Eyes and hands flickering, he went through the paper in thirty seconds, then tossed it down.

"No. I had thought perhaps a journalist I know there, that he would have found something – but no." He smiled at their politely blank faces and explained: "When he can find one thing, then I can write how it will affect Hungary. You see?"

O'Gilroy looked blank, knowing nothing of the journalistic round of liar-dice where one took another's story, added a fresh twist and republished it as new, so that another could take it, add a twist . . . Ranklin, more newspaper-wise, smiled politely and said: "It must be an important matter to affect all Hungary."

"It is still the affair of Colonel Redl. You have read about that?"

"Oh, something in the papers." He turned to O'Gilroy and asked blandly: "Did you?"

"Sure, something." The problem was that neither of them could now separate what was public knowledge from what they had picked up on the professional grapevine in Brussels. So they both put on expressions of interested ignorance.

"It has caused much trouble in our Parliaments and Minister Krobatin has tried to stop our Budapest papers from publishing so much . . . " He shrugged. "So we send it to Munich or Paris and then we can publish here that it is quite untrue what Munich and Paris say that Colonel Redl had given all our plans and codes for war to the Russians, and General Conrad did not lie to Parliament, he is an honourable man . . . our readers understand."

This "revelation by denial" was itself news to Ranklin. But in a country with official censorship – and probably a lot of unofficial pressure as well – journalists would need crafts beyond the mere stringing together of words.

"And do you know what secrets Redl did give to the Russians?" he asked.

"But no. The Army does not know – it gave Redl no time to confess. So General Conrad *did* lie to Parliament when he said the secrets Redl gave were not important, because he cannot be sure."

O'Gilroy said: "The Army should know what Redl knew. Then it would know what he might have given away."

"Of course." Hazay nodded emphatically. "But as deputy to military intelligence, he would know much. And as chief of staff to an army corps, the new work he had just moved to, he must know that Corps' plans for war, perhaps all the Army's plans."

"All in all," Ranklin summed up, "it sounds a good reason not to risk a war with Russia over Serbia just now."

"But yes," Hazay agreed. "You are interested in our politics, no?"

Ranklin was taken aback. O'Gilroy hastily rescued him, his voice muffled by cream cake: "Since when was politics and profit sleeping in different beds?"

"But of course."

"And who's pushing for war?" Ranklin asked, hoping it was a logical question at that point. "Apart from Archduke Franzie, of course."

"General Conrad, yes. Always. He would solve everything to send in the Army. Your wife is unfaithful? – send in the Army. A fly has bitten you? – send in the Army. And the Minister of War, Krobatin, you know? – and General Georgi . . . But the Archduke; he made Conrad Chief of Staff, it was said, so we think he believes as Conrad – but who really knows what a pig thinks except 'More mud, please,'?"

O'Gilroy was listening enchanted to this Hungarian view of Viennese authority – and of the Archduke, of course.

"Do you believe," Ranklin asked, "these stories about the Archduke's madness? Shooting a servant and so on?"

Hazay pondered, frowning, then decided to be frank. "I want to believe anything of the Archduke – but also I believe nothing that is said in Austria. So I have a problem, no?" He grinned.

"Well, if it's any help, he didn't look too mad yesterday."

Suddenly wary, Hazay asked: "Do you know the Archduke?"

O'Gilroy said abruptly: "Met him."

"He and his party tried to walk over us on the train," Ranklin explained. "Coming to Vienna."

"*He* was going to there?" Hazay was so eager that for a moment Ranklin feared he had let slip some self-betraying secret. But no, he reassured himself, it's just journalistic enthusiasm. I hope.

"Last evening; he got on at Salzburg."

"Who was with him? – please."

"Three men. Two in Army uniform. One – I'm not good at ranks – could have been a colonel."

"Colonel Doctor Bardolff, his aide." Hazay was blinking with excitement. "So he is today in Becs . . . " The Magyar name for Vienna seemed to sum up the attitude: "operatic, enchanting Becs" – it just wasn't quite the same. "Excuse, please, I have work – I will pay – "

"No, no, Mr Reynard Sherring will pay," Ranklin said expansively.

Hazay grinned. "Thank you. I buy him coffee, or beer, soon – yes? Excuse." He strode away.

O'Gilroy gazed after him. "Are we missing the main event somehow, then?"

"God knows, I think it's just journalism. Anyway, we gave him the tip so he should feel he owes us anything he finds out. I think we should stay – accidentally – in touch. But if he's still picking over Redl's bones after – what? nearly three months? – he's not making any friends in high places."

"Seems he's got most of the tale anyhow. Jest not how long the Colonel'd been working for the Russkies and the name of the Russkie himself Bat-what-was-it."

"Batjuschin. And Plan Three."

"Now, Captain, that was just talk. Nobody told us for sure he'd given away Plan Three. How would they know? – without the Russkies up and said it."

"Hmm. Well, I wouldn't risk an attack on Serbia if there was even a whisper the Russians might have the blueprint of it."

"Ah, if yer dragging common sense into it . . . And what are we doing now?"

Ranklin looked at his watch. "It's an hour and a half until we join the ladies – assuming we do. I'd better read the financial pages of any German-language papers, you could go and look at the shops. You'd better have some money."

O'Gilroy looked disdainfully at the grubby ten- and twenty-korona notes. "I know," Ranklin said, "but the bank was short of gold coins." He paused. "And *that's* not a good sign, either."

42

The New York café occupied the ground and basement corner of the New York building, mostly taken up by newspaper and publishing offices which liked the flavour of the name. America was clearly the Promised Land of Hungary and for hundreds of thousands who had emigrated there (some must have done well: how about persuading them to invest in their old country, with Sherring as the middleman? Damn it, Ranklin thought, I'm *thinking* like a blasted financier now. He dropped the idea).

Corinna and Lucy were drinking coffee at a small marble table under cascading chandeliers and the most thoroughly neo-Baroque ceiling Ranklin had ever seen; even a South American general couldn't have more twiddly gilt bits on him. Nor did it do anything to hush the political arguments which raged in normal Budapest fashion at most of the other tables without quite drowning the gypsy band.

"Is New York really like this?" Ranklin bellowed.

"No," Corinna shrieked back. "There you get silence at these prices. Hold it – " to a waiter who was bringing more chairs; she pointed to the floor; " – let's go downstairs and eat."

Down there, at least the political debate was interrupted by chewing and swallowing, though they were nearer the band.

"And how was the morning?" Ranklin asked politely. "I don't see you weighed down with parcels."

"You haven't seen the cloakroom," Corinna said.

"There really wasn't a *thing* to buy," Lucy complained.

"But we bought it anyway."

"What are we eating?" O'Gilroy asked. He had taken one look at the menu and laid it aside; even in translation it would mean nothing.

Ranklin said: "Something with pork and paprika and sour cream. Unless, of course, they've got something without pork and paprika and sour cream."

Corinna laid down her own menu. "I just love decisive men. Go ahead and order for us. Good practice," she added, "since you're taking Lucy out to dinner tonight while her father gives the private lecture. And Conall and I go over those import tariff figures."

Ranklin managed to smile at Lucy and say: "I'll be honoured," hoping Corinna got a quite different message about bloody impertinence and impromptu lies.

"I want," Lucy said, eyes bright, "to see a *real* gypsy haunt in the old town."

Well, you're not ruddy well going to; you're going to see a faked-up tourist version like everybody else because I'm not eating stewed cat and getting into knife fights just to please you. I need Hazay or Dr Klapka to recommend a place.

He smiled grimly at Corinna and ordered Gulasch for the four of them. "By the way, did you know that the German for 'field kitchen' is 'Gulaschkanone'?"

When they were waiting for an after-lunch coffee, Lucy took herself off to the ladies' room. Ranklin promptly leant across the table and hissed: "And why am I escorting her this evening? – am I to marry her off to a gypsy fiddler?"

Corinna smiled brightly. "No, no, I just want her out of the way while Conall and I burgle Hornbeam's room."

O'Gilroy woke up. "We do?"

"Well, probably more you than me – but I can keep watch, and his suite's next to mine."

"And what'll we be looking for?" O'Gilroy demanded.

"Look," Corinna turned serious, "Lucy's been rattling on about the Baroness who's taking up all of Hornbeam's time and some document he's got – probably from her – that's terribly terribly secret. That he doesn't want Lucy shouting from the rooftops, anyhow. I just think we ought to know what it is, that's all, so I thought while he's out lecturing . . . "

Ranklin was – had become – in favour of looking at secret documents, but: "Would it be too much of a strain to make ideas like this just *suggestions* until we've actually heard them?"

"Well, I started by *suggesting* to her that you could take her out and she said 'Why not just tell him to – he works for you, doesn't he?' She has a charmingly direct manner."

"Splendid. If there's one thing they appreciate in real gypsy haunts it's a charmingly direct manner."

Corinna's dark eyes got several shades darker. "You bring that dear girl home totally unharmed or I'll change your marriage prospects with a meat-axe. Is that understood?"

"You make yourself, if I may say so, almost vulgarly clear," Ranklin said in his most County voice, feeling a little better.

Finding Hazay again was easier than Ranklin had expected, since the café upstairs turned out to be infested with writers. This surprised him, but then he wondered if the management regarded them as an attraction to customers and whittled the price of their coffees accordingly; anything was possible in a city which put up statues to poets.

Within moments of the maître d'hotel passing on his request the room was an uproar of debate about where Hazay was last seen or might now be; within minutes Ranklin was speaking to him (where, he never knew) by telephone.

"I know of the place you must go," Hazay assured him. "The Panna Tavern."

"Splendid; would you care to join us?" Ranklin was eager to share the load of entertaining Lucy. "With Mr Sherring paying, of course."

"I begin to like your millionaire. Thank you, it is most kind. The Tavern is on Castle Hill, you go past . . . "

Ranklin and O'Gilroy got back to Margaret Island by a steam ferry that zigzagged from bank to bank just as the Kiel harbour ferries had done. Despite the river's width, they were butting against a fierce current – five knots, O'Gilroy estimated – and Ranklin noticed that the few rowing boats crept along in the shelter of the banks and jetties. How on earth had they managed in the days of sail?

The ferry put them down on a jetty only a brief walk through the trees from the hotel. There Ranklin announced they were back, in case anybody wanted them, then went outside again and flopped at a café table, already exhausted by the sun and the prospect of the evening.

O'Gilroy had managed to order lemon tea and cream cakes. "Lot of old folk around," he commented.

"Probably taking the cure." Ranklin nodded towards the up-stream tip of the island: "The building over there is a hot springs bath-house; Budapest's full of them. And the villas on the other side are probably mostly nursing homes."

"What does it cure?" O'Gilroy asked uneasily, having a primitive fear of illness.

"Your cash surplus." Ranklin's prejudices were more modern.

O'Gilroy smiled and relaxed. Hornbeam and the Baroness Schramm came out of the hotel, chattering like old friends, and sat at a nearby table.

"Good afternoon," Hornbeam called cheerily, at peace with the world. "Are you finding any time for sight-seeing?"

"Fitting it into the cracks, sir," Ranklin the diligent businessman called back, and smiled at the Baroness. But whoever she was at peace with, it wasn't him.

"Old biddy," O'Gilroy muttered. He sipped his tea. "So what've we learnt to keep Uncle Charlie happy?"

"Not much," Ranklin admitted. "The Redl case is still making news, people are hoarding gold; I wonder if the price of horses has gone up? – that's the other sign of a belief in war. No, it's the Consulate's job to report things like that. Perhaps you'll turn up something interesting in Hornbeam's papers tonight." Although privately he doubted it. "Perhaps we should be taking the business side and the Sherring link more seriously; such people have already got the international links and quick communications that the Bureau needs. Big money carves deep and secret rivers."

"I'm thinking ye mean 'canals', but 'rivers' is more of poetry." O'Gilroy was secretly amused at seeing the reluctant spy getting involved in how the Bureau was run.

"You know what I mean." Ranklin was annoyed at himself for

the flowery phrase. "My God, if we had the spy service people like the Rothschilds must have . . . "

The hotel wasn't really of millionaire standard and had probably been surprised at having such distinguished Americans thrust upon it. But the result was one that not even millionaires can count on buying: it tried. It had clearly stripped its unused rooms to cram their suites and the public rooms with the best furniture, polished its silver and bribed its staff until one shone and the other tried to.

In the evening, the guests naturally gathered in the lobby with its verandah and the cool, if not quite sanitary, wind that filtered through the trees from the river.

"For Heaven's sake," Ranklin was imploring Corinna, "don't let Lucy overdress. It won't be that sort of place. I'm going in a lounge suit."

"Is this the end of the empire? I thought Englishmen dressed for dinner in the jungle."

"If we were only going to meet monkeys, I wouldn't be bothered."

O'Gilroy wandered out onto the verandah to join them, a waiter at his heels like an eager dog. Ranklin took the opportunity to order another whisky.

"You'd better take my automobile," Corinna said disapprovingly. "You won't be fit to do much walking."

"Car?" Then Ranklin wished he hadn't asked: where Corinna went, could a hired car be far behind?

"He'll be here at seven; I'll have Lucy ready by then. Conall, try and keep him sober."

In fact, Ranklin was manipulating himself, trying to believe the evening would be so boring that it was bound to be better than he feared. And that he would be cheerful and talkative as a result. The whisky was insurance.

"About this secret document," he said. "You're sure there's no other way of getting a look at it?"

Corinna made a face. "Lucy says he keeps it in that briefcase – " And Ranklin could remember Hornbeam clutching it on the train; " – I guess we could hire some highwaymen to rob him when he goes . . . "

"All right, all right. You can burgle his room – if O'Gilroy thinks it's safe. He's in charge. And if he says No, then No it stays."

She began to pout.

"If you get caught," Ranklin said quickly, "and there's a rumpus, with you they'll say 'Girls will be girls' and assume it was O'Gilroy leading you astray. And even if Hornbeam doesn't get legal with us, from then on O'Gilroy, and I, will be under suspicion. The hotel may tell the police, they may become interested in us . . . we'd be better off on the next train back to Paris."

If you could persuade Corinna that she was wrong, that was an end to it. She wasted no time on grudges or regrets: that idea's dead, let's get on with the next. "You're right, of course. Okay, Conall, I'll take my time from you."

O'Gilroy smiled – partly from relief, Ranklin thought. He must have seen the risks himself, but just didn't know how to say so to someone like Corinna.

43

To find the roots of a continental city, look for the easily defended: the high ground, or the river-as-moat. Or in Buda, both. The rambling flat-topped ridge of Castle Hill rose only a few hundred feet above the river, but it rose sharply, stiffened by thick walls that by now seemed to grow out of the rock. The wide river hurried past less than a quarter of a mile away below, and from the ramparts a single field gun would dominate the whole area of Pest on the far side.

Behind the walls was a city in miniature, complete in grandeur and squalor. The Royal Palace with its eight hundred and sixty recently refurbished rooms waited for the Emperor to recall that he was also Hungary's King and drop in for a night, the Coronation Church (where he had dropped in long enough to be crowned, over sixty years ago) studded with needle spires like a startled hedgehog, a host of ministries, barracks, town houses originally built by Turkish merchants and alleyways that once housed the Danube fishermen.

And the Panna Tavern.

Hazay had met Ranklin's request perfectly. They entered from a crooked alleyway through a door in an ironbound gate, already plodding against a frothing tide of violin music. And there ahead of them, at the end of a small courtyard crammed with tables, was a vine-roofed bandstand with a gypsy band sawing and strumming for dear life. Or cash.

A waiter, obviously familiar with, and primed by, Hazay weaved them through the crowd to a side table with chairs for six. Seeing

Ranklin's surprise, Hazay explained: "I thought Miss Hornbeam would like to meet some of my friends – poets, writers – who might come by. If not," he shrugged and smiled, "they will go away."

"Why, I'd just love to meet your friends," Lucy smiled back, and Ranklin relaxed. Unless somebody found a cat bone in their chicken, the evening looked like being a success. He raised his wineglass and silently wished equal success to Hornbeam's lecture – and the burglary of his room.

"Of course they are all real gypsies," Hazay was telling Lucy. "Who will pretend to be a . . . an outcast, a wanderer, a thief? Myself," he added wickedly, "I do not believe the stories in the country villages that they are also blood-sucking – vampires – and cannibals."

Lucy was listening, wide-eyed, and Hazay was enjoying himself: gypsies were a journalist's dream people since whatever you said about them somebody had said – and believed – before, so you were only reporting, not inventing. The music swirled about them, alternately wild tavern dances and slow melancholy tunes that the locals seemed to soak up and appreciate without for one moment stopping their eating and arguing.

"Czermak, he was a nobleman who took his violin and joined the gypsies," Hazay was saying, "and Czinka Panna – this café is named for her – she was most rare, a woman violinist, that was nearly two centuries ago, and the great Bihari . . . who knows who was the best? Their music was never written down, nobody alive has heard them play, now it is only memories of memories . . . "

The band-leader violinist had worked his way towards them, playing a tune for each table that asked. He was authentically dark and swarthy, but short and tubby, too; Ranklin recognised his own unromantic shape. But when Hazay tore a banknote in two, licked one half (you're a braver man than I am, Ranklin thought) and stuck it to the leader's forehead and he began to play, he seemed to grow in dignity and even height. The music flowed out of him like a familiar tale from a natural storyteller. That was all it was, a simple retelling of simple musical emotions, and if the magic was in the ear of the behearer – and in the wine in the behearer, too – then Lucy seemed ready to settle for that.

The band-leader finished, got the second half of the banknote, and moved on with a deep bow to Lucy. Then they realised that two of the spare chairs were occupied, a new bottle of wine was on the table, and Hazay did the introductions. Miro was small, dark, with a thin face and jerky expressions, as if afraid he would be late with the appropriate one. Tibor was large, slow, bear-like, with what seemed like a fringe of fur rather than beard on his face. Both appeared to be that vague age of old students and young poets; Mitteleuropa café philosophers, Ranklin thought unkindly, not welcoming the effort of new acquaintances this late.

They greeted Lucy with great warmth, quickly establishing that she (a) thought Budapest was wonderful, and (b) didn't know Tibor's cousin in Brooklyn. But their real interest seemed to be in Hazay.

"Miro's worried about the peace talks in Bucharest," Tibor explained, as Miro and Hazay chattered quickly in Magyar. "Stefan knows all the latest news, and Miro is writing a poem."

"A poem?" Lucy couldn't see the connection; Tibor looked surprised at her surprise.

Ranklin intervened: "If he'd said a speech or an article, you wouldn't have thought it odd. Well, here a poem does the same thing."

Tibor beamed at Ranklin. "Yes, you understand. Why not a poem?"

"Why not?" Lucy agreed, smiling.

"He blames the warmongers in Vienna for urging Bulgaria into starting the war she has just lost . . . "

Miro broke off from Hazay to explain, found his English wasn't quick enough for his thoughts and switched into German, with Tibor interpreting: "No, he blames Russia – I am sorry, he blames both. Both wanted the war . . . Vienna wanted Bulgaria to win, Russia wanted her to lose, why? . . . I understand, so Turkey would grab back Adrianople herself but it will cause less trouble to take it from Turkey, who has no friends – "

"Except the Kaiser," Hazay suggested.

" – than from Bulgaria." Miro muttered something, Hazay laughed and Tibor tried to translate: "He says to . . . to do something rude to the Kaiser. That will not be in his poem, I think."

Miro said more.

" . . . so the Habsburgs and the Romanovs act in one royal conspiracy for opposite reasons . . . the sufferer is the ordinary soldier who has no illusions, who knows he will die on the battlefield . . . Pigshit!" Tibor bellowed. "The one illusion a soldier has is that we will live through anything! If he thinks he is going to die, he runs away!"

Nobody seemed to notice the shout except Lucy, and Ranklin who was thinking: so Tibor's been a soldier. But with conscription, so had every man in the café except the gypsy band and, it seemed, Miro. Now he sat silent and frowning, presumably recasting a verse.

Ranklin took advantage of the lull to ask Hazay: "What is the news of the peace conference?"

Hazay put on his diffident smile. "The Great Powers want a part in the final decision . . . "

"Ha! Let them stay out," Tibor grunted. "They were six months in London to make new frontiers and how long did they last? – six days. And if Miro is right, already two of your Great Powers worked to destroy the treaty before it is signed even."

"Count Berchtold says . . . "

"Tbe Foreign Minister in Vienna," Ranklin whispered to Lucy.

"I *know*," Lucy didn't whisper back.

" . . . he says that any agreement reached without Austria-Hungary can only be provisional."

"Let the Balkans settle their own frontiers," Tibor growled.

"That was what this last war was for, no?" Hazay said.

Ranklin felt he ought to say something; just sitting and listening could arouse suspicion. But he was pretty sure that anything he said would be wrong.

"No frontiers are ever going to be completely just," he said cautiously. "Or where do you stop before every village, every house, is a nation? The Balkans need to start exporting things they can sell, not just nationalist fervour."

Miro glared at him, pale-faced and dark-eyed; he obviously understood English better than he spoke it, and gabbled out an answer.

Tibor interpreted again: "He asks do you want a life of comfort or a road to travel? Do you want an armchair or a cause?"

Ranklin felt himself being dragged into the whirlpool. "Europe's elephant country. If you startle the elephants in Vienna and Berlin and Paris and St Petersburg – "

"And London?" Hazay suggested.

"Yes, and London, too – into a stampede, they won't watch where they put their feet."

Tibor leant his big arms on the table. "So, your fine grey men in London will tell these peoples that nationalism is dangerous, hey? These peoples whose *nationalism* has liberated them from four hundred years of Turkish rule? Come again in four hundred more years and tell them then – if you can also tell them how to untangle the flags of liberty and nationalism."

Yes, Ranklin thought sadly, I *was* wrong. Oh, I was *right*, but so in his own way is Tibor – and so, in many ways, are so many others. And suddenly, before he realised why, he felt a terrible fear, as if the courtyard had vanished to leave him alone in a vast cold desert.

Until that moment, like anyone else thinking about a European war, he had wondered what might start it. But he should have been like the man in the story who, shown Niagara Falls for the first time and told proudly how many millions of gallons of water poured over it, had asked simply: "What's to stop it?"

"Perhaps," he said, looking over their heads, perhaps to reassure himself of the courtyard walls; "we all have this disease of war. Only we're not showing all the symptoms yet and we haven't started dying." He looked at Tibor. "You and I could be enemies tomorrow."

Tibor sat back, smiling uneasily. "You would be a soldier?"

"For my nationalism? Oh yes. As you would for yours."

Hazay said: "Each on top of your elephant."

They grabbed the silly image gratefully and roared with laughter, then poured more wine and Ranklin offered round his case of English cigarettes and everyone lit one – even Lucy.

But after one more glass, Miro had to get away to his poem, and Tibor decided to go with him. He shook Ranklin's hand and then, on an impulse, hugged him. "So," he said, standing back, "we must meet at Philippi."

"Perhaps we'll neither of us find the way."

They took the evening with them. Ranklin paid the bill,

watching Hazay's expression to make sure he got the complicated division of the tip right, while Lucy asked: "Will he get his poem published?"

"Somewhere," Hazay said. "Perhaps not in *Nyugat*, but in some magazine. I will help if it is needed. And," he smiled at Ranklin, "if you wish to write a poem in answer, I will translate it for you."

And even when it seemed I was being honest, Ranklin thought, I was just hiding the fact that I am already your enemy. That's why I'm here.

"Thank you, but no. Poetry isn't really my style," he said.

44

The car was waiting for them in the square by the church, but Ranklin led the way past it to a bit of neo-Gothic nonsense called the Fishermen's Bastion. It was being built when Ranklin was last in Budapest and was nothing more than a lookout point across the river to Pest, but elaborated with steps, parapets, arches and needle spires.

"Why Fishermen's?" Lucy asked.

"They used to live around here, and their Guild had the job of defending this stretch of the city wall against besiegers. I don't know if they ever did, but that's the story."

"Everything seems to be war: wars in the past, wars just down the road now, war tomorrow . . . "

"I'm afraid that's Europe for you." It wasn't an answer. Perhaps he had hoped to see an answer in the peaceful twinkling lights of the city that, at night, could be any city with its ordinary butchers and bakers and candlestick-makers. But the view did the opposite: just emphasised how small and lonely their island of lights was, how endless the dark plain that surrounded it.

Lucy seemed to pick up the thought. "But why, why start a war in the middle of all this?" She gestured at the lights. "I know the politics are dreadfully complicated, but . . . "

"That might be one reason. I think a lot of people, ordinary people, in most European countries, feel that things are getting too complicated: that a simple outright war will clear the air."

"Would it?" she asked doubtfully.

"I don't know – it doesn't seem the best of reasons for a war."

She turned away towards the car. "If there is a war, would you really become a soldier?"

"Yes."

"But aren't you too old?" she asked with that charmingly direct manner Corrinna had mentioned.

Ranklin winced. "Well, I was a soldier – once. They'd probably take me back."

"An officer? I thought you had to be terribly grand to be an English officer."

"In the Guards or Cavalry, yes, but we've got generals who've risen from the ranks. Not that I did. But I wasn't a general, either."

"Why did you leave?"

"Oh – for a change. Nothing much happens in an army in peacetime."

They climbed into the back of the car, which started with a jerk towards the Vienna Gate.

"And how long have you known Corinna?" Lucy asked.

"Just a few months – since I started working for her father."

"Has she told you anything about her husband – Mr Finn?"

"No – " The word had trouble getting out of Ranklin's throat. He coughed. "Why should she?"

"Oh, you just seemed very friendly. I wondered if she'd told you anything."

"No." Then the oddness of her question sank in. "Don't you know him?"

"No. I heard – she didn't tell me – I *heard* he'd died in the San Francisco fire of '06. Either that or he keeps missing the train back, because I've known her nearly five years and never met him."

Ranklin put his hands on the seat to brace himself, and not only against the swaying of the car as they wound down off the Hill. I'll be damned, he thought dizzily: which of us is supposed to be leading a secret life?

"Mind," Lucy prattled on, "I don't blame her for not letting on his position's vacant, if it is. She'd have every fortune-hunter in Europe lining up at her door."

"Oh, yes, quite," Ranklin said brightly.

"But I think it's time she married again and settled down. It doesn't seem real *ladylike* to be so involved in business matters. I

sometimes feel quite ashamed with her when she starts talking
stocks and bonds to men."

Ranklin almost threw her out of the car. Shamed of Corinna?
You damnable little brat. I've changed my mind about what husband you need: it's one who wallops the daylight out of you for his
morning exercise.

Evening, too, he added.

When his feelings had simmered down, he said: "Really? I don't
find it unattractive for a woman to know something of the world
outside the drawing-room."

"Oh, but *real* men don't like it," she said with hobnailed confidence. "They like a lady to be sweet and scatter-brained."

I truly believe, Ranklin thought grimly, that you'll wind up with
the sort of husband I hope for you.

"And what will happen," Lucy went on, "when Pop Sherring
dies or gets too old? Can you see Corinna running the House of
Sherring? I don't think the law allows it. And quite right."

"Doesn't she have any brothers?"

"Oh, there's Andrew, but he's always doing things with ma-
chines. He's got no head for business. A great disappointment.
That's why Corinna has to be both hostess and business partner for
Pop."

"And Mrs Sherring?"

"Why, she divorced him years ago, it was in *all* the newspapers,
he had so many lady-friends and I don't mean ladies and I don't
mean just friends. Why, you don't know anything, do you?"

But I'm learning, Ranklin thought dazedly. I'm learning.

Corinna, O'Gilroy and the hotel's best coffee pot were waiting as
Lucy bounced in calling gaily: "Hello there, we've had a great
evening, we went to the weirdest place and met the weirdest
people; they write poems about politics – can you believe that? Is
Daddy back?"

"He just got in," Corinna said, smiling – perhaps a little relieved. "I think he's in the lounge with the Baroness."

"Oh, that old crow. I'll soon get rid of her." She turned back to
Ranklin and became formal. "Thank you kindly for a most enjoy-
able evening, Mr Ranklin. No – Matt; I can call you Matt now,

can't I? Thank you. Good night, all."

Corinna eyed Ranklin. "She can call you Matt now, hey?"

"She can call me anything she likes as long as she's saying goodbye."

She began to get stern, then relented. "Yes, you do look kind of ragged. Would you like some coffee?"

"No, I would like a real drink. I've had quite enough and I want some more." He collapsed into a sun-bleached basket chair already full of cushions while O'Gilroy aimed some well-practised sign language at a waiter.

Corinna stood up; she wore a very simple evening dress in burgundy silk and hardly any jewellery – dressing so as not to outshine Lucy, perhaps. Or by only a carefully modest amount, anyway. "I'll just tell the driver about tomorrow morning."

"So," Ranklin said to O'Gilroy, "how did the tariff figures look?"

"Not too good at all." O'Gilroy seemed quietly amused. "With him taking his case along to the speech-making."

Ranklin stared. "Oh hell's Christmas – d'you mean I had that whole evening for nothing?"

"Now, Captain dear, I'm sure ye enjoyed yeself in yer own quiet way." Corinna came back and O'Gilroy explained: "I was jest telling Matt what a peaceful evening we'd been having."

Ranklin groaned: "All for nothing."

"We couldn't get at his case if he'd taken it with him," she said truculently. "*You* didn't think of that."

"I didn't think of burgling his room in the first place."

"You approved."

"I approved of the promised result. To that end, I played my part impeccably, not to say heroically, wearing my sanity to the bone . . . Thank you," as the waiter delivered half a tumbler of brandy and a bottle of mineral water. "Not too much soda, just take the chill off . . . woah, stoppen sie, anhalten! Danke."

Corinna watched him drink. "If that's your reaction to a minor setback, you're on the way to becoming a lush."

O'Gilroy said: "When the women start talking about the men's drinking habits, it's time for bed. I'll bid ye both good night."

Corinna gave him a cheery wave and then sprawled herself – elegantly – on the sofa. "We can try again – when you're sober.

And I bet the evening wasn't all that terrible."

"It had its moments," Ranklin said sombrely. "And Lucy talked about your family."

"Oh? You've been prying, have you?"

"Do you need to stoke a volcano? If I'd been prying, I wouldn't be telling you."

"No, sorry. If Lucy has a fault, it's a tendency to gossip. Well, what did you learn?"

"Nothing more than most people who know you know. Including that your husband died in the San Francisco fire."

"Well, I didn't say he hadn't, did I?"

"No. I was just going to say I was very sorry. It must have been – "

"Oh, never mind. Long ago, forget it." But why the devil haven't you been prying into my life before? she thought indignantly. I suppose because gentlemen don't pry. But no wonder you need so much help as spies. "And learning about my family cast you into total gloom, did it?"

"What? No," Ranklin said hastily. "But . . . talking to some of Hazay's – that's the journalist – his friends, I suddenly got convinced we really are going to have a war."

"I thought you were busy preparing for one anyway."

Ranklin looked around, but the nearest waiter was at a safe distance in the shadows at the edge of the lobby. "That's what armies are supposed to do. No, I just suddenly saw all the nations and peoples of Europe each demanding liberty, territory and whatever they think are their 'rights'. And most of them justified, but all of it irreconcilable. And all of them ready to fight. What else *can* happen next?"

Corinna was silent for a while. Then she sat forward, tasted a cup of cold coffee, grimaced and reached for Ranklin's glass. "That isn't just the evening's wine talking?"

Ranklin shrugged. "In vino veritas? You travel Europe, at a more exalted level. What do you hear?"

She considered. "I guess it's 'If only Germany would realise . . . ' and 'If only England could understand . . . ' or if France would, or Russia or Austria. It's always the other guys who should do something. Are you going to report this to Pop? – or anyone?"

"Report what? Isn't it just a smell in the air? If it was a wicked plot . . . Perhaps I mean that life should be simpler."

Corinna smiled, stood and stretched. "Yes, growing up, you miss Santa Claus and the Devil both."

45

Ranklin was shaken from the very depths of sleep and came up mumbling and unfocused.

"Wake up, Matt, wake up, God damn it." He realised it was Corinna, holding a shaded oil lamp and wearing a striped kimono with her hair loose to her shoulders.

That woke him. "What the devil are you doing in here?"

"Well, *thank* you. That isn't the way I'm usually greeted in these circumstances. Get up, we're going burgling."

"Are we? What time is – "

"It's one o'clock. Just get *up* – all right, I'll turn my back – and get Conall."

He reached for his worn old woollen dressing-gown, and a few minutes later they were in Corinna's sitting room, plotting in whispers.

"Is he not there now?" O'Gilroy asked. "What's he doing?"

"A lady doesn't speculate, but he's doing it in the Baroness's room, so . . . "

"How do ye know?"

"I was half expecting this, so I stayed awake, listening – *and* I spilt some face powder. Look." She led them proudly back to the door and showed a faint dusting of powder – and the footprints in it – by both Hornbeam's and the Baroness's doors. "How's about that for evidence?" She closed the door again.

Ranklin said: "Most ingenious, but it doesn't tell us how long he'll be there."

"Being a lawyer I expect he'll spin things out as long as possible, but that doesn't mean we have to. Conall, you can . . . " but then she remembered their talk before dinner and turned it into a question: "Do you think it's safe to hop over that railing thing between our balconies? He's sure to have left a window open."

Ranklin and O'Gilroy looked at each other, then O'Gilroy nodded. He was more shy about taking off his dressing-gown in front of Corinna than getting caught in the burglary. But in a couple of minutes he was back, laying the brief-case under the lamplight and grabbing for his gown. "'Twas easier to bring it right back, seeing it was setting by his bed."

"Not even locked?" Corinna was surprised.

"Oh sure, but he hadn't taken his keys a-courting."

It was, Ranklin reflected, a new twist on the classic espionage ploy outlined by the Bureau: pinching the Secret Documents while the bearer is being seduced. Only here the seducer was their rival, not accomplice, and the documents they were lifting from the case probably belonged to her.

The top one was amateurishly typed in German, with many corrections, and laid out in numbered paragraphs and sub-paragraphs. Ranklin frowned, tasting the leaden legalisms: Gehinderungsfalle, it said; Vermächtnisnehmer. He turned back to the first page.

Corinna had picked up three pages of handwritten notes on the paper of the Hotel Imperial, Vienna. "This seems to be about some law case: 'could be argued that' . . . 'query constructive duress' . . . What have you got?"

Ranklin's whisper had become reverent. "I rather think I've got a copy of the Habsburg Family Law. Which I shouldn't have. And I'm damned sure Hornbeam shouldn't have, either." He put the document down as carefully as he would a suspect artillery cartridge. "May I see some of those notes?"

Corinna passed him a page and he read down it quickly, trying to find a train of thought. But couldn't. There were, however, several references to "Art 1" He turned a page of the Family Law and tried to decipher Article 1. It seemed to be about the composition of the family itself, perhaps a definition of who belonged. It certainly included a long list of titled families. But beyond that . . .

"This is hopeless," he said. "And we haven't got the time. Let's just copy out his notes. How many pencils have you got?"

"Let me just look at the Law." She read for half a minute, then said: "I'll round up some pencils."

Doing one page each, it took them about five minutes which seemed much longer to Ranklin. Then they had to remember in what order the papers had been arranged in the case – the Bureau had been crisp on that very matter – and hustle a de-dressing-gowned O'Gilroy out of the window again. But Ranklin's heart didn't slow down until O'Gilroy was back.

"Now then," Corinna said, "you seem to have something I don't . . . "

"If we're going to talk this over, may I invite you, this time, to my room? Assuming you don't want yours smelling of tobacco smoke and whatever I hope and trust O'Gilroy's got in his travelling flask."

So there was another scene of silent tiptoeing across the dim corridor, which so much reminded Corinna of the Comédie Française that she nearly broke down in giggles halfway. But finally they were settled in Ranklin's bedroom.

"When you take up a life of crime," he mused, "I imagine it's very important to know just what crimes you've taken up. We might get away with no more than a Hungarian version of trespass, but Hornbeam could be vulnerable for something like treason."

"Just for having that Family Law?" Corinna asked.

O'Gilroy added: "And what is it, anyways?"

"Remember, I haven't come across it until just now, but I've heard of it before. And it's what it says: the law of the Habsburgs. A rich, powerful, big – seventy archdukes or so – family that needs laws to decide who ranks after who, inheritance and succession."

Corinna made a face. "What's wrong with the ordinary law?"

"The Habsburgs don't see themselves as part of the Monarchy, the Empire: they see that as part of themselves. They've been one of the most important royal families in Europe for seven hundred years, far longer than most nations have lasted. They'd say they're the trunk of history: nations, frontiers, common laws are just leaves that have their season. So they need their own private law."

Corinna frowned into her well-watered brandy. Sure, she knew families, younger and brasher, and called Morgan and Rockefeller and Carnegie – and Sherring, come to that – who preferred their own codes to the laws of the common herd. And she had learnt plenty about the Habsburgs as characters in a play written by "history". But Ranklin, with his European perspective, was seeing the Habsburgs more as they saw themselves; chosen and burdened to lead. Not stripping off the beards and greasepaint when the curtain fell, because the curtain never did. And the blood on the Habsburg stage was not stage blood.

She nodded. "And is the Family Law really that secret?"

"In practice, it just can't be. All those archdukes and their lawyers. But it certainly isn't something you can buy in a legal bookshop. A badly typewritten copy is probably the best you could lay hands on, so I don't think Hornbeam went looking for it out of professional curiosity. I think it must have come to him, and for a purpose. It's that purpose I don't like thinking about."

"The Baroness's purpose, we assume, don't we? And what d'you figure it is?"

"I don't. Just the fact that he's looking at the Law and making notes about it suggest he's trying to interfere with it. And he shouldn't even be looking."

"Interfere how?"

"I don't know." He picked up the copied notes. "These don't tell us. We really need a lawyer."

"Dr Klapka?"

"Ummm. If there were any hint of treason, he might go straight to the police – just to protect himself."

"A lawyer doesn't discuss his clients' affairs. So, I shall hire him."

There must, Ranklin thought, be some problems that couldn't be solved by saying "I'll hire a car, a couple of spies, a lawyer . . . " But he had to admit it simplified life a great deal.

"As long as we're sure Klapka himself isn't involved."

"He doesn't like the Baroness one bit. He was spitting blood about her getting between him and Hornbeam this afternoon, thinks she's an interfering busybody. And now I can tell him just how busy her body's been."

O'Gilroy was sitting on the bed, elbows on knees with a tooth-mug of brandy in one hand and a cigarette in the other, and mostly just listening and nodding. Now he asked quietly: "And how will ye be explaining ye know he's got a copy of the Law?"

"Oh – he left his case around, and I saw a paper nearby that I thought must've fallen out, so I – I found the case was unlocked – so I opened it to put the paper back . . ." She was clearly making it up as she went along, and Ranklin shuddered.

O'Gilroy said: "And it being a dull afternoon, like, ye jest happened to copy out three pages of his notes. Ye think he'll believe it?"

"Lordie, no. But he'll be used to clients telling lies."

O'Gilroy took a thoughtful drag at his cigarette. "And are we thinking this is the whole reason of his being here – what ye was talking about on the train? To take a look at this Law?"

Ranklin looked at Corinna; neither of them had been thinking of the wider implications. Catching up with O'Gilroy, he said: "If it is, it goes far beyond the Baroness. Barons are just errand boys in court circles. So who recruited the Baroness?"

"Who'd know how to get hold of the Law?" O'Gilroy asked.

"And," Corinna added, her face serious now, "what sort of people would want a legal opinion of it? It wouldn't be the guy who sweeps the street crossings, that's for damn sure."

She shivered and glanced at the window curtains, but they hung still, there was no draught. Maybe she was just feeling suddenly far from home: it was a rare feeling for a Sherring.

On the other hand, she didn't feel like sleep yet. The thrill of the midnight burglary and speculating about its results would keep her awake for hours yet unless she soaked herself in laudanum. Brandy was healthier: she held out her glass.

Mock grudgingly, O'Gilroy poured from the big silver flask engraved with unknown initials. "Ye likely can't find stuff this good in this heathen country, and it hurts terrible to see ye mangling it with water. I'm back to bed."

A little larceny had never troubled O'Gilroy's sleep yet.

Then he added: "I'm sure ye can remember which yer own beds are," and closed the door very quietly.

"Now what d'you think he meant by that?" Corinna asked, enjoying Ranklin's embarrassment. "But you've got this place smelling like a dockside saloon. If you can leave that pipe behind, let's finish his precious flask in my sitting-room."

So once again they went through the tiptoe routine, but it was only to her *sitting* room, Ranklin excused himself, clutching the copies of Hornbeam's notes to remind himself of business.

"Here," he offered, "you'd better put these where the maids won't see them." And that reminded him: "What happened to your own maid?"

"Kitty? Oh, I sent her back to Paris. She got sick with the eastern cooking." That wasn't the whole truth; in fact it was very little of the truth. Corinna had found out that Kitty was also being paid by her father to report on her doings. She hadn't been shocked by that, hadn't really resented it; she just damned well wasn't going to put up with it. "So I'm here just on my poor little ownsome."

She dropped onto a sofa and flicked through the notes. "A year ago, would you have thought you'd be helping loot bedrooms for secret documents?"

"No-o," Ranklin agreed cautiously. How did she know he hadn't been doing just that a year ago?

"But it must be more fun than ordinary Army life."

"It isn't what I signed up for." Privately, Ranklin was thinking that if a spy, like a cat, had only nine lives, it was a pity to risk one trying to keep an American law professor out of trouble. The Habsburg Law wasn't exactly Plan Three.

"You really don't like being a spy, do you?"

Ranklin reached for the flask on the table – she had brought it across – and refilled the silver cap he was using. O'Gilroy was right: it was too good to be watered down. "It still wasn't what I signed up for."

She persisted: "But that doesn't mean you disapprove . . . "

He smiled, holding up his hand to cut off the question. "I know that argument; I've had it with myself. I certainly don't think espionage is taking an unsporting advantage or any nonsense like that. But I can approve of sweeping streets and unblocking drains without wanting to do them, either."

Hmm, she thought with a wry smile; is *that* how he sees his work? "What would you be doing in the Army if . . . if you weren't doing what you are doing?"

"Now, in August? Looking after the horses and ammunition for a battery on firing practice at Shoeburyness or Okehampton, probably."

"And you'd really rather be back holding horses and so on instead of all . . . *this?*" She flung out an arm, her kimono sleeve flaring in a world-sweeping gesture.

"It wasn't just horse-holding. It was the life, the friends – "

"Are they still your friends?" she asked shrewdly.

Ranklin said stubbornly: "It was the life I had chosen."

"Along with a few thousand others who can probably do it just as well because it's that sort of job. While you're in a job they couldn't do – but you despise it because *they* would. God Almighty, man, hadn't you noticed you're a hell of a smart guy? Because if you hadn't, Conall sure has: he wouldn't stick by you two minutes if you weren't, not in your trade."

A gentleman really ought to deflect any compliment from a lady, no matter how oddly phrased, with some modest but appreciative remark. However, this is difficult if the gentleman is suddenly wondering if he hasn't been wallowing in self-pity for the last six months, and also if he's never been called a hell of a smart guy before. None of the women who had drifted through Ranklin's life, and certainly not his family or the Army, had ever said such a thing. Not even an English translation of it.

Corinna had watched his bemused silence nervously, and found herself beginning to babble. "Lord, now I really did insult you, didn't I? – saying you were in a 'trade'. Suggesting you cared about that filthy stuff money which the English don't talk about. How the hell they can pretend that just beats me: you sit down to dinner in England and they never talk anything else – falling land values, agricultural prices, servants' wages, income tax, their mortgages, they all say they're broke but you know damn well they've never had real trouble like y . . .

"Oh hell." She sat up very straight and took a breath. "I guess I haven't been behaving like a gentleman. Conall told me – I *made* him – about your brother and how you landed in this job."

She was surprised to see Ranklin smiling, but he was rather surprised himself at feeling a sense of relief and not indignation. "O'Gilroy knew, then . . . But of course he would. I ought to stick to keeping secrets that really matter."

Reassured, she went on: "I got worse than that, I'm afraid. I had one of our London boys do some tracking in the City. He found they'd hauled up the drawbridge once you got into that Deed of Composition – was it your new bosses arranged that? – but he got the trail pretty clear up to there."

Still smiling, Ranklin hoped he'd remember to get that trail well muddied: if the House of Sherring could follow it, so could the Kundschaftstelle or the Nachrichtendienst.

"Matt," she said, "for the Lord's sake, if you – or your family – ever go buying gold shares again, ask me which mines to go for."

"I'm afraid that isn't exactly the family's problem at the moment, but I'll bear it in mind."

"And don't go signing guarantees you don't understand – please."

Ranklin nodded automatically. But then he paused and carefully took a big decision. "Did I?" he said.

"How d'you mean?"

"I'm really not so innocent that I don't know I'm innocent when it comes to City gentlemen and their pieces of paper."

She looked puzzled. "Just what do . . . "

"I've never told anybody," he said, almost dreamily. "Nobody else in the world knows this – but how do you tell your family that your brother, who's just killed himself because he lost pretty well all their – not just his, but their – inheritance, how do you tell them that he was a forger as well?"

She sat stunned. Then gradually the pieces fitted together in her mind. She had been thinking of this man as smart enough in his own world – she hadn't been flattering him there – but a bit of a fool in hers. And now she saw that he wasn't a fool but a hell of a nice guy as well as being smart and funny and, probably, brave (though she wasn't a schoolgirl, to be impressed by mere physical courage). And he hadn't been behaving according to some gentlemanly code; he'd just saved people he loved from hurt. For that, he'd let himself look a fool and put his career on the line. No, way below the line and in the ashcan.

She felt a sudden warmth towards him that really was that: a flush of loving excitement that tingled through her whole body. And a brief loathing for that brother of his, so intense she wanted to rip open his grave and stamp on his remains – only then I'd never have met Matt, she thought, and closed the grave again.

"Why don't you come and sit over here?" she said quietly.

Ranklin lay drifting in that luxurious space between sleep and waking, knowing he could choose either, reliving gently the sensations of Corinna's soft vigorous body that now slept beside him. Should I sleep or wake, remember or dream? The ceiling was dark above; there was no moon, only a slash of faint starlight on the part-opened curtains.

I suppose, looked at objectively, he thought, I have been seduced. He had been seduced once before, but that had been when he was a twenty-year-old subaltern, and by a senior officer's wife. A messy, clumsy business, he recalled, and best forgotten. But remembering it had woken him up and he slid carefully out of bed, found his dressing-gown, and lit a cigarette. Then stood by the half-open window to breathe smoke outside.

Not that that would fool the hotel staff; they'd know. The servants always knew.

"Are you planning to make a romantic escape through the window?" Corinna asked sleepily. "And break your stupid neck? Come back to bed."

"When I've finished my cigarette."

She rolled over and stared at the ceiling, the sheet spilling away from her left breast. "If we're confessing things, d'you want to hear one of mine?"

"Only if you want to tell me."

"I've never been married."

"Good God." Ranklin really was startled, and began hastily to re-examine his behaviour. And the re-examination told him only one thing: "Look, do you want . . . " This had gone from being perhaps his happiest hour to his most awkward; " . . . I mean, I'd be honoured if . . . "

"I'd marry you? Is this a proposal? Oh, poor Matt!" She began to laugh, choked, and had to sit up coughing herself breathless. Ranklin just stared, thinking: that was my first proposal, and . . . well, at least I know what being shot at dawn will be like: easy.

"My dear, dear boy," she gurgled at last. "I guess when I find a real gentleman, I get the full menu. No, I'm not trying to trap you." She flopped back again, now naked to the waist and giggling at the ceiling. "It's just I found out early that, in Europe, it's the married women and widows who have all the fun. So, I invented Mr Finn and a marriage in San Francisco. The great thing about the fire is that it burned up all the public records like marriages. So I can be Mrs Finn or the widow Finn, whatever fits the occasion."

"Good God," Ranklin said again, but not for the original reason.

"Con-men use it, too. If you get in a deal with anybody who says he was born in 'Frisco, be suspicious. Now forget about my honour and think about more interesting parts of me. Come back to bed.

"Mind," she added, "if you tell anyone about Mr Finn, I'll kill you."

Ranklin pitched his cigarette end through the window. "You've got a few secrets of mine I'm rather hoping you'll keep."

"That's right, I have, haven't I? I've got you in my power, Captain Ranklin. Come back to bed."

46

Breakfast, again out in the sun, was a busy time. Lucy, perhaps suspecting her father's beaming expression wasn't solely due to the success of the lawyers' dinner, was trying to get him alone. The Baroness was stopping that by sticking to Hornbeam like a leech. Dr Klapka also wanted to get Hornbeam alone for once, while Corinna was trying to arrange an urgent consultation with Klapka. And the waiters were run ragged trying to rematch the coffee cups to the breakfasters as they moved from seat to seat.

It was like the second act of a spy farce, and the spies stayed well clear of it. "Romania's turning the screws on Bulgaria," Ranklin translated loosely from a German-language newspaper. "Says she'll start the war again if there's no agreement on the new frontier . . . And Vienna's still hinting at intervention – Ah: they've approved an increase in Austro-Hungarian artillery, one new battery per regiment. But that'll take a while."

O'Gilroy took a spoonful of egg. "What guns?"

"Their own, they make 'em at the Skoda works in Pilsen. Good stuff, I believe; we bought some 75s to experiment with . . . "

Corinna flopped into a chair opposite, quickly followed by her faithful native bearer of coffee. She grinned at Ranklin, but then she grinned at O'Gilroy, too. "I finally pinned the little shyster down. In half an hour in my sitting-room. You can drop in ten minutes later, when I've broken the news to him. You'd probably like it to seem you've been dragged in unwillingly, wouldn't you?"

"Very thoughtful," Ranklin acknowledged.

O'Gilroy asked: "F'why are ye saying yer doing this?"

"I don't think I can improve on the truth," Corinna confessed. "That, as an American citizen, I'm worried that another one is getting imbrogled into a purely Austro-Hungarian matter – with international consequences." She glanced back at Hornbeam, who was still beaming. "If that's what the old fool's doing with his head in the clouds and his slippers under the wrong bed. So, your cue is forty minutes from now."

"What's everybody else doing?"

"The Baroness is meeting somebody coming in from Vienna, Hornbeam may or may not go along, Lucy may or may not have a touch of the vapours." She clearly felt she could handle only one Hornbeam problem at a time.

"If the Baroness is mixed in this," O'Gilroy said, "would we be wanting to know who she's meeting?"

Ranklin wished he'd thought of that. Corinna said: "How?"

"Yer car'll be along, will it? Then offer it to take her down while yer sending me on some errand. I'll be no help with talk on the law."

Corinna liked the thought, but: "Suppose she sees you hanging around?"

"She won't see him," Ranklin promised.

As the breakfast party broke up and the waiters began clearing the tables, Ranklin lit his pipe and stayed where he was. In the background, Corinna's car rolled up, she and O'Gilroy did some stage business with papers – and probably more impromptu inventions about local High Finance – then the Baroness and O'Gilroy got in and were driven off. Seizing her opportunity, Lucy was taking Hornbeam for a purposeful-looking stroll, perhaps to talk of rumours of his behaviour last night, or perhaps to discuss her dress allowance, unless the two subjects happened to coincide. Left standing alone, Corinna's shoulders sagged momentarily, then she braced for the meeting with Klapka and walked up into the hotel.

Already it was almost too hot, and small puffs of cloud were forming out of nowhere. Ranklin knew nothing of the local weather, but was prepared to bet on thunderstorms before teatime, and did a mental search for his umbrella. But mostly he just sat and enjoyed the warmth, and the inner glow of last night. Were they just lovers who passed in the night? Part of him yearned for it to be more than that, but another part knew how widely separated their worlds were. So much so that their bond was that they were strangers to everybody else, nobody had quite been *them* before. But that being so, anything was possible.

O'Gilroy had learnt to identify different types of women by their clothes in the streets of Cork and Dublin. This could not really be called a sense of fashion. However, he had gone from there virtually direct to the boulevards of Paris, where women's clothes and the messages they were supposed to be sending were a good deal more varied and subtle. And with his talent for observation and a desire to intercept whatever messages were going, he had begun to understand the code.

The Baroness, he reckoned, was dressed about three years behind the Paris times: her hem was barely off the ground and still slightly flared, her hat very wide and decorated with silk flowers. But the newness and craftsmanship showed this was deliberate: the message was quality, good taste, value for money, not fashionableness. And Hornbeam had liked the message, so who was he to criticise?

She sat rigidly upright in the back seat of the Benz, full-breasted – not just quality but a decent helping of it – hands resting on her furled sunshade and gazing out of the window. She totally ignored O'Gilroy until he asked politely: "And which station are ye wanting, m'lady?"

"The Westbahnhof." She didn't look at him.

"Mebbe I'll look up some trains meself. We should be seeing more of the country than jest Budapest."

"There is nothing to see in Hungary. Only some castles."

"I was thinking about trade, m'lady."

This time she did look at him. "I believe trade in Hungary is done by Jews."

"Is it so?" It was clear that he wasn't going to learn anything from cosy chat; on the other hand, it was just as clear that she wasn't interested in – or suspicious of – himself. So he chose to spend the rest of the drive reinforcing his pose as a business bore. "Did ye know that two-thirds of the machinery built in Hungary is for transport? – motor-cars, tram-cars, ships, trains and the like. Now that's a remarkable amount, when ye consider . . . "

At the Westbahnhof, a simple elegant iron-and-glass structure designed by Eiffel, of the Paris tower, they both got out. "When I've looked up the trains, I'll be walking to the bank," O'Gilroy said. "So ye keep the motor-car, m'lady."

She just managed to squeeze out a Thank you, told the driver to wait, and stalked into the station. O'Gilroy had never planned to keep the car and try to trail the Baroness in it: the sleek, high Benz was far too obvious in Budapest's mainly horse-drawn traffic. Better to let her drive in a landmark, and if he lost her, Corinna could demand of the driver where he had gone without seeming suspicious.

"Hello, Mr Ranklin, sit down. I've explained what I told you to Dr Klapka – and he's rather worried."

Indeed, Klapka was bubbling like a fondue, fingers drumming, feet shuffling, mouth opening and closing. "It is not believable," he burst out, waving the notes they had copied last night. "That somebody should ask . . . Dr Hornbeam is a great lawyer, yes, but he is not . . . not of our courts!"

"Oh, sure," Corinna soothed.

"To be asked for an opinion – on the Habsburg Law – Unbelievable!"

"The Law's secret, isn't it?" Corinna asked.

"Yes, but lawyers know it. It is not our concern, that is all."

Ranklin asked: "What do you think Hornbeam's trying to do to the Law, then?" He tried to sound businesslike and detached.

"To break it! To break the new amendment! To make it so the Archduke's wife can be Empress!" His arms waved with the enormity of it; his jacket moved reluctantly and differently, dissociating itself from the opinions of the arms.

Ranklin nodded calmly. "And can this be done?"

"I explain." Klapka took a deep breath. "Now: when the Archduke Franzie is married, no, before, he must sign that . . . No. I explain." He took another breath. "The old Article One says the Habsburg House is the Emperor, his consort, the Archdukes and Archduchesses, la-la, la-la . . . you see? His *consort*. If he marries

Sophie, only a Czech countess, she will be Empress when he becomes Emperor – and this they must change. So they make the amendment which is a list of the families in standesgemäss – you would say, of proper standing – whose women may be Empress. If he marries one of them, good, if not, pffft. It must be a morganatic marriage. You understand morganatic?"

"Sure," Corinna said. "Wife doesn't get husband's rank."

"Yes. It is first meaning 'the morning gift' that the husband gives after . . . after the first night, which says 'This is all you get from marrying me.' Very romantic, hein? So – this amendment the Archduke must sign if he is to become Emperor, with the Prince Archbishop holding up the cross of Ferdinand over him and all the House looking and then also signing. And after three days only, he marries his Sophie and the Prince Montenuovo, Obersthofmeister of the Court, declares there must be twelve days mourning for some cousin that nobody knows, so nobody can go to the wedding."

"That Montenuovo would be right at home in Tammany Hall," Corinna observed. It had just struck her that she, daughter of Reynard Sherring, would not be standesgemäss, was unworthy of becoming Empress, and her democratic blood was boiling. Not that she *wanted* to be, but . . .

Ranklin had put his empty pipe into his mouth so as to look even more thoughtful and detached. Now he took it out and asked: "And do you think Hornbeam can break this amendment – legally?"

Klapka's arms flew up again. "You do not *understand*! You English and American – I apologise, but – this is the *Habsburg* Law! Perhaps legally it does not work, there may be – you say a 'loophole' – but what matter? They get the lawyers, the Prince-Archbishop, the cross – they make a new amendment. Now no loophole."

They absorbed this, Ranklin less surprised than Corinna. He said: "But nobody – whoever nobody is – told Hornbeam this?"

"That is sure, yes – but still you do not understand. To ask a foreign lawyer – a great one, yes, but . . . to interfere in the Habsburg Law, this is bad. An insult. But to try *at all* to make Sophie the Empress, if this is known – " he threw the notes onto a table, " – then the Archduke never becomes Emperor."

The Baroness was sitting at a front table of the first-class buffet, so that she could watch the door. This had made it impossible for O'Gilroy to follow, so he resorted to inconspicuous time-wasting within sight of the door. He bought a newspaper he couldn't read, cigarettes which he hoped not to smoke, and an apple of which he ate half. He also changed his hat. He had come out wearing Ranklin's folding straw Panama; now he pocketed that and slipped on a flat cloth cap. But he had already realised he would have to be stark naked to look conspicuous in the crowd that changed with every train: landowners in tweeds with servants and gun cases, farmers with live chickens, soldiers in various operatic uniforms and peasant girls in traditional eleven-petticoat finery. And it was only the Baroness he had to fool.

Then suddenly it wasn't. She was out of the buffet and walking towards the street, escorted by the Military Attaché who had bought the code in Paris.

As the waiter went out, Corinna surveyed the tray. "That coffee pot seems to follow me around. How does anybody like their coffee? And if you want a cake, just grab. How can anybody decide that the Archduke *can't* become Emperor? I thought it was just a matter of birth . . . "

"You think like what you are: American. You have the rule of Law, we have the House of Habsburg. You must believe, if enough people do not want, then he will not be Emperor. And those people will be the Emperor himself, Prince Montenuovo, the Court, the House – and the Parliament in Hungary also, they do not like the Archduke Franzie. Last year, the Archduke's young brother, he married not to the standesgemäss. Now he is not an Archduke, he is not a general, he does not even have his medals. You must believe." He took a cream cake.

Corinna shook her head slowly. She had always assumed – insofar as she thought about it at all – that European royalty survived by playing by the rules, dopey though those rules might be. Now she saw it was the opposite: survival by playing *with* the rules – which wasn't nearly so dopey. She glanced at Ranklin.

He was clutching one end of his pipe and chewing the other, frowning intently in a way that always seemed faintly absurd for his boyish face. The poor man, she thought, stuck with a face that people will never quite take seriously. But not a bad face for what you really are, these days, because nobody takes your thinking seriously, either. Except me.

Abruptly, Ranklin said: "What do you know of the Baroness Schramm?"

Klapka blinked. "I do not know her at all, before this. But – if the Law comes from her, obviously she is connected with the Archduke. Or his advisers, Count Czernin, Bardolff . . . "

"You think they'd have the influence to get her into this job? It might still be worth asking about her. Quietly."

Klapka looked at Corinna for confirmation; she nodded.

"And," Ranklin went on, "what are you going to do yourself?"

Klapka blinked even harder and then waved his arms again. "To do? I must do nothing. Mrs Finn has employed me, and . . . and . . . " he seemed to cringe into the protection of his suit.

"You don't want to be involved?" Ranklin said soothingly. "Of course not. Better to let Dr Hornbeam's fellow countrywomen advise him that he's playing with fire and gunpowder."

"Of course." Klapka expanded to fill his suit again. "That is most best."

"And thank you very much for your time and excellent advice."

After that, Klapka had no choice but to go, despite Corinna's obvious flabbergastation. He was more accustomed to taking orders from men than from even the richest women.

As the door closed, Corinna turned to Ranklin and it was going to be thunder well before teatime.

He held up a hand. "I know, I know – it was unpardonable. *But* – so far he hasn't thought through to the next step, and perhaps he'll deliberately not think any more. He'll know he's close enough for fragment wounds if there's any scandal involving Hornbeam. Anyway, we're one step ahead at the moment so let's use that moment."

"*What* step?" She was far from soothed.

"Remembering the Archduke may be stupid but he's been a Habsburg all his life. He has to know the risk he'd be running by involving Hornbeam and the Law. Why not wait until he's Emperor, with an Emperor's clout, and see what he can do about the

Law then? *I* don't think he knows anything about this at all."

Corinna's mouth opened slowly, but she caught on quickly. "Then the Baroness isn't working for him but against him? And that's why you wanted to know what her connections are – that's pretty smart, and I forgive your masterfulness." She pondered. "Then this – trying to break the Amendment to the Law – must be planned to leak out. How?"

"That I can't guess. They can't have counted on your taste for burglary."

She grinned. "And that was pretty smart of me, too."

"And I forgive your instinctive immorality. But it has to leak out soon: they need Hornbeam himself – an independent witness, you might say – to confirm that it isn't just another Viennese café rumour."

"Maybe he'll announce it as part of his speech tonight: 'I bring good cheer: Duchess Sophie can be Empress after all.' Wow."

"Wow indeed," Ranklin whispered, awe-struck at the idea. But something like that seemed horribly likely: public and irrefutable.

Corinna's mind was off on a branch line. "Solving a legal problem and making a pretty lady into an Empress, that would really be gravy to an old dormouse from Harvard Yard. And the Baroness's beautiful white body to make doubly sure."

"Trebly: now she's snared him, they can threaten to tell his wife if he wants to back out. Or if you and Lucy tell him to."

"Wow some more." Now Corinna was being awe-struck. "This *is* big."

"Destroying the Emperor Presumptive usually is, I imagine. And because that's what we're talking about, I want you to promise to do and say nothing: nothing to Lucy, no telegram to Paris, *nothing* until we know more."

To promise inactivity was probably the hardest thing you could ask Corinna to do, but he believed her solemn nod.

Back in his own room, Ranklin pottered about looking for his folding Panama hat and trying to think of what more there might be for them to find. If the plotted "revelation" was intended to stop the Archduke becoming Emperor, then it had its risks. Suppose that Hornbeam, seeing what he had stirred up, told the whole story? Then suppose that pressure was brought on the Baroness to tell yet more? In time, the plot might well be revealed and its effect destroyed. After all, the job of Emperor wasn't open yet.

He remembered that O'Gilroy had borrowed the Panama, put on his straw boater, and started looking for his umbrella. Suppose, then, that the plot was not so much to destroy Franz Ferdinand's chance of becoming Emperor in the future as to throw him into temporary disgrace right *now*? This summer, this month, this war season. With the Archduke silenced, his influence gone, the war party would be badly weakened. Berchtold and his fellow peace-mongers at the Foreign Office might then be able to stop any invasion of Serbia, get the Army scattered back to its barracks. It would take too long to re-assemble for this season even if the plot leaked out and the Archduke regained his status.

He found his umbrella; a hot summer spent on the Continent meant he hadn't carried it in months. Now he twirled it expertly and its comforting familiarity improved his humour even more. Because now, he thought, as he trotted cheerfully down the stairs, I need do nothing – except confirm my theory. Let the peace party have its way: who could criticise that?

Well, Corinna could, if it meant letting a distinguished American make a diplomatic incident of himself. And it did mean just that, he realised, a shade less cheerfully; the plot had to succeed. Would it be fair to ask if she would rather see Europe ablaze with war? Perhaps he should just take charge of stopping the plot – and then bungle it and apologise. Hmm.

Out in the sunlight, he lifted the furled umbrella with a flick of his wrist and the dozing cabbie across the driveway woke immediately; even his horse seemed to stand to attention. If there was one thing at which the English still unquestionably led the world, it was handling umbrellas.

47

Ranklin had forgotten the name of the café, so just had the cabbie put him down at the statue of Petöfi. He was surprised to find how eagerly he was looking forward to a talk with Hazay. Was he overtrusting the young man's inside knowledge and cynical judgement? Certainly he was being overdependent on one friendly source in a strange city, a recognised pitfall for a lazy spy. But time was short, and anyway, he would judge anything Hazay said on its merits.

He sat pondering over a coffee and a copy of the *Neue Freie Presse*. Was there any way in which he could use Hazay and his access to the public? Obviously he couldn't give him the plot against the Archduke: that would wreck it – if the censors allowed it to be printed. But any other way? He shuddered suddenly at how cynical he himself was becoming, and picked up the newspaper. Anyway, he couldn't use the man unless the damned man turned up. The morning was wearing away.

He had just about given up hope when Tibor came along with his bear-like shamble. "Good day, Enemy," he grinned, leaning over to shake hands. "Stefan tells me to see if you are here. He is most sorry – " he broke off to order a drink, " – but he must go to Komárom to telegraph to Munich."

Komárom? That was the next proper town up the railway line to Vienna; he remembered passing through it.

"There," Tibor explained, "he misses the Budapest censors." Of course: the telegraph line followed the railway line in every country.

"But," Tibor added, shrugging, "the censors in Vienna will see it anyway. He asks me to give you this."

This was a page from a notebook covered in hasty handwriting. Ranklin deciphered it carefully. "So the Archduke went to Vienna the day before yesterday to see Count Berchtold at the Ballhausplatz." That was the Foreign Office. "And tomorrow Berchtold goes to Bad Ischl to an audience with the Emperor – sorry, King. How far is that?"

"Half a day," Tibor shrugged. "More, perhaps."

The Emperor spent much of the summer in the little mountain resort near Salzburg, playing (it was said) at being just an ordinary citizen and being surprised when everyone stepped aside and bowed.

"So Berchtold," Ranklin deduced, "will advise the Emp–, King, whether or not to accept the new frontiers in the peace treaty." He hastily indicated the newspaper, to excuse his knowledge. According to it, the treaty was almost ready for signing in Bucharest, but Austria disliked the way Serbia was gaining land to the west. It was another step towards seizing a port on the Adriatic – where a Russian fleet might one day drop anchor.

So there was a ready-made quarrel with Serbia – if the Emperor wanted to take it up. And the Archduke would have been urging Berchtold to advise the Emperor to do just that. If they let the treaty be signed without objecting, the excuse for war was gone by default.

"And is that what Hazay is telegraphing to the Munich newspaper?"

But Tibor was frowning suspiciously. Ranklin offered his cigarettes and Tibor took one, but it didn't stop him wondering why a business adviser was so interested in the detail of Balkan politics. But then a waiter arrived with two glasses and Tibor scattered some coins in return. Ranklin hadn't realised the order had included him, and distrusted small glasses of almost clear liquid.

"Szilva," Tibor explained: plum brandy. "Egészségére!" He swallowed half in a gulp; Ranklin sipped cautiously. "'Why do you like to talk with Stefan?"

"He knows more than he can get printed. And my employer – you know who I mean?" Tibor nodded, thinking he did know;

" – well, he doesn't pay me to tell him what he can read for himself."

"He wants to know all about this?" Tibor waved a hand at the newspaper.

"I'll tell you what he wants to know, perhaps you can answer him," Ranklin said boldly. "Is there going to be a war? When? Who's going to be involved? And who's going to win?"

Tibor sat back in his chair. Then he said: "Capitalists."

"He'd agree. What about the peasant with half a dozen gold pieces buried under his hearth? He wants to know whether to move his money, too."

"But the peasant does not care if everybody else knows also," Tibor said shrewdly. "The capitalist wants to know in secret, to move before others move. He wants truth, but to hide it for himself. But – " he finished his brandy; " – Stefan does not telegraph about the treaty, it is about Colonel Redl."

"Ah."

"You know about the Colonel?"

"What I read in the papers – and Stefan was talking about him yesterday." He daren't seem too interested: what would Sherring care about an intelligence scandal?

But, perhaps for the same reason, Tibor insisted on "boring" him with what Hazay had uncovered. "He has learnt of a meeting between the Archduke Franzie and General Conrad, after Redl has shot himself. Franzie talks to him as if he is a *common soldier*." Tibor relished that. "He makes him stand to attention and tells him he is a pig-head to make Redl kill himself and not answer any question. That now they cannot know what Serbia, what Russia, knows about their Army and its plans. And also, that it is wicked to make a good Catholic do a mortal sin."

Now that, a complete irrelevance to Ranklin's non-Catholic mind, had the truth of a detail nobody would think to invent. "Really?" he said, his uninterested tone hiding his thoughts. If true, *if* true, that confrontation meant the Archduke was well aware of the danger in starting a war here and now. So could he really have been advising one?

"So now," Tibor said, "you will tell your Capitalist this truth also?"

"Perhaps – but only if the censors stop it being published." And he could see just why those censors wouldn't want such dissension in the high command made public. "Why is Hazay taking such a risk? – it must be a risk."

"They cannot shoot him for it. And he does it for truth, so everybody will know, not just capitalists."

Ranklin nodded absently and sipped his brandy. "Would you ask Hazay to telephone me at the Margaret Island hotel?"

"He says he will see you tonight, if you go to the American's speech."

"He'll be there?"

"All journalists are invited." So somebody wanted to make sure that Hornbeam got well and undeniably reported.

"All the same, I'd like to talk to him as soon as he gets back from – from Komárom. I might have some extra truth he'd be interested in," he added as bait.

Tibor stared at him without expression, then said: "All right – Enemy." He lumbered away and Ranklin watched without really seeing.

Damn, he was thinking. And damn again. This may change everything.

Dr Ignatz Brull's stern-but-kindly expression changed into one of astonished horror. "You are telling me that Professor Hornbeam will announce that the Habsburg Law can be broken! – to make Duchess Sophie become Empress? Du Liebe Gott!" Although the British Consul, Brull's origins had obviously been German-speaking. His accent was now just a constant mild flavour – except when he got astonished.

"I fear the papers his daughter found allow of no other conclusion," Ranklin said sadly. He had cleaned up the details of the discovery.

"And you say that the Archduke himself sent a copy of the Law to Dr Hornbeam? Then surely he must be mad. He will destroy himself."

"Er – no; I said it could *appear* that the Archduke was behind it all. For myself, I rather doubt that. I fear it may be a move to discredit the Archduke, destroy his influence . . . But I'm probably wrong. As Consul here you know far more about such matters."

Dr Brull acknowledged this with a nod and then sat frowning with thought. Apart from the length of his moustache, he looked like a – no, *the* bank manager of a county town: comfortable, reliable, knowing his job and knowing his table would be kept free at his lunchtime restaurant. He did not look as if he dabbled much in international intrigue, but he was all Ranklin had.

Budapest was a Consul-General's post but was awaiting a new C.-G. being sent from London; Dr Brull was just keeping the seat warm for his new chief. It was, Ranklin feared, a reasonable guess that he wouldn't want that chief to find the seat too hot.

Dr Brull took off his thick-lensed spectacles and tapped them on the table. "I believe you are correct, Mr Ranklin. The Archduke's advisers – and he would have to communicate with Professor Hornbeam through them – would never permit him to do anything so foolish."

"But to the man in the street," Ranklin said, "to the reader of tomorrow's newspapers, that thought might not occur."

"It might not occur to the Emperor, either," Dr Brull ruminated. "And some of *his* advisers might not hurry to point it out. The Archduke seems to be in good standing with the Emperor at the moment. There is a rumour – I trust you will not pass this on – that the Emperor plans, on his birthday next week, to make the Archduke the Inspector General of the Army."

Which would give him the right – officially, not just as a Habsburg – to curb General Conrad's ambitions. Ranklin said: "But that would go by the board if . . . "

"I fear so." Dr Brull put his spectacles back on and focused on Ranklin. "You did right to bring this to my attention."

"My patriotic duty," Ranklin simpered hopefully.

"But of course, this is none of our concern."

Ranklin stared. "But – don't you feel that this is political news that should be sent to the Ambassador in Vienna? Or even direct to London?"

Dr Brull smiled indulgently. He was used to agitated British citizens coming in with "news" (usually café gossip) that should immediately be telegraphed to the Foreign Secretary *personally*. Like a good bank manager, it was his duty to be polite – but firm.

"But what news, Mr Ranklin? Nothing, as yet, has actually happened. It may not happen – "

"But if this is an attempt to destroy the Archduke's influence at this time . . . "

"Many would say that was not a bad thing, Mr Ranklin. The Archduke has a reputation for advocating warlike solutions to political problems."

"But the . . . " No: there was no point in bringing up the Redl affair. You learnt this from a friend of a journalist who's trying to get it published in Munich, Mr Ranklin? Well, well; we'll just have to wait and see, then, won't we?

"May I ask," Dr Brull said, "if you have sent this *news* to your employer?"

That's exactly what I'm trying to do, Ranklin thought impatiently – and then realised that Brull meant Reynard Sherring.

"He, ah . . . his representative . . . "

"I see," Ranklin saw, too: Brull suspected him of using the Consular Service to spread rumours so that Sherring could make a killing in the stock market. Just as Tibor had suspected. It was really rather hard when all you were trying to do was a decent, honest bit of spying.

Ranklin found O'Gilroy in his bedroom, staring down at the gravel forecourt. "Are you feeling all right? What are you doing hiding away up here?"

"Yer wicked past's caught up with *me*," O'Gilroy said gloomily. "Ye recall the Austrian Major I sold the code to in Paris? – well, 'twas him the Baroness was meeting this morning."

"Oh dear me." Ranklin sat heavily on the bed. "Did he see you?"

"No, and might not be knowing me 'cept for me voice."

There was the snag: Irish accents were rare in European society. Most Irishmen rich enough to travel had only got that way by adopting English attitudes and accent.

Ranklin nodded. "What happened, then?"

"I followed them across the bridge heading for Castle Hill. I was in a cab. Then we lost them, but found the car outside of the officers' mess at the barracks on the Hill. I couldn't be following when they came out, but he'd changed into plain clothes and left his luggage so that's where he's staying, thank God, and not here. I came on back quickish."

"Yes. Damn. But I suppose it fits: him in Paris on a temporary attachment to meet Hornbeam and see him doing his lecture at the Embassy, then coming here for the Grand Finale – No, of course, you don't know about that. Talking to Klapka the lawyer . . . " He brought O'Gilroy up to date on the morning's doings and discoveries, ending up: "So there's no hope of any advice from Uncle Charlie. We're on our own."

"Ye think so?" A car crunched the gravel below and Ranklin peeked cautiously around the window frame to see the Baroness and the lithe, moustachioed Major step down from the hired Benz.

48

"You know the Baroness Schramm," Corinna said, "but I don't think you've met Major Stanzer. Her *cousin*." They didn't know Corinna well, so Ranklin hoped they hadn't caught the disbelief in her tone. He bowed to the Major across the table and sat down.

"Have you come to hear Professor Hornbeam speak tonight?" he asked to keep the conversation going while he looked Stanzer over. A man of action was the first impression: muscular and restless. A handsome face with a quick smile and a fair moustache that was as well tended as any Englishman's lawn. He wore a hairy country suit that showed his opinion of Budapest.

"That is so," he said. "I have heard him in Paris, but now I understand more about international law, so perhaps I ask him a question, no?"

Ah, Ranklin thought, is *that* how Hornbeam's announcement is going to be triggered? He said: "I hope he knows the answer."

"I am sure the Herr Professor knows all answers," and Stanzer gave his quick smile that didn't seem to mean much.

"Is Conall lunching?" Corinna asked Ranklin.

"He's still working on the tariff figures. I asked for something to be sent up to him."

While Corinna was being baffled by this return of her own fiction, the Baroness muttered to Stanzer: "Herr Ranklin und Herr Gilroy sind Kaufleute." She didn't need to emphasise that "businessmen": Stanzer's smile showed he forgave Ranklin for having crawled from under his rock before nightfall.

But Corinna's hearing and German were just as good. "Major

Stanzer," she beamed, "makes his living by riding horses. Isn't that *clever* of him?"

Ranklin cringed inside; we should ask the waiters, when they come, to save us trouble by throwing the food for us. And he was quite content to be despised by the cavalry officer: you aren't suspicious of those you despise.

Well, well, he thought; my attitudes really are changing.

"We believe there are great business opportunities in Hungary," he announced. "Primarily it's a matter of increasing efficiency in the fledgling industries you already have. Take pig iron production, for example. Here you produce only sixty pounds a year per worker, while in Germany the figure is over five hundred and in the USA . . . "

By the time the first course arrived he had lowered the emotional temperature to near zero. And nobody could fail to despise his devotion to business.

They were halfway through the main courses – stuffed pepper, for Ranklin – when a young man came round the corner of the building, paused to look around the tables, then hurried over to Stanzer. From his deference and stiffness of pose, Ranklin reckoned he was another Army officer.

Stanzer stood up, bowed to them all, and said: "I am most sorry, please excuse . . . It is urgent . . . " He murmured something to the Baroness that Ranklin couldn't catch, and hurried off.

"Dear me," Corinna said brightly. "I do hope his horse isn't feeling unwell."

The Baroness gave her a look that was pure paprika – but she was worried. After picking at her lunch for a minute or two, she threw down her napkin and walked back into the hotel.

"Any more of this," Corinna said, "and the chef's going to have a nervous collapse. Have you any idea what that was about?"

Ranklin shook his head. "I think it may be time for what your original countrymen would call a pow-wow."

Corinna nodded. "Cousin, my ass."

"Meeting of the British Secret Service, House of Sherring branch, will come to order," Corinna announced brightly.

"For God's sake . . . " Ranklin winced.

She grinned, then called: "Conall, are you with us?"

O'Gilroy was standing at one of the windows of the billiard room, staring up at the tops of the thunderclouds moving in from the north-west. He was always fascinated by their detail, by the exquisite fineness of every last curl, that existed simply to cloak a drifting inferno. Perhaps it gave perspective to his thoughts – only the thoughts swilling around him were pretty big and awesome already.

"I'm with ye." He turned back to the room.

"And we all know what Dr Klapka said, what Matt deduced and what he's done and been told?" She sat in a high wing chair against the wall by the marker board, occasionally and impatiently swatting the soggy air with her fan. The room was low-ceilinged, dark and smelt of dust. From the café by the baths a military band was marching the late lunchers through their pudding and coffee.

"And about this Austrian Major Stanzer?" Corinna added.

"He's part of it," Ranklin said. "The next link in the chain up from the Baroness, we assume. But we don't know why he went tearing off in the middle of lunch."

"There was a couple of fellers in a car come to pick him up." O'Gilroy had been watching from his bedroom.

"Really?" Ranklin considered this. He had abandoned his jacket and perched himself on the billiard table, rolling a ball off two cushions and back to his hand, over and over.

"D'you want to sum up, Matt?" Corinna offered.

Ranklin hesitated, then began abruptly: "The plot begins at a very high level, perhaps in the Army, certainly the Army's involved. That's where Major Stanzer comes in."

Corinna made a face; Ranklin looked to O'Gilroy: "What would you say of him?"

"He's more'n the fancy boy he looks," O'Gilroy admitted, and when Corinna looked puzzled, went on: "I had some dealings with him in Paris; business, ye might say . . . " His voice trailed off.

Corinna smiled lopsidedly. "So that's why you were lunching alone."

Ranklin took over: "I assume he's Army Intelligence, from the way he can jump from place to place." He smiled suddenly. "If he *is*, I wonder if it's occurred to him that Colonel Redl must have had a say in his selection. And since the Colonel was working for the Russians, he wouldn't be selecting the best and brainiest . . . However, if all Stanzer's here to do is ask a question at the lecture, he should manage that without tripping over his moustache.

"*Anyway*, I think the idea isn't so much to stop the Archduke becoming Emperor as to discredit him right now – just temporarily – when the Emperor's taking advice on whether or not to accept the Bucharest peace treaty. Whether to opt for war or peace, in effect. And I'm told the Emperor thinks highly of the Archduke – and, presumably, his advice – at this moment. And, though I'm less sure about this, I think the Archduke may be advising peace – on purely military grounds."

"That bastard," O'Gilroy muttered.

Corinna frowned as she worked through this. "So we're not just talking about who gets the big part in the next Habsburg play, but a whole European war? – that's what you believe, isn't it?"

Ranklin nodded, and she looked at O'Gilroy. "Conall?"

O'Gilroy shrugged. "Whatever the Captain says. I'm way over me head in matters this size."

She looked back at Ranklin. "Well, last night you thought things would be simpler if it were a nice big plot. Today it seems it is. Only we aren't quite sure where the Archduke stands; do we need to be?"

"It would be nice to know if this is a plot to start a war or to stop one."

The room darkened, as abruptly as if a curtain had been pulled, as the clouds overtook the sun.

"But how much," Corinna asked, "do we really know about the Archduke?"

"That's the trouble. So much is Vienna society gossip – his mad rages, shooting servants and so on – but Vienna society doesn't know him. He never goes near them. And if he's really no more than pig-headed and bad-mannered then he's no worse than most generals I've met. And as a general, he could see it's lunacy to risk a war with Russia when Redl might have given them the Monarchy's Plan Three – their war plans."

O'Gilroy objected: "But ye said the Chief of Staff – and he must be a general – he wants a war."

"Conrad, yes. But he might feel his career needs one: he's been in post some years now and never ordered a shot fired. He might even want a war to restore the Army's morale after the Redl affair. But a war now won't do the Archduke any good. He's so close to becoming Emperor – the old boy's nearly eighty-three – that all he has to do is wait and then he can have all the wars he wants – and total direction of them besides. He's got far more to gain from keeping the peace now – if we can credit him with the sense to see that."

There had been no hint, no distant mutter, of thunder. But like a besieging army, it had crept up on them, laid its mines in silence and then detonated them all at once in an enormous explosion that rattled the windows and squeezed their eardrums. Ranklin knew he had jumped, and suspected the other two had as well. For a full minute, as the explosions rolled and echoed on, they just stared at the shuddering windows, with no point in trying to speak.

When there was something nearer silence, Corinna said: "Operatic and overdone."

"Your criticism is minuted," Ranklin said gravely.

O'Gilroy asked: "So ye think mebbe it's that General Conrad behind of all this?"

It was a difficult question, and Corinna came in with her answer while Ranklin was still puzzling at it. "It can happen sometimes that an important man's aides and sidekicks can set something going that they *think* the boss wants but won't want to know about. To keep his hands clean. All very self-sacrificing and self-advancing of them, and it can be one hell of a nuisance."

She said it with quiet fervour and they both knew whom she was talking about. Ranklin summed up: "It's being run from Vienna by somebody well up the ladder from Stanzer, but there's no point in guessing who. And nothing, nobody, can take away the cause of war, it's just there, in the air, in everything that's going on."

"But," Corinna said, "if we can stop Hornbeam being the occasion for it, maybe we'll stop it for this war season. Maybe something will happen, a miracle, before the next season comes around . . . " She glared at him. "One thing we can sure do is talk to Hornbeam. If it all depends on what he says tonight and we can stop him saying it – hallelujah!"

Ranklin nodded, but not as enthusiastically as she had expected, and went back to rolling the billiard ball.

Outside, the rain began: at first just a rattle of heavy drops, but in seconds the noise became a roar and the windows waterfalls. Corinna walked to one and pressed her nose against the glass, playing the childhood game of being warm and dry just a fraction of an inch from the streaming flood.

"We'd better try and catch him as soon as we can," she went on, turning from the window.

"It means tipping our hand somewhat," Ranklin said.

"Okay, so what else do you want us to do?"

Ranklin frowned down at the tabletop. "The problem is that spies are supposed just to find out, not to *do*. It tends to make them conspicuous. And there's another good reason," he went on quickly. "A spy's always working with incomplete knowledge, deliberately so. We don't get sent into the field knowing all our bosses know, what our side's plans are – for obvious reasons."

"But you can't think your bosses *want* a war."

He sighed. "No, I don't think they do, although they wouldn't tell us anyway."

They were silent for a while, listening to the steady rain and the now distant soft-edged growls of thunder. O'Gilroy looked tensed, Corinna more perplexed.

"Then," she said finally, "you don't really want to speak to Hornbeam, either?"

"No, I'll come with you on that. But I really don't see what more we – O'Gilroy and I – can do. We've been acting nosy enough to get people wondering about us. If we do anything more blatant, we might give ourselves away completely."

"Captain – " O'Gilroy's voice was low and trembling with, perhaps, reined-in anger; " – I think we're here for different reasons. Mebbe yer saving the British Empire, but ye know I've no part in that. I'm here because I chose, though – " he shrugged; " – the reason for that I wouldn't say I knew. I do know ye've told me often enough ye think spying's a dirty business – and mebbe it is for the likes of yerself. But I'm telling ye it's just *because* we're spies that we're knowing this plot and can mebbe do something to stop it. And I recall what ye told me of the war ye saw, and fought, in

Greece and what yer guns can do. And I say if ye run from the chancest to stop that happening in the towns and countries ye've shown me, then they'll have to dig a new pit in Hell to make it deep enough to hold ye!"

Corinna turned her head slowly from watching O'Gilroy and her face was troubled and, though she tried to hide it, disappointed. "Matt," she appealed, "isn't there anything, just anything, you can . . . ?"

"You just don't see," Ranklin said wearily. "Not either of you. It isn't as *easy* as sacrificing ourselves. It needs just a hint, just one, that the British Secret Service is opposing them, and the war party's won hands down."

After a time, Corinna said in a voice that was subdued but somehow relieved: "Conall, next time let's remember there's a good reason why they put this guy in charge."

"You won't," Ranklin growled.

49

They found Hornbeam in his room. In his shirtsleeves and with a wad of papers in his hand, he had obviously been pacing about practising his lecture which, since he had given versions of it four times already on this trip, was truly conscientious of him.

"We aren't interrupting, are we, Professor?" Corinna asked demurely.

"No, no, I've just been pitting my puny voice against that of the gods." He waved at the open window, beyond which the rain still streamed down and the thunder muttered. "A useful rehearsal for the coughs and snores of my audience. Sit yourselves down."

He was in a jovial mood – and why not? This would be the last night of a tour that was a personal triumph, a phrase that might stretch to include the Baroness. And he would top it all with a surprise high C of judicial revelation; it was cream enough for the fattest of cats.

"Professor," Corinna began diffidently, "we've picked up a rumour, I don't know if it's true, that you've been asked to give a legal opinion on the Habsburg Family Law – "

"Where did you learn this?" Hornbeam's manner had changed abruptly.

"It is true, then," she sighed.

"This is a gossipy part of the world, sir," Ranklin put in. "And I imagine quite a lot of people must have been involved in getting the Law to you."

"This is – was supposed to be – a highly confidential matter between myself and a . . . a certain distinguished party,"

Hornbeam said heatedly. "I must insist that you mention this to nobody, absolutely nobody. Happily it's only for a few hours now, but in the meantime . . . "

Corinna said: "Professor, we came here to ask you to keep it to yourself, not to give any opinion on the Law in public. Nor in private, if it can be attributed to you."

Having blown hot, Hornbeam drew himself up and turned icy. "Mrs Finn, you are intruding into a matter between a client and his legal adviser, sacred ground to a professional man. I beg you to trespass no further."

"But have you considered the political aspect, sir?" Ranklin asked.

"Political aspect? There is no political aspect. This is a matter of a . . . certain lady being entitled to share her husband's rank when . . . in a certain circumstance. A private matter."

Ranklin stared, puzzled. "But this concerns the ruling branch of the Habsburg family, and if that isn't political – "

"Would you say, sir, that such people are denied a private life? Excluded from the basic rights of ordinary citizens?"

It suddenly dawned on Ranklin that, in Hornbeam's academic, cloistered but essentially democratic view, the Habsburgs simply didn't matter. They must be a quaint old ritual, kept alive to amuse and distract the populace on feast days; real power, obviously, had to lie with the witty and urbane ministers and administrators who had clustered round him in Vienna and now Budapest. The idea that an aged Emperor pottering about the streets of Bad Ischl in the thin guise of a commoner should actually hold the reins of peace and war was patently absurd.

As indeed it is, Ranklin agreed. But, God help us, it's also true. Yet how, in a few moments, can I persuade him that here in the Dual Monarchy dinosaurs still survive, still red in tooth and claw?

He didn't even get the chance to try. There was a distant rapping on another door and a voice called: "Herr Ranklin, Herr Ranklin. Telefon . . . "

"Blast, that'll be Hazay. I have to talk to him, but I'll try and get back – "

"Please don't trouble yourself on my account." Hornbeam was freezingly dismissive. "I regard this conversation as ended."

It wasn't Hazay, it was Tibor again. And sounding more agitated than mere inexperience with the telephone should make him. "Come to the Petöfi statue," he bawled. "I meet you there soon. Now." And he hung up.

Ranklin glared exasperatedly at the ceiling, then ran to find O'Gilroy.

The storm had left Pest with the look of fresh paint: the colours more vivid, the shadows more intense, the streets and pavements shining and steaming. Even the trams threw festive showers of sparks from damp overhead cables.

Ranklin picked his way primly among the puddles and flooding gutters, with O'Gilroy ambling along a hundred yards back – or so he assumed; by now he knew not to look. Tibor was waiting by the Petöfi statue, not sitting, just shifting from one wet foot to the other and sucking impatiently on a long cigarette.

He threw the cigarette away and headed straight off into the town as Ranklin came up, directly away from the river. He still moved like a bear, but now a bristly damp one; he had been caught in at least part of the storm without any topcoat.

"May I ask where we are going?" Ranklin said, striding out to keep up.

"See Stefan," Tibor growled.

Ranklin looked at him sharply. "What's happened to him?"

Tibor glanced at him with at least equal suspicion. "What have you been making him to do?"

"Do? Nothing. Just asking him for information. Damnation!" He had dropped his furled umbrella in a puddle. He picked it up gingerly, shook it and flicked scraps of rubbish off it while Tibor stomped about and O'Gilroy, on the other side of the street, had time to close up. Ranklin was sure he was being led into something, and wanted his reserves right at hand.

They passed through the university and museum district, un-crowded now with most students on vacation and tourists still waiting for the streets to dry. Tibor turned into a narrower street, then through a carriage arch into the courtyard of an apartment building. Continental cities were full of identical buildings – it was a way of life, not a style of architecture – only here the stucco was painted the inevitable Habsburg yellow.

Ranklin stopped. "What about the concierge? – gatekeeper?"

"Not in afternoon." Tibor headed for a stone staircase in one corner; Ranklin peered cautiously into the concierge's room, but it was quiet and dark.

At the top of one flight of stairs, Tibor pushed open a heavy door, took a few paces down a hallway and opened another door.

"Now see what you have made to happen."

By now, Ranklin was well braced, but it's never enough. A close-up gunshot to the head is particularly nasty, since it empties much of the skull and swells the eyeballs nearly out of their sockets. The surroundings get messy, too.

Ranklin stood, swallowing hard and looking not too hard; luckily the room overlooked the courtyard and was rather dark. The outer door creaked, and Ranklin called softly: "Come on in – and be ready for a shock."

"Jayzus," O'Gilroy breathed over his shoulder.

"Who is this?" Tibor demanded, looking ready to start throwing punches.

"A colleague, a friend."

"You did not trust me!"

"Have you been acting trustworthily? Why didn't you just tell me what had happened?"

Probably the answer was that Tibor didn't know. Something terrible had happened and he was ready to blame the nearest bystander.

O'Gilroy moved forward, peering at the body sprawled across the table from a wooden elbow chair. Hazay's right hand clutched a small semi-automatic pistol. Next to it was a notepad with writing on it; the blood and brains had mostly blown the other way, over the papers on the far end of the table.

O'Gilroy passed the notepad to Ranklin and asked Tibor: "Would this be his pistol?"

"He had a gun, for travelling in the south . . . "

O'Gilroy began moving quickly but carefully, opening drawers and cupboards. Ranklin read the scrawl on the notepad. In German, it said:

> *I have been deceived into betraying the Monarchy by the*
> *secret planning of a Great Prince who is unworthy of his*
> *destiny. Forgive me, my friends.*

"Is this Hazay's writing?" he asked Tibor.

"Yes, I believe . . . " But there was plenty of Hazay's writing scattered around the table: it looked genuine. Only most of the rest was in Magyar.

Ranklin sat down in another chair, tapping the notepad against his knee and thinking desperately. O'Gilroy came back from the hallway holding a grease-soaked little cardboard box of cartridges.

"In with his shoes."

"Do they match?"

O'Gilroy squinted at the weapon on the table. "Looks like the same bore."

"Right." Ranklin took a deep breath and said to Tibor: "Now do you believe he shot himself?"

Tibor let his mouth hang open. What he had seen – could see – was so horrible and vivid that mere thoughts could make no impact on it. The scene just *was*, he couldn't see it as composed of details yet, let alone ones that might be false.

Ranklin tried to supply them. "This morning, so you told me, he was all fired up about telegraphing an article to Munich, but expected trouble with the censors. A few hours later you find him dead, leaving a suicide letter in German. A letter for friends, like you; would you have expected it to be in Magyar?"

Tibor nodded slowly.

"So somebody, several somebodies, could have forced him to produce the pistol, write the letter in German because they couldn't read Magyar – then shot him. Do you agree this could have happened?"

"Yes," Tibor said huskily.

"Right. Then let's get the devil out of here."

O'Gilroy let out a long breath of relief. But Tibor, catching on to the implications of murder, was searching the desktop with his eyes. "I find his notes, then I prove the story he sends is true . . . "

"*They'll* have thought of that. As for proof – " he jerked his head at Hazay; " – that's convinced me."

"But while I'm sure you've found a loophole, a weakness in the Family Law," Corinna was saying, "how can you stop them re-amending it to plug the hole before the Archduke succeeds to the throne?"

Hornbeam smiled paternally. "The very fact of my making the announcement so publicly, my dear. Their tame lawyers would never dare do anything so cynical in the broad daylight of the public gaze, and particularly since the legal opinion comes from a source – myself – representing, one might say, the gaze of the international public. Of course, we are still talking hypothetically." He still hadn't admitted he believed he had been hired by the Archduke.

"Of course," Corinna said automatically. So *that's* the argument they've fed him. Never mind that if the Habsburgs cared a bugger for anybody else's opinion they wouldn't now be wondering whether or not to start a war.

She tried another approach. "Then could you accept, hypothetically, that if there is the slightest chance that our theory is correct – and after all, you haven't actually met the Archduke, only people claiming to represent him – you might wait a few days before making a public statement?"

"My dear Mrs Finn, tonight's lecture is by far the most public . . . Come in," he called to a knock on the door.

The Baroness came in, saw Corinna, and said: "Ah, I am most sorry you are . . . "

"No, no," Hornbeam assured her. "Be seated, my dear. This concerns you as much as anybody. I fear our little secret has leaked out – " the Baroness gave Corinna a sharp but apprehensive look; " – and Mrs Finn, misguided I fear by her father's business adviser, seems to believe it is all a plot to bring the Archduke into disrepute. I seem quite unable to disabuse her of this fancy."

Say what you would about the Baroness – and Corinna was ready to say a great deal – she had poise. "My dear child, you cannot know our Monarchy so well after just a few days. It is not a place of mysterious plots and, how do you say it, blood and thunder. That *businessman* who follows you everywhere is just telling you romantic . . . "

"Shut your face," Corinna said. "You, Professor, are as

hidebound as a horse's ass and have about as much vision . . . "
Listening to her own voice, she knew it wouldn't do her any good.
But for the moment, it didn't feel that way.

Ranklin let O'Gilroy saunter out into the street first, then they
followed a couple of minutes later, heading in the opposite direction. It was a sensible move to perplex any watchers but, naturally,
it did nothing to calm Tibor's suspicions about them.

Making left turns while O'Gilroy made rights, they met up again
a street away. O'Gilroy shook his head and Ranklin agreed: Hazay's
street had been deserted, and being lined with similar apartment
houses, left no place for snoopers to loiter.

"We need some inconspicuous place for a talk," Ranklin said,
and whether or not he understood "inconspicuous", Tibor led them
quickly through a zigzag of back streets, out in Deák Place, and
down a short flight of steps to Budapest's single underground train
line. It might be amateurish of him, Ranklin reflected, but he did
indeed feel safe and unobserved in a burrow, even an electrified
one.

"What do we do about Stefan?" Tibor demanded.

"We just have to leave him. Somebody'll find him." Ranklin
didn't envy the somebody.

"But you do not want to tell the police?"

O'Gilroy snorted. "Ye can say I'm old-fashioned, but I've no
wish to commit suicide meself."

Tibor eyed him cautiously, he didn't know what to make of
O'Gilroy – and because of that, was newly suspicious of Ranklin as
well. Just then a little square-ended carriage rattled in and they got
aboard, heading out towards the Town Park.

"I think," Tibor said, "I must tell them myself."

"I hope that before that," Ranklin said, as quietly serious as he
could be in the rumble and creak of the carriage, "you'll remember
saying this morning that Hazay couldn't be shot for trying to bypass
the censors – but a few hours later, he was. So who did the censors
tell? Who decided he should be killed? Who actually did it? *I* don't
know, but obviously some authority must be involved. So who can
you trust?"

He had hoped that Tibor's young-rebel-writer attitude had made him anti-authority. And probably he was – but when things get sudden and nasty you want an authority to turn to. Ranklin wanted that authority to be the Secret Service Bureau, but saying so would hardly help.

Tibor considered. "But . . . what do we do?"

"You know what we want: to know if it's to be war or peace. And peace is better for international trade, I'm sure you'll agree. But we think there's a plot to besmirch the Archduke Franz Ferdinand. And that Stefan was killed because his article would have shown that the Archduke would oppose a war – and that would reveal the motive for the plot. So if we can prevent this plot succeeding then we carry on Stefan's work and perhaps unmask his assassins." Or perhaps not, of course, but he had to hammer the idea of avenging Hazay.

"So perhaps you know who kills Stefan?"

That was too big a leap of logic for Ranklin, but O'Gilroy asked: "What time was it ye first found him dead?"

Tibor tried to remember, he even took out a big gun-metal watch and stared at it. "Soon before I telephone you . . . "

"You telephoned at about a quarter to three," Ranklin said. "A quarter of an hour before? Half an hour?" Finding and using a telephone wouldn't be an everyday event for Tibor.

O'Gilroy said: "Anyway, plenty of time for a feller leaving the hotel jest after one o'clock in a motor-car *with* a coupla other fellers to get down there and – bang."

"Woah, hold on now," Ranklin warned – but the timing and Stanzer's behaviour made him a very likely suspect. And if so, he had very good lines-of-communication behind him: from the censors picking up Hazay's telegram to the gunshot must have been no more than two hours. Well, he'd already pointed that out – and now it gave him an idea. But it meant scurrying back to the hotel and he didn't want to leave Tibor alone, angry and bewildered and likely to start an elephant stampede on his own. Or a few more "suicides".

"Look," he said, "I want to try something, but it means me nipping back to the hotel. Can you two amuse yourselves for . . . No, I tell you what you can do: find out the *home* address of the British Consul, Dr I. Brull, for me. Can you do that?"

"But now," Tibor said, "he is at his office, no? He must be there until . . . "

"It's still his home address I want. I'll meet you at the Petöfi statue."

50

"It wasn't locked against you," Ranklin assured Corinna, relocking his bedroom door behind her. "I'm working on something . . . How did it go with Hornbeam? Not very well?" Her expression had already told him.

"God damn it!" she exploded. "Why are we landed with the one eminent American who's never run for elective office? He knows no more of politicking than . . . than a Harvard law professor. He's cold certain he's doing the right, the noble, the American thing, championing the Duchess Sophie's democratic right to be Empress – so *that's* what George Washington was fighting you bastards for – then riding into the sunset to the cheers of the mob."

"Is there any point in me tackling him again?"

"No," she said too quickly.

"You wouldn't happen to have said, just in passing, something a little bit unforgivable?"

"He didn't seem to mind what I said about him personally," she reflected, "but when I called Harvard Law School a rest home for punctured windbags . . . I insulted the Baroness quite thoroughly, too."

"She was there? Hmm. You seem to have put every shot in the bull."

"So how did you get on?"

Ranklin took a breath. "You'd better sit down."

"I . . . what?"

"Sit down, please." She obediently sat on the bed. "The game's turned rough: Hazay's been murdered."

363

"God Almighty." She clutched at the bedpost for support. "But . . . how? Why?"

"A faked suicide. And it may have been what Major Stanzer left lunch to do: the timing fits. Obviously somebody didn't like what Hazay was trying to telegraph out. Here – " she had turned frighteningly pale; " – let me see if there's any brandy in O'Gilroy's – "

"No, no, I'm all right. But . . . Stanzer can't just have got up from lunch and gone off and . . . "

Ranklin shrugged. "What we think they're plotting is going to kill tens of thousands. Why not just one now?"

Staring at the floor, she whispered: "Matt, we just *have* to stop these people."

"I'm trying a new scheme; it's too complicated to explain it all but I'll give you a broad outline . . . "

She stood up. "But, Matt – what about you? *They* may know you've been seeing Hazay, that you're involved . . . "

Ranklin reached into his trousers pocket and showed a stubby nickel-plated revolver. "Just a normal accoutrement of an English gentleman travelling in these parts. Before they get me to go Hazay's way, it'll cost them something."

"And what damned use has men saying things like that ever been to a woman?"

Even with a consul-general to share the load, Dr Brull would have counted this a hard day. The holiday season had brought the usual crop of tourists who had lost their passports, their money, everything but their voices; businessmen wanting to know if it was safe to travel on south and exactly what effect the coming Peace Treaty would have on the flax trade – and then Mr Ranklin with his wild (but quite possibly true) tale of plots against the Archduke.

And now, dear God, he had him again.

"Dr Brull," Ranklin said soothingly, "before we do anything else, would you telephone to your home?"

Brull frowned. "But what do you . . . "

"Just telephone home. Then you'll begin to understand."

The very weirdness of the demand, and the unease that brought, stopped Brull arguing further, and he lifted the telephone. But when a strange voice answered from his home in a – sort of –

English, he was struck dumb.

Ranklin took the handpiece from him. "Con? All's well. Twenty minutes should do it." He hung up.

"A colleague of mine," he explained. "He's *looking after* your wife and household whilst you and I complete a very simple task."

"Dear God – what sort of man are you?"

"A desperate one, I suppose," Ranklin said reflectively. "But not, I hope, to the point of impoliteness. However, all I ask is that we stroll down to the telegraph office and send, with your authority, a coded telegram to our Embassy in Vienna. What could be simpler than that?"

Now Dr Brull was completely bewildered. "To the Embassy? But you must not believe I will show you our code book . . . "

"Oh dear me, no. I'm sorry, I should have explained. The telegram's already encoded. It's just that they won't accept something in code from me but they will from you. Now, I expect you'll be anxious to get this over with, so shall we . . . ?"

They hardly spoke during the short walk to the telegraph office and the flurry of signings and stampings that saw the message off at the Most Urgent rate. Outside again on the Varoshaz Utcza, Ranklin hailed a cab and gave Dr Brull's address.

"I'll just come along and collect my colleague," he explained, sitting down beside the Consul. "I'm sure you'll find he's behaved with perfect propriety. And, as you see, all I wanted was to communicate, confidentially, with our Embassy."

"But if you had confided properly in me, explained your particular situation, I would undoubtedly have . . . "

"Would you, Doctor?" Ranklin smiled politely, still convinced that any such explanation would have got him thrown bodily out of the Consulate. "Perhaps you would, and I acted too hastily. So I hope you'll take me as an example of how *not* to behave and restrict your complaints – and you most certainly have grounds for such – to our own official circles. If you involved the Budapest authorities it would make trouble for me, of course, but also for Britain – and perhaps yourself, your name being on that telegram . . . Dear me, what sombre thoughts.

"Oh yes," he felt in a pocket. "A little something as poor compensation for the worry to which we've put your wife. I'm

afraid I knew nothing of her colouring, so it had to be diamonds."
The comment about colouring, the actual brooch and the very
thought itself had, of course, all come from Corinna.

Ranklin added: "And by the way, should the Embassy start
complaining that the telegram is indecipherable, say it was all a
silly prank by a code clerk. Or something. The right person will
have seen it, never fear."

"I hope your new code is also indecipherable to others." Dr
Brull's confidence was returning, along with the properly superior
attitude to what he now knew Ranklin to be. "The Kundschaftstelle in Vienna prides itself on its code-breaking expertise."

"Really? Ah well, perhaps this will keep them amused for a while
. . . This is your house, I think? Yes, there's my colleague at the
window. You'll forgive me for not coming in to apologise personally
to your good wife . . . "

"You know, it's served a lot more purposes than whoever drew it up
ever intended," Ranklin said.

"And more'n I fancy ye'd have 'em know," O'Gilroy smiled.

"Indeed. But I think it would be tempting fate to hang onto it
any longer, so . . . " He threw the shoe-bag holding Code X and a
number of heavy stones out into the fast deep Danube, and they
walked back along the jetty towards the hotel.

51

Tucked away in the trees just south of the hotel were the low walls of a ruined convent. A few late-afternoon holiday-makers and patients from the thermal baths pottered about but whoever had ruined the convent had done a very thorough job and the most interesting sight was two men and a woman, obviously foreign, sitting on one of the walls staring gloomily at nothing. The House of Sherring branch of the British Secret Service was back in session.

"So the way they'll play it," Corinna was saying, "is that when Hornbeam's finished and asked for questions, Major Stanzer – whom he thinks is the Archduke's man – asks if he's any views on the Duchess Sophie, and Hornbeam says Yes and starts a war.

"Could we maybe," she added, "push Stanzer in the river first?"

"It would be pleasure and not work," Ranklin said, "but it wouldn't stop the Baroness or one of Stanzer's chums asking instead. They'll find a way to give Hornbeam his cue – unless they get word from Vienna telling them not to."

"Jest what was yer telegram saying?" O'Gilroy asked.

"That we (I didn't specify who 'we' were, the Consul will get the blame) had reliable information from the Russian Embassy in Belgrade that they had all of Plan Three – from Redl – and were only too happy for Austria-Hungary to start a war based on that plan. Please pass on to interested departments in London and so forth."

"But how," Corinna asked, "can you be sure the Austrians will be able to decode it?"

"Ah – a bit complicated, but we're sure it's a code that's been compromised."

"Mebbe," O'Gilroy said, "some rotten money-grubbing bastard sold it to them."

"Quite so," Ranklin said hastily.

"But," Corinna mused, "you can't be sure how quickly they'll do it, or get word to Major Stanzer in time."

Ranklin took his pipe out of his mouth to nod. "But the only other approach is the one that's failed: getting Hornbeam not to say anything."

"Maybe we should kidnap Lucy – or the Baroness," Corinna said dreamily, "and tell Hornbeam that if he talks, he gets her back in little blood-stained parcels."

There was a pause, then Ranklin asked: "Just what did they teach in that Swiss finishing school of yours?"

But O'Gilroy was considering the idea seriously. "With a thing like that, ye need good planning – and anyways, they're likely dressing for the shebang already."

Corinna glanced at her wristwatch. "Lordie, yes." She stood up. "Why have they pitched the lecture so early?" They began strolling back through the trees.

"Perhaps so the journalists have all the time they need," Ranklin suggested. "Make sure it's headline news in Vienna tomorrow. And Bad Ischl."

"If they hadn't killed . . . Hazay," Corinna said, "he might . . . Do you think they killed him to stop him breaking this story publicly?"

"He didn't know it. And no editor would print anything about the plot on the evidence we could give him – unless we said exactly who we are. No," Ranklin shook his head; "don't be misled by the public aspect of all this. It's all being done to influence the views of one man: the Emperor. He's all that matters, his opinion of the Archduke and hence of the Archduke's advice. That's what Hornbeam can't grasp. It'll be part of the Archduke's disgrace that he seemed to be washing Habsburg linen in public. But the opinion of the public, all fifty million of it, doesn't count a whisker."

They had reached the edge of the trees, with a stretch of grass and then the gravel drive to cross before the hotel.

"You stay back," Ranklin told O'Gilroy, "I'll give you a wave from my room when I'm sure Stanzer isn't around."

"You really don't want to meet this guy, do you?" Corinna said to O'Gilroy. "Well, I don't blame you. So we won't see you until after the lecture. Wish us – Europe – good luck."

Ranklin nudged her into moving. There was just her hired car in the driveway, along with a couple of one-horse cabs. No sign of any car that might be Stanzer's, nor the one that would come to collect Hornbeam and Lucy.

A couple of minutes later, Ranklin came out onto his tiny balcony and waved at the trees; he'd seen no sign of Stanzer, nor of the Baroness. But when O'Gilroy was halfway across the drive, it occurred to him that he needn't go up to his room anyway. He stopped and called up to the open window and Ranklin reappeared, now half out of his shirt.

"Is it all right with ye if I jest take a cab down the town right now?"

Preoccupied, Ranklin nodded and vanished. And Major Stanzer, already in civilian dress clothes, stepped out onto the Baroness's balcony and looked down at O'Gilroy. Then he smiled, put a finger to his lips and gestured O'Gilroy around to the main entrance.

The hotel cooks glanced curiously out of their open windows onto the little courtyard stacked with vegetable baskets and strewn with old cabbage leaves, but didn't interfere. The muscular one with the Austrian moustache looked like an officer, and if he wanted a private place for a talk with the thin dark Englishman, so be it.

"I do not hear an Irish voice so much," Stanzer said, "so it is most easy to remember. So the Herr Ranklin is your drunken master, no?" O'Gilroy could sense the delight with which Stanzer fingered this new revelation, squeezing it, fondling it. He himself was trying to imitate the potato he was standing on.

"And also Mrs . . . the daughter of Sherring? She is also an agent?"

At least O'Gilroy could react honestly to that. "Herself? – ye must be joking, Major. She's disguise, and not the worst idea me master's had. Who'd think she'd be carting round a coupla British spies? She'd have fits to know it herself."

Stanzer half smiled; he hadn't been serious about Corinna. "But also, who would believe that a good Irishman works for the English Secret Service?"

O'Gilroy's mood changed. "Isn't that what they think themselves?" and he didn't think he was lying yet. "So when they caught me and me brother with the bomb . . . well, he's rotting in Kilmainham jail and no worse. But if they think now I'm not working for them with all me soul, he swings."

"Swings?"

"Gets hanged."

Stanzer nodded. He already believed the best way to control an agent was power, not trust. Hadn't the Redl case proved that?

"So," O'Gilroy said, with a hint of defiance, "any idea ye have for me changing sides, I'll do nothing to put that rope round me brother's neck."

"But already that risk you take," Stanzer pointed out gently, "when you sold to me the code. If the English knew that . . . "

"Mebbe so." The defiance was gone. "But a man gets . . . "

"You must fight back, no? – but secretly. I understand. That is all I want you to do now."

"Anyways," O'Gilroy's spirit seemed to return, "the code's no good for ye if ye tell 'em I sold it. Ye said that much yerself."

"That is true. But codes do not for ever last. They must be changed because just perhaps they are – you say 'broken', I think. Or sold."

O'Gilroy shrugged, his defiance turning sullen. The cooks knew no English and wished the pair would talk more with their hands. But the English never did, and the Austrian's officer-training had rendered him almost dumb. So they went on concentrating on O'Gilroy's fluent changes of expression.

"So – " Stanzer had a problem sounding smooth in an alien language; " – there must also be more work, to be sure your brother does not 'swing'. Why are you coming to Budapest?"

"I wisht I knew. But," O'Gilroy went on quickly, "he was

wanting to see some feller – "

"Do not lie to me! I am an officer of the Emperor, it is my *duty* to report you for spies! But I have no duty for your brother . . . So, I know your Herr Ranklin is telling the Herr Professor he must not say – *something* at his lecture. Why does he do this?"

The cooks appreciated O'Gilroy's look of utter bewilderment – but not the acting that went into it. This could be the moment of decision: Stanzer could choose to strengthen the war party's case, as Ranklin had feared, by denouncing them as spies. But then he would lose not only the code but an even bigger personal prize: a hidden door leading into the British Secret Service. That way lay promotion, if Stanzer could only see it.

"Ah, *that* . . . " The cooks saw that O'Gilroy had remembered something, though not a very important something. "That's all Mrs Finn herself, saying the Professor's meddling with laws that's none of his concern, and like to make a fool of himself and Americans like herself. She thinks she owns the world, her with her money."

Stanzer hadn't forgotten Corinna's jibes at lunchtime; he nodded. "But your Herr Ranklin?"

"He's never my Herr Ranklin!" O'Gilroy snapped. "Ye can have him yeself any time, long's ye do it without it seeming my work . . . " His eyes gleamed as the idea appeared to take root. "Why not that, then? I can help ye lay a trap, like, and ye snap him up and let me go? Would there be money in that for me?"

Stanzer smiled as O'Gilroy seemed to bare his twisted soul. But he could hardly say that O'Gilroy himself was only any use as a channel to Ranklin, not if the man was too stupid to realise it already.

"Perhaps," he temporised, "but not yet. So why does Herr Ranklin argue with the Professor?"

"Mrs Finn told him to. What does he care about Americans? – and him tearing to be away to see this feller, and taking the code book and the Consul besides . . . "

"What fellow is this? Your master is sending a message in code?" Galloping down the new track, Stanzer couldn't hide all his eagerness.

"Ah, jest some feller . . . mebbe Russian, or was it about Russia?

What's the big town down the river, Bel-something? Is that in Russia?"

"Belgrad? In Serbia?"

"That's the place, sure – something about Russia from there. Jayzus! – d'ye think he tells me these things? He's more like tell his dog."

Stanzer would probably have disbelieved a clear-cut tale; certainly he would have picked it apart with suspicion. But leave him to work it out for himself, now . . . And Stanzer was working, all right: Belgrade was a cesspit of Russian influence and intrigue – so a message from there – then the code book . . . and the Consul to authorise the telegram . . .

"Where is the telephone in this hovel?" he demanded.

"Holy Mary!" O'Gilroy took fright. "Yer never turning us in to the police?"

"No, no, no. You are safe – if what you tell me is true. You are my secret now. You do not leave Budapest soon? I send you a message . . . I call myself . . . " He thought quickly. "Danilo. You know that? Danilo. But – " he felt a reminder was called for; "I do not forget all my duty. Now, telephone."

As Stanzer hurried off, the pastry cook announced that it must all have been about money: no Englishman nor Austrian got that excited about women. The vegetable cook thought it had been about horses, but kept the thought quiet; pastry cooks have artistic temperaments.

Strolling back to the more recently painted side of the hotel, O'Gilroy reckoned they were safe – for the moment. Stanzer clearly thought he had recruited O'Gilroy as an informer, what with all that talk of "Danilo" as his code-name for messages. And that meant Stanzer would protect him: not mention him to whoever he was telephoning, nor to the Baroness. Spies, they had been told, are very possessive about the agents they collect. Perhaps it was a desire to build their own secret empire, not merely be part of someone else's.

But moments, like codes, don't last for ever. And now he had no need to hide from Stanzer, he could go anywhere – even, eventually, to the lecture at the Palace. He went up to his room to change. And once there, he unwrapped his pistol. Unlike

Ranklin's distinctively British "Bull-Dog" revolver, this weapon had no nationality. It was an American design manufactured in Belgium and, O'Gilroy felt sure, quite untraceable. Little things like that could sometimes be quite important.

52

If it had really been used as a Royal Palace, it would have been a good one: a warren of offices, barracks, kitchens, stables, treasury – anything and everything as well as the royal apartments – a grandiose village with corridors for streets. Use and bustle would have been everything: unused, it had little more elegance than a deserted village, since its only grandeur was its hilltop site, and that less than half a mile from the Panna Tavern. The rest was a neo-Gothic pile of statues, carved stonework, wrought-iron gates, lamps and fountains, and a big bronze bird that Ranklin knew wasn't an eagle but couldn't remember what it really was.

As they got out of the car they were saluted by two Palace Gardeoffiziere in uniforms so embroidered, even on the breeches, that they reminded Ranklin of the Cockney "Pearly Kings" in suits covered with shiny buttons.

"Nice of them to lend Hornbeam this little place," Corinna observed. "But I wonder what they're doing with the other eight hundred and fifty-nine rooms tonight?" Unlike the other women of the audience, whose clothes showed they expected an evening of the very best boredom, Corinna was dressed for death or glory. She wore a very simple off-the-shoulder gown of her favourite dark red silk with a gold-mounted ruby dangling above her breast, and a white fur stole that she treated like a dishrag. Whatever happened, she was ready to go down with flags flying, and Ranklin glowed with pride as a man and cringed from the limelight as a spy.

As they paused by the great doorway – nobody was rushing to

claim a front seat – Dr Klapka scurried up.

"Do you talk with the Herr Professor?" he asked anxiously. "Is he to say . . . " But he choked on the dreaded words.

"We talked to him," Ranklin said, "but . . . "

"Stupid old goat," Corinna said.

Klapka interpreted this correctly and his already drooping moustache sagged further. "And so he will . . . " He shook his head. "And I have thought. I think now the Archduke cannot know of this. Perhaps it is someone who thinks to do a good thing for the Archduke who is so stupid . . . Or someone who wishes to do him harm, even . . . "

"Did you learn anything about the Baroness Schramm?" Corinna asked.

Klapka shook his head again. "I look in Almanac de Gotha, but . . . it is perhaps a French title, or even Belgian, or – "

"Or the lady's just dreamt it up," Corinna said crisply. "She could get away with it – if barons come by the cartload, as you said."

Ranklin, who hadn't *quite* said that, looked embarrassed. But Klapka reverted to gloom. "It will be a most terrible thing."

And they couldn't even share their one hope with him. "Perhaps he'll have second thoughts after all," Ranklin offered feebly, but Klapka went away still shaking his head.

A car rolled up bringing the Baroness, Lucy and a clean-limbed young lawyer whom the Budapest Bar had deputed to squire her. The Baroness ignored Ranklin and Corinna, but Lucy clearly hadn't heard of the disagreement with her father because she started chattering immediately. Ranklin's gaze wandered until he picked up the jaunty figure of Major Stanzer striding across the courtyard. He was at first surprised Stanzer wasn't in Cuirassiers' mess kit, then realised he would probably want to ask his question anonymously, not implicating the Army.

But anyway, he didn't look as if he'd just got a bad news telegram from Vienna. Yet.

Lucy was saying: " . . . going to be the most important lecture he's ever given, but he won't tell me why! Isn't that exciting? Come on." She dragged her squire inside.

Corinna looked at Ranklin. "Well, once more into the breach, dear boy . . . No, that isn't quite apt. Something from Dante, maybe. Abandon hope all ye who enter here . . . No, I'm damned if I will. Shall we go in?"

"A Turul," Ranklin said suddenly.

"What?"

"That bird on the plinth back there. It isn't an eagle, it's a Turul. Legendary or mythical."

"And what's it supposed to do?"

"Sit on plinths outside Royal Palaces, as far as I can tell."

They walked in just behind Stanzer.

"The Treaty of Westphalia in 1648 put an end to the destructive and, above all, undisciplined wars which had wracked Europe in the preceding century. It did this by acknowledging the existence of a number of relatively stable nation states, most obviously France, which shared common values and hence customs. Thereafter the Law of Custom was to . . . "

Hornbeam's voice produced a slight but clattery echo, perhaps more so because he was speaking in German. Ranklin knew he must read the language in which so much philosophy and law (including the Habsburg Family version) was written, but hadn't guessed he would dare lecture in it. But it made it easier to stop listening and gaze around.

Apart from the ponderous crystal chandeliers, the hall was pure Hansel and Gretel, all marzipan and cake icing. Even the Corinthian pillars along the walls had wreaths carved around their waists, and plaster scrolls writhed across the ceiling like tree snakes. Just what use the place had been intended for, he had no idea, but tonight it held a stage with Hornbeam and the city's legal bigwigs aboard, and hard small chairs set in two blocks with a central gangway. Corinna and Ranklin sat well forward, just behind the Baroness and Lucy, but Stanzer had picked a seat right at the back on the gangway and close to a doorway. Perhaps he planned to vanish just after his question; meanwhile it made him awkward to keep an eye on.

" . . . what philosophers and jurists had hitherto cited as the Natural or God-given Law in seeking justification for any given war became largely irrelevant in the eighteenth century, which

accepted war as a matter of policy, needing no specific justification . . . "

At that point Corinna nudged Ranklin. He first thought she was
just making sure he was awake, but then looked past her and was
appalled to see O'Gilroy, in proper dress clothes, sauntering along
the side of the hall in full view of everyone, Stanzer included.
O'Gilroy caught Ranklin's look, smiled reassuringly, and found a
seat at the end of the row just behind them. Ranklin turned back to
the stage, heart and mind racing.

Could O'Gilroy somehow have misunderstood the whole situation? He tried reassuring himself that O'Gilroy was no fool,
particularly where his own skin was concerned. So the situation
itself must have changed – but since he had no idea how, that
thought was hardly reassuring at all.

" . . . and since these wars were concerned mainly with frontier
disputes they posed no threat to the values and customs which the
warring states held in common. Moreover, they were fought by
a separate class of disciplined mercenaries led by warrior aristo-
crats . . . "

"Just like dear old England right now," Corinna murmured.

" . . . so society and state became separate entities in time of
war, allowing society to become the forum of conscience in which
the Kriegsmanier of the states, their customs of war, would be
adjudged. This stable, if hardly ideal, system was disrupted initially
by the actions of the British Navy – "

Corinna was about to whisper flippant agreement when she
realised that everybody else really did agree: a mutter, almost a
growl, rippled through the hall. You could do no wrong, she saw,
by denouncing the Royal Navy to a Continental audience.

While Hornbeam paused, Ranklin glanced back towards Stanzer
and saw a young officer with a light blue jacket slung cavalry-
fashion from his shoulder wandering slowly past the back rows.
Stanzer beckoned him and after a whispered conversation, the
officer handed over an envelope.

"What's happening?" Corinna demanded.

"Stanzer's got a message."

She turned her full-power stare on the back of the hall, forcing
an elderly gentlemen just behind her to lean hastily out of its way.

"He's reading it," she reported. "He doesn't like it . . . he's reading it *again* . . . "

"It's bad manners to stare," Ranklin muttered uncomfortably.

"Pigshit, as they say in this town." But she stopped her reportage. Stanzer dismissed the officer with a nod, crumpled the paper and bowed his head over clasped hands, frowning with thought.

Corinna faced front again, wearing a shining grin, and squeezed Ranklin's hand. "We've *won*," her whisper gloated. "You clever man, we've won!"

"When Hornbeam's closed down for the night, perhaps," Ranklin's natural pessimism warned.

" . . . when the use of blockade, inevitably an indiscriminate weapon, spread the effects of war to society and threatened its values, war lost its inherent justification as an act of policy, legal thinkers were forced to turn back to the Kriegsraison to seek a means of controlling what had become so much more destructive . . . "

Get *on* with it! Ranklin's inner voice screamed, while earlier it had been willing Hornbeam to drag it out all night. But that was before the message arrived (which could be to say they'd found his lost cuff-link . . . No, he'd looked too serious for that. But it could be that his horse or mother was ill . . .) Now he wanted a decision, war or peace, and a train ticket for Paris in either case . . .

No, if it were war, they'd have to stay to get the news out ahead of them. But make sure Corinna was on the first train . . .

A wave of applause woke him: Hornbeam had finished, and Ranklin had no idea of how much longer he'd taken. But now Corinna was muttering: "No questions, no questions, get off the stage you old fossil," so perhaps Ranklin's nervousness was catching.

But there had to be questions, the first asking whether the necessity of war could be held to exist in peace, that is, whether it is possible to anticipate necessity, in other words, whether necessity was dependent on conditions which . . . The second asked more simply whether Pufendorf's concept of the state as imbued with the same conscience as the natural man could be equated with St Augustine's view that . . .

"*Forget* Pufendorf and St Augustine," Corinna raged quietly. "Their supper's not getting cold but yours is. Think of *that*."

Pretending to look at a questioner towards the back, Ranklin saw Stanzer with his arms folded, staring at the seat in front with a grim expression. So far, so good – but Stanzer would make sure his question was the last one anyway.

Then nobody was asking a question and a restless, perhaps hungry, murmur filled the hall. Hornbeam asked hopefully: "Are there any more questions?"

There was a pause, then the Baroness half rose in her seat to frown across the rows of faces at Stanzer. But he gave a slow shake of his head and went on sitting stolidly.

So it's over, Ranklin thought. The legal ringmaster who had introduced Hornbeam began getting up to propose a vote of thanks.

But the Baroness was still on her feet, and now upright and looking more like a ship's figurehead than ever. "Herr Professor, I have a question, although it is not strictly concerning international law."

My God! Ranklin realised that Stanzer may have got the message but the Baroness knew nothing about it. She thought he was just suffering from cold feet and was going to ask the question herself.

"Please proceed, Baroness," Hornbeam smiled down at her.

"Nein! – lass das!" a voice yelled from the back, and Ranklin saw Stanzer on his feet, arms waving. "Nichts – "

The shots rattled together, too fast to count. Stanzer's outflung arms stiffened, his mouth gaped in a last gasp, then he crashed onto the row in front.

A hundred women started screaming and overturning their chairs. A few men, who had been under fire before, threw themselves flat but quickly realised flat was no place to be in a stampede. Ranklin grabbed Corinna's arm and dragged her forward into the lee of the stage.

O'Gilroy eased out of the swirling, shrieking crowd and stood protecting Corinna from the other side. "Ah, but that was a dreadful and calamitous thing."

He said it with such calm satisfaction that Corinna and Ranklin both stared at him. But he hadn't been sitting anywhere near

Stanzer; the shots, Ranklin reckoned, had come from the doorway at the very back.

Gradually the crowd eddied to a stop in quaking groups spread round the walls; the women had stopped screaming – except for one having hysterics – but the male instinct for shouting orders at each other had taken over. A reluctant Gardeoffizier and a more purposeful man, possibly a doctor, picked their way through the chairs towards Stanzer's body.

"Who was that? – the man who got shot?" Hornbeam was down off the stage and with his arm round Lucy, who was sobbing – but not so loudly that she couldn't hear anything interesting.

"Wasn't it Major Stanzer?" Ranklin said to the Baroness, now standing nearby. "Your cousin?"

She gave a tiny nod and went on looking grim.

"My God!" Hornbeam seemed stunned. "But . . . but why?"

"I don't know if you saw," Ranklin said, "but the Major got a message – brought by an officer – a little while ago." He wanted the Baroness to get that message, too: the plot was *over*.

"I saw that," Hornbeam exclaimed. "I saw the officer. But did that . . . ? I mean . . . what was it about?"

"Foreign assassins," the Baroness said and walked away.

By now, men in every sort of uniform were flooding into the hall or running back and forth beyond the doorways. A small group of rather shaken legal grandees had gathered and was about to descend on Hornbeam with apologies, reassurances . . .

While he still had Hornbeam's attention, Ranklin said quickly: "It would hardly be assassins, for a mere major. But in this country, you can't tell what's political and what isn't. I think it's wiser not to get involved in their affairs – particularly not at high level."

The police investigation was "helped" by the Gardeoffiziere (the Palace being their responsibility) and officers from the nearby barracks (since the victim had been one of their kind), and Ranklin didn't envy them the job. Neither did the police once they realised that half the men in the audience were Budapest's top lawyers and the rest just as distinguished in their own ways. And then it turned out that most of the journalists had already bribed their way through the guarded doors to spread the news . . .

During this, Corinna wisely kept them close to Hornbeam and his protective aura as Guest of Honour, where they listened to rumours: an arrest had been made (false) – fired cartridges had been found just outside the hall (true) – a man had been seen running through the corridors and then the gardens – young, from his speed, and "bear-like" . . . The police asked anybody who had seen anything to please tell them, and let the rest go.

They picked up one more rumour from Corinna's chauffeur, who had been chatting to policemen while he waited. "They found a pistol," Ranklin translated to O'Gilroy; " . . . dropped or thrown away . . . had been fired . . . an American type but made in Belgium."

"Find them anywhere," O'Gilroy said.

"Oh, good. So if somebody had one, and lost – or lent – it, he'd be able to pick up a replacement easily. That's reassuring."

53

They drove back to the hotel in silence, but as they got out, Corinna said: "Hornbeam and Lucy are heading back to Paris tomorrow. Is there any reason for us to stay on?"

Ranklin glanced at O'Gilroy, then shook his head. "I think it's all over here. Tomorrow Berchtold goes to Bad Ischl to advise the Emperor . . . If you can get us invited to tea at the Imperial Villa there . . . "

O'Gilroy went inside, probably to make sure the brandy corks hadn't jammed in the bottles, while Corinna gave the chauffeur instructions for the morning.

Then she turned to Ranklin, puffed out a long breath and let her shoulders sag theatrically. "Wasn't it your Duke of Wellington who said it had been 'a damned close-run thing'? But, apart from the bad guy getting shot in the last scene, I guess I'll never know just all of what happened back there."

Ranklin said thoughtfully: "I fancy Hazay had a lot of friends in Budapest. But some questions are better left unasked."

"Thank you kindly, sir," she said coolly.

"I was talking to myself."

After a moment, she said: "Ah, it's that way, is it?" and took his arm as they walked up the steps and into the lobby.

After Corinna had gone upstairs, they sat on with their second glasses. The lobby was deserted except for a politely distant waiter, Hornbeam, Lucy and the Baroness had gone straight to bed, Dr Klapka would be at home by now . . . Ranklin would probably see them all in the morning, but his mind had already let them go, they were fading, their lines spoken. The play was ended.

"A short run, but a busy one," he muttered, and O'Gilroy glanced at him. Ranklin roused himself. "Tomorrow I'll have to start thinking about a report on all this."

"What ye going to say in it?"

"God knows. If I tell a quarter of the truth, we'll find ourselves selling matches down the Strand."

"I doubt that, Captain." O'Gilroy smiled comfortably. "With what ye know now, they'd never let ye go discontented. Least they'll do is send ye back to yer big guns – mebbe as a major, too. And that's what yer wanting, isn't it?"

Ranklin leant back in his chair, hands thrust into his pockets and frowning down past his stomach. "I don't know, now . . . But what sort of man *likes* being a spy?"

O'Gilroy looked contentedly at the pearl studs in the shirt over his own, flatter, stomach. "Depends where he starts, mebbe. Me, 'twas the bottom of Spy Hill . . . seems a long ways, now. And seems to me, if yer good at a job – and yer surviving, which must count good in this trade – mebbe ye got a duty to do it, rather'n let some feller not so good wreck the job and himself both."

"Perhaps," Ranklin agreed. Then he looked up suspiciously. "Where did you get that thought?"

"Ah, now, Captain, would I ever be remembering jest what . . . "

"And don't try your round-the-houses Irishness on me. It was Corinna, wasn't it?"

"She's a gracious lady with her favours, I'm thinking, so mebbe she threw a small thought in the way of meself."

Ranklin reached for his brandy. "Go to bed, you black-hearted chancer. I've got a report to worry about."

"With not too much truth in it?"

"Hardly a word."